UNGODLY

UNGODLY

THE GODDESS WAR: BOOK THREE

KENDARE BLAKE

TOR*
TEEN

A TOM DOHERTY ASSOCIATES BOOK
NEW YORK

To Athena and Izzy,
the two coolest teens at Centralia Library

UNGODLY

Copyright © 2015 by Kendare Blake

All rights reserved.

A Tor Teen Book
Published by Tom Doherty Associates, LLC
175 Fifth Avenue
New York, NY 10010

www.tor-forge.com

Tor® is a registered trademark of Tom Doherty Associates, LLC.

The Library of Congress Cataloging-in-Publication Data
is available upon request.

ISBN 978-0-7653-3445-9 (hardcover)
ISBN 978-1-4668-1223-9 (e-book)

Our books may be purchased in bulk for promotional,
educational, or business use. Please contact your local bookseller
or the Macmillan Corporate and Premium Sales Department
at (800) 221-7945, extension 5442, or by e-mail at
MacmillanSpecialMarkets@macmillan.com.

First Edition: September 2015

Printed in the United States of America

0 9 8 7 6 5 4 3 2 1

PART I

THREE QUESTS

I

AT LARGE

The California coast. Soft, hot sand beneath her feet and an expanse of blue before her eyes. Cassandra pulled a deep breath in through her nose: dry heat, and oil from the fryer in the café behind her. A hint of engine exhaust, too, from somewhere, and underneath all the rest, barely detectable on the edges of the air, the smell of salt and deep, dark cold.

Deep, and dark. And blue. But I know what moves farther out underneath the currents. Behind the waves. I've seen their fins, and their lidless eyes. I've tasted their blood.

Her eyes tracked the water for ripples and shadows, but saw nothing. None of Poseidon's Nereids, or Leviathans. Not even a shark. Nothing to wade into the shallows and meet, to fill her nose with fish and rot. Nothing for her to pop like a blister.

"It's been months since your Aidan killed Poseidon. Maybe they're gone. Dead, like him."

Cassandra turned. Calypso bent over a wooden table, arms laden with red plastic baskets of French fries and turkey club sandwiches. *Dead like him*, she'd said. She meant dead like Poseidon, not dead like Aidan. But that's what Cassandra heard. Her mouth opened, ready to spit out something bitter, to say Aidan wasn't *her* Aidan. That he never had been. But he had belonged to her as much as any god could belong to anyone.

"If they were dead, they'd wash up on the beaches," Cassandra said. "They'd be lined up for me to see. Black, bloated bodies to crack under the sun and be torn apart by seagulls."

Calypso pushed a sandwich toward her.

"Their deaths on display for you. Their corpses for your approval. You think they owe you that, do you?"

"It doesn't matter. They're not dead." Cassandra pulled a toothpick from the turkey club and pointed at a tomato. Calypso took it and added it to her own. They'd been on the road for a month, since Cassandra had dragged them both out of flooding Olympus. Only she'd taken a wrong turn. When they emerged on dry, cold dirt in the back of an anonymous cave, they had been hundreds of miles from Kincade, New York, and when they turned back, the cave wall was just a cave wall no matter how she'd tried to pry her way back inside. Olympus was gone. So she'd had to let Aphrodite and Ares go, while she growled and gritted her teeth and screamed loud enough to drown out Calypso's wails for Odysseus. Odysseus, who lay ruined on rocks somewhere outside of time with Achilles' sword through his chest.

And Athena is lying just as ruined right beside him.

She clenched her jaw. She hated that Odysseus' death

should be twisted through with a god's, that hate spread thick and covered everything. Even him. Her friend. She tried to smile at Calypso.

"Thanks for the sandwich."

"You're welcome." Calypso smiled back, and small wrinkles appeared beside her eyes. The skin of her face was softer, and drawn thinner. The price of Cassandra's touch when she'd dragged her to safety. A streak of gray had appeared in her hair in the space of a blink inside the cave, just behind her ear, bright white against the brown waves. Now she kept it gathered together in one piece, and twisted it through a new braid. In the sun it looked shiny and separate, pretty as pulled taffy.

Calypso nodded toward Cassandra's basket.

"You should eat more. You're getting thin. And you need to sleep. You need to do something to sleep better."

"We're not going back," Cassandra said. "And we're not calling them. Not yet."

"Not yet," Calypso repeated. "They think you're dead."

"Not everyone. Not my parents." When they left that cave in Texas, she decided she wasn't going back to Kincade. Not to a mess and grief and confusion. Not to watch Hermes panic and try to regroup. She had work to do, the work of killing gods, and she wanted to do it alone. Or so she told herself. But the first time she had Internet access, she scoured the web for news from Kincade. Andie and Henry's Twitter feeds were both jammed with speculation about why she'd run away. There was nothing else. The papers didn't write up runaways. Only Andie and Henry thought she was dead. And so far they hadn't let anyone else in on the suspicion.

"But your brother," Calypso frowned. "And poor Andie."

"They'll understand. When it's over." *When all the gods are dead, and we have our lives back.*

As if we could ever have our lives back.

Calypso raised her brows.

"You'd feel better if you called them."

"No I wouldn't. I'd feel heavy, and guilty, and I would miss them."

"You miss them anyway. At least if you spoke to them you might have some comfort."

"The only thing that comforts me—the only thing that gives me an ounce of comfort—is the thought of Hera sinking like a stone in that underwater cave." Cassandra threw a tomato onto her napkin. "I hear the sound of it, the *clink*, *clink*, *clink* of her body against the bottom. I hear it in my dreams, and I sleep like an angel."

"You don't sleep at all."

The nymph's steady eyes hung on her, heavy and so damn thorough. An almost constant irritant these days. Calypso saw everything. Half the time it felt like she could read Cassandra's mind.

"It's almost time to go," Cassandra said. "Are you sure he'll be there?"

Calypso glanced at her watch and brushed crumbs from her palms.

"Yes. If he wants to keep my friendship. Which he does."

"Good." She watched Calypso clear the baskets and discarded napkins without trying to help. She would've only been batted away. Calypso acted very much like a servant sometimes.

Cassandra frowned. It would have been nicer to have a friend.

"You don't have to do everything, you know."

"Yes, I do," Calypso said.

"You pay, and you're helping. You're not a slave. And I shouldn't snap at you all the time."

Calypso stopped, and crunched an aluminum can of Fanta in her fist.

"Cassandra. Don't forget your promise. Our bargain."

Cassandra lowered her eyes. "I won't."

"Look at me when you say so."

"Okay. I won't."

"Say it again."

The gravity of those green eyes held her up and down all at once. But Cassandra did as she was asked.

"You'll help me. And when all the work is done, and the gods are dead, I'll kill you, too."

2

POST-OLYMPUS

Andie was a master at lugging grocery bags. She looped plastic over her wrists and hugged paper to her chest and was altogether blind by the time she started making her way toward the door. Hermes watched from the window. He could've helped of course, but it was early April, and the ice on the walk had melted so it wasn't like she was going to fall. He did open the door, though, when he heard her start to grunt.

"Andie."

"I saw you in the window, lazy ass. You want to start doing your own shopping?" She threw a bag into his chest. It appeared to be filled with nothing but Oreos and E.L. Fudge cookies. "There's a lot here, and more in the backseat. If you supplement with Stanley's Wok, maybe it'll last you a week."

The five bags wouldn't last three days, but Hermes smiled at her anyway.

"You know I'd be just as happy ordering pizza."

"You would not," she said, walking into the kitchen. "There are some super fatty steaks in here." She dug them out and put them in the refrigerator. "So don't argue."

"Henry coming over later?" he asked. "We could put some of those on the grill. Have a feast." He almost didn't need to ask. Since Olympus, Andie and Henry barely gave him five minutes to himself. As if he were the one who needed looking after.

Andie shook her head.

"He's with his parents. For the duration, I think."

"It won't be much longer before they'll want real answers."

"It won't be long until we'll have them. Until they'll be back. Right?" She paused her unpacking and looked at him with big eyes over a box of cereal.

"Right," he said, and turned away so she wouldn't see the falsity on his face. Around his eyes. Around his mouth. He was usually a much better liar.

But this time they should know the truth. That I don't know what I'm doing. That I'm not sure if we'll ever see Athena or Cassandra again.

It was easy enough at first to pass off the story that Cassandra, Athena, and Odysseus had taken off together. To Cabo, or Cancun. In the months preceding, Cassandra had become enough of a delinquent for her parents to buy it. But then weeks passed and they didn't come back, and concern slowly burned into panic.

"Tom was here again today," he said. "Asking if I'd heard from my sister."

"What did you tell him?"

"That Athena left a message a few days ago." He swallowed. "I made it sound like it's all about Aidan. That Cassandra had to get away for awhile."

Andie pulled her black hair back over her shoulder. "That's good. But don't sound so guilty when you say it. You're saving their skins. When they come back they'll thank you."

"They're not all coming back. Odysseus is dead. Remember?"

Andie paused less than a second before stacking boxes of cookies next to the microwave. Sometimes Hermes wondered if she had come to believe the Cabo story just as much as Henry and Cassandra's parents.

"I want to go over for awhile and see how Henry's doing," she said. "You'll be all right here, won't you?"

"I'm a god," Hermes said. "I think I can hold my own for an evening. It should be me following you around everywhere, making sure Ares or the Fates don't pop up and squish you like mosquitoes."

Andie gestured vaguely around the empty kitchen.

"I know. It's just that—you're all alone. Without her here. And—" Her eyes flickered over his emaciated body. "I don't want you to get bored and skip town. It's one more week until spring break. Then we can go find Demeter, and she'll lead us to Cassandra and Athena. I don't want anything to happen before then."

"Like me falling dead to the floor in a pile of papery, sagging skin and bones?" He chuckled.

"That's not funny."

Except it was, a little. He was so thin that the whole mess would look like a pile of T-shirts and a basketball. That's all that would remain. They could bury him in a knapsack. But it wouldn't happen anytime soon. Strength still heated his fingers when he made a fist, even if that fist wasn't much more than knuckles and tendon.

"Hermes? Where do you think they are?"

He took a deep breath. The last time he'd glimpsed Athena, she was clutching a bloodied Odysseus to her chest and throwing herself off of Olympus. He couldn't feel her anywhere, didn't know if she was still slogging through sorrow or if the rage had taken over. Because it would.

"Maybe she and Cassandra have already found each other," he said. But they hadn't. If they had, he'd have heard. They would trail a wake of god's blood a mile wide. The Fates would be screaming.

"But what if Demeter's wrong? What if they really are dead?"

Hermes shook his head. "She's not wrong."

"How do you know?"

"Because we need her to be right."

Henry stood at the end of his driveway holding a white plastic bag of trash. On the way back up to the house he'd get the mail. He glanced up at the spring sky. There weren't many clouds. After dinner there might be enough light to work on cleaning up the yard.

His new list of self-imposed chores made the days go by, he could say that at least. Picking up the slack that Cassandra used to tow, so his parents wouldn't have to worry about one more thing. He'd been in overdrive since she'd been gone, taking on some of his dad's tasks and his mom's, too.

It was easier than he thought to be two kids instead of one. It was easy to get lost in it.

Beside him, Lux shoved his black nose into Henry's elbow, asking why they never played anymore.

He dropped the garbage into the can and closed the lid, and thought of how many chores he could get Cassandra to do when she got home. He'd never have to clean his room again. He'd make her drive up to State to clean his college dorm. That would really piss her off, if she got back.

When she gets back. Cassandra's not lost.

A car horn sounded, and Lux ducked as from a gunshot. He hid behind Henry's leg as the vehicle slowed, and he didn't jump up to greet it, not even when the girl rolled the window down. Henry knelt and scratched him, treading lightly on his surgery scars.

"Hey." The girl inside leaned across the seat and turned down her radio. "Cute dog. What's his name?"

"Lux."

"Here, Lux!" She held out her hand, and Lux retreated farther behind Henry's pant leg. Since Ares' wolves attacked that winter, Lux hadn't been the same. All the bluster had gone out of him. It had taken Henry a while to get used to the fact that Lux was a new dog, one that shied away from corgis in the park and only barked for people he knew.

"He's a little shy." The girl in the car was Ariel Moreau. They'd been partners on a history project first term.

"What are you doing here?" He tried to smile so it wouldn't sound so rude, but she didn't seem to notice one way or the other.

"Mary lives over on Red Oak." She gestured back the way she'd come. "I was on my way home, and saw you."

Her voice took a big upswing at the end, as though seeing him had been the best thing to happen to her all day. It was actually a nice thought. Almost made him smile for real.

"What are you doing?" she asked.

He pointed at the garbage can, and she blushed.

"Oh. So, nothing cool."

"No," he agreed. "Nothing cool."

"Still no news from your sister?"

"No."

"But you're pretty sure she's okay?"

"Pretty sure."

Ariel made a sympathetic face. "Must suck though, still. Not knowing. I bet your parents are clamping down on you pretty hard. Are they really worried?" She exhaled and smiled. "Sorry. Stupid question."

"It's okay. I should get back inside. Before Lux starts drooling all over your door."

"I don't mind. He seems sweet. He didn't jump up or anything." She reached out again, and the dog whined. She looked back at Henry. "I'm not upsetting you, am I? When I stopped I didn't mean to ask about your sister. It just popped out."

"Don't worry about it." He shrugged. "It would've been weird if you hadn't mentioned it. But why did you stop, then?"

"I don't know." She looked away, down at her steering wheel and the front of her jacket. "Do you want to . . . go get something to eat or something?"

Henry blinked. He hadn't expected that. But she was pretty. And seemed cool. And it had been a while.

Ariel giggled nervously. "What? If you'd rather not—"

"No. It's just that I just realized I haven't been on a date since Jennifer Sanford this fall. And before that, the two—"

"—week thing with Melissa Miller," she finished for him.

"You've been paying attention." Between them, Lux whined and twisted away to bark at an approaching car: Andie's silver Saturn. She pulled up and flipped on her blinker, but Ariel was blocking the driveway.

"I guess I should get going." Ariel smiled. "Maybe some other time?"

Henry nodded. "Sure."

Andie honked once, long and loud. Ariel waved at her as she drove past.

"Who was that?" Andie asked once she'd parked and gotten out.

"Ariel Moreau. She's in my class."

"Oh." She scrunched her face. "What'd *she* want?"

Henry snorted. "Nothing. What do *you* want?"

"Nothing. I was just over at Hermes' place. Stocking the shelves, as they say. Hey, I was thinking about trying to get some assignments in advance. For after spring break. In case we don't get back on time. Are you going to?"

Henry looked down at Lux, who leaned heavily against Andie's legs. The longer he stayed silent, the more Andie talked.

"I mean, who knows how long it'll take. Or how far we'll have to go. Hermes says it'll take days just to find Demeter, and then if she's not sure where they are—let's face it. We could be talking summer school."

"I don't think I should go."

"Noted. So are you going to get your homework or not?"

Henry sighed and stared down the road.

"You have to go," Andie said. "We have to find them. Besides, you can't stay here by yourself. We don't know where Ares is, or that asshole Achilles." Her fists clenched when she said his name.

"Andie, will you shut up for five minutes?"

"Not effing likely."

Henry took a breath to quell the urge to throw her in a headlock and roll her around the yard.

"I'm pulled in a lot of different directions right now, if you haven't noticed," he said. "My parents, school, the parts of my life that aren't freaking insane."

"You're not the only one. But we have to go. There isn't a choice."

"There's been a choice this whole time. Just nobody's made the right ones. I'm not going." He frowned. It was a shitty situation they were in. That they were all in. "I'm sorry. My parents would worry themselves to death. With Cassandra missing . . . and then me . . ."

Of course, they'd forgive him if he could bring Cassandra home.

Andie's glare made him hold his breath.

"Of course I noticed," she said. "You idiot. What do you think I was doing here?" She opened her door and ducked inside.

"Andie."

If she heard she didn't show it. She just backed out and drove away.

3

UNDERNEATH

The dark is not total. There is some light still, and movement of air that isn't my breath, and isn't yours. There's still time, before the light sets on another passing day, or week, or hour, whatever arbitrary chunk of time she's decided to turn into a cycle. There's still time for you to open your eyes.

Athena trembled, cold despite the warm blood on her arms. Odysseus lay before her on soft, slate-colored sand. His eyes were closed. Achilles' sword was still lodged in his chest. She'd tilted him onto his side to accommodate it.

"I can hear his blood, singing down the edge of that blade."

"Shut up, Persephone." Athena jerked her head in time to see the trailing edge of her cousin's dark dress. Persephone laughed, and Athena bit her tongue, saving whatever strength she had inside a body that felt clammy and pliant. Persephone couldn't hurt him here. Not where

Athena had set him, on the far bank of the river Styx, in the hinterland between the living and the dead. Not while he still breathed. Even the queen of the underworld had limits. But Persephone could send things: shades, and worse than shades, across the river in the night. Athena swallowed. The light around them faded like a waning candle, and when it was gone, she'd have to be ready to fight again.

"You can't keep this up forever, Athena."

"Watch me."

"He won't live here."

"But he won't die, either." Odysseus would breathe, and lay unconscious and shivering, with a monster's blade through his chest. A bead of sweat, or a tear, rolled down Athena's cheek. She held his hand gently and there was no letting go. Over and over her mind replayed those last seconds inside of Olympus. She saw Achilles walk to Hera and the Moirae. Saw him smile. Had it been a sudden betrayal? Or had he played them all along?

It doesn't matter. Whatever it was, it came easy. And I should have known.

"Is that what you really want?" Persephone asked. "For him to linger here, half dead and always dying?"

Athena laughed weakly. "Half dead and always dying. He'll be just like you. And you don't seem to mind it much."

The wind changed, and carried the scent of sweet decay to Athena's nostrils. She kept her breath shallow to stave off gagging. It hadn't come from Odysseus. His wounds bled, but were no worse. He remained trapped in between. The smell could have been from anything else in the underworld. From whatever beast Persephone intended to send across the river that night, or from Persephone herself, from the half of her body that was still wet and rotting. Or perhaps it came from the Styx, the river of hate. Often Athena thought she caught a hint of what she imagined hate must smell like. Hot and metallic.

She passed a hand across Odysseus' forehead. She was so tired. Bone tired.

When the light returns I'll lie down beside you. I'll lie beside you, and you'll keep me, for a little while.

The light would return. She didn't know when. Sometimes the blackness felt so long, and the cuts on her arms and throbs in her joints weighed her down until she wanted to scream. Until she did scream. And then she would blink, and the light would be back. She could see what it was she fought, and she would fight on. Athena didn't know how long they'd been there. It wasn't worth trying to measure the cycles of light and dark. The light wasn't morning. It was barely real light. And it didn't matter. She and Odysseus were there, and there they would remain.

"Odysseus," Athena whispered, and watched him as the dark came. When she could no longer see him, she got to her feet and clenched her fists.

4

THE GODS OF DEATH

The doors of the bar stood wide open and let in a swath of bright light. Which was good, because there wasn't much light from anywhere else. Just a green glass lamp hanging over the pool table and a few yellow bulbs behind the cash register. Cassandra looked at herself in the slivers of mirror visible between bottles of Pucker and vodka. She looked as young as she suspected she looked.

"Stop fidgeting," Calypso said into her drink. "You might as well be a blinking neon underage sign."

"Sorry. There aren't a lot of bars back in Kincade where sophomores like to hang out." Cassandra wrinkled her nose. The interior smelled like smoke and old wood, open doors or not.

"As long as you don't order your beer in a red plastic cup, you'll be fine." Calypso smiled prettily at the bartender.

Cassandra wouldn't order anything, but as long as Calypso kept flirting, it wouldn't make a difference.

"Where is this guy?" Cassandra glanced around the room. It wasn't exactly a happening scene in the middle of the day. Maybe it never was. The place was a dive, with chipped tables and a Metroid pinball machine in the corner. The kind of bar that saw the same two dozen regulars on rotating nights.

"He'll be here." Calypso took a sip of her gin and tonic. "Don't look too eager. You'll chase him away."

"I'll do my best." The knowledge of Cassandra's powers had spread surprisingly fast through the gods' subculture, considering how disjointed they were and how poorly they kept in touch. This was the third lead that Calypso had tracked down. The first two had hissed and scurried for cover, burying themselves deep within human crowds before she could even tell them what she wanted. It was a lot of trouble to go through for fake IDs and passports. A lot of trouble for the trails of gods.

But it would be worth every minute when she found them.

Frustrated, she eyed the bartender and considered ordering a beer. He might let her slide, if for no other reason than to curry favor with Calypso. And Cassandra could use it. The tension of waiting was getting on her nerves. The guy was twenty-five minutes late already. Maybe he'd seen her from the door and changed his mind. Maybe she shouldn't have come.

Cassandra sighed and looked at Calypso. The nymph stirred her drink listlessly.

"What? Is it Odysseus?"

"No," Calypso replied. "Yes. But I'll be with Odysseus soon enough."

"Then what is it?" Cassandra asked. "You look really depressed."

Calypso smiled. "It's stupid. But it is depressing." She fingered the brown and white twist in her hair. "I look my age."

"You do not." Cassandra snorted. "If you looked your age, you'd look like dust." She laughed, relieved that it was something so foolish. Of all the things to worry about. Though she supposed that to Calypso, it was important. Beauty defined her. Cassandra watched her tap her hair, almost distractedly. Saying she was still beautiful would do no good. What bothered her was the fact that she had changed. She had changed, and she would change still more. When she died she would wear an aged face. A stranger's face.

"Tell me about your friend," Cassandra said. "Something besides that he's afraid of me. *Should* he be afraid of me?"

Calypso shrugged and brightened a little. "He's a satyr. He doesn't kill. But he does have appetites."

"What kind of appetites?"

"He sleeps with lots of girls and doesn't call them in the morning. Is that something you can forgive?"

Cassandra shrugged. "He sleeps with girls."

"Lots of girls."

She shrugged again. "So would Hermes if Athena wasn't watching him all the time. And not just girls, but boys and probably congressmen."

Calypso shook her head slowly. "But you're going to kill Hermes, too. Aren't you?"

Cassandra said nothing. She'd pushed the idea of killing

Hermes into the back of her mind. Aside from Aidan, he was the only god she loved as well as hated.

It doesn't matter. All gods must die. Whether I love them or not.

Loud, almost clanging footsteps snapped her out of her thoughts. Beside her, Calypso smiled and gestured for the figure in the doorway to come closer. After a second of staring at him, Cassandra did, too, with a slight nod of her head. *Come on. It's safe. I won't put my hands on you and turn you into mutton.* And she wouldn't unless he gave her real cause. He was only a satyr. Not a god. Not even a nymph like Calypso. His death was probably so accelerated that he only had a few more years anyway.

As he hugged Calypso and kissed her cheek, Cassandra studied his body and every inch of exposed skin. All seemed healthy and California tan. His olive undertones made his brown T-shirt look green.

"David. This is Cassandra."

Cassandra held her hand out, and watched him debate whether to touch her or to risk pissing her off by not touching her.

"It's okay," she said, and put her hand back on the bar.

"Sorry I'm late." He gave no excuse as to why, and signaled to the bartender for a beer. "Should we get a table?"

They moved to the back, out of the shaft of sunlight and into the dusty yellow of the billiard lamp. David slid into a chair and tossed a small manila envelope onto the table. Calypso opened it and took out a stack of fake passports and driver's licenses. The way she flipped through them so casually made Cassandra glance back to check the bartender. But he had his eyes where they should be, on the glasses he was washing. He knew what it meant when his patrons retreated to the back corner.

Calypso frowned.

"You made me twenty-seven."

David shrugged. "The photos you sent looked twenty-seven. It's a good age. You want them to last, don't you?"

Calypso passed Cassandra hers.

"He made you twenty-one."

"And that was a stretch." David took a drink. "You look all of about fifteen."

All of about fifteen. But she was almost seventeen. And could have killed him by caressing his cheek. She tucked the IDs into her pocket and looked David over, noting the faint lines around his mouth and the looseness of his skin. A burly patch of chest hair was visible at his collar, shot through with gray. Cassandra scrutinized his head. That black hair of his wasn't quite so naturally black anymore. Poor David. He would be sleeping with and not calling fewer and fewer girls in the coming months.

"So. Ladies. Is that it? Because not that it isn't a kick to see you, Cally, but . . ."

"No, that's not it." Cassandra interjected. "What have you heard of the other gods? And—don't lie. And don't make me 'bad cop' you either. I'd feel ridiculous."

David paused. He looked sort of amused, but no less nervous.

"I'm just a satyr," he said. "A lower being. Why would I know anything?"

Cassandra glanced at Calypso. As a nymph, she was half a lower being herself. And the farther down you were on the godly ladder, the closer you paid attention. Lowers minded the uppers, in case the uppers decided to cause trouble.

"What have you heard?" Cassandra asked again.

"What have *I* heard?" David snorted. "What have *you* heard?"

"I've heard that Artemis is dead," Cassandra said. "Not by my hand. And Poseidon is dead. Not mine either. Aidan—" she swallowed. "Apollo is dead. Hera is dead. She was mine. Athena's probably dead, too." She couldn't tell if any of it surprised or saddened David. He wore his masks well.

"Who do you want?" he asked.

"I want Aphrodite. And Ares, since he'll probably be there anyway."

David shook his head. "Not a chance. Those two took off so fast they left behind a dust trail. Nobody's heard a thing from them. Besides, by all accounts, Aphrodite's in pretty bad shape. She'll probably die on her own. Save you the trouble."

No. Aphrodite would die screaming at her hands, and it wouldn't be any trouble at all. Cassandra's palms burned quietly, and she brushed them against the cool fabric of her jeans.

"He's not lying," Calypso said after a few seconds.

"I know," Cassandra replied.

He was too afraid to lie. Nothing he would protect could hurt him worse than she could. Still, the idea that Aphrodite had gone to ground, out of her reach, made her stomach twist.

We'll find them, someday. They can't hide forever. Someone will have seen them.

"What about Hades?" she asked. God of the underworld. God of death. When she'd gone to the underworld looking for Aidan, Persephone said that Hades' death would be a blight on the world. That he would die in a blast of virus and disease. An entire city would fall around him to some unspeakable plague. One last tribute, she'd called it. But not if Cassandra could help it. If she couldn't have Aphrodite, then she'd settle for him.

Calypso and David stared.

"Hades?"

Cassandra nodded. The idea of him walking in a city somewhere, ticking down like a biological weapon, had been in the back of her mind since she'd returned from the underworld. More than once she'd dreamed of a man clothed in black, surrounded by thousands of corpses, blackened and bleeding from the eyes. The first time she woke in a panic, and flipped through every news channel she could find. But it hadn't been a vision. Only a nightmare. It was harder and harder to tell the difference.

David laughed and drew his hand roughly over his chin.

"Cally, your friend has big balls for such a little girl."

Calypso made a face. "Don't be gross, David. Have you heard anything about Hades, or not?"

He sighed. "He's not on this continent. He doesn't like it. Except for Mexico, when the Aztecs were there, and then he came north for the frontier. That's the last I heard of him here."

Cassandra rolled her eyes. It didn't matter if Hades wasn't in the United States when David had just supplied them with passports.

"I can't get you to Hades," he said finally. "But if you're after the god of death, why not try the real thing?"

"The real thing?"

Cassandra searched the whole of her mind all the way to Troy and back but couldn't discern who he referenced.

"Thanatos?" Calypso asked, and David nodded.

"Thanatos. Death embodied. If you want Hades, he'll know where to find him."

"And?" Cassandra snapped. "Where is this . . . Thanatos?"

David finished his beer and stood. "You're in luck. He loves Los Angeles."

"Don't you know how to do your hair? I thought all girls today would know at least how to do a fancy ponytail."

Cassandra stared at her reflection in the hotel mirror. The girl who stared back had a face clean of makeup and slightly tanned shoulders from time spent under unfamiliar sun. Brown hair hung down to her elbows. It hadn't been cut in months.

"I don't want to do my hair. And I don't want to wear this." The dress Calypso had put her in stuck to her in every place that would make her self-conscious. It was black, but a shadow of gray patterning across her chest and down her hip suggested a leopard's spots. They might have stripped it off of any wasted Hollywood socialite.

"We won't get in if you don't wear that." Calypso stepped behind her and swept her hair back over her shoulders. Four quick twists and what felt like a dozen bobby pins threaded through Cassandra's scalp made it almost presentable.

"I don't like the idea of that, either." She squirmed as Calypso applied makeup to her eyes and lips. "I don't need this. You'd be enough. I could sneak by in your shadow." Calypso wore light blue silk. Somehow it made her eyes greener and her skin more honeyed. She patted Cassandra's cheek.

"This is the price to meet the god of death."

Cassandra frowned. The price to meet the god of death was animal print. But she would bear it to get close to him, so he might get her closer to the other gods. Her heart hammered at the thought, and her hands hadn't stopped itching all day. She'd had to watch herself to make certain she didn't touch Calypso and accidentally add another line to her face.

"Come on. The cab will be here in a few minutes." Calypso's warm smile was almost infectious. But not quite. Not so very long ago, a night like this would have been thrilling. To hit the clubs in a strange town. Not so long ago, it would've been Cassandra in the mirror, trying to get Andie to put on at least a little eyeliner.

But I still wouldn't have worn this stupid dress.

She glanced down at her chest.

Might've been fun to get Andie to wear it.

The name of the club was Haze Park. On the drive from the hotel, Cassandra tried to track the streets, but lost the thread after four turns. Every inch of Los Angeles looked the same to her, especially at night. It was all so dry and spare compared with back home. She never thought she would miss the mud and gray slop of a Kincade spring. By now the whole yard would be wet. Lux would roll around in the melt puddles and come out smelling awful. Their mom would shriek and chase him off of the furniture until Henry caught him and threw him into the tub.

The cab pulled up to the curb, past a long line of people waiting behind ropes. It was on the tip of her tongue to tell Calypso they could just wait with everyone else, that they'd never cut to the front of the line. That it only happened in movies. But the second Calypso stuck a leg out the door, the bouncer motioned with his fingers for them to come ahead.

"How do people not hate you?" Cassandra asked, careful to avoid eye contact with anyone waiting.

Calypso shrugged.

"Some do," she said. "Athena did."

"Well, you hated her, too."

Calypso stopped short inside the door, and Cassandra surveyed the interior: blues and blacks and silvers. Loud music and gyrating bodies. All very good-looking gyrating bodies.

"I didn't hate her," Calypso said. "I don't hate anyone."

"Not even Achilles?"

Calypso looked at her carefully. "I'm not made for vengeance. Not everyone is like you and Athena."

Hearing their names grouped together made Cassandra's hackles rise, but she swallowed and turned away. Calypso hadn't meant anything by it, and besides, they had work to do. Thanatos, god of death, was there somewhere. According to Satyr David, he'd been at Haze Park every Saturday night for the last two months. Satyr David also said they'd know him when they saw him.

Cassandra squinted, barely able to see a thing around the

obstruction of so many already tall girls stacked up by four-inch heels. The blue lighting didn't help much, either.

"Do you think your friend told him we were coming?" she asked.

"I don't think so," Calypso replied, and Cassandra figured she was right. David hadn't given the impression that he was on close terms with Thanatos, or that they even spoke. The Satyr was a pigeon. He watched and he ferried messages.

They threaded their way through the crowd, trying to catch a glimpse of whatever Death looked like. Was he a hunched-over man at the bar dragging an oxygen tank? Someone with clothing covering most of his skin to hide sores and rot? It was unlikely that either one would get into a club like Haze Park, no matter how much money he had.

Then again, maybe he paid to be kept in the back.

"Calypso. Check the doors and"—Cassandra gestured to the second level—"those funky beaded curtains. Find the VIPs." She was tempted to let Calypso do everything. No one would try to stop her; all she'd have to do was bat an eyelash. She touched the nymph's arm. "I'll go up to the left." Calypso nodded, and Cassandra watched her head toward the back of the club. She took a breath and glanced down. The dress still clung, and the skin of her chest and shoulder shimmered. Body glitter. She brushed at it irritably, but Calypso hadn't snuck it on. It had rubbed off of someone else.

"Fine," she muttered. She scanned the length of the bar, part searching, part considering whether to try her fake ID for some liquid courage. She had no idea what she'd order.

She didn't even feel like drinking. But having something in her clammy palms to stop her fidgeting seemed like a good idea. A few more feet and she'd reach the stairway that twisted up along the wall. It led to beaded curtains and a balcony overlooking the main level.

Maybe it's just the bathroom. But there is the balcony . . .

It would give her a much better vantage point at least. Cassandra gripped the banister, careful to keep her ankles straight in the delicately heeled shoes.

The second she stood against the rail and looked down on the main level, she felt better. The whole place was too close for comfort. Even there, above it all, the sound was a constant cloak. She couldn't hear anything except the music, the beat, and the closest shouts. Certainly not the rattling whisper of the beaded curtain when Death walked through it.

But she felt him, like the cool of a breeze without any wind. A still kind of cold, like a lake that didn't ripple.

"You don't—" she shouted, and stopped. *You don't want to touch me*, is what she'd meant to say. *You don't want to touch me, because I don't want you to crumble like a pillar of wet sugar before you tell me anything.* She hadn't needed to speak. Her arms and hands felt about as threatening as wet rags.

The being who stood before her was no eighty-year-old on oxygen. He was no cloaked monster covered in leprous sores. Instead, Death was beautiful, if a bit extreme. His hair was black. His eyes were black. His skin was pale white. Or maybe that was just a trick of the blue lights. If it wasn't for the green tones of his shirt, he might've been made out of newsprint.

He didn't say anything, just slid onto the rail beside her and looked down into the crowd. A few lovely faces turned up toward his like flowers tracking sunlight. Cassandra glanced back through the beaded curtain, still swaying from his exit. More beautiful faces were in there, watching his back. A tiny spark lit in Cassandra's wrists.

"What are you doing with those girls?" she asked.

"Drinking. Talking. Dancing, when I can't avoid it." He smiled. She didn't know whether to swoon or scream. "The rest is none of your business."

"Thanatos."

"At your service."

She studied his face, and the way the girls, and some guys, seemed drawn to him like a magnet. Already there was movement toward the stairs. If they stayed much longer they'd be surrounded.

"They're drawn to you," she said quietly. So quietly she was surprised when he answered.

"Yes. Some of them are. Many of them. Even if they don't know it."

"And you let them find you."

He shrugged. His eyes had a slight squint. She couldn't decide whether it made him look dishonest, or just mischievous.

"Everyone finds me," he said. "Eventually. Except the immortals." He smiled again. "But then, I suppose, *they* find *you*. We can't talk here," he said before she could speak. "We've got to go." He looked down into the crowd. Cassandra followed his eyes and saw Calypso, staring up at him as though she'd been there for days. When he tilted his head toward the exit, she nodded.

"Wait," Cassandra said, but when he slipped his arm around her waist she found herself walking calmly down the stairs.

It wouldn't do to fight anyway. If I struggle, I might burn him to a crisp.

"It's a short drive to my place. You don't mind? Calypso will come, too, of course."

Cassandra nodded. In the back of her mind her power to kill gods sat quietly, comforting as a gun under her pillow.

"You have nothing to fear from me." He smiled.

"Of course I don't," she said.

He slid his hand into hers and led her from the club and down the street to his parked car, Calypso trailing behind at a safe distance. To the waiting line they would look like a pair of lovers, excited to be going home.

"Calypso," Thanatos said, and opened the door for her to climb into the backseat.

"Thanatos," she replied, and glanced at Cassandra. But this was why they'd come. Cassandra nodded, and she got in.

The drive was indeed short. Perhaps because the god of death had a sports car and no use for speed limits. The car hugged the turns, tires squealing. By the time they pulled into his secluded driveway, Cassandra's stomach was wrapped trembling around her heart.

"Well?" he asked. "What do you think?"

Cassandra surveyed the yard. The house was beautiful, with wide windows and a view of the hills. It was isolated, and softly lit. The kind of house you'd expect a very rich serial killer to have. She pried her fingers away from the door handle she'd been clutching.

"I think you're lucky my power doesn't work on cars. Else your oh-shit handle would be toast."

He chuckled.

"You're not surprised to see me," she said.

"I've been around a long time. There isn't much that can surprise me. Come inside."

Inside, the house was clean and sparely decorated. A few interesting modern art sculptures adorned the corners, and the couches and chairs were either white fabric or smooth black leather. Calypso came with her, in through the entry-way and toward the open kitchen. Their heels clicked loudly on stone tile. Cassandra took a deep sniff and couldn't detect a single scent. She frowned.

"You thought it might smell of flowers?" Thanatos asked. "Like a funeral home? That'd be a little on the nose, don't you think?" He took off his jacket and laid it across the couch, then walked to the bar and poured three glasses of what Cassandra figured was brandy. She shook her head when he offered it.

"No thank you, on the date-rape brandy."

Thanatos shrugged, and handed it to Calypso. Calypso went to lounge on a chair, and Cassandra blinked. They needed to stay on guard in the house of death. In the mellow light, his black eyes looked amused, and more human. The curve of his lip was seductive and soft. She crossed her arms.

"It's obscene," she said. "That you look this way."

"Does that mean you like it? I hope so. Because I like this." He gestured up and down at her dress. "The print, like an animal's skin. It makes you look like the huntress you are."

"It was my idea," Calypso said.

"I'm not a huntress," Cassandra snapped.

"Oh? You didn't come here to find out what I knew of the other gods, so you can kill them? If you don't think that constitutes hunting then you'd better get a dictionary." He walked casually to the fireplace and lit it with a button. "It's strange having you here. You're like a big, bright, blinking light in my living room. To think I first heard of you such a long time ago."

"Where? From who?"

He shrugged, and pushed black hair back from his eyes. "But I sensed *you* first in the club." He sat beside Calypso.

"Me?" she asked in her soft, musical voice. "Why me?"

"Because you want me more than anyone else. More than anything." He leaned in close. "Your longing is like a song."

"Get away from her." Cassandra stepped forward, but neither Thanatos nor Calypso moved. Calypso didn't even look up. "Calypso. Don't. You promised."

Calypso blinked slowly. She looked so suddenly miserable that Cassandra's throat tightened with guilt.

"You're right," she said. "I promised."

"She promised she would stay," Thanatos said to Cassandra. "What did you promise her? Because you better have promised her something."

Under the intensity of his stare, Cassandra's cheeks reddened.

"I promised I would kill her."

Thanatos turned to Calypso and laughed.

"But I could do it for her now. She's no god; she's always been able to be killed. Always. Even when she wasn't so delicately aging." He reached out and drew his fingers along her face and down her neck. "I could lay her back and kiss her, and there she could remain."

Calypso brushed his hand aside.

"I made a promise to Cassandra."

"Are you sure? My way is cleaner."

Cleaner. What did that even mean? Dead was dead. Cassandra rubbed her bare arms. Being inside the house felt wrong. Death clung to every surface. Shades of murdered girls were probably strung up in every corner.

But that's sexist. There must be shades of boys. People of all ages. And puppies and geraniums, too.

And despite Thanatos' handsome appearance, she doubted they had all died by way of a gentle kiss. Her feet twisted painfully in her heels, imagining downstairs rooms lined with plastic and blood spatter, a walk-in freezer with dead clubbers hung on meat hooks. Maybe an entire pantry full of peeled eyeballs.

Stop it. This is California. There probably is no downstairs.

"I want to know," she said, "what you know about the other gods."

Thanatos swirled the brandy in his glass and looked at Calypso from under his brow.

"Would you excuse us? Don't worry about the girl," he said before either could object. "If I start to scare her, she'll just kill me."

Calypso regarded Cassandra with caution, but slid off the chair.

"Go take a swim in the pool. It's heated." Thanatos gestured down the dark hall behind them. "You'll find it lit." After the clicking of Calypso's heels had grown faint, he turned back to Cassandra. "She never could resist a swim.

Nymphs." He leaned forward. "I want you to do some tricks for me. I want to see your gifts in action. What do you need?"

She curled her fists.

"What do you mean, 'my gifts in action'?"

"Not the power in those deadly hands," he said. "Your other gift. Now, what do you need?"

She answered reluctantly. "A coin. I can call it in the air."

He reached into his pocket and pulled one out, fat and gold. No regular quarters or silver dollars here. It was probably a freaking doubloon.

"Why did you want us to be alone?" she asked.

He smiled. "I didn't think you were the kind of girl who would enjoy being on display."

"I don't mind it at all, actually," she said softly. "Depending on who's watching."

"Very well," he said. "Then let's play a game. For every correct prediction, I'll tell you something. Do we have a deal?"

She didn't like that phrasing. A deal. Like if he welched, she'd get a shiny fiddle made of gold. She looked into his dark eyes, always with their hint of a smile, and felt dizzy. But he was the god of death. Not the devil.

"Deal."

He tossed the coin; it flashed in the firelight.

"Tails."

He caught it and slapped it down on the back of his hand.

"Tails indeed." He studied the coin with amusement, rather stupidly, she thought, because it was his damn coin. "An interesting little gift. You received it from Lachesis.

I think you would know her as the Moirae on the right. With long, silver-blond hair."

"I got it from Apollo."

"He bestowed it. But it traces back to the Moirae."

"Whatever. What do you know about Ares and Aphrodite? Or Hades?"

Thanatos held up the coin. Too many questions. Fine. She rolled her eyes and motioned for him to flip, then called "tails" as soon as it left his fingers. Right again. Of course.

"The Moirae on the left is Clotho. Wild, red hair. Many witches share her blood, or at least those good at midwifery and past-life regression."

Cassandra glared.

"That's not what I asked."

"I never said I'd give you answers." He shrugged. "I said I'd tell you something. But I will give you answers. Eventually."

She did her best to hide her bubbling frustration.

"Should I just ask about the Moirae in the middle, so I'll feel like I'm making progress?" She eyed the coin. "Heads. Heads. Heads. Tails. Heads. Tails."

His smile was genuinely delighted, and he flipped the coin six times. Cassandra swallowed. She'd never been able to do that before. The call had always come into her head after the coin was tossed. She was getting better. Stronger.

"Atropos is the one I miss the most," said Thanatos. "The raven-haired beauty in the middle."

"Not so beautiful anymore."

Thanatos chuckled. "She'll always be beautiful. A god of death. Like me." He looked at Cassandra. "There aren't actually that many creatures who understand what it is to end life. Like we do."

"This is a stupid game," she said, and moved toward the fireplace to escape his gaze.

"It's over, anyway."

Irritated heat shot through her wrists, into her palms, and down each finger. She felt ridiculous, in this house, clacking around in heels that were too high and a dress that was too tight.

"Tell me what you know. If you know where Ares and Aphrodite are, tell me."

"Or what?" he asked.

"Or I *will* kill you."

He twisted on the sofa to keep her in view.

"Try."

"What?"

He put his brandy down and stood.

"I want you to try. You would do it eventually anyway, wouldn't you? Or were you planning on sparing the god of death, just because I turned state's evidence?"

"I don't know. It could be arranged that you would just wither and fade on your own. Not how I would do it." Bargaining. It sounded like bargaining, when she'd come with every intention of threatening. If she was honest, she'd come with every intention of putting him down. But with each step closer he took, she had to fight to keep from running.

Fire licked up her arms to the elbows, but her heart pounded. She couldn't deny that death was a draw. She wanted to kill him, and fall against him while she did it.

"You don't want this," she said. "Trust me. Or go see for yourself; Hera's frozen stone face tells the story way better than I can." She felt his cold again, and resented it, forced more heat into her hands. But he didn't heed her warning.

"I'm not afraid. Touch me." He smiled slightly. "Anywhere you want."

She almost laughed, and almost slapped him across the face. He wouldn't give in, and she wouldn't be stalked through the house like a cornered rabbit.

"Just a little bit," she whispered. "Just enough so you'll know what your eventual death will feel like."

"But not enough to turn me to dust?"

"Not while I still need you." He was close enough that she could feel his breath. She could smell his cologne.

"A preview then," he said, inches away. "Do I need to make you angry?"

"You've been doing that all night." She studied his exposed skin. Her eyes moved over his angular face, down his neck, to his chest, or at least what was visible above his shirt buttons. "Roll up your sleeve." Something passed across his features. Disappointment? But then it was gone, and he rolled his shirt up to the elbow. Cassandra flexed her fingers. It would feel good for the heat to have somewhere to go. She wondered what would happen to his flesh beneath her hand. He seemed so cold that perhaps he'd crack into layers of frozen meat and skin.

Look into his eyes when you do it. Don't be a coward.

Her fingers curled around his wrist. She'd only hold him until he screamed. Waves pulsed out of her and into him; she thought of the feathers blossoming out of Athena like a bracelet. Maybe Thanatos would just decay. Maybe when she drew her hand away most of his wrist would come with it, oozing and stuck to her fingers. She looked into his eyes.

And he looked back into hers. Nothing happened. The shock extinguished her like a bucket of water. For a second she squeezed his wrist harder; tried to will it to break. But it held.

Thanatos shrugged.

"Don't feel bad," he said, rolling his sleeve back down. "It was impossible. You can't kill Death. Though I'll admit, I was curious. And this begs the question of what you're going to do with Atropos. . . ."

He turned away, and Cassandra backed up quickly. Her heels skidded until she ran into the sofa and stumbled to a sit. She couldn't kill him. Couldn't even make him sweat, while he could kill anything with a kiss. With a thought. And she was alone with him in his house.

"Calypso!"

"Don't!" Thanatos held up his hands. "Everything's fine. I don't want to hurt you, Cassandra. I never wanted to hurt you. But don't make Calypso come running. I suspect she's been skinny-dipping this whole time." He made a face, reconsidering. "On second thought, do call her."

"Shut up," Cassandra said. "If you don't want to hurt me, then what do you want?"

"It's not what I want," he said softly. "It's what I'm going to do." He picked up his brandy and downed it in one gulp. "You're going after Hades, and I'm going with you."

5

HELLO DESERT, MY OLD FRIEND

Hermes packed for hot and cold. Temps in the desert fluctuated wildly between night and day. There was a big bottle of sunscreen on the table, too, and aloe vera gel for Andie's inevitable sunburn. They could buy a case of water when they got there.

Packing was a lot harder with a mortal tagging along. If it were just him, he'd fill two canteens and throw two T-shirts into a bag before stuffing the rest full with food. But Andie refused to be left behind. And honestly, he was glad for the company.

Maybe leathery old Demeter will like her better than she likes me. Maybe we'll get real answers out of her this time.

He snorted. Not likely. But he'd weed through a *Da Vinci Code*'s worth of her ciphers and riddles if it meant finding out what happened to his sister and Cassandra.

Athena. How pissed she would be if she knew he wasn't

hitchhiking cross-country. How she would seethe over their first-class plane tickets to Utah. He smiled.

"Hey." Andie came through the front door without knocking, her backpack over her shoulder.

"You made it."

"Of course I made it."

She sounded indignant, but Hermes knew it must've taken a presentation with pie charts and begging for her mother to let her go. Henry and Cassandra's parents weren't the only ones holding on tighter in the wake of Cassandra's disappearance.

"My mom trusts me to a fault," Andie said. "I've never messed up, and I tell her everything." She tilted her head. "Or at least everything that wouldn't blow her mind. Besides, with just the two of us around, she has to trust me. Our lives wouldn't work otherwise."

"And you don't feel the least bit guilty lying?"

"I don't have to, as long as you get me home safe." Her hands moved methodically over their supplies, tucking the sunscreen and aloe into Hermes' suitcase.

"Still no word from Henry?"

She shook her head.

"He doesn't think he should come," she said. "And maybe he's right. I don't think his parents would let him come any-way."

Henry came through the door carrying a bag.

"What?" he asked as they stared at him in surprise.

"How . . . how did you get them to let you?" Andie asked.

"I told them the truth. That we had a chance to find Cassandra. That Hermes thought he knew where Athena might hole up." He let out a stressed breath. "The hardest part was convincing them it would be a bad idea for them to come along." His big, dark eyes were steely and still. "I hate seeing them like this, almost as much as I'm worried about Cassandra. This has to work."

They drove for as long as they dared. It would've been nice to drive straight to the eye, but they were just as likely to run over it, and besides, Hermes doubted that Demeter would take kindly to tire marks on her hide. So they ditched the rented SUV and shouldered their packs, ready to walk until they hit Demeter's skin, stretched across the desert.

"You sure you remember the way?" Andie asked.

Hermes nodded. He remembered the way. Just not exactly how far they'd had to go to get there. And he didn't have the option of a handy little owl guide if things went awry.

I really hope I haven't dragged them both out here to dehydrate.

"What if she moved?" Henry looked out across the landscape and Hermes followed his eyes. It was hot. Cacti in the distance seemed to waver, covered in haze.

"Not likely. She seemed pretty dug in the last time we were here." A disturbing image reared its head: Demeter shaking loose and scuttling across the hard-packed dirt like a manta ray at the bottom of the sea. "Besides, I think she wants us to find her. Why else would she make contact?"

"Maybe she was just sympathizing," Henry said. "Trying to be a good aunt. Maybe she doesn't really know anything, and they're dead."

Hermes' shoulders slumped. "You know, you're a real ball of sunshine sometimes, Henry."

"Don't start bickering," Andie said. "You're both sort of annoying me already."

Henry shook his head and they started off. It wasn't long before he overtook them both with long strides.

"Don't mind him," she muttered to Hermes. "He's just practical. He doesn't want us to get our hopes up."

"I don't know why," Hermes muttered back, "when hope's all we've got."

The walk was long, and hot. All three were soaked with sweat in under an hour. A light wind kicked up now and then, just to pepper them with dirt and dust. Andie and Henry's black hair was dull with it. Talk died off except to ask for water. No one asked to stop for a break. Soon enough the sun tipped behind the horizon, and the desert began to grow cold.

"Hold up." Andie stripped out of her backpack and dug inside it, then pulled out a hooded sweatshirt.

"Good idea," Henry agreed.

"I don't even want to put this on my dirty, sweaty arms," Andie grumbled. "But it's so cold."

It was cold. And to Hermes it felt unseasonably so, after having a sheen of sweat on his skin all afternoon. Andie and Henry shivered, though they tried to hide it. It wouldn't be much longer before they'd have to stop, and he'd have to track down fuel for a fire.

Not like when Athena and I were here. Back to back through the night. Two godly Popsicles.

"Hey!"

Hermes jumped up. Henry had shouted so abruptly his voice squeaked.

"I think . . ." He scuffed his sole gently against the ground. "Is this her?"

Hermes zipped to where Henry stood and brushed sand and small stones away from the leather that disappeared into the dirt. His smile spread ear to ear, and he bent his head to the earth and kissed her.

"Ew." Andie toed Demeter gently. "I mean, you said what she would be like, but . . . ew."

"It's like someone stretched an elephant rug out over the ground," said Henry.

Andie reached down and touched the skin. "More like . . . E.T. Like someone made a giant rug out of a bunch of E.T.s. Yuck. E.T. was so gross. I don't know why people liked that movie."

"Because it's a classic, that's why." Hermes swatted her hand away. "And watch what you say. If you think she can't hear you, you're wrong. And if you think she can't lift up out of the sand and slap you to a pancake, you're wrong about that, too."

Hermes led the way across the skin, and had to focus hard to keep his legs moving at a pace Andie and Henry could manage. They were so close. Close to finding answers, and then to finding his sister. He was going to strangle Athena when he found her. And he was going to hug her tight. He was going to strangle-hug her.

The nerve of you, jumping off that mountain, leaving me there between the Fates and Ares. I'd kill you if I wasn't so glad you haven't killed yourself.

"Hermes?"

"What?" He heard Andie's breath behind him, but got no reply. When he turned, they both stumbled forward, eyes wide. "What's the matter with—" He stopped, and felt like an idiot. They'd lost the light. He might be able to see and navigate by the quarter moon, but to Andie and Henry it was pitch black. He smiled at them fondly. Who knew how long they'd been soldiering along, trying to follow him with ears alone. And they were both shivering hard.

"Wait here." He put a hand on each of their shoulders. "I'm going to go find wood somewhere. Be back in a few minutes."

They insulated Demeter from the fire with several loads of dirt carried in Hermes' jacket. It didn't take long for him to gather the wood and scrub kindling, and even less time for Henry to get a decent fire going.

"Let me guess. You were an Eagle Scout." Hermes sat down on the skin and passed around a bag of taffy while cans of stew warmed in the coals.

"I wasn't, actually," Henry said. "But we take family camping trips every summer."

"That fire feels so good." Andie groaned. She'd stretched out on the skin and snuggled into it for warmth. It was a little weird, but Hermes and Henry only exchanged a silent smirk. "I don't know if I even have the energy to eat."

"Try," Hermes said. "You'll need the fuel for tomorrow. We've still got another few hours on the skin, and then a trek to who knows where."

Henry leaned forward and stirred the fire, careful to keep all coals inside the sand trap.

"Is this weird to anyone else?" he asked. "We're here on her skin, and she's somewhere over that way." He jerked his head over his shoulder. "But she knows we're here, and we're camping on her."

Andie rolled her head toward him.

"Henry. Just about everything about this is weird."

"Want to add another dimension?" Hermes asked. "Sit still and feel very closely." He watched their faces turn horrified. "That's her pulse through your butts." They groaned and he laughed, but they couldn't get away from it. Everywhere Andie rolled, the pulse followed. Hermes reached into the coals for a can of stew, double-wrapped it in a sock, and handed it to Henry. "Eat up, and get some rest. Tomorrow we'll have our answers."

Today is the day, big sister. Today we pick up your trail. And Cassandra's trail. But yours first. Hope the mortals don't have a problem with that.

Hermes stretched languidly. The sun had started to warm the air, but Andie and Henry would probably still wake up shivering. In the early pink hours, he'd let the fire burn down to coals as a sort of alarm clock.

They'll have to see the logic of it. If we go for Athena first, we're safer. And who better to get to Cassandra fast than Athena?

It sounded good in his head. But he could just imagine Henry's stubborn face: jaw set, eyebrows squeezed so close together they formed a line. They'd come around. But they'd argue first. Another reason they needed his sister. They never would have argued with her.

A different sort of thrum resonated through Demeter's skin. Henry's footsteps.

"Morning," Hermes said as Henry came to stand shoulder to shoulder with him. "Sleep well?"

Henry nodded and blushed a little. Hermes stifled a smirk. When he'd left the campsite, Henry had been locked together with Andie in a very solid spoon.

"She makes a better mattress than I thought she would, actually," Henry said.

Hermes laughed. "I'm going to assume you're talking about Demeter and not Andie."

Henry stuffed his hands into his pockets. The muscles in his jaw clenched and reclenched.

"Let's just wake Andie up so we can get going."

Andie didn't say much when they woke her, except to ask for some water and a piece of gum, but Hermes noticed she didn't look in Henry's direction the entire time they were packing up their gear.

So much tension. Maybe I shouldn't have rolled them together last night after all.

"Hey." He tossed Andie the bottle of sunblock. "Reapply. You, too, Henry."

She reluctantly squeezed some into her palm, and made a face rubbing it in. It must've felt disgusting after the sweat, the dirt, and the night in the cold desert, but it was better than winding up red and peely.

"You're in a good mood," she muttered.

"Of course I am."

"Aren't you the least bit worried about what she'll say?"

Of course he was. He was worried about a million things. Athena. Cassandra. The condition of them both when they were finally found. Athena's feathers. The Fates. His own thinning body. Leading Andie and Henry into danger. He was worried, with a side of sadness and outright fatigue. But what good did it do, when they needed him? He was all that was left.

"Let's just go meet my aunt."

Demeter's enormous, leather-lidded eye swept up, down, and over the two mortals and one filthy god. They stood around it in a semicircle, quietly tolerating the appraisal. Hermes thanked the stars that Andie didn't have any visible tattoos or piercings. Not even in her ears. But her sweat-stretched tank top didn't do much to hide her ample chest, either. He glanced at her nervously, noting her tired face shaded underneath a ridiculous floppy hat. Maybe Demeter would just focus on that.

"I was too hard on Athena before," Demeter said. "Apparently everyone dresses like this." She fixed her eye on Andie, and Andie squinted.

"What's that supposed to mean?"

"Nothing," Hermes said quickly. "She's old. She likes collars buttoned to your chin and long sleeves."

Demeter chuckled, or at least it sounded like a chuckle. A lot of air moved across their faces, and the skin rattled beneath their feet.

"I'm not as bad as all that, Messenger."

Henry craned his neck and looked around.

"Where is your voice coming from?"

Demeter's eye swiveled his way, and Hermes braced. The mortals were bold and flippant. It was his own damn fault, and Athena's, too, for befriending them and taking their jibes. But Demeter didn't seem angry. The eye had an almost affectionate tilt.

"I hardly know anymore, Hector. From my mouth. But where that is . . . I've been stretched so far it's hard to feel."

"But you're not in pain?" Henry asked.

Her eye blinked slowly.

"No. Not in particular. I sleep. Often. I dream."

Hermes nodded along with the polite conversation until he couldn't anymore, particles of dust falling out of his hair.

"Where's Athena?" he blurted.

All five eyes snapped to his face, but come on, they hadn't walked across miles and miles of skin and sand to talk about his aunt's aches and Andie's exposed bra straps. This was what they wanted to know. It was all they wanted to know. And he feared the answer the second the question left his lips.

"She's in the underworld. Fighting my daughter."

The underworld. The words flickered into his head in neon lights. But that was so easy. He could get there. He could get there in less than a day. All he needed was water, a river maybe, and a boat . . . and blood. Always blood. Only there had to be more. Something else. Demeter never spoke so plainly.

Except when it doesn't matter. When there's nothing to be done about it.

"Is she dead?" His voice trembled. "She's in the underworld. But is she dead?"

"If she's dead . . ." Andie whispered.

"We'll pull her out anyway!" It had been done before. By

him, on occasion. Of course, that had been under orders. Demeter's eye narrowed and she scoffed.

"You? Pull her out? Messenger of skin and bones is going to stand against my daughter and the king of the underworld? Hades doesn't let the dead go. And you've never been anything, compared to him."

You old rag. You don't know what I would do for her. What I could still do, for any of them.

Rage bubbled up his throat and sang down to his toes. He could tear her to ribbons before she knew what was happening. Before she had a chance to pull her edges in. His anger was hot enough to almost make him believe it, but his knuckles rattled in his hands like dice and kept him still. He could only lie to himself until he looked in a mirror.

Andie crossed her arms over her chest and shouted down at the eye.

"Why did you bring us out here, then, if there's nothing we can do? Where's Cassandra? Where is she, you . . . saddlebag made of E.T.—"

"Andie!" Henry grabbed her and pulled her back. "Fricken zip it!"

"Don't tell me to zip it. She's my best friend. I'd be crying right now if I had any liquid left in my body!"

Henry looked at Hermes angrily, demanding he do something, but aside from grabbing them both and whisking them off of the skin, and dropping another two pounds in the process, there was nothing Hermes could do.

Demeter took a deep breath and lifted them five inches.

"Cassandra is alive," she said. "I told you that much. And I didn't bring you here. That was your idea. If Hermes told you there'd be easy answers, or the answers that you wanted, then he's still the same silver-tongued liar I was always so fond of." She glanced his way. It was as close to an olive branch as he was likely to get.

"But where is she?" Henry asked. "Why doesn't she come home?"

"Because she has work to do. You're thinking too much about these errant girls. You have work of your own."

Hermes bent down and rested his knee against her warm surface. The day had grown hot again, and bright, and relentless. He pitied her, stretched thin every day to bake, and for dry winds to rake over.

"Our work is to find our sisters," he said.

"Your sisters will find their ways home. Your job is to still be alive when they get there." Her eye narrowed again. "Do you not dream, Messenger? Do you not sleep and see the shears shining in the dark? Can't you hear the sound they make when they cut down through your skin and bones?" She sighed. "That is all I dream of, now. Atropos and her blood-ringed eyes."

"Atropos?" Andie asked.

"Atropos," Hermes replied. "The Moirae in the middle. The black-haired one, sucking life from her shriveling sisters. The Moirae of death." He brushed pebbles and grit from Demeter's skin. "I wouldn't be afraid of those shears, if I were you, Aunt. I've seen the Fates, and as they are, they're not much of a threat to anyone. Joined at the legs, their limbs grown together like a pile of melted plastic dolls. It's one sad-looking potato-sack race. They could certainly never catch me."

"Your own blood will catch you. It races through your veins and feeds on every tissue it touches. It's the water of a riverbed, carrying away sand and wearing down rock." She let her eye move over his chest. "If you took off that shirt, I'd be able to see your organs."

He pushed back on his haunches. "You could not." He looked at Andie and Henry, who were trying to learn X-ray vision. "You can not."

"And who will save Hector and Andromache, when you're dead?" Demeter went on. "You have to do it now. While you have the strength."

"You want me to lead a fight against the Moirae, when Athena couldn't?"

It was more than ridiculous. It was impossible.

"You must want me to end up with a pair of shears in each eye."

"Athena didn't know what she fought," Demeter said. "You will."

"I'm not a leader. I'm the god of thieves."

"Hermes. There's no one else. There's no one left."

Just him. Only him, until Athena made it back. If she ever made it back.

"Hold on," Henry said. "Why don't we just wait for Athena? And my sister, if they're coming back?"

Demeter regarded the boy warily.

"This is how a warrior speaks?"

"Yes," Henry said, eyes dark. "If he wants to win. If waiting is smarter, then we wait. And if running is smarter, we do that, too."

"Stop." Hermes closed his eyes. The flat plane of the

desert seemed to tilt. They'd come for solutions and instead found another fight. Another set of odds. And bad ones at that.

This isn't real. The Moirae are a puddle of twisted bodies. I haven't dreamed about them, and even if I had, they can't come through my dreams and shear me in my sleep.

"You're trying to push me into something," he said. "Something where there's no winning."

Demeter chuckled, and her eye scrunched up. Somewhere in the distance, what remained of her mouth was smiling.

"I can't fight the Moirae," Hermes said. "Nobody can. Not Athena. Not anybody. Definitely not me."

"Why not?" Demeter asked.

"Because you just don't. Because you can't."

"Because my brother Zeus said you couldn't?"

Hermes pursed his lips. Zeus deferred to the Moirae. They all deferred to the Moirae. It was how a god learned to bow his head. Their only hard limit.

The very idea of fighting them seemed mad.

"I can't win," he said quietly.

Demeter lifted, and flopped back into the dirt: the rug's equivalent of a shrug.

"You might not," she said. "But sometimes you don't fight to win. Sometimes you fight to fight."

6

OUT OF THE BLACK

Athena knelt beside Odysseus, watching his chest rise and fall around the blade that still protruded from his chest and back. In the strange red-orange light of the underworld, the blood around the wound was visible, and still wet. He'd bled no more once they'd landed in Hades. It was the same blood in the same pattern, the same rhythm to his breath. Nothing changed, and he never spoke. She couldn't remember why she'd thought he would.

Sometimes she whispered to him, mostly nonsense and foolish promises, apologies for slights and mistakes she made thousands of years ago. But the words died inches from her lips. The air ate the sound so quickly she wasn't sure if it ever reached his ears.

Athena brushed his dark hair gently away from his eyes and paused at the sight of her fingers. Three of her nails were cracked. The one on her index finger had split down the middle, a casualty of an unlucky grab. It had slid against some water-bound creature's scales. Slid, and then scraped and then split.

"But no feathers." She fluttered the wounds before Odysseus' closed lids. The feathers were fewer, if there were any at all. Being in the bounds of the underworld seemed to slow them.

"We should have come here from the start," she said. "We should've come here, all of us, and left you alone." But they hadn't, and Achilles had put a sword through Odysseus' chest.

That was my decision. My choice to bring Achilles back with us. My plan to force Hera into a fight. And now my choice to hide from everything that happened.

More often, her thoughts turned to the others. To Cassandra, and Hermes. Andie and Henry. She'd left them. But they survived. Somehow she knew that. Persephone would have been quick to gloat if they hadn't.

Athena stretched herself out on the cold sand and rested her head against Odysseus' shoulder. His warmth flowed into her, and she felt his heart thumping. But it wouldn't forever. She couldn't let him linger between worlds.

You're already dead. And no matter how stubborn I am, or how many monsters I fight, I can't change that. You were dead when I put my arms around you on Olympus. You're dead now, with your heart beating against my cheek.

She took a deep breath. Her head felt heavy as lead when she tried to lift it from him, but she did it.

"I could deny this forever," she whispered. "And I might, if it wasn't for my brother and the others. I'll never really know if I would've been strong enough to do this if not for them." Her hand wrapped around the hilt of the sword.

I'm sorry.

The sword dragged free in one long, slow motion. It yanked him toward her and fresh blood splashed across his skin. He screamed. She hadn't thought he would scream, and by the end Athena's face was soaked in sweat and tears, and she was screaming, too. Odysseus gulped air and stiffened. His hands hooked into claws, and she pressed him back into the sand, shushing him with the blade raised over her head.

His eyes fluttered open.

"Remember this," Athena said. "He didn't kill you. Do you understand? It was me. It was my fault, and I let you go."

Her arm swung down, ready to strike clean, and she held her eyes wide open. But the blade never hit. A hand grabbed her wrist and jerked it back.

"You'll thank me for this later," Ares said, and struck Athena hard across the face.

7

THANATOS

"I don't want him to come. He can't come." Cassandra pushed wisps of brown hair away from her face. The beach wind kept blowing it into her eyes and into her mouth when she talked. What people loved so much about the beach she'd never understand. The sand burned her feet when it rose past the edges of her sandals, and the sun made her squint. Every time the wind changed, it smelled like fish. She missed home, and mild silver light with maybe the trees and ditches starting to green. Beside her, Calypso didn't feel the same. She looked like a girl in a '90s music video, traipsing along the surf as though she'd just been borne of it.

"You want to find Hades, don't you?" Calypso said. "Thanatos can help. And besides, he isn't giving us a choice." She cocked her head and kicked sea spray toward Cassandra with her toes. "And you have no power over him, so . . ."

Cassandra winced from the water.

"Stop doing that." She crossed her arms. "I didn't start this quest to kill gods to make another one my ally. And the god of death, no less."

"But since you can't kill him . . ."

"Yet. I get stronger every day." *But probably not strong enough to kill fricken death.*

"We can go home if you want," Calypso said gently. "To Kincade."

A tempting idea. The urges to throw her arms around her mother's neck, to kiss her father's cheek, and to punch Henry were starting to weigh heavy. The urge to see them all, somewhere other than in her memory.

She shook it off.

"None of them are safe," she said, "until the gods are dead."

Calypso sighed and whispered something disapproving. Cassandra turned on her.

"How can you not want them dead?" Cassandra shouted. "After what happened to Odysseus!"

Calypso grew still. Her eyes darkened. It was the closest she'd ever come to looking truly dangerous.

"Don't speak to me of Odysseus," she said, "when you have not shed one tear for him."

They stared at each other a long time. But it was Cassandra's shoulders that slumped first, and her feet that awkwardly kicked the sand.

"I shouldn't have said that," Cassandra said. "I'm sorry. I didn't mean it."

"I'm sorry, too," said Calypso. "I know that you can't cry. That the anger is a mask for tears. The anger will carry you through."

"The anger will carry me through. And when it's over, when they're all safe, then I'll weep for Odysseus. I'll weep buckets, for him and for everyone that I've lost."

"For him and for yourself, then?" Calypso asked.

"Calypso," she said, and turned away to scan the beach, and the depths of the water besides. Thanatos was coming, and she wasn't going to allow him to snake his way up to her again undetected. "There's no going back now."

Calypso raised her chin.

"There he is." She nodded toward the sloping path from the parking lot.

He looked different than he had at the club. With his black hair blowing lightly back from his face and the sun lending color to his cheeks, he looked younger. Almost her age. Cassandra bristled, and felt fire rush to her palms. But her power couldn't do anything to him. The heat in her hands, the tingling, was embarrassing. She tried to make it go away, discreetly flexing her fingers.

"You look younger today," he said. "Without the makeup and your leopard-skin dress." He looked at the white shirt she wore and she wished she hadn't chosen such an innocent color.

"I was thinking something similar about you," she said. "It made me want to punch you in the face."

He laughed. "This trip we're taking . . . it's going to be interesting."

"You invited yourself along. I never said you could come."

Calypso cleared her throat. "This day of sea salt puts me in mind for a fish taco. There's a stand across the street. I'll bring some back." She brushed past them, her skirt gathered in one hand and her sandals hanging from her fingers.

"She has excellent ideas," said Thanatos. "Do you like fish tacos? I can't help getting the impression you're not from around here."

"We're not going to stand around and talk about fish tacos," Cassandra said, glaring. "Though for the record, I've never had one and they sound disgusting."

"All right. Should we take a walk then, or go up that hill and get a table?" He pointed toward tables and chairs in the distance. Both options sounded too congenial, but she stalked toward the tables. As she went, she felt his eyes on every inch of her as clearly as if they were his hands. But when she snapped her head back to look, he was staring serenely out at the ocean.

Maybe I was imagining it. Or maybe he was groping me with his death brain tentacles.

That thought was dumb enough to make her stumble. He caught her by the arm and pulled her back to her feet.

"Your hand," she said. "Get it off me."

He shrugged and let her go, then led the way to a table and pulled out a chair for her. She almost snubbed him and pulled one out for herself, but sat down instead. Defiance had its limits. He sat across from her and began to spin a coin like a child's top. The same fat gold coin he'd made her call the night before. His eyes followed it thoughtfully. Downcast, they lost their arrogant, mirthful squint. Downcast, they looked almost sad.

"Why do you want to come with us?" she asked.

He didn't look up when he answered.

"Because though I've never had much fondness for the other gods, or them for me, I'm the god of death. If their time has come, I should be there."

"You don't want to save them? Sabotage me? Kill me?"

He slapped the coin down on the table and smiled. "That's a lot of questions. But the answer to all is no."

"Forgive me if I don't believe you."

"You're forgiven. But I like you, Cassandra. Can't decide yet if I like you better in heels and skintight leopard or like this, brown hair loose, beach clothes, eyes shooting daggers at my face."

She swallowed. Where the hell was Calypso? The way he looked at her, it was impossible to keep color from creeping into her cheeks.

"You don't even know me," she said.

He shrugged.

"I will. And besides, I can tell already that you're not like most of the girls who seek me out. All they want is to know about death."

"You did not just make fun of suicidal girls."

"You misunderstand. Suicidal girls don't need me. Except for, perhaps, poor Calypso." He raised his brow and she narrowed her eyes. "The truth is, lots of people are curious about death. They want to know it without knowing it. I can only keep it up for so long. The dance gets old."

"So you don't . . . kill them?"

His black eyes sparkled, and for the tenth time she wished she could tell whether they were dishonest or charming.

"No. I don't kill them. Except on those rare occasions when it really is their time. I'm Thanatos, not Jeffrey Dahmer."

"But you're the god of death. Death embodied. Don't you need to be killing things?"

He leaned back in his chair and laughed.

"I'm killing things right now. Things die, and are dying, all the time. Everywhere. Plants. Fish. Someone in an apartment twelve blocks from here. I don't have to be there. I don't have to choke the life out of them. Atropos, the Fate of death, decrees, and I am her hand, but the phrase 'the touch of death' is still just an expression."

Cassandra's eyes moved over nearby buildings. Someone dying in an apartment twelve blocks away? The thought filled her with dread and a spike of adrenaline.

"But you have," she said. "Killed with your hands before."

He looked into her eyes.

"I have. I won't make excuses for what I am. Not even for a pretty girl."

She didn't know what to say to that, but didn't have to, as Calypso finally returned with several tacos wrapped in brown paper. They ate in relative silence, and Cassandra was pleasantly surprised to find that she liked the food. Lots of salsa, and the fish was fresh. She watched Thanatos exchange godly small talk with Calypso. Maybe it was the daylight playing tricks with her eyes and mind, but he didn't seem so bad. Certainly not as coldly menacing as he had in the club and in the serial killer's pad he kept.

I've come this far. And I knew it was going to be dangerous anyway.

"Thanatos," she said, and the laughter at the table died off. "I've made up my mind. You can come."

After lunch, they checked out of their hotel and took their scant belongings to Thanatos' house in the hills. The second she dropped her bags in one of his guest rooms, which was just as neutral and sparely decorated as the rest of the house, she felt like a fly beginning to notice bits of web sticking to her feet. But when he said it would be easier to make their plans if they were all together, she couldn't think of a single reasonable objection.

She studied the floor-to-ceiling mirrors in the guest bath, and the oversized claw-foot bathtub. She walked the long hardwood hallways and let her eyes crawl up the walls to the vaulted ceiling. When she got back to the kitchen, he'd poured them glasses of sparkling water.

"What story do you tell?" she asked. "People must wonder who you are, to have all this. And they must notice you have no job besides . . . seducing girls with slightly self-destructive tendencies."

"Lots of people have the same," he replied. "I think it helps that no one can really tell how old I am. Everyone in this town can play from sixteen to thirty-five." He shrugged. Standing behind the counter cutting limes, he looked not only human, but domestic. "Cassandra?"

"Yes?"

"How long are you going to study me like that?"

Her mouth dropped open, but he didn't look up to see.

"It's all right," he said. "I sort of like it. At least when you're not doing it with your eyes narrowed."

"You can stop that any time," she said. "I'm never going to smile at you."

Calypso chuckled into her glass, and moved to the living room to sit. Thanatos went after her.

"You haven't told us where we're going," Cassandra said. "Where Hades is."

He and Calypso exchanged a look, and Cassandra ground

her teeth. Their little god-moments were starting to get on her nerves. *Oh, listen to the little mortal. Isn't she cute? Isn't she just precious, now that she can't kill us?*

But there had to be some way to kill him. Every god in the world was showing their underbelly. The god of death had to have one, too.

And I'll find it. I might not be able to kill him with my hands, but I'll kill him with something.

"Come and sit down for a few minutes," he said. "Rest."

"I don't want to rest. I want to kill Hades, and all the gods I can find, so I can go home." But not only that. Who knew what condition Hades was in. If he was already spreading disease wherever he went, then she didn't have time to waste. Certainly not time to spend sipping sparkling lime water in Death's living room.

Thanatos stood.

"As you wish. Come to the basement."

So there is a basement.

The access was through the garage. As they descended the stairs Cassandra tried to put all thoughts of peeled eyeballs and girls on meat hooks out of her mind, but the unfinished state of the stairs didn't help. Neither did the rough stone walls. It was such a sharp contrast to the rest of the house that it almost felt like descending into a cave.

Like descending into Olympus.

That one stupid day. The foolish pride of it and the disaster that awaited them. She and Athena had been no more than dogs with the scent of blood in their noses. They'd gone blindly, seeking meat in their teeth, and they'd paid the price.

On impulse, she reached back, slipped her hand into Calypso's, and squeezed. The walk to the basement had to be bringing up similar memories for her, and hers were much worse.

I'll get vengeance for Odysseus, too. I promise. Somehow.

She pulled her hand free before her thoughts turned too dark. She wanted to comfort Calypso, not turn her to dust.

"Isn't there any better lighting?" Cassandra asked. "I can barely see my feet to keep from falling down the stairs."

"Here. I know the way well." Thanatos reached for her arm and drew her closer to his back. His fingers slid against her palm, testing the heat there as if he was trying to feel the rage licking through her fingers.

They descended the last step and hit a floor of hard-packed damp dirt. Thanatos moved away quickly, and Cassandra spun in the pitch black, half-certain her shoulder was going to bump into a hanging corpse. Then he lit a torch, and yellow light flooded the small room.

No corpses. Not much of anything, really. A few shelves of dusty books. An old stone table. Some candles. He moved along the walls, using his torch to light other torches, and made some lame joke about an earthquake striking at that instant and burying them all.

"Your sense of humor is even more twisted than Athena's," Cassandra said, and Calypso blinked.

"Athena didn't have a sense of humor."

Cassandra shrugged. She ran her hands down her legs, smoothing her skirt. Her most recent wave of anger had subsided and left her cold. She took a breath. The air in the basement smelled of worms and water.

"What are we doing down here?"

"Looking for a map," Thanatos replied.

"To Hades? You need a map?" Her nose crinkled. "I thought you knew where he was."

"It's not as easy as all that. They don't call him the Unseen One for nothing."

Calypso laughed. "I thought they were just making fun of his helmet of invisibility."

Thanatos laughed, too, then made a stern face. "Don't get smart. This is going to be nasty business."

"How's that?" Cassandra asked. "How can looking for a map be 'nasty business'?"

"Because our map is nasty business. It's one of the Erinyes. One of the Furies. And she's not going to be pleased when we bait her here. She'll be even less pleased when I drink her blood."

"What?"

"A little vampiric, I know. But the Furies belong to Hades. They're his favorite daughters. His most loved pets. They always know where he is, and their blood will sing the song to me." He paused. "Like a really gory GPS."

Cassandra willed her stomach to be still. She was the killer of gods. Losing her lunch in front of Thanatos wouldn't do.

"So where is she?" There didn't appear to be anyplace in the basement to hide a Fury. It was one room with no doors.

"I don't know. But we're about to summon her."

Summoning. The word sounded ominous. Dangerous. Cassandra glanced at Calypso, but she didn't seem the slightest bit concerned. She barely seemed curious.

Maybe I'm an idiot for using her as a litmus test. Maybe I'm stupid for thinking she might care about what happens to

me at all. She hasn't really cared about anything since Odys-
seus died.

But those were paranoid, unfair thoughts. Calypso had taken care of her, fed her, counseled her. Brushed her hair and tried to make her laugh. And she asked for nothing in return except for one good death, when everything was over.

"You can help by lighting candles." Thanatos tossed her a box of matches. He didn't tell her which candles to light, so she began to light them all, each tiny flame adding yellow to the brown and gray room.

"Is this just for ambiance? Or are we about to do some"—she made some ridiculous flourish with her hands—"magic?"

"You get very sarcastic when you're nervous." He moved toward the back wall and bent down, feeling the packed dirt with his hands. "Calypso, will you help me with these?" They knelt together, and Cassandra watched as they pulled a massive set of chains with cuffed ends out of the ground. The chains were fixed somewhere down deep. Maybe to the bedrock. She swallowed. Nothing disturbing about that.

"Can you handle these?" Thanatos asked, and Calypso tested the chains' weight in her hands.

"Yes."

"Don't even give her a chance to speak, when we bring her in."

The sight of Calypso with the chains made everything suddenly real, and it was moving too fast. They were about to summon a thing, a Fury, that was strong enough to need to be bound by chains with four-inch-thick links. It could be a trap. A lie. Thanatos could be summoning one of his own pets. A quick vision of her insides splashed against the wall and soaking into the dirt of the floor popped into Cassandra's head.

Not a real vision. Just the product of too many horror movies with Andie.

She closed her eyes. This time something flashed behind her lids, in the dark part of her mind that always felt open. Just a glimpse of a leathery wing, claws, and an eye so red all the vessels must have burst.

She stepped back and sucked in cool air through her nostrils. That was a Fury?

Calypso had better be goddamn fast with those chains, or Cassandra's insides really would end up splattered on the walls.

Comforting heat curled into Cassandra's fingers and soothed her stomach. Anger followed so quickly behind fear these days. She made a fist and gripped the heat like a handful of sand, ready to throw it into a bloodied eye.

Anything that kills me, kills itself.

"Thanatos," Cassandra said hotly. "What else have you used those chains for?"

"All manner of underworld beasts. A couple of Furies, a Gorgon." He leafed through a book she hadn't noticed him pick up. "A volleyball player from UCLA."

"What?"

"Relax. It was voluntary. All very *Fifty Shades*." He looked up and nodded at Calypso. "Once I read the incantation, the path opens. So. Who do you want? Any preferences? Now's the time to make requests."

"Requests for what?" Cassandra asked.

"Which Fury, of course. There are lots of them, but some

are shinier than others. I thought you, Princess of Troy, might want Alecto. She was ecstatic about your city falling and your brother dying."

"Alecto?" Cassandra's brain reached into her past but found no memory. Back then she'd been a doomed prophetess. Nowhere near as involved with the gods' machinations as she was now. Ah, simpler times.

"Alecto of the Unceasing Anger."

"That's what they call her?"

Calypso rattled her chains. "Perhaps one of the lesser Furies might be better."

Thanatos clapped his book closed.

"I hate to tell you this," he said, "but we won't get much lesser. When you've got the killer of the gods and the god of death putting out the call, who do you think is going to answer?"

Calypso let her chains droop and cocked her brow at him.

"We could always try to color the request," she said. "Put out the right bait."

Cassandra looked from the nymph to the god. "What do you mean, put out the right bait?"

"Well, you wouldn't try to catch a shark with ice cream," said Calypso, "any more than you'd try to catch a butterfly with a leg of goat."

Thanatos looked at Calypso like she'd broken his favorite toy. He'd been holding that bit back. For what? His own amusement? Or was he really trying to get one of them killed?

I suppose I shouldn't be surprised, considering what he is.

"So." She passed Thanatos with a look and spoke to

Calypso. "How do we put out ice cream? I think the ice cream–loving breed of Fury is the kind we're looking for."

Calypso transferred the chains to one hand so she could secure her braids, and the dirt on her fingers tinged the white braid brown. It made her look tired already, and they hadn't even started. But if Calypso wasn't strong enough for the job, it was Cassandra's fault, because of the damage she'd done to her dragging her out of Olympus.

"Unfortunately, Thanatos is right," Calypso said. "With the two of you calling, we can't hold out much hope for a minor Fury. More likely it will be one of the Erinyes who shows up. The original Erinyes. And that means Alecto, Megaera, or Tisiphone.

"Knowing you as I do, I wouldn't be surprised if it *was* Alecto of the Unceasing Anger. But with Thanatos by your side, it might be Tisiphone, the Avenger of Murder."

"Death isn't murder," Thanatos mumbled.

"The one you want," Calypso continued, "is Megaera. Mild compared to the other two. They call her the Jealous One."

The Jealous One. That didn't sound so bad.

"She tends to show up in times of infidelity, or lust."

"What do you mean, 'lust'?" Cassandra eyed Thanatos, who chuckled.

"Who's the one sabotaging you now?" he asked. "But come on. It's not like I'm bad to look at."

Cassandra crossed her arms. There was no denying that. He was incredibly easy to look at. Beautiful, and terrible, like they all were.

Except Aidan.

Her eyes moved across his chest, over his shoulders and

up to his amused expression. He was so dark and cold. He didn't have any of the warmth that Aidan had. Aidan's smile was dashing and open. Thanatos had a secret smirk.

But Thanatos hasn't betrayed me, driven me insane, and gotten me locked in a basket, either.

She squared her shoulders. Their differences didn't matter. It wasn't a contest. It wasn't real. Whatever happened in the next few minutes was only a ruse. Bait at the end of a hook.

She stepped close to Thanatos and looked up into his eyes. The sound of her breath was loud. After a moment, his hand came up to touch her face.

"I'm not kissing you!" She jerked back. "I'm not here to die."

He pulled away and rolled his eyes, muttering about stereotypes. "Not all of my kisses kill," he said. "But you're really starting to tempt me."

"Thanatos." Calypso shook her head. "Don't joke. Not now."

"Why don't you try with me?" he said to the nymph, but Calypso shook her head.

"It has to be real," Calypso replied. "And I feel nothing, now that Odysseus is gone. But Cassandra, I will help you."

"Help me," Cassandra said. She wasn't sure if she could do it. Lusting for death was not her style. But what was the alternative? To let Calypso try to lasso something called the Unceasing Anger? She took a deep breath and closed her eyes. After a few moments, she felt Thanatos' hands settle on her hips.

"Make it real," Calypso whispered. "It has to *be* real."

It felt impossible. The cold from Thanatos seeped into

the air and wound around Cassandra's body. And there was nothing romantic about standing in the middle of a stone and dirt basement, waiting for a leather-winged hell-beast to burst in between them.

Slow and easy, Calypso's voice began to weave through the room like a melody. Cassandra wanted to ask what she was saying, but could barely form the thought, and besides, the song didn't sound like words. It sounded like sunlight filtered through clear water. It sounded like island flowers.

Thanatos pulled Cassandra closer. He didn't feel so cold anymore, and a tug had started in her chest, sweet and warm. When she pressed against him it felt natural. His fingers slipped into her hair. He whispered something, and she leaned in close to hear.

"Cassandra, be ready."

She blinked. His voice was strained, as though he'd run a mile.

"The path is open."

Calypso's chant was gone, and slowly, Cassandra's body sank back into her shoes, leaving her to wonder where it had been. Her fingers were clenched onto the sides of Thanatos' shirt, and for the moment she didn't let go. She was too busy listening, and studying the change in the room.

Everything had crystallized. The air was clearer and somehow brighter. The stone of the walls and even the dirt floor seemed sharper. It was like standing inside of a mirror's reflection.

A beautiful girl materialized beside them. She wore a short black dress and black boots. Hair the color of wet sand tumbled to her waist. And before she could speak a word, Calypso threw the chain around her neck and pulled.

The image of the girl disappeared faster than Cassandra could have imagined. The girl's tanned arm turned shriveled, the skin loose and ropey with veins. Her lovely mouth morphed into a bat's mouth, too full of teeth and tongue. And her brown eyes rolled so red it was a wonder they didn't burst and bleed down her cheeks.

The Fury screeched and bucked, but Calypso maneuvered the chains as if she'd practiced for years: a quick loop there to secure an arm, a hard jerk here to throw the Fury off balance. A cuff closed around its right wrist and Thanatos moved in to help, pulling the slack chain taut. It was none too soon. The Fury bit down on air inches from Cassandra's face. She could smell the decay on its breath.

Wings burst from the Fury's back and battered Calypso and Thanatos both, but Calypso looped more chain around its body and then jumped onto the wings.

"Thanatos! Secure the legs!"

Before he could, the Fury kicked, and its talons caught Calypso in the shin, tearing a bright red line. And then Thanatos had the cuffs on and Calypso rolled away, leaving the beast to seethe and writhe on the floor.

"Cally! Your leg." Cassandra held her hands out, to help her walk or apply pressure, but Calypso waved her away.

"It's all right. It's shallow." But blood ran freely down to her ankle and into her sandal.

Thanatos stepped up beside them and looked down on the Fury. He seemed exhilarated, more than anything.

"Wrapped up nicely as a Christmas package." He dusted his hands off on his jeans. "Let's go upstairs awhile. Let her mellow. I'd rather not have to suck the blood out of something that looks like that."

8

LIKE EXCALIBUR

"Achilles will come for Hector. It's all he's ever wanted. That, and to be a god. You can bet that the Moirae have promised him both. He'll come with all their strength at his heel. You won't be able to protect Hector. The Fates will hold you down, press you to the ground, and turn your head to watch."

"Great. So what are we supposed to do? Achilles can't be killed. You kill him once, and he pops right back up to be killed again."

"Only because it isn't the right death."

"What the hell does that mean?"

"It means the boy who can put Achilles to rest is the boy standing right next to you. And he is the only one."

Hermes sat behind the wheel of the rented SUV, driving back toward the road and on to the airport, and home to

Kincade. No one had spoken since they got into the car, but the words of Demeter filled the cab. He could hear Andie and Henry replaying it in their heads so clearly he might as well have been telepathic.

"Why Henry? Why does it have to be him?"

"Their destinies are intertwined. All the way to Troy and back again, it is one or the other. There are threads of Achilles inside Hector and threads of Hector inside Achilles. This time will be like the time before. They will face each other. And you have to hurry, if you want to help him."

"How am I supposed to do that? How can I help him?"

"By making him equal to the task. No mortal man could best Achilles. Not then, and not now. But then, Achilles was only a mortal himself. Find the edge that he once carried, and give it to Hector."

"The edge that he once carried. You want me to drag Henry to the underworld and dunk him in the river Styx?"

He was lucky Demeter hadn't had arms then, or she'd have cuffed him in the head. But she said no more. She waited, and breathed, and blinked her elephant-lashed eye patiently.

"The edge he carried. The edge he carried . . . Like a sword. Like Excalibur. But Achilles didn't have a magic sword. He had the Styx dip and he had . . . a shield. A shield forged by the gods. The Shield of Achilles."

"Very good, Messenger. Now all you have to do is find it."

Find it. All he had to do was find it, a legendary shield that hadn't been seen for a few thousand years.

"My god," he said softly.

"What?" Andie asked. She sat up fast in the passenger seat and scanned the windows as though Demeter or something worse might be flying up after them. Hermes gripped the wheel grimly.

"I might have to do research."

A day after they returned from their failed trip to the desert, Henry lay on his bed, idly rolling a hockey puck between his fingers. Lux lay on the floor chewing a strip of rawhide. It was the only noise in the house, even though his parents were downstairs.

He, Hermes, and Andie had made it back days before the end of spring break. He wished they'd stayed in the desert longer. Coming back so soon without Cassandra and facing his parents was harder than Henry had imagined. Their faces when he walked through the door showed how much they'd hoped. They'd thought he might be able to bring her home, and he'd thought so, too.

Lux heard the sound of Andie's Saturn and scrambled up off the floor. Andie knocked once and let herself in, calling out a tremulous "hello" that was met with mostly silence. The house was joyless. Sometimes Henry couldn't help being pissed off at Cassandra for just how joyless it was.

"Hey." Andie poked her head through his door. "You finally get the dust out of your hair?"

"It only took three showers." He sat up on the bed to make room.

"I told my mom what we 'found'," she said, and made air quotation marks. "That by the time we got there they were gone. But they left word that they were safe, and would come home soon." She pulled her black hair out of its ponytail and snapped the binder between her fingers. "My mom went on this tirade about how irresponsible they were. How inconsiderate they were of everyone's feelings."

"My parents said the same thing."

"I couldn't even disagree. I mean, I do feel like that sometimes, even though I know the truth. Not about Athena, because she's doing who knows what in the underworld, but then again, she effing *left* us on that hellhole of a mountain—"

"Andie. You're rambling." He tossed the hockey puck onto his desk. "But I know what you mean."

"Why won't they just come back?" she asked.

"They will."

"I don't think Demeter really knows that." Andie sat down heavily on the edge of his bed, then tilted up again. "I sat on your phone. Here, it's ringing. It's . . . Ariel. What's she want?"

"Give me that." He looked at it briefly, and wished she'd called at any other time. "Hello?" He turned slightly and tried to listen, laughed in all the right places, asked follow-up questions, all the while with one ear tuned to Andie, who was not so subtly rubbernecking over his shoulder. It was distracting, but he got the gist of the conversation. Party at Ariel's house. Come whenever he wanted.

"What was that about?"

"Nothing." He put the phone in his pocket. He and Andie could just hang out, the two of them. Watch a movie. Be miserable together. He sighed, and got up off the bed. "Want to go to a party?"

"A party at Ariel Moreau's," Andie mused as they pulled up to her house. It was in the same wealthy neighborhood as their friend Sam, who hosted epic Halloween shindigs. "What's she even doing home? Shouldn't she be spring breaking in Cancun or something?"

Henry smiled. "Don't be a jerk."

"Tall order. Maybe I shouldn't have come. This isn't exactly my crowd."

"I'm your crowd."

"If you say so," Andie said. "But if you disappear for three hours to make out with Ariel, I'll be none too pleased."

Henry watched her get out of the car and start up the street toward the driveway. "Not much chance of that," he said quietly.

Inside the house, Andie stuck to him for approximately five minutes. Then she was off, talking to everyone and no one. She had a way of making herself seem comfortable even when she wasn't.

Henry stood with his friends from hockey and drank a beer. There was enough music and enough conversation to keep him from thinking about his sister for five minutes at a stretch. It wasn't the same with Achilles, though. He thought of that fight every time he looked at Andie.

Henry didn't remember the first fight with Achilles, that grand duel in the sands outside Troy. He wondered if he would be even more afraid if he did, or if it would be boring, like it was just more of the same.

But boring was the wrong word. He didn't imagine the prospect of getting a spear rammed through one's chest could ever be boring.

"Hey."

He turned and found Ariel with her head cocked flirtatiously. She seemed a little drunk. "You brought a girl to my party," she said.

"No, he didn't," Max Bauer interjected. "He brought Big Andie. She doesn't count." Everyone laughed.

"Don't let her hear you say that," Henry said through a fake smile. "She could kill you."

"I sort of want her to. Remember Sam Burress' Halloween party? If she smothers me to death with her rack then I'm all for it."

Henry's grip tightened around the beer bottle, but Ariel turned him away.

"Do you need another drink?" she asked.

"No, this one's almost full. And I have to drive home later."

She looked disappointed, and put her hand on his arm. "My parents are out of town. You don't have to drive home. You could stay."

Snickers and victorious whispers broke out behind him. He could stay at Ariel's house. Probably in her room. Likely in her bed. He looked across the party to where Andie was taking a shot of something. She was going to need him, before the night was over.

"No, I think I'd better stay sober. Get Andie home safe."

Ariel shrugged, surprised, and walked away.

That might be it. The end of his phone calls from Ariel Moreau.

Henry looked at Andie and realized that he didn't care.

In the end, Andie had a better time than he did. Maybe too good a time, judging from the way she stumbled on the walk back to the Mustang.

"My mom's going to kill me if I wake up hungover tomorrow. She'll kill me tonight if she's still up. Whoops—"

She stumbled again. Henry caught her and threw her arm around his shoulders.

"You can stay at our place if you want. Just text her and let her know. She probably won't mind."

"Stay? At your place? Your parents won't care?"

"You've been staying over at our house since you were seven." They reached the car and he maneuvered her toward the passenger side. It took some doing, but he got her in and managed to drive them both home.

When they got to his house, it was dark. His parents hadn't even left the outside lights on. They were home, though, inside sleeping—or at least pretending to. He did his best to be quiet going in, but Lux was ecstatic to find not one but two family members to greet, and his snuffling nose in the entryway made it a special chore to get Andie out of her shoes and jacket.

"Wait," she said when they stood before the open door of Cassandra's bedroom. "I don't think I want to go in there."

"Andie. It's late." But he couldn't say he blamed her. The room looked darker than dark, and deserted. The air inside didn't feel like it belonged to the rest of the house anymore.

"Can I sleep in your room?" she asked, then wrinkled her nose. "Your bed's not super dirty, is it?"

"It won't be unless you barf in it."

He brought her into his room and closed the door behind the dog, who looked perplexed by their extra company. Andie wasted no time getting under his blankets. He was just about to go to his closet for a sleeping bag to put on the floor when she moved toward the wall and turned the covers down.

"Okay," he said, and shut the lights off. His bed had never creaked as loud and gracelessly as it did when he got in beside her. But they lay back and listened to Lux turn in a circle before he sacked out on the floor.

"Henry?"

"Yeah?"

"I don't want you to fight Achilles."

He was about to say *me neither* when she threw her arm over his chest and pulled him close.

"I'm scared of it," she whispered, and he wrapped his arms around her and held her tight.

"It's okay," he said.

Sure it was. He'd have some magic shield and he'd stare down that blond, god-obsessed monster just like he did before. Just like it happened before. Only this time he wouldn't let Andie be there to see it. He didn't know how Hector could have done it back then, how he could have let her see it and carry the sight with her forever afterward.

——

"How do you find a magical shield that's two thousand years missing?" Hermes paced back and forth across the balcony outside Athena's bedroom. "How do you find a magical shield that's two thousand years missing?" He'd gone to Athena's room after an hour of asking the same question in the living room, in the hopes that a little of her wisdom remained. Just enough to float the answer into his brain. But the only answer that came was:

You don't. You don't find a magical shield that's two thousand years missing, any more than you find Excalibur, or the Holy Grail, or the last living unicorn. There was no trail to follow, no leads, no sightings. Maybe if Athena were there, she'd have a plan.

"But she isn't. I am." He felt the balcony rattle under his feet and slowed his pace. Without noticing it, he'd started to use his speed. To any passersby, he would've looked like a human-colored set of lines streaking back and forth. Oops.

He gripped the railing. This little game of What Would Athena Do? wasn't getting him anywhere. So what would Hermes do?

"That's easy. Hermes would run." Except that after their trip to the desert, he'd been exhausted and slept for twenty hours. He wouldn't be able to run for much longer. And Henry and Andie would be unlikely to run with him willingly and leave their families defenseless in the blast radius.

"So we can't run. What else? Play to my strengths. What do I do if I can't run?" He thought back. The last time he couldn't run or steal his way out of a problem had been when he noticed he was losing weight. And then he'd still run. Straight to Athena. Straight to—

"Someone else who can take care of the problem."

He stood, careful not to move too much and disrupt the thought that had started to form between his ears. The problem wasn't *finding* the shield, which seemed fairly damned impossible, it was *having* a shield. Having the advantage given to Achilles by the gods. Given by Hephaestus, god of fire, craftsmen, and metalwork.

A spark of hope started in Hermes' chest and worked its way outward, making his whole body vibrate. Hephaestus. A god. A god he'd just seen, less than two hundred years ago.

"Screw that shield. The shield of Achilles. We'll make a new one. A better one. A shield of Henry." He winced. Of course, they'd have to give it a better name.

9

DEALS

When Athena woke, it was full dark. It took several blinks
just to figure out her eyes were open, and several more to
remember what happened. The Ares' fist–shaped bruise on
her jaw helped in that department.

Ares had stopped her from putting Odysseus out of his
misery. Why? She'd had the sword in her hand. She'd
finally been ready.

The sword. It was gone. She groped the cool, hard sand
around her and found nothing. But she heard things. Pad-
ded paw steps. Soft yips and sniffing.

Ares' wolves.

But where was Odysseus? Athena's throat tightened. If
Ares had finished what she'd started— She pushed herself up on her elbows and tested her legs. Her boot heel
scraped loudly against the sand.

"Awake already? I must not hit as hard as I used to."

"Where is he?" Athena got her feet underneath her but remained in a crouch. Ares' voice hadn't come from that far away, and her eyes still hadn't adjusted. She thought she saw a shadow move, and in the distance, the rippling of the river.

"He's here," Ares said. "Not far. Come this way."

She scuttled like a crab, hands in front of her until she felt Odysseus' arm. He was still warm. Still breathing. She pulled him into her lap as gently as she could, and then sharpened her ears to the dark. Two separate creatures moved. Probably the wolves, but the count didn't mean much. Ares himself was probably standing stone still, and Oblivion could go days without so much as a twitch.

"What do you want?" she asked.

Ares snorted.

"Always to the point, aren't you sister? Not a hello. Or a 'glad to see you're not dead like your mother.'"

Athena inhaled sharply. Hera was dead? What the hell had happened on Olympus?

"I didn't know she was dead."

"That's right," Ares said. "I forgot. You jumped over the edge before that part. Before your little assassin made her into a statue. What did you think you were doing bringing her there? Training mortals against us."

"It's a war, you idiot," replied Athena. "We're trying to kill each other. You take the advantages you can get." Odysseus lay full across her lap, safe for the moment. Athena kept as much acid out of her voice as she could. Ares was trying to control his formidable temper. Until she knew what it was that he wanted, she would do the same.

"We see eye to eye on that much, at least," he said.

She felt him move closer, and the air move as he crouched down.

"It's why I'm here."

Athena's ears scanned the dark. After a few moments, she caught the movement of the wolves. One she knew was Panic, because its paws were skittish. The other could have been Famine, or Oblivion. Pain wasn't there. She'd have been able to smell the blood, and the open sores in its fur.

So two wolves for certain, and possibly three. Plus Ares. But she heard no monsters or beasts fording the river to take chunks from her arms and shear strips of skin from her back. Wherever dear Persephone was, she didn't seem to be causing any trouble at the moment.

"Who's with you?" Athena asked.

"Oblivion and Panic. The two wolves who remain. Famine and Pain fell in the fight on Olympus."

"I'm sorry," she said.

"Are you?"

"Well, I'm sorrier about them than I am about your mother."

"You should watch your mouth," he growled, and he was right. Odysseus lay prone on Athena's lap, and she was un-armed. Ares probably held the sword, and between him and two wolves, they could take Odysseus apart.

"What do you want, Ares?"

"The same thing you do. To survive."

"Then why aren't you back on Olympus, hiding behind the Moirae's twisted skirts?"

Movement in the dark: a shuffle of feet, a shrug of shoulders; Athena couldn't tell.

"The Moirae let my mother die." Ares exhaled hard

through his nose, as though he still couldn't believe it. "They stood by and let that girl murder her. They didn't defend any of us. Aphrodite was the one who cleared the mountain, and when the water receded and we looked around, they were gone. Disappeared with their new pet."

Their new pet. Achilles. Athena's hand trailed over Odysseus' chest and pressed down on the wound.

"What do you mean, 'cleared the mountain'?" Athena asked. "What happened to my brother and the others?"

"What do you think happened?" Ares sneered. "They ran. Hermes always runs. And I suppose the Moirae did, too, when they understood they couldn't control that girl. I don't know how they managed it, with their legs melded together. Or at least I don't like to picture it."

It had been a loss on both sides, then. Maybe it was petty, but that made Athena feel better. The Fates were forced to scuttle off, and Ares had lost Hera.

"So now you're looking for another shadow to cower in?" Athena asked. "Thinking maybe if you help me out of here, I might let you hide in mine?"

"You're not throwing much of a shadow these days, sister. In case you haven't noticed."

Athena gripped Odysseus' shoulders, ashamed. Even though the idea choked her, Ares was right. He'd been right when he warned her not to go to Olympus, and he was right that she was less. The goddess of wisdom and battle strategy had rushed in and been swatted like a child. And instead of regrouping she'd run away to wallow, half-mad in the underworld. For once Athena was glad of the dark. Ares couldn't see the wetness in her eyes.

"You came to make a deal, Ares," she said. "So spit it out."

"I'll help you get your boy toy out of here in one piece," he said. "And once we're out, you'll help me and mine should it come to blows with the Moirae and their unkillable bodyguard."

"Should it come to blows with the Moirae," Athena repeated, and chuckled. Ares sounded terrified. Under the wing of the Moirae he'd been safe. Unbeatable. Now he was just as fucked as the rest of them.

"You and yours," she said. "I suppose that means the wolves and Aphrodite."

"Yes."

The wolves and Aphrodite were the things that Henry and Cassandra hated the most. If Athena took the deal, she'd wind up fighting two wars: one against the Moirae, and the other against the killer of gods. She didn't know which she was less likely to win.

"How do I know you're true to your word?" Athena asked.

"You don't. But I'm running out of sisters to lie to."

"That's not enough assurance."

"Then how about an act of good faith?" Ares moved, and she heard an odd sound, something uncorked or uncapped. He stayed low, and slow, and she tightened all over. But she let him press the leather skin to Odysseus' lips, and listened to the liquid pour out. The scent of it wafted up in a cloud. It smelled like fruit juice tainted with lead.

"Say his name," Ares said. "Wake him up."

It couldn't be that easy. It had to be a trick. She'd say his name and Ares would laugh. His wolves would howl her gullibility all the way up to Olympus.

"Odysseus?" Athena bit down hard on her lip and tasted blood. "Can you hear me?"

"Yes," Odysseus said, and she struggled to keep herself from crying out and crushing him to her. "And it's just the voice I wanted to hear."

"What was that?" Athena asked Ares. "What was that you gave him?" She tilted Odysseus' head up and he winced.

"Whatever it was, it tastes like balls."

"Just water." Ares shrugged. "Of course, waters from the rivers and streams on the eastern side of Olympus can do . . . lots of incredible shit for wounded mortals." He stood and stepped away. The light was coming back. Athena looked down at Odysseus.

"That smile," Odysseus said. "Never seen it on your face before."

She laughed and pressed her hand against the wound in his chest. It bled only slightly.

"I hate you," she said.

He grasped her hand and held it, made to kiss it but recoiled at the sight of her mangled nails and knuckles.

"What the hell have you been up to?"

"Doesn't matter." She looked at Ares. "Thank you."

"I had to go far enough to get it," Ares said. "Sneaking back onto that mountain. It felt like robbing my own house. You should have thought of that yourself, Athena. Instead of getting stuck in Uncle Hades' web."

"There wasn't time," Athena said. "He'd have died before I got him there."

Ares snorted again. In truth, the waters of Olympus

hadn't even crossed her mind. Not until the moment Ares mentioned them. When the sword went through Odysseus' chest, it was as if Athena had disappeared.

Or maybe she had disappeared even before that, when she convinced herself the Fates were with her, and she was invincible.

Ares watched his wolves pad lightly in a small perimeter, red fur and black.

"Speaking of Uncle Hades," he said. "You know how he gets, when someone tries to pull the dead out of the underworld without permission. He had a claim on that one"—he pointed to Odysseus—"and he's not going to like what we've done. We're going to need leverage, and fast."

"What do you propose?" Athena asked.

"I propose that you and I ford that river and take Persephone."

"Are you sure you're up to this?" Ares asked.

"Are you?"

Athena walked side by side with him through the Styx. The river of hate rose up to her thighs and rippled away like oil no matter how hard she kicked. There was no froth. No splash. Its scent hung heavy and sweet, like old pennies tossed into bad wine. She remembered the taste of it from her trip with Cassandra. At least then they'd had a boat.

Another few moments and they'd be forced to swim, necks strained to keep the water out of their eyes and mouths. Athena felt Ares' eyes on her bruises and scabs and wondered if she'd have enough strength to take on both him and Persephone if he double-crossed her. She doubted it. Whatever had transpired on Olympus, Ares didn't look any worse than he had the last time she'd seen him.

He wore a black T-shirt and no visible bandages. The only cut showing was on his forearm, and it had healed to a dry, red line.

"Hurry up." Ares pushed out and started to swim. "I don't want to be in this river without my feet touching sand for long. Who knows what might drag us under."

Athena pushed off. She knew what might drag them under. Enormous deepwater serpents, their fins and sides lit with phosphorescence. And once they were down there, other things would fight the serpents for possession. Bigger things. Things with gullets big enough to swallow them whole.

She kicked her legs hard, and smiled when Ares kicked his harder, trying to stay ahead. When their feet touched the bottom on the other side, both breathed heavy from exertion and relief.

"Where's Persephone? And where's the dog?" Athena asked, referring to Cerberus, Hades' three-headed hound. Though he'd been down to two heads the last time she'd seen him. The third head had already died and been picked clean of meat and fur by the other two.

Maybe by now he'd be down to one.

Athena looked farther inland, deeper into the caverns and tunnels of the underworld. Persephone was nowhere to be seen. And she hadn't sent anything across the river after them during the dark hours the night before.

"She knows we're here." Ares pushed water off his arms as though his hands were squeegees, and shook them dry with distaste. "But she doesn't know why."

"We?"

"Yeah, we. You didn't think I'd leave her alone above, did you?"

Aphrodite's slender leg poked into Athena's peripheral vision, as if she'd only been waiting for her introduction. Athena turned and took her in: the mad goddess, still marred with purple bruises, her blue-green dress torn and stained with mud.

"Fan-fucking-tastic."

"Not happy to see me, sister?" Aphrodite asked. "It's all right. I wasn't expecting tears and embraces." Aphrodite smiled a small smile; it shivered sadly in her beautiful face. "But you have accepted our offer?"

"I have. But you both know it doesn't matter."

"Why?"

Athena ground her teeth. Aphrodite knew damned well why. The minute Athena burst into that chamber on Olympus and saw the Moirae, she knew that they were finished. The Moirae were gods to the gods. Gods to her father.

But Aphrodite's innocent, stupid face sang of denial.

So let her hold on to it. She'll be more use busting out of here if she has hope.

"Because you killed Aidan, that's why," Athena said. "You killed Apollo, and the girl who can kill every one of us loved him. She wants you dead more than anyone, and she might not care too much what my opinion is."

"I thought you were her friend," Aphrodite said.

"I am her friend. But she isn't mine."

Ares reached out and pulled Aphrodite close to his side.

"You'll do whatever you can, Athena," he said. "For now, let's worry about our uncle. And our half-corpse aunt."

Athena cocked her head. "You seem less crazy here, Aphrodite."

"You seem less bitchy," Aphrodite said, and Athena curled her lip.

"Persephone is strong," Athena warned. "Maybe stronger here than we are."

"I'm not worried about that," said Ares. "The hardest thing is going to be finding her. But don't worry. I've got a plan." He and Aphrodite headed farther in, toward the labyrinth of tunnels.

I might be an idiot, following those two. Or we might all be idiots, going in there.

Athena looked over her shoulder to where Odysseus lay propped against a stone, watching. Oblivion sat by his side. Panic paced near the edge of the river.

"Don't worry about him," said Ares. "They'll make sure he's safe. And they won't kill him, either."

"If they take so much as a nibble, I'll eat my fill of red and black wolf." Athena said it loud, and saw Oblivion flash his fangs.

It felt stupid to go. To leave Odysseus in a den of enemies.

But she had no other choice.

Athena stayed behind them by a few steps, feeling safer with Ares and Aphrodite in her sight line. Except that meant that she would be the one Persephone sank her teeth into first, if she came upon them from behind. There was no winning.

The walls of the underworld stretched up on all sides,

translucent, pale, and cut through with dark veins of rock. Or was it oil? Red-orange light played off the surface and made the whole thing seem to move. It reminded Athena of an old person's skin, or of Persephone's decaying half. As she watched, a shadow passed close to the surface and made her jump.

Ares heard, and chuckled over his shoulder.

The dead roamed the walls in numbers beyond counting. But they were only shadows. Stuck shadows.

"You all right back there?" Ares asked.

"Shut up, Ares. And that goes for both of you. The way you're walking you might as well be a herd of cattle. Have you forgotten how to hunt?"

Ares made no attempt to lessen the audible crunching of his shoes on the ground. If anything, he got louder.

"I never learned to hunt," he said. "I learned to kill."

"Whatever you say, Chuck Norris."

Aphrodite looked back, but when she spoke it was to Ares, not Athena.

"She's gotten so adorably human, hasn't she? In love with a mortal. Perhaps not even a virgin anymore."

"Where are we going?" Athena asked, ignoring her. "Not past the palace?"

If Hades had returned home, that's where he would be. And if he was pissed, he'd have called the Judges home as well.

The Judges. If we manage to get out of here without facing them, I'll hug Ares. Hell, I'll hug them both.

"No," Ares replied. "We're going to the lake."

The dead tended to gather near the lake to wander, to try to drink, and to remember who they were. It was a sad, horrible place, the air choked with equal parts frustration and despair.

They were close, if the scenery could be trusted. Small sprigs of asphodel had begun to crop up along the walls, having twisted their way through cracks. The banks of the lake were covered with it: small, pale blossoms of delicate beauty with no scent. The sight of the bloom filled the dead with hope only to tear it away when they buried their noses in the flowers and smelled nothing.

When they came upon the lake, it lay still and coldly black, stretching out into the distance. Asphodel carpeted the banks. A few ambitious sprouts had even flowered in the shallows. Athena kept herself from sniffing. It was difficult, even though she knew better. After a few seconds, she moved her eyes to the water, unable to look at the flowers anymore.

"What are we doing here, Ares?" she asked. "Don't keep me in suspense."

"We're looking for some dead to do a job for us."

Athena scanned the lake. They were alone. No shades. Perhaps their presence had frightened them off.

"I don't see any dead."

Ares smiled and drew a knife from his pocket.

"That's because we haven't called them."

10

FURY

The Fury railed against the chains in the basement. Her rage shook the foundation of Thanatos' house, and every time she screamed, Cassandra's spine tried to crawl out of her back and take up residence on the ceiling.

"Maybe we should have taped her mouth," Calypso suggested.

Thanatos leaned against the bookshelves in his living room.

"Make a note for next time," he said.

They closed their eyes as she shrieked again. It felt indecent. Cassandra imagined the Fury down there, bound and writhing on the floor. Kicking her claws into the stone walls, the chains cutting into her skin. While they sat upstairs on leather sofas and chairs, sipping lime water.

"You're sure no one can hear her screaming?" Cassandra asked.

Thanatos waved his hand; a don't-worry-about-it gesture. He hadn't spoken to her since whatever spell Calypso had used to make them lust for each other had worn off. He hadn't really looked at her, either, which was the only reason she felt safe looking at him. Whatever Calypso had done, it was strong. It still tingled in her chest. It made her fixate on the details of his face: the darkness of his lashes against his cheek. The muscular curve of his shoulder.

Calypso sat alone on the sofa with her legs tucked up, pleased as a cat despite a quickly forming bruise along her jaw.

"I think I'm going to go outside for a minute." Cassandra set her water glass on the table. "It feels cold in here."

Outside, the sun baked into her arms and face. She wished she'd worn a black shirt. White reflected too much heat. She walked through the yard toward the pool and looked out over the hills. In the basement, the Fury's screams grew less insistent, and less frequent.

"Your stomach doesn't want to hold still, does it?" Thanatos asked. He walked up behind her, along the stone tiles beside the pool. "You can't keep your mind off her," he said, "can't help but pity her a little. Even though you think she's a monster."

His words weren't cruel, nor were they an accusation. It struck her as strange that he wouldn't see pity as weakness.

"She is a monster," Cassandra said.

"No. She's a Fury. She is as she was made. But you don't fool me. Your feeling for that creature borders on compassion. It's not what I was expecting. Not what I had heard about the girl who kills gods."

"What have you heard about me?"

"Whispers." He shrugged. "Most of which I ignored. Some tales of a reincarnated prophetess. Rumor had it that gods were looking for you. I didn't really pay attention until the gods showed their hand. That they were dying. Then my ears pricked. And then you started killing them. Imagine my delight when a satyr whispered you were headed my way."

Cassandra cursed under her breath. "Satyr David."

"Of course. But I don't know why he thought he had to warn me about a young girl from small-town New York."

"Because you weren't sure," she said, scrutinizing him. "Not a hundred percent. I might have been able to kill you. I might be able to still, one day."

"Don't be so full of yourself. You're not that different from a thousand angry girls before you. Tracking me down with bloodied, broken hearts clenched in your fingers. Wanting someone to pay. Wanting to pay yourselves."

Psych 101 from the god of death. What a treat.

"You know about Aidan," she said.

"I do."

"Well excuse me for saying so, but you don't know *shit* about Aidan." She turned to face him, and her heart pounded to her fingertips. Not with anger. If her skirt had pockets, she'd have stuffed them inside. Anything to keep her hands from his shoulders, and her arms from snaking around his neck.

"Damn Calypso," he whispered, staring at her lips.

"It'll wear off, won't it?" Cassandra asked, and clenched her teeth. She was getting angry now, and the anger made it worse.

"Yes. I think so."

"Good. Because I really want to—" She paused and looked at his chest, rising and falling fast with his breath. "Put my hands underneath your shirt."

"And I want to throw you to the ground. But it'll have to wait. We've got a Fury to bleed."

The candles in the basement had burned down to nubs. A few had gone out. The torches, too, burned low. Instead of relighting them, or exchanging the candles for fresh ones, Thanatos pulled a chain and lit dusty, yellow sixty-watt lightbulbs screwed into the ceiling. Cassandra didn't know why they hadn't used them before. Maybe because it changed the entire mood—from ritualistic to interrogation chamber in the pull of a cord. Two detectives from the '70s might come out any minute and straddle backward chairs.

The Fury had also altered the room: She'd heated it to the point of being suffocating. But the heat had a used-up feel. It must've been ten times worse at the height of the Fury's rages. Now she knelt at the ends of her chains, having somehow gotten her legs underneath her. Her wings and sinewy veins were nowhere to be seen. She was just a girl in a short black dress and boots.

The claws would come back soon enough, though. When Thanatos took her blood.

Cassandra could hardly blame her.

Calypso drew Cassandra to the side and nodded toward the Fury.

"Don't be fooled," she said. "Don't get too close. Let Thanatos take the lead."

"Okay." Cassandra poked her arm. "But you and I are

going to have words about whatever it was you did to us down here."

"I did what I needed to do," Calypso said innocently. "You should be glad I did it. Or we'd never have gotten Megaera."

"*That's* Megaera?" Cassandra blinked. That twisting creature of blood and rage was the Fury they called the Jealous One?

"Of course that's Megaera. If she was Tisiphone, I'd be sporting more than a bruised chin and a cut leg. And if she was Alecto"—Calypso shrugged—"I'd probably be dead."

Cassandra felt a tickle on the back of her neck. When she looked back, Megaera was watching. The Fury's eyes were still full of blood—so much blood the irises had been completely obliterated. Only the black dots of her pupils remained.

She'd thought the eyes were part of the creature's form, like the wings and the veins. Now it seemed more likely that the eyes were some kind of wound. Another symptom of the deaths of the immortals.

"Who are you?" Megaera asked.

"Don't answer that." Thanatos pulled on the end of the chain and drew the Fury to her feet. Her arms were bound tight to her sides, secured twice with shackles at the wrists. When she stood, she wobbled.

"I know who you are, boy." Megaera's eyes swiveled toward him. "I can smell the death on you. I can smell the death in this room. And just as I know that, I know you didn't call me here for you. So who is it? The nymph?" Megaera's red eyes twitched to Calypso. "No. The nymph is along for the ride. So it must be the girl."

"I—"

"Don't talk to her," Thanatos cautioned. "We don't need to talk to her." The Fury shuffled backward as he continued to tug and shorten her chains. It was strangely sad to see her so bound. So powerless.

"No need to talk?" Megaera bared her teeth. Rope-like veins popped beneath the skin of her face, but disappeared again. "There aren't many reasons to summon one of the Erinyes. Someone must need punishment. Tell me who, and quickly, and I'll forget how rude you were in the asking."

"No one needs punishment," Thanatos said soothingly, and took a knife off of a shelf, along with a smooth, black bowl. He sliced into Megaera's wrist before she knew what he was up to, and blood ran down her fingers. It splashed against the sides of the bowl and collected in a fast puddle, flowing so thick and so quickly it made Cassandra's head spin. But it was worse when he decided he had enough, and withdrew the bowl to let the blood drip and spatter onto the dirt floor.

"You're healing slower these days, Megaera." Thanatos wiped the blade of his knife on a towel and set it back on the shelf. "I figured on having to cut you twice. But look. A bowl full, and you're still bleeding."

The Fury's bloodied eyes followed the bowl.

She knows what we're after. But how can she? There have to be other uses for the blood of a Fury.

Or perhaps not. Megaera jerked toward Cassandra with such sudden force that they all stepped back, half-certain the chains would snap. They held, but the walls shed dust from the effort.

"You. You're the girl who kills gods. And you think now

to track back to *him*. To *Hades*." Before Cassandra could say anything, Megaera screamed. The sound was terrible, infinitely worse than what they'd heard through layers of stone and floorboards. It was a million gears ground backward; it was silver fillings come loose and gnashed between teeth.

Cassandra's knees buckled. She felt Calypso's arms around her, catching her just short of hitting the cold dirt floor. And then she was back on her feet, and Thanatos held her by the shoulders.

"Open your eyes," he shouted over the noise. Cassandra pried her eyes open. Megaera had become a true Fury again. Veined wings writhed underneath the chains. Strange bones stuck out at odd angles, and Cassandra heard one snap. Megaera would tear herself apart, getting free. But she would get free.

"Kill her!" Thanatos shouted.

"What?" Cassandra jerked. He wanted her to kill the Fury. To lay her hands on a tip of one wing, and watch the red eyes burst inside her skull. He wanted Megaera dead so she wouldn't be on their trail, and so she couldn't warn Hades that they were coming.

It would only take seconds, and the screeching would stop. They would all be able to think again. And breathe. Cassandra's hands clenched into fists, but she felt no heat.

"You do it!" she shouted, but he shook his head.

"I'll do it." Calypso dashed to the shelf and took up the knife. In two quick strides she positioned herself behind Megaera and drove the knife through the base of her skull, up into the brain. She twisted the blade and sawed her head off. It happened so quickly. Cassandra hadn't even thought to look away.

"Worthless gods of death," Calypso said, and tossed the Fury's head into a corner.

The bowl of blood sat heavily between Cassandra and Thanatos on his kitchen island. Blood filled the lower third, still and thick as a dark red soup. Cassandra wasn't sure, but she thought she could smell it, as if it had already started to rot.

Calypso remained down below, annoyed with both of them for not acting sooner. She'd volunteered to bury the body, and occasionally Cassandra thought she heard the strike of the spade, or the thumping of the corpse as Calypso rolled it into its shallow grave.

"Are you sure this is going to work?" Cassandra asked.

Thanatos shrugged. "You know the old saying. 'Find a Fury, drink its blood, all day long you'll have good luck.'"

"That's 'find a penny, pick it up.' And that blood better last more than a day, because I don't want to summon another one of those things."

Thanatos' lips pressed together in a grim line. She got the feeling he was annoyed with her, too.

"Do we need to do anything to it? To prepare it?" she asked.

"Nope. Just drink it."

"Am I going to have to watch?"

His dark eyes flashed.

"You're the one who's set on vengeance. You should have to be the one to do it," he said. "You should want to do it."

"What's your problem? Are you seriously pissed that I didn't kill the Fury in the basement? Because you're the flipping god of death, so—"

"It's not that you didn't. It's that you couldn't." He placed his hands on the counter on either side of the bowl. "You couldn't."

"Whatever this is"—she fluttered her fingers—"it doesn't work the way I . . . It's like my visions. It does what it wants." But Cassandra could hear the lie in her own voice. The visions came from outside of her. From some other force that showed her what would be. When she killed gods, she drew their deaths right out of their centers. It was her will, like a sword.

Thanatos grabbed her hand.

"Whatever this is," he said, "it comes from rage. From hate, and from pain."

She waited for him to throw her hand back, but he didn't. Instead his touch softened and he slid his cool fingers against her palm.

"And that makes it dangerous," he said. "It makes it corrupt."

"You're the expert." She curled her lip. "But this? It's not about death. It's about killing. And there's a big goddamn difference."

Thanatos' eyes were sad. "Yes. There is."

The door to the garage opened and closed. Calypso had finished the burial. Cassandra pulled her hand free before Calypso turned the corner into the kitchen.

"The blood is still in the bowl," Calypso said, and flicked irritated beach-glass eyes in both their directions. She pushed sweaty strands of hair off her forehead. Her fingers left dark streaks of dirt and blood. "I'm going to use your shower," she said, and left.

"We should probably have the blood out of the bowl by the time she gets out," Cassandra said.

"She grows impatient," said Thanatos. "She wants it over. She wants to be dead." He went to his cupboards and pulled out a dark blue metallic sport cup. Roughly half the blood went into it, and then into the refrigerator. The other half he poured into a glass tumbler.

Cassandra swallowed. She fought the urge to look away or to ask for more sparkling water to calm her stomach.

"Bottoms up." He swallowed the blood in one long gulp. It took forever to leave the glass. So much longer than it took to run out of the Fury's wrist. When he finished, he looked even paler than when he started.

"Thanatos?"

He buckled, and Cassandra reached for him across the counter. But his weight was too much. It pulled her halfway up and over. Her elbow upended the mostly empty tumbler of blood and it leaked a large, dark dot onto the white countertop.

"I can't hold you!" She jerked him hard to the right so she could clamber around the end. Thanatos convulsed. She held him, even though the blood coating his teeth made her want to retch.

"Are you all right?" she asked. "Should I do something?"

He didn't answer, so she lowered him to the floor and went to the sink to wet a towel with cold water. By the time she pressed it to his forehead, the convulsions had mostly stopped.

"Something to drink," he said. "Something strong."

She ran to the bar and poured a large snifter of brandy.

"Date-rape brandy to the rescue," she said, and pulled his head into her lap so he could drink.

"I would never—" He sipped. "—roofie anyone. Don't be insulting or I'll barf Fury blood all over your skirt."

"I was kidding." She brushed her fingers across his forehead. "And you should have warned me about the seizure."

"I've never had a reaction like that before."

"Was it because she was dying? I noticed her eyes. All the vessels looked like they'd burst."

"No," he said. "It wasn't the death, but who put it there. Another god. Atropos. I could taste her corruption." Cassandra pressed the brandy to his lips again. "She's the one. The Moirae of death. She's the source."

The source. Cassandra sucked in breath.

"What do you mean?" she asked. "Do you mean she's the source of the gods' deaths?"

"Yes," Thanatos said. "It all stems from Atropos. And trickles down."

"Do the other gods know?" She was fairly sure Athena didn't.

"I'm not sure. Maybe some suspect."

"Does that mean they'll survive? If they kill her? They won't be dying anymore?"

He blinked at her slowly. The panic in her voice had been hard to miss.

"Yes," he said. "But don't worry. They'll never be able to kill her."

II

THE INDUSTRIALIST

A Shield of Hector to replace the lost Shield of Achilles. It wasn't exactly an easy task, but certainly more attainable than finding the real thing. Hermes sat impatiently in front of his laptop. He'd been searching and printing for the last thirty minutes, ever since he got off the phone with Andie, Henry, and the take-out guys from Stanley's Wok and Napoli Pizza.

Damn slow Internet.

Everything except his own fingers and mind seemed slow at the moment. He tapped his toes and looked at the growing pile of paper, then at the wall clock. What the hell was taking Andie and Henry so long? Henry lived three streets away, for Pete's sake.

Someone pulled into the driveway and killed the engine.

Damn it. Not pizza. Delivery guys never turn their cars off.

"Andie!" he said when she walked in. "What took you so long? And why do you look so pale?"

"I went to a party last night." She waved her hand to keep him from asking more. "Why are you talking so fast? What's happening?"

"Not until Henry gets here. And at least one of the take-out guys. I ordered a couple of garlic chickens and a Mediterranean special. And the left half of the Stanley's Wok menu, as usual."

She made a face.

"No food." She sat down hard on the sofa and put her hand over her eyes. It was, he surmised, what the mortals called a hangover. Great. She'd be irritable, uncomfortable, and mostly useless for hours. A fine way mortals had of ruining the day after a good party.

Two more cars rolled into the driveway. One was particularly loud. Henry's Mustang. He came into the house laden with boxes and bags.

"Hey." Henry nodded. "You wanna go pay them? From the looks of it you owe them hundreds of dollars."

"They've got my credit cards. I just have to tip the drivers."

"Don't worry about that. I took care of it."

"Thanks."

Henry shrugged. "You're always feeding us, so." He walked through to the kitchen and started assembling an eclectic plate of egg rolls, sweet-and-sour pork, and two slices of garlic chicken pizza.

"I take it you didn't go to the party with Andie last night." Hermes stuffed a slice of Mediterranean into his mouth. Olives and feta cheese popped on his tongue.

"I did. I just didn't drink as much."

"Hmm." Hermes chewed thoughtfully. "Normally I would find the blush that's creeping up your neck absolutely fascinating. But we've got things." He jerked his head toward the living room, where Andie waited with a pillow over her face.

"Don't tell me," she said, her voice muffled and miserable. "You have a lead on the Shield of Achilles."

"Don't be ridiculous. We were never going to find that thing."

She pulled the pillow off her face.

"What do you mean? Then what are we going to do?"

"We're going to make our own." Hermes sat and explained his plan to forge a new shield. A new set of weapons, given by the gods. And all they needed to do was find Hephaestus, the godly blacksmith, and make him do it.

"Hephaestus?" Henry frowned. "You mean Hera's other son? The one she made all by herself in competition with Zeus? When he created Athena on his own and hatched her fully formed from his head?"

"And he was Aphrodite's husband!" Andie added.

Hermes sighed. The mortals had been studying. How unfortunate.

"He's a good god," Hermes assured them. "I promise. He's not going to be thrilled about what happened to his mother, but he'll understand. As for the marriage, it was crap. Aphrodite was plastered all over Ares every time Hephaestus turned his back."

"This is your only idea?" Andie asked.

"It's *the* only idea."

Henry and Andie exchanged a doubtful look.

"Even if we can convince him to do it," Henry said, "which isn't likely, how is finding Hephaestus any easier than finding the shield?"

"Ha! That's the beauty." Hermes went to his laptop and grabbed the stack of papers. He'd already been through it with a highlighter to pull out the pertinent information. "Here. Look at this. I know who he is. Or at least, who he was."

Andie flipped through the first few pages and then put the pillow back on her face.

"Can you summarize?"

"I ran across Hephaestus in Germany during the Industrial Revolution. He was there making deals, touring factories. We ate white asparagus. We drank questionable German wine. I never saw him again after that one night. But I remember his name. Alexander Derby."

Henry picked up the papers and leafed through them. What he held was essentially a comprehensive family history of the Derbys, from Alexander to Alexander Derby the second and third, to Alistair Derby the first through the third, and so on. They were titans of metallurgy. They built bridges, instituted innovations in the smelting process.

"So you're saying that all of these guys . . . are Hephaestus?" Henry asked.

"No. Not all of them. That's the interesting part. He's fashioned himself a sort of family. But every generation or so, one Derby shows up who outshines the rest. He comes out of nowhere, a heretofore unmentioned relation, and dominates the industry for ten, sometimes twenty years before disappearing. Those Derbys in particular. They're Hephaestus."

"And you know which Derby he is now?" Andie asked.

Hermes nodded. "Rather cosmically, he's come back around to Alexander. And he lives in a very big, very old house, just a few hours from here. Come on." Hermes clapped his hands and jumped up.

Andie dropped the pillow and regarded him with eyes as large as one of Athena's owls'.

"You want us to go now? Are you nuts?" She took a deep breath and made to push off of the sofa. "Okay."

"No." Hermes put his hand up. Of course they shouldn't go now. They shouldn't go at all. Who knew what Hephaestus might have waiting for them, especially if he'd heard about their part in his mother's death. Who knew what state he was in, grappling with a death of his own. Just because they'd met as friends a couple hundred years ago didn't mean they would do it again. Hephaestus might not even be sane anymore.

Hermes shut his eyes. How stupid of him, to rush in. How typical.

"I'll go myself first," he said. "I just meant, get up and get out, because I'm leaving as soon as I eat the rest of the Chinese and pizza."

"Are you sure?" Henry asked. "I could go at least. I'm not hungover."

"No. It's not that. I have to be sure it's safe first. And I'll hurry, so you're not left unwatched here long."

Henry did his best to pay attention during History. It wasn't easy. It never was, but just coming off a vacation made it worse. Everyone in the room fidgeted, discreetly texting photos and tales of wild spring breaks. Henry's phone had buzzed in his pocket no less than ten times in that period alone. He finally took it out on the eleventh and read a text from Jen Thomsen, a friend of Ariel's.

What was with you leaving Ariel's with Andie?

Henry texted back.

She needed a ride home.

His phone buzzed again.

Oh. So you 2 not dating? Good.

And again, before he could reply.

I knew you weren't. She's in tenth and you know.

Henry frowned.

You know what?

A delay this time, and then,

Well she's not exactly hot and Ariels totally into you.

The urge to tell her what he really thought, that Andie was more beautiful than Ariel and all her friends put together, wrestled with the urge to tell her to shove it. Instead, he shut his phone off and tried to pay attention to Mr. Fisher. Strangely enough, Mr. Fisher was lecturing on the Industrial Revolution, and mentioned the Derby family at length. It took all Henry's remaining restraint not to raise his hand and say, *Yeah. And they're also Hephaestus.*

When the bell finally rang, he walked to his locker and scanned the halls for Andie. Two days had passed since Hermes left. He should've been back by now. They should have gone with him. If anything happened to Hermes, they would be stuck in Kincade, rudderless.

But that was stupid. If something could take out Hermes, who was faster than a cheetah and still strong, what the hell did he think he would be able to do about it?

But maybe I could, if I really had that shield.

The idea had crept into his head more than once since Demeter suggested it. Half the time it sounded ridiculous, as if one weapon could suddenly make him the equal of Achilles. He'd seen Achilles fight. He'd seen the inhuman strength Achilles had, and how fast he moved.

But Henry couldn't deny that he wished it would. He wondered what it would feel like to have that kind of strength. That kind of confidence. To be able to stand against Achilles and not be afraid. To be able to win.

"Henry."

He turned and saw Max and Matt Bauer. He nodded, mostly toward Matt. Max's comments about Andie's rack at the party had almost earned him a punch in the face.

"What's going on?" Henry asked.

"Nothing, man," Max said, and leaned against the lockers. "What's going on with you? Ariel's pretty pissed about you leaving."

"Ariel's not my girlfriend. Let her be pissed. I don't care."

"I know, right? And what's she got to be pissed about anyway? You just left with Big Andie."

"Stop calling her that. You're not going to make it stick."

Max and Matt laughed, oblivious to his darkening expression.

"Wanna bet? There she is. Hey, Big Andie!" He waved to her, and Henry turned. The look on Andie's face was carefully balanced. Only someone who knew her like Henry did could tell that Max's jibe had gotten to her.

Come over here and pound him. Come on. I'll help.

But she didn't. She nodded their way and turned to go.

"Oh, come on, Big Andie!" Max shouted. "Come hang with the rest of us guys!"

Henry slammed his locker shut. He didn't call her name, and he didn't think. He just jogged after her and spun her around. And kissed her.

After an initial gasp, the hall around them went silent, but Henry didn't care. He wasn't aware of anything but the warmth of her lips, and the increasing rate of his heartbeat. When he pulled away, he braced himself for anything. Yelling. Glaring. Her fist to his face. What he got instead was her arm slipped around his neck. She pulled him back and kissed him again.

"We're not them," she said quietly. "Not Hector. Not Andromache."

"We're not. We're us." He smiled, and they walked down the hall together. Ariel and Max be damned.

Buffalo, New York. Hermes took a breath and savored the smell of Lake Erie before blowing it out again. The city was still ugly from snowmelt. And around every corner was the whisper of decline. It was a city that knew what it used to be. A city that wept rust. A city that Hephaestus would like.

Last fall, Athena and Odysseus had passed through on their way to Kincade. Strange how close they'd come to another one of their brothers. He wondered what it meant, that Athena hadn't detected him so nearby. He wondered if Hephaestus had known they were there.

Hermes had traveled north from Kincade in style, hiring a private car and driver, but he'd left them at the edge of the city (the backseat littered with an odd juxtaposition of caviar jars and fast-food bags, champagne bottles and Mello Yello) and walked into town on foot. He'd wasted no time and gone directly to Alexander Derby's last known address. And he'd waited there on and off for the last two days. Watching and listening to the people who came and went.

Almost no one came and went. Only one man and one woman in two days, both of whom returned with groceries and packages wrapped in brown paper. He'd stood in the shadows for two days watching housekeepers.

And not one time has my god-dar gone off. Not even a blip. And no movement from any of the million windows, either.

He looked up to the top floors, which rose well above the trees. The place looked less like a home than a museum. Several stories of gray-brown brick and white window moldings. It took up an entire corner of a city block.

And all that's rattling around in there is one god and two housekeepers?

Or maybe no god at all. Maybe he'd come too late, and Hephaestus was already dead. He'd hoped to watch the house and see a well-dressed gentleman walk down the front steps with a silver-handled cane and a bad limp. He'd hoped they would catch each other's eye and smile. They'd have a drink, and share some food. Talk about old times. And then he'd forge Henry a new shield, a better shield than that flimsy Frisbee Achilles toted around. And Hermes would go home.

Just once, couldn't it be that easy?

There was only one way to find out. The soles of Hermes' shoes seemed loud as he crossed the street. He had his hand raised in a fist to knock before he remembered that he was the god of thieves, and broke in.

He stepped into the foyer, feet soft on the marble floor. The interior looked like any other massively expensive house might. High ceilings, walls painted robin's egg blue, and a striped silk chaise. He moved farther in and sniffed the air. A light scent of iron lingered in the rooms, and his pulse quickened with hope.

As he passed by open doorways he noted the rich furnishings: Chinese vases, long oak dining tables, a study full of books and bronze busts. But his mind galloped ahead to Hephaestus. His old friend. The god that Zeus had deemed the most sturdy. The most reasonable.

He can't possibly be that pissed about Hera. She kicked him off Olympus because she was ashamed of his shriveled foot.

Hermes swallowed. She had done that. But she was still his mother.

The sound of footsteps made him freeze, then zip down another hallway. But it was only the woman. He heard her humming in what he assumed was the kitchen. He listened to cabinets and drawers open and close, and sniffed the air again. No iron this time, but chicken with sage and butter. Enough for an extra guest? He glanced at his emaciated stomach. Maybe enough for one extra guest, but never enough for him.

Have to hurry. It would be rude to interrupt his lunch.

He darted into the hall and up a set of stairs, following the faint hint of metal in his nose. The farther he got into the house, the less it looked like a house. Rooms grew larger and hallways shorter. They doubled back on themselves. Twice he found himself in the same hallway and three times in the same room. And everything seemed to skirt the outside edges. There didn't seem to be anything in the center. The architecture was clever; you wouldn't even notice if you weren't already suspicious and paying too much attention. But all the rooms and stairways he'd been through left a rather large square empty in the middle of the building. Sweat broke out on his forehead. He was close to lost.

There has to be a way to the center. And what will I find when I get there?

Images of all kinds flashed through his head. He imagined ten bellows, an entire smelting operation. A wide, gray, empty room, and at the center a contorted, withered corpse that was unrecognizable as anything resembling a god or human. And then he opened a door on his right, and stumbled through.

The space was massive, walls covered with books and paintings. Great chandeliers lit it, casting a yellowed parchment color across the marble floor. Hermes leaned against a railing three floors up and looked down on it. Above him were another four floors.

"Hermes."

Hephaestus sat in a leather wingback chair, his lap covered with a blanket. Behind him, a fireplace roughly the size of a Chevy sedan blasted heat through the space.

"Hephaestus?"

His friend smiled. "What took you so long? Is the messenger of the gods slowing down? I felt you come in twenty minutes ago. And I felt you lurking outside my walls for two days before that."

Hermes leapt over the rail and dropped to the floor, in too big a hurry to bother with stairs or a ladder.

"All that time you knew I was here, and you didn't come out to welcome me?" Hermes tried to smile. But the longer Hephaestus stayed in that chair, the more his apprehension grew. The other god looked all of about twenty-five except for his strange widow's peak hairline, but he sat at an odd angle, one shoulder jutted up much higher than the other. Hermes' eyes flickered to his legs, hidden under the blanket. "You look like a cartoon villain in that chair."

Hephaestus reached to the side and gripped a long silver crutch that attached to his elbow and shoulder, then pushed to the other side and attached its mate. When he stood, Hermes saw the extent of the damage. His spine had twisted cruelly. The joints in his hands bulged, warping the finger bones. He could barely hold his arm braces, but he kicked aside the blanket. His legs were encased in bands of metal.

"Get that look off your face," Hephaestus said gruffly. "Watch." He stepped forward, and the mechanisms on his leg whirred. Despite his contorted form, the motion seemed effortless.

"You're . . . Iron Man."

"Ha!" Hephaestus grinned. "Tony Stark gets no credit. These are my own design."

"You look good, old friend," Hermes said. "All things considered."

"All things considered, we both do. Both of us still handsome, from the neck up."

A faint knock sounded and the young woman Hermes had seen leaving and returning entered, pushing a cart of silver platters. She parked it beside a dark dining table in the north end of the room.

Hephaestus walked to the table, leg braces whirring. The

combination of movements with the metal arm crutches gave the impression of an ungainly silver spider. A very strong ungainly silver spider.

"Stay for lunch?" Hephaestus asked. The woman, who really wasn't much more than a girl on closer inspection, lifted silver covers to reveal a platter of six roasted chickens and two more of white asparagus bathed in hollandaise. "I sent them out for it specially. For old times' sake."

"Next you'll tell me you've got some of that odd German wine."

Hephaestus' eyes widened in horror. "Let's try a nice New York white this time. Marie, two bottles of the Chateau Frank Riesling."

Over the course of the meal, Hermes tried not to stuff himself, but it was difficult. He also tried not to drink too much, which was even more difficult. The Riesling paired well with the food, and being inside the grand house brought back memories of their time spent in Hephaestus' fine German hotel.

"So, the Derbys. Are they really your family? Or just mortals you befriended and bewitched with roasted chicken?"

"They really are," Hephaestus said. "Or at least, they're my descendants. The first Alexander Derby II was my biological son. I've lived a whole saga here. Heartbreak and triumph. Wars fought and won. Generations of family." He frowned. "And then this." He held up his twisted and curled hand. "Now my real family comes knocking."

"Athena was here," Hermes said. "At the end of this past summer. Briefly."

"I know. I felt her, luckily, before she felt me."

"So far before?" Hermes asked. "No offense, but, steel robot legs or not, you don't look like you can make a speedy getaway."

"My body is twistier, that's for certain," Hephaestus replied. "But the limp is nothing new, and I've learned the need for escape plans. There are ways out of here, my friend, that you can't even imagine. Be careful what doors you go through."

"Sounds ominous," Hermes said, and stuffed another bite of chicken into his mouth.

"So it does. But it's a necessity."

"I didn't want to find you this way," Hermes said. "I imagined you in a suit not so different from the one you're wearing now. But there were no crutches, or braces. I thought . . . I hoped, that maybe you had a bigger cane. Maybe one of those canes with four feet at the bottom."

"And I hoped you'd somehow been able to outrun the whole mess." Hephaestus chuckled. "But here we are. And here it is."

Here it is. And damn it, how I hate to ruin such a nice lunch.

"You've heard about the war, haven't you," Hermes said quietly. "And you've heard about your mother."

Hephaestus looked down, and picked up his wine.

"Yes," he said. "Hera has fallen. Shall we pour a libation for her out on the floor?" He shook his head. "I heard."

"She didn't try to contact you? Didn't try to get you to come over to her side?"

"She didn't. And I would have said no, anyway. Dying gods tearing each other's throats out just to be the last gods standing. Even if you win, what kind of survival is that? What kind of victory? It's vulgar. No, when Mother needed help, she didn't turn to me. She went to her favorite son, like she always does. Like my own damned wife does, for that matter."

Ares and Aphrodite. They always enjoyed humiliating you.

· "I thought you gave Aphrodite back," Hermes said.

"Zeus wouldn't take back the bride-price. He said I was stuck with her."

Hermes laughed. Nothing remained on any of the platters except chicken bones and a few sprigs of asparagus. Both bottles of wine were dry. And he needed to get back to Andie and Henry. He'd been gone too long already.

"I'm in the war, Hephaestus. I need your help. That's why I came."

"I just told you. I don't want to be involved."

"I know. And I wish I didn't have to beg." He leaned forward, elbows on the table, and stared into his empty plate. "I don't want to die."

Hephaestus sat quietly for a long time. Then he set his wineglass down with a clink.

"What do you think I can do for you?"

"I need you to forge us a shield for Hector of Troy."

12

THE KIDNAPPING OF PERSEPHONE, REDUX

The knife in Ares' hand shone dull silver. Athena tensed. He'd gotten the drop on her, but if he thought he and Aphrodite would get out of it clean, he was kidding himself. When he took one step forward, she would spring. And that knife might just end up buried in his gut. She might just saw the blade clear up to his throat.

Aphrodite stepped between them and slapped Ares' hand.

"Don't," she said. "Don't joke. Do you think because she's unarmed she can do no damage?" She turned to Athena and apologized.

"A joke?" Athena asked. "That's supposed to be funny? I could've torn your hand off."

"Torn my hand off?" Ares laughed. "Weeks of fighting monsters have made you overconfident."

Weeks of fighting monsters. Had it been that long that

she'd spent tearing scales and claws off of beasts at the banks of the Styx? Had that much time passed in the dark? She didn't know. It could have been days and it could have been forever.

"It wasn't all a joke, either, Aphrodite," Ares said. "This is going to take a lot of blood."

He drew the blade across his hand and flicked a few red drops into the lake. He shook blood in all directions, flinging it onto petals of asphodel and into the mud of the bank. Athena recoiled as some of it landed on her face, but it was smart. The dead would smell it, and come for a taste. It wouldn't take long.

"Why are we doing this?" Athena asked, wiping her cheek.

"Have you noticed how Persephone is nowhere near?" Ares asked. "How she seems to hang out by the river border, and near her palace? I think it's because she's mostly dead now. Mostly a shade herself. I don't think the dead are quite as obedient as they used to be."

As Athena looked out across the still lake, a pale head poked out of one of the tunnels. A pale arm followed it, and then another, until a parade of waxy corpses lurched toward them, so many that Athena wished Ares had put out less bait. They came from everywhere, even from the corridor they'd come down, their legs stiff and jerking, vacant eyes bright at the prospect of food. Of life.

Aphrodite moved close to Ares and took his arm. So many dead were disconcerting. Men, women, youths, all shuffled closer with their mouths slightly open.

"They won't hurt you," Ares whispered into Aphrodite's hair.

"You sure?" Athena asked irritably. "What's the second part of the plan?" The first of the dead touched her: a whisper against her shoulder. Then a weak, groping hand.

Athena pushed her panic down. They were only shades. Only the dead, and she could force her way through thousands if she had to.

Which she would, if she wanted to get free. Hundreds of pale shades had already assembled in only a few seconds.

"All right, before there are too many." Ares' voice was loud, and not quite as calm as before.

"Ares, hurry," Aphrodite pressed.

He dragged the blade across his wrist and reached for the head of the nearest dead. He forced his wrist against its mouth and let it drink. "Here." He tossed Athena the knife. "Feed as many as you can."

Athena watched the corpse lap and suck on Ares' blood. Color quickly returned to its hair, its cheeks, and even the rags it wore. The eyes blinked to something like life.

Turncoats. They were making turncoats. The blood of whoever fed the dead would bind the dead to them.

Athena made a quick cut in her palm and shoved it in the face of the nearest shambling body.

"Give me the knife," Aphrodite said.

Athena handed it over, and Aphrodite followed their lead. When they started, Athena feared an onslaught, a rush of bodies crushing them and pushing them back into the lake. But the corpses just shuffled without much aim. All except those being fed.

Ares had finished with two, and held both of them by the shoulder.

"Your mistress is dead now, like you," he said. "She isn't your queen any longer, but a shade who walks the halls. Find her. Bring her to us."

Athena lay back on a bed of asphodel. The wounds on her wrists and hands had scabbed over, but she'd given up so much blood that her head swam. How much blood could a god bleed before they passed out? She still didn't know. But she, Ares, and Aphrodite had pressed the issue. Aphrodite lay somewhere in the flowers beside her, and Ares sat wearily on a rock.

"Does anyone have anything to eat?" Aphrodite asked. "Some fruit?"

"No," Athena replied. "And I wouldn't eat anything you find down here, if I were you." She turned her face away from the scentless blossoms. No food. No water. They'd just have to wait for their heads to stop pounding.

"How long do you think they'll take?" Aphrodite sighed. "To get back, I mean. Do you think it will take them long to find Persephone?"

"Not as long as you'd think."

Athena sat up when she heard Odysseus' voice. At first she thought it was a trick of her bleary eyes and swimmy head. But there he was. Standing. And more than that, walking, damp from the shoulders down from swimming across the Styx. The sword that Achilles had forced through his chest was now strapped to his back.

"Judging by the speed of that massive herd of dead people I just passed, she could be here within the hour." Ares' wolves stood on either side of him until their master beckoned and they trotted forward to have their heads scratched.

"What are you doing here?" Athena asked. "How are you healed?"

"Sorry for not waiting," Odysseus said. "I didn't trust these two." He nodded toward Ares and Aphrodite. "And I really wanted to see Oblivion dog paddle."

Oblivion growled low in its throat. Athena pressed her hand to Odysseus' chest through the tear in his shirt. Her fingers expected blood and a raw wound. Instead she found a warm, purple scar.

"This shouldn't be."

Odysseus smiled and kissed her fingertips. "You'd rather I stick the sword back in then?"

Ares stood and walked around Odysseus in a wide circle.

"That is some fast healing, even on the banks of the underworld," Ares said warily.

Odysseus watched him out of the corner of his eye.

Athena took his hand.

"Come on."

She led him down the corridor they'd come through, ears pointed backward to make sure Ares and Aphrodite weren't following. But they were weak from feeding a horde of shades. Their heads probably hurt too much to make mischief.

The dark veined walls didn't move as much as when they'd first passed. Perhaps they were nearly empty of dead, since so many were scouring the tunnels with fresh gods' blood in their cheeks. As they walked, Athena kept one hand on Odysseus. She was afraid to let go.

I should tell him a hundred things. A thousand. I should tell him everything again that I whispered in the dark.

"You do heal fast," she said. "And you move fast. Faster than you used to. You fight better, too. Even better than when I used to help you."

"So you've figured it out, then," Odysseus said, and grinned. "That I'm Mortal with a capital *M*, and clever enough to keep the secret from the goddess of wisdom."

They stopped, and Athena turned and traced the scar on his chest. It had faded still more.

"I should have known sooner," Athena said. "As soon as we met Achilles. As soon as I choked Cassandra. Even then I hadn't guessed how far it went. I thought you were dead. I would've killed you last night, had Ares not stayed my hand. *Ares*, of all gods."

"Don't tell me any more," Odysseus said. "I'm indebted to the prig enough as it is."

She pressed her palm to his chest.

"I'm sorry. I'm sorry that I let this happen to you."

"It wasn't your fault. It wasn't your sword."

"It was my fight!" Athena ground her teeth, and backed away. "I lost it," she said. "Whatever I was. I'm not that anymore."

"Athena. What are you talking about?"

"It doesn't matter," she said. "It matters that you're here. My fuckup didn't cost me someone else."

"So the others," he said. "They're safe?"

"I don't know. But if they are that's not the point. Andie and Henry. Cassandra. My brother. They all could have been killed."

"But they weren't," Odysseus said. "And you're wrong

about Cassandra. I don't think she was in much danger at all. We've never had to test the theory, but I suspect that Cassandra would be even harder to kill than I am."

"Why do you think that?" Athena asked.

She had figured it out—it had gradually worked its way into her head after she caught a glimpse of his more-than-human quickness. The ones who had fallen and been brought back—Odysseus, Cassandra, and Achilles—they were more than they had been when they died. And they were more than they had been when they lived before. They were two bodies in one. The hero and the myth. So Achilles being stronger, Athena understood. But Cassandra was no great warrior.

"Cassandra and Achilles," Odysseus explained, "are archetypes. Touched by the gods. I was a traveler, with a good head on my shoulders and the finest patron goddess a man could ask for. But I was still only a man. Not divine."

Athena nodded. Achilles was once a near invincible fighter. Now he was unkillable. And Cassandra, once an oracle, had seemed to become almost as Fate itself.

"We're ourselves," Odysseus said. "And we're the old myths."

"But you can't kill gods?" Athena asked.

Odysseus smiled. "I'm not a weapon. Just an old hero. Although I may have been imbued with the powers of supersmartness."

Athena thought back to Demeter's words. *Make her remember and she'll be more. They still are what they were.*

"The Fates are responsible for this," she said, "but I don't know why. Achilles I understand. But why would they put Cassandra in motion when they can't control her?"

Odysseus shrugged.

"Maybe the Fates are like the rest of you lot. Maybe they can't agree."

Behind them in the tunnel, closer than Athena thought possible, Ares cleared his throat.

"Had enough of your reunion?" Ares asked. "We don't exactly have the time to waste."

"Why not?" Aphrodite asked from his arm. "All we're doing is waiting for the dead to bring us Persephone." She looked at Athena and Odysseus with surprising fondness. "Let them have their time. Our reunion lasted for days, remember?"

Ares tugged her close. They looked happy and miserable all at once. Passion edged with resentment. But that was how they'd always been.

Athena pursed her lips. She stepped away from Odysseus. After all this time, she'd finally blundered into Aphrodite's domain. Love. It felt dangerous. Foolish. As if all the wisdom gained from watching mortals wear their hearts on their sleeves and ruin themselves meant nothing.

Persephone's scream cut through the corridor, and Athena tensed. Aphrodite trembled and closed her eyes. She clamped her hands down over her ears like a child. It was the first sign of instability she'd shown in the underworld.

"We should probably move." Odysseus craned his neck around a curve in the wall. What would they see when Persephone rounded the corner? A mass of blood-rushed dead swarming all over her? Or perhaps they'd be driving her from the rear like cattle.

Athena looked at Ares. "Where did you intend to take her?"

"The only place we can hold her," Ares said. "Across the river."

Persephone crossed the river screaming curses, boiling from the center of an army of corpses. Their arms and legs writhed like a bed of snakes. If Persephone hadn't been a goddess, she would've been pulled apart, or drowned. They all might have been. But Athena and the others were able to stay just ahead of the pack, swimming fast across the Styx, splashing and squinting with closed mouths.

Athena waded as quickly as she could toward shore. Her legs felt like logs, still weak from the loss of blood. Beside her, Aphrodite stumbled and Athena caught her by the arm before she could go under.

"Stay up!" Athena shouted. "Wolves, help!" For a second she thought they wouldn't obey, but then both Panic and Oblivion turned and let Aphrodite grab onto the shoulders of their coats.

"Athena!" Ares called.

He was still hip deep in the river. Persephone hissed and struggled in the arms of the dead a few feet beyond.

"The dead can't cross the Styx," he said. "The rest of the way is up to us."

Great.

Odysseus drew the sword from his back, but Ares shook his head.

"I don't think Hades will entertain making any deals if

you take his bride's arm off." He motioned for Odysseus to go up onto the bank. It would just be the gods of war. Ares would probably take the close quarters as an opportunity to throw a few elbows into Athena's eye.

I can throw them right back. Let's just get this done.

Persephone stilled when she saw them coming. Bits of the half of her that was fully dead and rotten floated in the Styx like so much fish food, scraped off by the grips of the shades. Her one usable, yellowed eye tracked their movements, while the milky-white rotten one twitched distractingly. Athena swallowed. She would have to grip those decaying arms. The fully dead side wouldn't be so terrible, but on the still-rotting side the skin would slough off in Athena's hands.

There was no time to get squeamish.

"Go!" Athena shouted at Ares, and he, always the gentleman, surged forward and punched Persephone square in the face. Athena heard Persephone's teeth rattle, but the punch didn't do much and she struck, slicing five deep gashes into Ares' chest with her fingernails.

Athena grabbed Persephone's mushy, rotting wrist and twisted it behind her back. The shoulder joint went farther than she expected and she almost let go, thinking it would come loose from the socket and tear free.

"Get the other arm, Ares!" Athena shouted.

He yanked it across his body and grabbed the back of Persephone's head with his other hand to dunk her under the water. Athena ground her teeth.

Good plan, moron. Let her drink up some extra hate. It's not like she needs to breathe!

Slowly, they dragged her toward the shore. As they neared the border between the living and the dead, Persephone weakened, but it still felt like wrangling a marlin. She jerked and thrashed and bit down hard into Athena's bicep. Something in the half-dead saliva made the muscle go slack. But they were close to shore. The water rose to the middle of their thighs. Once they got to dry land on the far bank, Persephone would be easier to handle.

Ares roared. He dragged Persephone the rest of the way in heaving, enormous strides. Before he threw her on the bank, he drew his hand back to strike.

"Ares!" Aphrodite forced her way between them and shoved him hard. Knocking Persephone out was unnecessary. Once her feet left the water, she collapsed like a sack of rags. Athena and Odysseus watched Aphrodite help her up and lean her against the black rocks.

"Aphrodite's a lot sweeter than I remember," Odysseus said, and Athena regarded her grimly. Aphrodite could be tender, when she wanted to be. When she was sane enough to be.

"Just remember that she can turn back into a raging bitch at the drop of a hat."

Odysseus nodded. He hadn't forgotten the sight of her shoving a makeshift spear through Aidan's back any more than Athena had. The mad, victorious light in her eyes. Athena couldn't get it out of her head.

"She's sweet because she needs us," Athena said. "Because we suit her purpose. Don't trust it. Don't ever trust either of them." She looked at Ares as he wrung the river out of his shirt. "And don't care about them, either."

Odysseus stared at Aphrodite, and narrowed his eyes. "No chance of that."

Athena smiled slightly.

Odysseus nudged her with his shoulder. "Now what?"

"Now we wait for Hades. It shouldn't take long."

13

HUNTERS

Cassandra stared at the television. An actress she knew spoke on the screen, but she had no idea what she was watching. She didn't even remember when she'd stopped aimlessly flipping through channels. Outside, the light through the window showed orange. Another lost day. After swallowing the Fury's blood, Thanatos had taken to his bed ill. That had been two days ago.

The back door opened and closed. Calypso's soft footsteps echoed down the hall, and then the door to her guest room clicked shut. They hadn't spoken much since Calypso killed the Fury in the basement. Calypso spent most of her time in the pool, swimming and swimming and swimming, and when she wasn't in the pool, she was in her room. For the first time since leaving the cave, Cassandra was lonely. She'd gotten used to the nymph's company.

So go talk to her. It takes two people for the silent treatment to work.

She shoved herself off of the sofa and went to the kitchen to assemble a tray of papaya juice. The ice rattled in the glasses as she carried it to Calypso's door. She had to knock with her toe.

Calypso answered wrapped in a white bathrobe. Her brown braids dripped and smelled faintly of chlorine.

"Papaya juice?" Cassandra offered up the tray.

Calypso shook her head.

"Come on. Please? There's only so much to do in this place, you know? Only so many shows to pretend to watch. So many books to pretend to read."

"Then why don't you really read them?" Calypso asked.

"I can't concentrate."

Calypso stepped back to allow Cassandra inside.

"I don't want any juice," she said as Cassandra set the tray down and started to pour.

"Why are you so mad at me?" Cassandra asked. "It's not like the Fury gave you much trouble. You've obviously had experience killing something like that before."

Calypso's movements had been fast and coldly precise. As businesslike as a cat breaking the back of a mouse.

"You should've done it," Calypso said.

Cassandra sat on the edge of the bed.

"Maybe I should have. Everyone certainly seems to think so. But it still got done."

"This is your war," Calypso said loudly.

"*My* war? I'm not the one who showed up on your door-step."

"*You* are the one who seeks to kill gods. I don't care about

[140]

it. And Thanatos cares about nothing. Yet I'm the one who severed Megaera's head, and Thanatos lies in pain. You're behaving like a spoiled child."

"No," Cassandra said. "I was a spoiled child. Before this. Now I'm behaving the only way I can."

She poured juice into both glasses. Calypso could drink it or not drink it. But to her surprise, Calypso picked it up, and sat down beside her.

"You couldn't kill that Fury," Calypso said softly. "How do you expect to be able to kill me?"

"I'll be stronger then," Cassandra said. "I'll be better."

She looked away. That was a lie. Cassandra didn't really believe she'd ever have to make good on their bargain. She thought that if enough time passed, Calypso would heal, and want to stay.

"There's nothing for me here anymore, Cassandra."

"You're wrong. There is. It's just hard to see right now."

Calypso sighed wearily.

"I've lived a very long time. I know when to leave. Don't presume to know better." She stood and stepped to the side of the open door. "Take some juice to Thanatos. Get him up. It's time we got going. Though I don't know how you intend to kill Lord Hades, when he's bound to be more charming than the Fury in the basement."

Cassandra quietly opened the door to Thanatos' room and set the tray down on the first thing she bumped into. With the curtains closed, the room was nearly pitch black.

"Thanatos?"

"Yes?"

"Are you just sitting in here awake?"

"With a massive headache," he said.

She closed the door and fumbled her way through to the windows, then pulled the curtain back by inches to let in a sliver of fading light. Thanatos watched with equal parts curiosity and irritation. She kept on pulling until he groaned and swung his legs over the side of the bed, elbows on his knees and head resting in his hands.

"Cassandra. What the hell are you doing in here?"

"Getting you moving," she barked, suddenly irritated. "Now do you want some juice, or just a kick in the ass?"

"Careful," he said as she handed him the glass. "Your temper will melt the ice." He took a sip and set it on the bedside table. "What's the matter?"

"Nothing. I'm just pitching a tantrum because you stayed in bed too long."

"You're a bad liar," he said. "I like that."

"Because it gives you an advantage?" Cassandra's lip curled. "Gods. You're all the same. Calypso thinks I won't be able to kill Hades because he'll charm me into thinking he's good. But none of you are good. I'll hate him the minute I lay eyes on him. I hate him already, just knowing what he is. Killing him will be easy."

Thanatos watched her with steady eyes. The heat in her hands and chest ebbed.

"Why are you so angry?" he asked.

"That's a stupid question."

"So give me a stupid answer."

"But you already know, don't you?" she asked. "You already know what I am. Who I was."

She paused, but he didn't move. He held her with those dark, steady eyes until she went on.

"They cursed me and murdered my family. They put an axe in my chest. They betrayed me, strangled me in a field! Blew up buildings full of people. Made it so I can't go home."

Her voice went lower and grew louder with every word. Every memory. An image of Aidan flashed inside her brain and she squeezed her fists to crush it out.

"It's more than enough reason to hate them," she said. "More than enough reason for them to die. And that's the truth."

"That's the truth," he said softly. "But it's not the whole truth."

"Finish your juice and get up." She walked out of the room. "I've got gods to kill."

Cassandra's anger kept her warm for most of an hour, long after she'd finished stuffing her scant belongings into a bag. Anger felt good. Safe. When it started to wane, she imagined Ares' face bleeding under her hands. And then Athena's. And then Aphrodite's, and the fire surged up fresh.

Calypso stepped into her open doorway.

"Did you wake Thanatos?" Calypso asked. "Is he well again?"

"I don't know if he's well. But he's up."

Calypso seemed to have calmed since their encounter in her bedroom, but said nothing else before walking away. Cassandra's heart sank. Her anger fizzled, and without it she felt cold and alone again.

I want to go home.

"She just wants assurances," Thanatos said.

He leaned against her door, looking down the hall after Calypso.

"Assurances that you'll do what you promised," he said. "That you're more than a shaken little girl whose anger won't carry her as far as she thinks it will." He shrugged. "I tried to tell her you are. But she didn't seem to believe me. Right now I don't think you'd believe me, either."

"Stop *pressing* me."

She glared at him. The god of death looked too smug and too innocent. The effects of the Fury's blood still clung to him, and the slight hitch in his movements and grimace on his face made him seem more human. He'd abandoned his slacks for jeans and a dark gray T-shirt. He wore the costume well.

"Did your headache go away?" she asked.

"No. But I'm out of bed now."

He held his hand out. Cassandra shouldered her bag and walked past it.

"I had another day and a half before we really needed to get moving," he said. "But if you insist."

"What do you mean? Why a day and a half?"

He slid past her in the hallway. "That's the earliest we can expect to be hunted down by one of Megaera's avenging sisters."

"Her what?"

"You didn't think they'd just let that go? They'll be on our trail every step of the way to Hades. And even if I don't come back to this house for a decade, one of them will be here waiting when I do. Unless they're all dead. The Erinyes have patience to spare."

Cassandra paused in the living room and looked out over the darkness of the hills, at the thousand tiny points of light from mortal houses. She thought she detected movement in a few of the closest and, standing in front of the large windows with the neon glow from the kitchen bathing her back, she felt suddenly exposed.

Relax. There's no Fury standing in the bushes with leathery wings and bloody eyes. She blinked and focused in on a particularly tall shadow. *That's just a tree, idiot.*

Thanatos moved around in the kitchen, stuffing supplies into a bag. The extra Fury blood went into a cooler with a couple of ice packs. He seemed calm. Sure of his timeline. But maybe he was always calm. Death had nothing to fear.

"Does this mean you can't come back to this house?" Cassandra asked. "Did you give up your house for this?"

He nodded.

"It's just a house," he said. "And I will come back. As soon as you're strong enough to come with me and scare the Furies out of my basement." He closed the last of his cabinets and picked up his bags. "Time to go. Taking the car east."

"Is that where Hades is?"

"Must be. That's the way my arteries are straining."

Thanatos drove fast through the nighttime desert. Too fast for Cassandra's taste, but he seemed at home behind the wheel, and it was nowhere near as gut-wrenching as driving up the steep, curving road to his home. Behind them,

Calypso reclined in the backseat, twisting her white-tainted braid around her finger and looking at the stars.

"Where do you think he is?" Cassandra asked Thanatos. "Do you have any guesses?"

Thanatos cocked his head. "If I had to guess? I'm leaning toward Greece. If the god of the underworld is dying, it might have made him a little homesick. Or at least nostalgic."

"We're going to Greece?"

"Or somewhere else in Europe. Maybe Africa. He loves those places best. They're where all his favorite plagues happened." He glanced her way and smiled. There was something so disarming about it that she almost smiled back.

"You know how creepy that is, right?" she asked. "Talking about plagues that killed thousands and then grinning like a goon?"

"Millions," he corrected her. "They killed millions. And it isn't me who loves the plagues. It's Hades. They fill his halls. He loves his dead."

"Shouldn't the god of death love the dead?"

"No," he said. "It's a difficult thing to understand. You wouldn't comprehend it even if I told you. But I think you will, someday."

Cassandra rolled her eyes. Gods. They acted like they knew everything, but they were some of the most obtuse creatures she'd ever met.

"There is one thing I don't get," she said. "Why do you exist? If Hades is lord of the dead, and Atropos is the Fate of death, why does there need to be another?"

"Hades is lord of the underworld. Like a shepherd. And Atropos is a Fate. The decider. I am death embodied. I am the hand, and if you want to get specific, I'm the hand of gentle death. There are," he said, and eyed her sideways, "many of us. All different sorts."

"What a lovely thought."

Thanatos shrugged and pressed down on the accelerator a little harder.

"Would you slow down?" Cassandra asked. "We're going to run out of gas before we get to a station."

"I've got extra gas. In the trunk."

"Fantastic. When we flip over, we'll make an *extra* big explosion." She mimed a car accident and subsequent fireball with her hands, and Thanatos laughed. She laughed, too, until a wing beat against her window.

"What was that?" she asked.

There was no time to say anything else before the Fury's heavy body struck the side and the car started to spin.

Thanatos swore and squeezed the brakes, trying to steer into it. Dust and grit from the shoulder of the highway flew up on all sides and hit the window in a rain of pebbles. Cassandra's head spun as the car twisted and fishtailed. She gripped the door handle hard, knowing the impact would come in the next moment. One hard jerk and one black thud, and maybe she would wake up afterward and maybe she wouldn't.

The dark part of her mind clicked open: she saw the car spinning as if from above, as if she was outside of it, and saw not one but two Furies latched onto the roof, wings unfurled like sails. Two more sets of wings flapped into view. If they attached, the car would flip.

"Two more!" she shouted. "Get them off the roof!"

The car slowed, but Thanatos couldn't do much besides

control the fishtail. Cassandra fumbled for the window button and failed, but Calypso got hers down and snaked her torso through, knife in hand. She cut one of the Furies and it tumbled off of the car. With it gone, Thanatos hit the brakes hard. The car careened to the side as they stopped. Cassandra was thrown against the door. Calypso was thrown out.

"Calypso!" Cassandra wrestled with her seat belt.

"No! Stay inside!"

"But—" Before she could protest, Thanatos was out and over the hood. He dove for Calypso and scooped her up. She had her right arm gripped tight to her body, but otherwise seemed all right. Cassandra tried to catch her breath. Every inch of her felt as though it was made of loose Jell-O. Her heartbeat vibrated in her ears.

"Where are they?" she asked, and in answer, heard a boot heel stomp on the roof of the car. She looked out the back window, into the weak red of the taillights.

Two Furies walked the road. They weren't in their creature form. They wore the same short black dresses and tall boots that Megaera had, when she hadn't been sporting claws and leathery wings. The Fury that Calypso had knocked off the car followed behind, still hideous, perhaps too injured to affect the change. One of her legs dragged as she crawled and scratched toward them.

"Thanatos," the first Fury said. "What have you done with our sister?"

"And not only our sister, but one of the Erinyes," said the second.

A third voice came from the roof of the car.

"Return Megaera's body and her blood. Give us the nymph. They are ours."

Thanatos shook his head. Beside him, Calypso grimaced and let go of her hurt arm. Her small knife glinted in the car's headlights. It wouldn't do much if one of the Furies decided to rush her. This time they weren't shackled to a wall.

"The blood I keep," Thanatos said. "I went to enough trouble to get it. And I'm keeping the nymph as well. The body, though, you're welcome to. It's buried in my basement."

Every Fury seethed. They hissed and roared. Wings popped through the skin of their backs and veins bounced across their cheeks and arms.

"Quit while you're ahead," he went on. "And don't take it so personal. Furies can die. I've killed you before."

But not her. Not Megaera. Cassandra could see the rage unspoken on the faces of every one. That had been the wrong thing to say.

Two of the Furies rushed Thanatos, claws digging into his chest and shoulders. They dragged him away from the car in a storm of beating wings. Every time the light caught their claws, they were covered with more and more blood. His arm lifted; he had one of their heads in his hand and crushed it. The Fury dropped, twitching, and the roof of the car bounced as the Fury on top of it flew to take her place.

"Thanatos!" Cassandra cried.

"Not me!" he shouted. "Calypso!"

"What?" Cassandra shouted back. She turned away from the attack, and saw Calypso struggling underneath the Fury they'd thrown from the car, her teeth bared with the effort of holding the fangs and claws at bay. Calypso had one good arm. The other looked broken, and bled from four deep cuts.

Cassandra jerked the car door open and stumbled out on unsteady legs, but adrenaline made her move fast. She felt outside of her body. Out of control. The Fury bit down on Calypso's forearm, razor teeth hitting bone, and Calypso screamed.

"Get off of her!"

Cassandra didn't think. She grabbed the Fury by the wing and shoulder and its eyes burst inside its skull. She wanted it away from Calypso, away and dead, a harmless corpse on the side of the road. Heat flooded her palms. She heard her own voice, shouting. She pushed the Fury up against the side of the car and kept pushing. She kept pushing as it shrieked. She kept pushing until it popped like a blister.

There were no bones. No internal organs. No teeth, or claws, barely a trace of wings and skin. It was all liquid. Red, and viscous, and laced through with something like mucus. It covered the rear quarter panel of the car and splattered up onto the roof. It coated Cassandra from her hair to her knees. She kept her lips pressed tightly closed, but could still taste it, salty and bitter, warm but cooling fast. Her hands flapped; droplets shook free and struck the ground.

"Don't move."

Cassandra closed her eyes as the Fury's blood began to drip.

Car doors opened. Whatever Thanatos was doing, it took forever. A scream built in Cassandra's throat: half rage, half disgust. Her hands still throbbed, full of steam. But it lessened. The shock of the Fury's sudden demise worked like a reset button.

A wet towel scraped along her eyes and mouth.

"It's only water on the towel. Don't open your eyes yet. Wait. There."

Cassandra opened her eyes to a puddle of red at her feet. It was as if the Fury had been nothing but a leather, winged bag of blood. Thanatos and Calypso wiped her as clean as they could.

"Where are the others?" she asked.

"I killed two," said Thanatos. "The third fled. Calypso, get her new clothes. And more water to rinse her hair." His hands moved to her shirt and started to tug at it. She almost slapped him away, but she had to get the Fury's mess off of her. That was more important than shyness or modesty. He stripped her shirt over her head. The night air hit her skin and made her shiver.

"Don't make her carry so much." Cassandra looked at Calypso. "I'm fine. I can rinse my own hair. Help her with her arm."

Thanatos released her reluctantly and handed her two bottles of water.

"Calypso, show me your arm," he said. "We need to splint it and find something to use as a sling."

Cassandra tilted her head back and carefully poured water into her hair. It was freezing cold, and blood and mucus slipped under her fingers as she rinsed. Her teeth clacked together with shivers and nausea. The last of the water she used to rinse her face and arms.

Calypso gave a small yelp as Thanatos set her arm into the makeshift splint. Even in the dark, a ring of purple bruises was visible against her skin. But they were lucky. The bone hadn't broken through.

"Are you all right?" Cassandra asked.

Calypso nodded, and smiled at her for the first time in what felt like a week. "I'll heal," she said. "You did well."

"Yeah. If I'd known the thing was going to explode like a water balloon, I might've pulled it back a little." Cassandra crossed her arms over her exposed chest, but Thanatos kept his eyes on the ground. He hadn't snuck so much as a peek. She walked around to the clean side of the car and dug inside her bag for a dry shirt. Something black, to keep from getting stained by the blood she knew was still on her. She slipped out of her destroyed jeans, too, and after a second's hesitation, tossed them into the ditch.

Calypso came around the car and leaned against the door as Cassandra pulled on a pair of pajama pants.

"Are you all right?" Calypso asked. "You didn't swallow any of the Fury's blood?"

"Nope. But I have new respect for Thanatos for downing an entire cup." She drew a shaky breath. Her next shower couldn't come soon enough. "Shouldn't you be mad at me? Wouldn't you rather the Fury killed you?"

"No," Calypso said. "I made you a promise, and I keep my promises. I'll die in the way of my own choosing."

"Calypso," Cassandra said sadly. "Listen, I—I promised you I would . . . because I was angry. Because I needed you. But you asked out of grief and—"

A vision slipped over Calypso's face: her brown hair faded to white and fell from her scalp like ashes. The skin of her face wrinkled, and darkened, and tightened against the bone until it might have been mummified. Her eyelids disappeared and her lips shrank back from her teeth. Cassandra saw her hands on Calypso's shoulders.

"Cassandra? Are you all right? What's the matter?"

"I'll do it," Cassandra said. Her voice was blank. The vision let go with a jerk and a rush of weakness. It was a true one, but it didn't seem possible.

I do it. I kill her. But how? How can I?

Calypso kissed her gently on the forehead.

"I know you will." She walked back to the front of the car and left Cassandra to slump against the rear panel. Thanatos cleared his throat. He kept his eyes low, and when he was close enough, Cassandra grabbed his arm.

"What is it?" he asked. "What's wrong?"

She didn't know. Maybe it wasn't wrong. It was what Calypso wanted. But it felt wrong. As wrong as the cold seeping into her fingers from Thanatos' skin.

I wish he was Aidan. If Aidan were here, none of this would be happening. If Aidan were here, I wouldn't have to worry.

But those thoughts were fairy tales. They weren't true, and even if they were, Aidan wasn't there. He was dead. Dead before the gods' war had a chance to turn from bad to worse. Dead before she really needed him.

Thanatos brushed wet hair from her cheek, and she inched away.

"You can't make me warm," she said.

"I could too," he said softly. "One irritating word from me and you'd be burning like a furnace. There. I saw that. Half a smile is better than nothing."

"This was a bad night."

"It was. I didn't think they'd come so fast. But it's not going to get any easier."

He glanced up at the stars. The desert was cold and quiet, lit by a bright moon. No visible movement in any direction. No cars. No flapping leather wings.

"These little beauties weren't even the cavalry," he said. "They were cannon fodder. If it had been Alecto, or even Tisiphone, you and Calypso would be dead. I would be strewn across the highway in annoying, painful pieces. And that's exactly who's coming."

"So what do we do?" Cassandra asked.

"Get a decent night's rest. And then fly out of here on the first plane we can find."

14

SHIELD OF HEROES

Henry lay on his bed beside Andie. Since the kiss in the hall, they'd gotten away with a lot. Plenty of time spent in his bedroom behind closed doors. Time to discover how her body felt against his, and to wonder at how that discovery felt like remembering. He'd kissed girls before. He'd had years of first kisses, kisses where he didn't have a brain cell free to feel it, too preoccupied wondering if he was doing it right, or what it meant, or how far it would go.

But Andie was different. And thanks to a very distracted set of parents, who would never in a million years think anything was going on in his room besides intense hockey debate, they had ample opportunity to enjoy just how different it was.

"Cassandra's going to flip when she gets home," said Andie.

"Good." He ran his fingers underneath her shirt, up

and down the bare skin of her back. He hoped Cassandra did freak out. It would serve her right. But he didn't think she would. He didn't want to say so to Andie, but he was beginning to think that the sister who came back wouldn't be the same person as the one who left. That whatever Cassandra was doing out there, whatever kept her from coming home, it couldn't be good.

Maybe we should be glad she's gone.

Maybe she would stay gone, and draw the gods away like insects after a blinking light. The Fates could drag Achilles in her direction, and make him forget all about their old feud.

"Hey." Andie poked him in the chest. "What's wrong?"

"Nothing," he said. "I'm good. Better than good."

"Good." Andie nipped his ear, and his pocket buzzed.

"Damn." He pulled the phone out. "It's Hermes."

Hermes didn't wait for a hello before speaking.

"Henry, excellent. I'm in your driveway. We've got to go to Buffalo. I found Hephaestus. I'm going to come in and tell your parents I have an appointment with a specialist and you need to drive me. Go with it." He hung up without waiting for a goodbye. Henry sighed.

"What is it?"

"Guess we're going to Buffalo."

"Your parents look good," Hermes lied as Henry backed the Mustang out of the driveway. He waved to Maureen in the kitchen and she raised her hand without smiling. Both she and Tom were like ghosts, thin and gray and sullen. They said all the right things, asked about his health, about the specialist and what he hoped to learn there. Asked if he was all right in the house by himself. But the words had nothing behind them. They were just preprogrammed sounds.

"They do," Henry lied back. "So, what are we going to Buffalo for? What's going on with Hephaestus?"

"He wants to meet you. Both of you. It was lucky that Andie was at the house. Saves us a stop at her place." Behind the steering wheel, Henry hid a smile. In the backseat, Andie didn't bother to hide hers.

"Oh." Hermes smirked. "Finally."

"Why does he want to meet us?" Andie asked.

"To make sure you're worthy of a new shield."

They parked the Mustang on the street in front of Hephaestus' massive, museumlike house. When they got out, neither Henry nor Andie could take their eyes off it.

"Millionaire industrialist, right?" Hermes smiled.

"No kidding." Henry glanced down at his sweatshirt. "Maybe we should have dressed better for this."

"In what?" Andie walked around to the driver's side. "Leather armor and one of those helmets with the tufts on them?" She snorted.

Hermes watched her carefully. She was uneasy. She hadn't liked it when she asked how Hephaestus was going to determine their worthiness and he hadn't had an answer. And she hated it whenever anyone implied she had something to prove.

But you do. We all do.

Hermes made a fist and felt his bones strain together under the skin. Practically no meat remained in his hands.

He told himself it was because he'd been on the move, and hadn't been able to eat the twenty thousand calories he could at home. But that wasn't true.

I ate all those chickens. All that caviar and fast food.

When he took off his shirt his heartbeat was visible through his chest. If he was a mortal, he'd be dead already. But he was a god. So he had a few more weeks.

The hell with that. I haven't come so far to leave them unprotected. I haven't come so far to never see my sister again.

He would live until Athena returned. And Andie and Henry could still use him. What he began to lack in strength, he still made up for in speed.

"Hermes?" Andie asked. "Are you okay?"

He moved away before she could put a hand on his bony shoulder.

"Fine. Now come on. I want to introduce you to my old friend."

Hephaestus welcomed them himself. No servants. No pretty blond maid. And no leg braces, that Hermes could see. He greeted them in a motorized chair, a blanket over his lap.

"I recognize them," he said after two awkward handshakes. Henry did a decent job of it, but Andie couldn't figure out how to lace her fingers through his gnarled grip. "But they don't recognize me."

"They don't have their old memories. But they know who they are."

Hermes nudged Andie discreetly. She hadn't blinked since they'd walked through the door.

"He's kind of . . . handsome," she whispered after Hephaestus turned his chair away and went down the hall with Henry. "I thought he was supposed to be an ugly god."

"He is, I suppose. Ugly for a god. But all that meant on Olympus was that he had a club foot. And I wouldn't mention that foot, if I were you."

Andie made a face. "He was hot from the ankle up and you called him ugly? You guys are dicks."

"Yes, that's a real news flash." Hermes took her by the arm and pulled her along. They walked a few steps behind as Hephaestus led them through the various hallways and connected rooms, giving them a tour of sorts. There was a story around every corner, some architectural tidbit or the tale of this or that chunk of worked metal. They walked, and he whirred, most of his attention on Henry.

"This feels like a maze," Andie whispered. "If I lived here I'd have to mark my way with string."

They paused at a set of stairs. But before anyone could look uncomfortable, Hephaestus maneuvered his chair toward the wall, and it engaged with a lift mechanism. And so the tour continued, until they reached the fourth floor.

"Just how many floors does this place have?" Hermes asked.

"Not nearly as many above as it does below," Hephaestus answered. "Why? Are you getting tired?" He looked back jovially, but his smile faltered as Hermes wiped sweat from his brow. "Just a few more rooms."

By the time they turned through the last, Hermes had begun to agree with Andie, who suspected that the house didn't obey any physical laws. But then they walked through the last door, and Hermes found himself looking down on the large central room where he'd dined with Hephaestus on his first visit. It was lit with the same combination of fireplaces and lamps, giving the marble floor a parchment yellow glow.

"Here we are," Hephaestus announced.

"Back to the center," Hermes mused. "How do we get down? Is there lunch?"

Hephaestus chuckled. He took Henry by the arm and gestured up. Hermes looked as well. What he saw almost made his stomach drop into his shoes.

The Shield of Achilles was mounted to the center of the ceiling, where a skylight might normally be. Instead the metal caught only the barest reflection of light. To Henry and Andie, it probably looked like nothing more than a black circle. Only Hermes' immortal eyes could detect the intricate detail work: the world laid out in each ring, from the constellations and cosmos to the vast ocean. And in between, cities and cattle and war. Farmers reaping their fields. Peace and strife.

"Is that real?" Hermes asked.

"Of course it is," Hephaestus replied. "It's my finest work. It was never lost. When the mortal world no longer required it, I took it back." Hephaestus studied the shield and its housing with pride. "I mounted it there in one day."

The shield sat in the middle of a system of steel girders, welded and arranged at angles so that they formed a lattice-work, similar to a spider web. The last of the girders attached to the wall just above their shoulders, and similar pieces attached to the doorway on the opposite side of the open room. No doubt Hephaestus had done all the welding and construction himself. To him, no skylight could have ever been more beautiful than this dark one, reflecting mellow orange flames.

"But now let's go down to the main level." Hephaestus moved his chair back into the twisting hallways. "And discuss a new shield."

Inside the large, ground-level room, Hermes began to despair of scoring another gourmet lunch. He hadn't seen a single servant since they'd arrived, and hadn't heard anyone humming in any room that might be a kitchen. The air smelled like iron and faintly of sulfur. He walked the length of the room restlessly, half an ear cast toward whatever dull industrial story Hephaestus was telling Henry at the moment. Henry, to his credit, appeared enthralled. Andie just seemed bored. After the initial handshake, she'd been largely ignored. Hermes wondered why Hephaestus had even asked her to come.

Maybe he'll get to her next. Or maybe he's just too taken with Henry.

Hermes smiled. That was good. It meant a better shield. He tapped his foot, and looked over the oil paintings on the walls and down into the shadowy corners. His eyes narrowed. What first appeared to be a black rectangle painted onto the floor was on closer inspection a stairway cut through the marble. Hermes walked toward it and sniffed. If Hephaestus kept his bellows down there, he couldn't smell them, or detect any heat.

"Hephaestus." Hermes gestured toward the stairs. "Does that lead to your bellows?"

Hephaestus turned his chair away from Henry and stared down into the dark space.

"I have no bellows, anymore."

Hermes blinked. No bellows. No forge?

"I suppose not." He looked at the robotics of the motorized chair. "You must have new ways of doing things. As long as it comes from your hand, the shield will have no equal."

He waited for his friend to say something else, but the silence stretched out. Hermes' stomach began to tighten.

"Hephaestus? What's going on?"

"Hermes," Hephaestus said quietly. "You always run in too soon."

Andie and Henry looked up in alarm. Too soon. Too soon and too careless.

A house empty of servants. How many of these doors have locked behind us?

"What have you done?" Hermes asked.

But Hephaestus didn't need to answer. On the opposite side of the room, from the opposite side of the house, a large set of doors opened on Achilles and the twisted, conjoined form of the Moirae. Achilles entered half-smiling, and the Moirae walked in behind him.

Walked was a strong word. Joined as they were, it was less a walk than a jerking shuffle. Each limb operated on its own in a left to right sequence. Clotho, Atropos, and Lachesis. Or more accurately, Atropos, and the emptying yolk sacs that were once Clotho and Lachesis. Clotho's arm twisted around her dark sister's back and disappeared into her skin. Both Lachesis' arms were still visible, but the one nearest Atropos had joined to her rib cage. Sooty purple rags draped across their parts to preserve modesty and hide whatever monstrous melding had taken place at their hips and legs.

Hermes could barely think. The only thing that popped into his head was the image of a brick wall, as if that could somehow bar the Moirae from entering his mind. One brick wall, that they'd chip and chisel at until the mortar gave and it tumbled down around his ears.

Stop. Be yourself. Be quick. Before they freeze your legs and you're all dead.

But his legs wouldn't budge. Whether it was due to fear or the Fates' interference didn't seem to matter.

Seeing Achilles again was the last thing Henry had expected. But he'd thought about it plenty. About what he would say. What it would be like to come face-to-face with the boy who betrayed them. The boy who killed Odysseus, and who had killed Henry, too, in their other life. In Henry's imagination, their meeting was always the same. Achilles won. Now Achilles was here, and it took everything Henry had not to turn tail and run. But he was acutely aware of Andie, standing on the other side of the room. Andie, who would probably do something very brave, and very stupid.

The fists that hung by his sides clenched tighter. No one would lay a hand on her, as long as he stood.

Achilles paced lightly in front of him, the walk of a caged lion. His eyes never left Henry's. Not for one second. Demeter had been right. Killing Henry was all he wanted.

"You're unarmed," Henry said.

Achilles stopped and held out his empty hands.

"No spear in your chest today. Nothing so easy. This time I want to do it up close."

"All that time we trained together this winter," Henry said. "You know I don't remember being Hector. I guess that doesn't make a difference."

"Not a bit. No amount of time is going to make me forget what I lost. What you took. My best friend. And you thought you were killing *me*."

Henry wondered what part stung Achilles worse. The loss of Patroclus, or the idea that Hector had thought, however briefly, that he was the better fighter.

"What would you know about friendship?" Andie shouted. "Odysseus was your friend!"

"Our sides weren't the same," Achilles replied, as if that explained everything.

But that was how Achilles worked. In simple terms. With or against. Not in complex terms like right or wrong. Henry wasn't sure how he knew that, but he did. Another ghost of a memory, tattooed into his skin.

"It must have been hard," Henry said, "to throw that sword into Odysseus instead of me. It must've been hard to pretend that you could become a friend."

"Pretending?" Achilles asked. "Is that what you think I did?" He shook his head, almost sadly.

"I would have stayed with Athena, had she been strong enough. I thought that she was the one. The goddess of battle!" He threw up his arms and grinned. "Who could beat that?"

Behind him, the Moirae writhed. They seemed larger than they had on Olympus. They would have towered over Athena. As they towered over Achilles.

"The sad fact is," Achilles said, "I did like you, *Henry*. And I loved Odysseus. As for that dark beauty there," he winked at Andie, "who knows what might have happened?"

Andie made a crude gesture and spit on the floor.

"I think I liked your sister the best, though," Achilles said. "She's a scrapper. And she'll be coming round to our side, soon enough. Where she was always meant to be."

"No," Henry said. "She won't."

"I suppose it's hard to grasp," Achilles said. He pointed over his shoulder toward the Moirae. "They are the Fates, but Fate is a thing. It's an 'it,' and a 'they.'" He shrugged. "Doesn't matter. I'm one of their weapons, and Cassandra is the other. You can't fight Fate, Hector. You knew that once. I think I read somewhere that you knew that once."

"Stop calling me that. It's not my name."

"It's always going to be your name," Achilles said.

"No it isn't. I don't have to be back in Troy, and you don't, either. We can do something different. Have different lives than the shitty ones they gave us."

For just a moment, something changed in Achilles' eyes. The crook of his mouth faltered, and he looked somber, almost soft. They could shake hands and walk out of there. Things could change. For just that moment, Achilles considered it. Maybe he even wished for it.

"Come on," Henry said. "Don't let them collar you."

Achilles' teeth flashed white.

"Collar me?" he asked. "You just don't get it, do you? We could have been friends. Lived our mortal lives. I could have forgiven you." He smiled. "But now I don't have to. I get to be a god."

"Cassandra was right about you," Andie said. "You're a real shit."

Achilles chuckled, but his jaw flexed hard. The fierceness of him made Henry take a step backward.

"Hephaestus!" Hermes shouted from the far corner. "You said you would forge us a new shield!" Poor, hurt Hermes. Sometimes he sounded as innocently disappointed as a child.

"Does it look like I'm in any condition to forge a new shield?" Hephaestus asked, and held up his gnarled hands. "With this damn death?"

He looked at Henry meaningfully.

"The only shield by my hand that will ever exist," Hephaestus said, glancing upward, "is that one."

Achilles followed the god's gaze. When he saw the shield, greed and joy transformed his features. He ran to the wall and jumped, latched on to a ladder, and climbed to the first-level railing. He kept going that way, leaping from rail to rail, until he reached the third floor. But the distance between the third and fourth levels was too great, and the surface of the joining wall was carefully smooth. Achilles slapped his hands against it in vain.

Henry looked up at the shield, and at the door on the fourth floor near the crisscrossing system of steel girders.

"It's not yours anymore, Achilles," he shouted, and ran back the way they'd come, into the maze of hallways and rooms.

Hermes watched Henry go, still frozen. Andie called after him, but he yelled for her to stay with Hermes, which wasn't a bad suggestion. Hermes had no desire to be left the only fly in a room full of spiders.

"Wait! What are you doing? Where are you going?" Andie shouted, but Hermes suspected that she knew. Her shouts were reactionary. Henry was going to find his way back up to the fourth floor for the shield, to beat Achilles to it and claim it for his own. It would be one brief, shining moment of sticking it in Achilles' face.

But that's all it would be. One shield wasn't going to save them.

"How could you do this?" Hermes asked Hephaestus. "We met as friends. We've always met as friends."

"And we are. But none of that matters in the face of the Moirae." Hephaestus sat motionless in his chair, but as the Moirae drew close to him on their jerking legs, he had to stiffen to keep from recoiling. Atropos reached out and touched his hand. Hermes saw the joints stretch and pop back into place. He saw the wonder in Hephaestus' eyes as he flexed his rejuvenated fist without struggle or pain.

Hermes glared at the Moirae, at Lachesis, and it almost seemed that she looked back. Even as her head lolled on her wrinkled, sunken neck, it almost seemed that she winked.

Above them, Achilles still fought the wall, trying in vain to climb it or tear it down. His impotent rage drowned out almost everything else.

(ON YOUR KNEES, MESSENGER.)

Atropos thundered between his ears, and Hermes' knees hit the marble with a sharp crack. He hadn't even felt his muscles give way.

"Get out of my head," he whispered, and heard Andie's footsteps as she ran to his side.

"Leave him alone!"

He wanted to drag her down, clamp his hand over her mouth, and provide what cover he could. He waited with held breath for her to hit the ground, too, or worse, to explode in a mist of pink. Instead, she smarted off, as insubordinate as ever.

"Can't get into my head, can you!" she taunted. "And with your guardian hanging orangutan-style from the walls, maybe I'll just shove a spear through your faces." She ran to one of the standing lamps and yanked it from its socket. If any one of the Moirae got a hit in, even one who wasn't much more than an emptying bag, they would take her head clean from her shoulders. Hermes couldn't keep his eyes off her.

Under pressure, these mortals rose up. They became something more.

Henry ran through the house as fast as he could, back to the foyer where they'd started. He had to start at the beginning, or he'd lose his way. But he had to go fast, or he'd never beat Achilles to the fourth level. And if they both started climbing girders at the same time, he knew which way it would go.

He retraced their steps through two rooms and hallways, turning right at a vase painted with Chinese shar-peis, bred to be protectors of the Chinese royal family, Hephaestus said. He ran fast through a study with a bust of Homer, and took one quick left and another right down the hall. Sweat stood out on his forehead, but his legs felt fresh, springy and steady as a rubber tire. Remembering the way was easier than he'd thought. He'd paid attention to Hephaestus during the tour. In each room, he'd singled out a piece of art or furniture. The stories played out in Henry's head as he went, laying an invisible thread through the house.

"Faster," he said, and willed his legs to run.

Henry burst through the fourth-floor door before Andie had a chance to try out her lamp-spear on the Moirae. Hermes watched him start to climb, and almost whooped, but the weight of Atropos' will sat on his shoulders like a stone, pressing him to his knees. Her words in his mind were law.

Andie shouted to Henry and switched her target. She launched the lamp at Achilles' back and struck a clean blow, knocking him off the railing to land face down on the third-floor carpet.

"Hermes, get up!"

Andie grabbed books off the shelves and began to lob them at Achilles as hard as she could. He batted them away and screamed in fury as he watched Henry climb closer and closer to the shield.

"I can't," Hermes whispered. Was she mad? It was the Moirae that held him. His own gods who held him down.

"Yes you can! They're dying. They're nothing. Now get up and help me!"

Hermes shook his head. He didn't know what was greater, the fear of them or the weight, but he couldn't move. The thought of their eyes on him made him want to weep. Andie was wrong. In the face of the Moirae, all any god could do was obey.

Hephaestus knew it. He knew it, and I can't blame him for that.

Something flew past Hermes' ear. A book. Flung end over end like the blade of a hatchet. It struck the Moirae with a heavy thud and a flutter of paper.

"Look at that!" Andie hissed. "Look at them! They're nothing now, Hermes! They're monsters." Her voice went low, menacing, and full of hate. "And they're afraid. They're more fucking afraid than all of us put together."

He listened to her voice. Saw another book fly and heard it hit. Andie. Andromache. Her name meant "man of war," and she earned every letter.

She fights my gods for me.

"They can't hold you down anymore, Hermes," she said. "They're nothing."

Hermes swallowed hard. Sweat ran down his nose and he hadn't even started trying to rise yet. He breathed deep, and felt Andie's strength in his own guts. He raised his head and looked into Atropos' eyes. He saw the way they blazed at Andie's words.

It's true. They're less. They're not our gods anymore.

He clenched his teeth and pushed hard against the weight on his shoulders.

(STAY DOWN.)

"No." It might have been easier if he still had muscle in his legs, but cartilage and bone would have to do. He pushed and kept pushing, and the longer he did, the lighter he felt. He rose, hunched over, and inched his feet forward.

"Go, Henry!" he shouted. "Climb!" The elation at getting his feet under him was so great that he laughed, even though just inching forward felt like walking on Jupiter. The Moirae were less, but they were still the Moirae. Atropos still held him down.

But not on his knees.

"Not like that, Achilles!" Hephaestus called up toward the third level. "You'll never get to it that way. You have to go through the house!"

Hermes looked up and saw Achilles dart through the doors on the third floor.

"Hephaestus, you shit!" he shouted, and glared at his friend. Hephaestus said nothing, but winked slowly with his right eye. A real wink. Impossible to miss.

Henry didn't look down. Even when he heard Achilles slamming his way through the opposite side of the house. Any minute he'd burst through the door on the fourth floor and start climbing for the shield. Henry needed to have it in his hands by then.

Climbing the girders wasn't that difficult. His balance was good, and better on adrenaline. But it wasn't fast. The shield was still twenty feet and nine girders away. He braced in the center of a steel X and jumped across to an inverted T. His arms wrapped around the base. Just once, he allowed himself a glance to the ground and was rewarded by seeing it spin. Andie was in his ear, shouting encouragement. Hermes, too. They were still alive. He still had time.

Across the house, Achilles bellowed. Something shattered that sounded like pottery, or plates. He was lost. His footsteps sounded across the third floor, back and forth and back again.

Guess he didn't pay attention on the tour. Or maybe he didn't get one.

Maybe Hephaestus hadn't betrayed them after all. Henry crawled and climbed across three more girders. Then another. One foot, and one grip at a time. Until his hand closed on the edge of the shield.

The Moirae advanced, ready to put Hermes on his knees for good. He edged his feet out to a wider stance.

Fine. Let them come. Give Andie and Henry a chance to get out with the shield.

Up close, they were massive. A mountain blotting out the sun. Especially since he still stood hunched. Hermes made himself study every inch. They would know he wasn't afraid. Beneath Clotho's dangling arm, and between waves of wild red hair, he could see Hephaestus, and smiled.

Hephaestus smiled back. He threw off his blanket and rose from his chair. The braces on his legs were smaller than the ones he had worn during Hermes' first visit, and better balanced. He could walk without arm supports. He could run, and leap, straight onto the backs of the Moirae.

"Hephaestus!"

"I'll hold them as long as I can! Get them out! Go where they won't follow!" He gripped Atropos' black hair with his freshly repaired hand. How kind of her to fix it for him.

"Hermes!" He looked up and saw Henry waving the shield. "Catch!"

The shield fell, a heavy, shining circle, and Hermes caught it and swept it up to his chest. With it before him, the influence of the Moirae was weaker. He could stand straight and even advance. He could bash Atropos in the face.

The Moirae stumbled back, facing an onslaught from Hephaestus behind and an armed Hermes in the front.

"It's a great shield, friend," Hermes said, and bashed her again.

"Of course it is." Hephaestus used his good hand to punch Clotho in the temple. He shouldn't have let go of Atropos. She reached back and dragged his legs over her shoulder. The sound of his joints stretching and popping was almost as terrible as his scream.

"Hephaestus!"

"Henry!" Andie shouted. "Over the rail! Dangle and drop! I'll get the ladder to you!"

Henry had climbed down from the girders. He threw his legs over the fourth-floor railing and dropped down to hang before letting go and sliding across the smooth wall to the third floor. It was a long drop; he shouted when he hit. But when Andie rolled the ladder to him he was on it, climbing and sliding the rest of the way down.

"Hermes, come on!" They ran toward the way they'd come in.

"No! Not to the car!" Not to Kincade, where they were still defenseless. He looked at the dark rectangle of stairs, cut into the marble floor. "There! Go!"

They changed direction and made for the staircase.

"Hermes!" Andie waved for him to follow.

"I can't leave Hephaestus!"

"Go, friend," Hephaestus said. He struggled with Atropos, but the fight was lost. In the scant seconds it took for Henry to reach the ground level, she had already turned one of his elbows around the wrong way, and stripped him of one of his leg braces. He looked at Hermes sadly, and smiled. "Come back for me, if you find her."

"I will," he replied. *I will.*

"Move, move!" he shouted to Andie, and she and Henry fled down the stairs. Down, and down, and down into the dark. The house had not near so many floors above as it had below, Hephaestus said. Hephaestus had no shortage of escape routes, and the stairs would take them far away from the grip of the Moirae. They would take them all the way to the underworld.

15

HADES

"It's like being inside a snow globe."

"What is?" Athena asked.

"This place." Odysseus gestured around, careful to keep his eyes from lingering too long on the black forever above their heads. "It feels contained. I can't stop thinking about up there. Or out there. The real world. I've never wanted to smash through something so much as I do these walls."

Athena studied the underworld, tall rock in uneven colors of red and orange, gray and rotten purple. Blue and black in the shadows. The creeping, silent river that ran to nowhere in both directions. The dying gods who sat nearby, one of whom looked like a pet corpse they'd been dragging around for a month in warm weather.

"It's only an illusion," she said. "The world still exists outside. It still breathes. It's still green. The edges do touch, in places."

"That's what makes it so maddening, I guess. The memory of it. Knowing that it's there. Death would be kinder if we forgot."

Across the river, a few shades lingered, hopeful of another taste of blood. Just one more drop, to quicken them and give them will. They circled and sniffed like dogs beneath an empty table.

Death would be kinder if they forgot. But death was rarely kind.

"The edges still touch," Athena said once more, to make herself believe it. She should've said that they weren't dead. Being there so long, even she had begun to despair of ever getting loose. She couldn't imagine what it was like for Odysseus, a living mortal, to sit there stuck. He'd only been conscious for a little while, and already seemed halfway to tearing free of his own skin, just to be free of something.

"Tell me we'll get out," he said.

"We'll get out."

He smiled. "I almost believe you."

"Believe me. You've been here before. You know there are ways."

"This time feels different." He scratched at his wrist. "This feels . . . like it won't end."

This time was different. This time the way was shut. Wherever Uncle Hades was, he knew they'd toyed with his boundaries. They'd taken back Odysseus without permission. So now they had to sit until they paid for their transgression. Or until they struck a decent bargain.

Athena felt Persephone's dead eyes on them, dead eyes made eerier by the fact that Persephone was, in fact, alive.

"God," Odysseus whispered, barely moving his lips. "I wish she would blink."

Athena snorted. "I'm just glad she's tied up." Persephone sat silent, a good little bargaining chip, all bones in a black, rotten shroud, wrists bound loosely with strips torn from Aphrodite's dress. At first it had seemed like a waste of time. But Persephone's stillness wasn't a beaten stillness. She'd move quick enough if they weren't looking. A dead-eyed doll sneaking up behind the rocks.

Hades would come for Persephone soon. Athena wondered how he would be when he got there. Would he arrive in a cloud of rage and disease, bleeding filth?

This is his place. He can come however he likes.

"Hey," Odysseus said, and pushed Athena's hair back over her shoulder. She'd seen him do the same to Cassandra, and to Calypso. It shouldn't bother her that he did the same thing to her. It shouldn't make her feel so strangely jealous.

"I need to walk." She stood.

"I'll keep an eye on the undead princess." Odysseus made a face. "Don't be gone long."

She nodded and went, not sure where or how far she intended to go. But walking didn't feel as good as she'd hoped. Passing by the strangely shadowed walls and listening to the hateful whisper of the Styx should have felt better. Even the complete lack of wind across her face and arms should've felt amazing, because Odysseus was alive.

Alive for the time being. And not of her doing, but Ares'. Ares, and Aphrodite, and she'd probably been a fool to accept their help.

Except for maybe the first time in his life, Ares had been

a gift, and you didn't look a gift god in the mouth even if he was a treacherous, violent, hateful ass. No matter how many problems it was going to cause with Cassandra. No matter how little Athena actually trusted them. Even the traitorous feeling she got every second she allowed Aphrodite to live was worth it for Odysseus.

"You shouldn't wander so far. Not with Hades on his way."

Athena turned. Aphrodite stood a few steps behind. She'd always been light and quiet on her feet.

"I didn't wander far," Athena said, but in truth she had no idea. Distance played tricks in the underworld, just like time did. She shouldn't have gone off by herself at all.

Aphrodite stared into her face, big blue eyes steady and somehow just as disturbing to Athena as if they'd been rolling and mad.

"What?" Athena asked.

"There are too many emotions running through you. Set some down."

"Just because you got a few of your marbles back doesn't mean you can psych me," Athena said. "Be careful what you say now."

"I'm only trying to help," Aphrodite said, and frowned. "You need to talk."

"Not to you."

"To who then? Dear as he is, Ares doesn't solve problems with words. And Odysseus you would never show your belly to. I know you, Athena, as sure as I've always disliked you. I just never understood you until now."

Athena narrowed her eyes.

"I fall in love and suddenly I'm relatable."

"Yes," Aphrodite said. "Part of you is mine now, and that bothers you more than anything. You're not above me. Not better than me." A little heat snuck into her voice. A trace of bitterness. "Part of you wants to turn him away just to prove me wrong. But don't. I've always known about your envy. The same way you always knew about mine."

"I never envied you," Athena said. "And you have a one-track mind, as usual."

"I know that's not the only thing." Aphrodite shrugged. "There's fear, too. And guilt."

"Fear?" Athena asked skeptically.

"Yes. So many new things for you," Aphrodite said. "You're guilty because you dove off of Olympus and left them alone to fight. And you're afraid because even if you hadn't, they would have lost anyway. Goddess of battle. You're not what you once were. None of us are what we once were."

The words stung. Athena still had so much pride. Even though she knew that it was her pride that had almost cost them everything.

"Those moments outside Olympus," Athena said. "I replay them over and over. I try to stop myself from running in. Try to make myself listen."

Aphrodite inclined her head sympathetically.

"I used them like soldiers," Athena said, "when I had no right to. I still thought of myself as their god. But their fates aren't mine. I'm not worthy of them anymore, if I ever was."

"Now we make mortal mistakes," Aphrodite said, nodding. "Now we have consequences." She twisted the filthy fabric of her skirt between her hands. "It's . . . unpleasant. I don't enjoy it."

Athena laughed, and Aphrodite looked up in surprise.

"I'm not laughing *at* you," Athena said, and they paused. It was as close as they'd ever come to a warm moment. But it didn't last. Aphrodite was saner in the underworld, but still not sane, and Athena's laughter put her on edge. Her blue eyes wobbled.

"I'm sorry," Aphrodite said. "I didn't know what I was doing, when I killed him."

"You mean when you killed my brother. Aidan."

"My brother," Aphrodite moaned. "Our brother." She clutched the sides of her head. "It went right through him. But I didn't know. Forgive me."

"Forgiveness for that isn't something you ask for," Athena muttered. "You either get it or you don't. And it isn't up to me. It's up to the girl you stole him from."

"I didn't know," Aphrodite said again.

"Explain it to Cassandra."

Athena brushed past Aphrodite to return to the river-bank. Aphrodite seemed about ready to weep, and Athena had no wish to be moved to sympathy. Not about that. Not yet.

But before she could go, Aphrodite grasped her arm.

"You have to protect him," Aphrodite cried.

"Who?"

"Ares. You promised."

Athena scoffed.

"He didn't have to come here," Aphrodite said. "And he doesn't have to stay. He can leave whenever he likes and let you deal with Hades. Leave you alone to bargain for Odysseus."

"Except he won't," Athena said, tugging free. "Because he needs me to stand between you and Cassandra." She paused. "You keep saying 'him.' 'Him' and not 'us.' Not 'we.'" She looked at Aphrodite, and Aphrodite looked back, imploring her to figure it out so she wouldn't have to confess. But reading emotion wasn't a skill Athena had much practice in.

"I'm not going back with you," Aphrodite whispered. "I'm staying here. Where I'm sane. I want to be sane, for as long as I can be."

"Down here? With Persephone? Just the two of you, doing what? Playing bridge?" The words didn't have the heat Athena had intended. They came out gentle and filled with more wonder than malice. To stay in the underworld— to be functionally dead—seemed like torture.

"Up there you can't trust me. Up there I'm useless," Aphrodite said. "Up there I'm *mad*."

"You don't think we stand a chance. Against the Moirae."

Aphrodite's eyes drifted toward Ares.

"I think some of us need to fight to the end," she said. "And some of us don't."

"Does he know?" Athena asked, and Aphrodite shook her head. Ares wouldn't be happy when he found out. But Aphrodite was right. Without the borders of the underworld to keep her death in check, she was a wild dog.

"You probably think I'm a coward now," Aphrodite said. "Not that you ever thought I was anything else."

Athena looked at Aphrodite's torn dress and the bruises that spotted her skin from ankle to cheek.

"I think you're conniving," she said. "And silly. And a

bitch." She watched Aphrodite bite her tongue on every retort. That Athena was cold. Self-righteous. Also a bitch. "But never a coward."

Persephone gave away Hades' arrival. Not even her deadest eye could hide its brightness, its happiness at his homecoming. Athena, too, felt something dense and heavy the moment he crossed over, a black hole opening up in the back of her head. Ares leapt quickly to Persephone and dragged her to her feet. His wolves circled around them both.

"It feels different now," Odysseus said. "Not so empty."

"It isn't empty anymore," Athena said. "He's home."

A shadow flashed in her mind: Hades, black as a bat's wing, titanic as his sister Demeter stretched across miles of desert. In her mind he wrapped them in cold, and spit them out as bones.

"He'll let us go, right? We're fighting for his side." Odysseus drew his sword, for all the good it would do. It didn't matter that they fought for the side of the gods. It didn't matter that Athena had been a good niece up till then, and had gone out of her way to keep from pissing him off. She'd stolen one of the dead, and the dead were his. It was his only rule.

When Hades came into view, he looked as young and handsome as Ares or Aidan. Not a walking embodiment of death or disease. It hadn't taken him over like it had his brother Poseidon. But Athena knew that what she'd seen in the back of her mind was the true Hades: a great, black shadow contained in skin and an expensive shirt. Just the sight of him made her mouth go dry. His voice made her shudder, even though he didn't address them.

"Persephone. Are you all right?"

Odd thing to ask when she looks six months into her coffin.

"As well as one can be, when one is held prisoner in one's own home," Persephone replied.

Hades looked over every inch of his bride with affection in his eyes. He didn't flinch from a single, terrible bit, not the purplish wrinkles in her skin or the bare red spots in her scalp. His gaze lingered on her face and, finally, on her bound wrists.

We should untie her. We shouldn't have tied her.

Ares apparently thought the same thing; his hand twitched over the knots where he held her fast to him, like a human shield. Aphrodite went to his side and put a hand on Persephone's shoulder.

"We haven't harmed her," she said sweetly.

"That's the only reason you're still wearing your skin," said Hades.

Athena and Ares exchanged a glance. *Tread carefully. He could burst out from under that boy-shaped mask anytime he wants. And that's all it is. All it ever was. But what's underneath it now is far worse than what used to be.*

"My dog lies shivering at my palace steps and my wife stands a hostage. And *that* is my dead boy."

"I was never dead," Odysseus said quietly.

"You're still dead. The breath in you is stolen. And dead boys don't speak to me." Hades turned toward him, and blood poured from Odysseus' mouth. He fell before Athena could catch him, and his sword clattered to the rocks.

"Stop it!" She went to her knees. Odysseus' hands pressed to his eyes and red leaked through his fingers. He bled from his nose and his ears, sprayed blood from his mouth like water from a blowhole. Virus blackened his skin and ate it away as she watched.

Athena grabbed the sword and leapt for Persephone. It was skewered through her side before anyone had time to block Athena's way. Persephone didn't cry out. Stabbing her was like running a blade through a loaf of dry bread. But Hades paid attention, and Odysseus stopped bleeding.

"Don't do that again," Hades warned.

"Don't make me."

"We just want to walk out of here, with Odysseus." Ares spoke boldly, but his eyes were ringed with white. Seeing a sword shoved through their cousin had rattled him, but what did he think a hostage was for?

"You shouldn't have taken her," said Hades.

"It was the only way to get you to bargain," Athena said.

Odysseus had regained his feet. He spat blood onto the rocks. It still dripped from one ear and blinked from his eyes like tears, but that was just leftovers. Ares' wolves fussed around him in a circle and stole licks from his clothes and fingers.

"So let's bargain." Hades motioned for them to cross the river.

"Not so fast," said Ares. "Not until a deal's in place. We walk out of here, and cut her loose at the threshold."

Hades shook his head. "You can't trade him for her. She is already mine. He is already mine. Mine for mine. It doesn't play."

"We don't have anything else." Athena thought of Aphrodite but dismissed the idea quickly. It was going to be hard enough for Ares to leave Aphrodite behind as a voluntary guest, let alone as traded chattel, and Athena didn't fancy having a brother-sister spat about it in front of their uncle.

"Not a trade at all, then." Odysseus stepped forward and wiped blood from his nose onto the back of his arm. Athena half wanted to throttle him for opening his mouth, to ask him if he enjoyed hemorrhaging from all the holes in his face. But her other half was proud. Her Odysseus. Bold and two steps ahead of himself, as usual.

"Not a trade," Athena agreed. "But a task. You've been known to lay tasks before, Uncle. They say you did it for Heracles lots of times, and he was only your half-nephew."

"A task." Hades smiled. Just enough time passed as he thought about it for Athena to dread putting it into his head. "A task it is. So here are the terms. The way up is through my palace. It is the only way up that will be allowed to you. And Persephone is released to me on the steps."

"That's it?"

"That's it. After that, you'll be free to leave. If you can fight your way out."

Athena pulled the sword out of Persephone's side and threw it to Odysseus, trying to ignore the dry bits of flesh that stuck to the blade.

"Nothing starts until we reach the palace," Athena said, and nudged Persephone forward to cross the Styx again. Hades showed his palms and agreed, backing away from the shore to let them come. Athena looked past Persephone at

Ares, and back at Odysseus. She'd fought everything the underworld had thrown at her in the dark and she'd done it bare-fisted and mostly blind. Now she had another god of war, and a hero with nine lives. It could work. They could make it.

Or they could wind up in pieces with Odysseus' ghost sucking blood off their severed stumps.

They left the river, soaked through with hate for what felt like the hundredth time, and followed Hades through tunnels and past fields of asphodel. It wasn't long until they'd left the tunnels completely, headed toward the massive marble columns of Hades' palace. Like everything else in the underworld, the palace was half-illusion. It appeared as a great rectangle. But the closer they walked, the larger it became. Columns stretched up farther and the shadows between grew darker. It was easier to look at than the walls of the tunnels, at least, constructed of plain white marble rather than shifting, iridescent stones, but at its steps it blotted out everything else. Athena wouldn't have been able to see the top had she craned her head all the way back.

This place sucks. I've never liked it. Never. Not even as a guest.

She looked back at Aphrodite, who stood at Persephone's shoulder, absently stroking the half-dead goddess' strawlike hair.

How could you ever think I would call you a coward for choosing to stay here?

A dog barked, and barked a second time. Cerberus emerged from behind a column and wagged his tail, then bared both sets of teeth when he saw Ares' wolves. Oblivion and Panic flashed fangs of their own, but neither they nor Cerberus attacked.

Hades placed his foot on the first step and turned. Aphrodite gently untied the knots of Persephone's bonds and let them flutter to the floor. Persephone rubbed her wrists, out of habit more than any real discomfort, Athena thought. In such an advanced state of decay, she doubted if Persephone felt much of anything anymore.

"There," Ares said. "She's free. And now you'll let us pass."

"If you can." Hades nodded. Ares looked at Athena and placed a cautious foot on the steps. Hades did nothing. His word was solid. He still believed in the scales tipping even.

"Come on." Ares beckoned Aphrodite as he backed up the steps. "It's all right."

Athena walked up the steps beside Odysseus and didn't look back. She didn't want to see anything that passed between Ares and Aphrodite. She didn't want to be softened. But she couldn't keep from hearing.

"I'm staying," Aphrodite said gently. "With Persephone. I'm not going up to fight with you. I'm no use."

Ares kept his voice hushed and his words ran together. For a moment Athena thought he'd take her anyway, that he'd abduct her from the underworld like Hades had abducted Persephone from above. But he didn't, and Aphrodite wouldn't change her mind.

"I never get to keep you very long," Ares said softly.

"So it seems. You'll come back for me, if you can."

"Don't I always?"

Athena tried not to listen as they embraced, and tried not to hear the emotion in Aphrodite's voice when she said, "Go with her now. Bitch that she is, she's your best chance."

"And you, Hades," Athena said over her shoulder. "You won't harm her?"

"If Aphrodite wishes to stay as my guest, then she will be treated as one."

Athena nodded as Ares brushed past. She and Odysseus followed behind, watching the wolves press their muzzles into his hands. None of them looked back. Enemy or true love, none could bear the sight of Aphrodite left behind in that dead place.

"Hades got the raw deal," Odysseus commented as they walked through the bleak, empty halls.

Athena had always been inclined to agree. When the world was divided, Zeus took the heavens for himself and Poseidon the seas. The underworld and the dead they gave to Hades.

"It suits him." Ares shrugged.

But had it always? Maybe in the beginning, Hades had been as bright and as full of laughter as his brothers. Maybe he'd been turned to morbidity slowly, from days and nights and centuries of the same gray nothing inside his palace. The same shifting red-orange light and the mourning dead crowded into his walls.

Or maybe he'd always loved the decadence of decay. The aggression of disease. The despair of no time passing. In any case, he loved them plenty now.

"Why doesn't he put things here?" Odysseus asked. "Furniture. Art. Candles." The light inside the palace was dull and washed the color out of their skin. They might have been a rerun of a '50s TV show. Perhaps the one where the fat guy was constantly threatening to slug his wife. *To the moon, Alice. To the moon.* Athena took a deep breath. The moon would've been a welcome trip.

"He has homes topside for that," Ares replied. "This place he wants pure. Desolate. So if you kill yourself to get here you'll wish you could kill yourself again."

"Poor Persephone." Odysseus cleared his throat. Poor Persephone. And now poor Aphrodite. Athena still wasn't sure if Aphrodite had made the right choice. The underworld was just as likely to drive her mad as her sickness. And it would be a crueler mad. Rats in an endless maze mad. Picking your brain out through your ear mad.

"I'm sure she'll be all right," Odysseus said. "There are two of them now, to keep company. They can play Pickle in the Middle with the two-headed dog." He stopped. They'd come to a long set of wall-to-wall stairs. "Do you think that's it?"

"I doubt it," Athena muttered. All the way through the hall she'd been waiting for something to come at them. A horde of shades maybe, freshly amped up on Hades' blood. That would've been fitting, a fine case of turnabout. But nothing came. Oblivion swept his nose back and forth along the ground. Panic's ears flicked in all directions. The wolves didn't sense anything, either.

Up was the only way to go, so they took the stairs, Odysseus by two and then three when Ares and Panic began to compete. Athena followed them up slowly with Oblivion. At the top of the stairs was a door.

And behind that door is a monster. Or an axe rigged up at head level. Or another door.

"Don't just run in," she said when they both looked about to. They gave her their best patronizing faces, but waited and moved, each to one side, while she checked it over. No trip wires or visible triggers. She chewed her lip. Open it low and slow, or kick it in and dodge? She felt Ares' smug eyes on her, and kicked hard.

Nothing but yellow light spilled out onto their faces.

"This is all getting pretty anticlimactic," Odysseus said as he walked into the new room, and promptly stopped talking. He also stopped dead in his tracks, causing Athena and Ares to run up against his back, but no one complained. The wolves whined. Athena's eyes widened.

The room they'd walked into was an arena, and in the arena stood three behemoths.

"The Judges." She clenched her teeth. *Son of a bitch.*

The three judges of the underworld, Hades' generals, who decided the fates of the dead and guarded the borders within. She hadn't thought he'd pull them from their posts, but there they stood. Rhadamanthys, Aeacus, and Minos.

"They're bigger than I remember," Ares said quietly. They were bigger than Athena remembered, too. Aeacus and Rhadamanthys seemed as large as trees and Minos, though smaller, looked more bull than man, from his cloven feet to his beautiful set of curving black goring horns. He even smelled like an animal: coarse, musky, and salty.

Along the walls of the room a few sad spears and shields lay littered in the corners. Provided for their benefit? Or leftover from the last heroes the Judges squished between their meaty hands? It didn't seem that the weapons could be of much use, anyway. Aeacus' and Rhadamanthys' skin was a dense-looking ivory-gray, and looked hard enough to shatter a spear like glass.

"There's one for each of us," Odysseus said. "I'll take a big one. Big and dumb is sort of my specialty."

"They're big, but they're not dumb," Athena said.

Hades had tasked the Judges with determining their worthiness, and that was exactly what they would do. Athena's palms began to sweat. No single one seemed a more appealing prospect than the others, and staring them down would be no more effective than staring down a mountain you had to climb.

"This is going to hurt," she said. "A lot."

"I'll lend you a wolf," Ares said to Odysseus. "Pick one."

"I should be able to pick both. You're a god. I'm a legally dead mortal. Panic, Oblivion." He motioned with his head for them to come, and they went to his side. "But you're thinking about this wrong. We don't need to beat them. We need to fight our way out. Our way through. To that tiny door, up those stairs."

Athena followed the tip of his sword to a stairway in the far right of the arena. It led to a door, the only other door in the room. From that distance, it looked about the size of the door Alice had to wedge herself through in Wonderland. But that was just a trick of the eye.

Odysseus made to move and she heard his name squeak out of her in a tone she hadn't known she could make. Aphrodite was right. Fear was getting the better of her. She cleared her throat.

"I didn't fight river monsters all this time only to have you torn apart now," she said.

Odysseus smiled his crooked smile.

"If you could see your face," he said. "So tender. So worried. You'd hate it." He reached out and touched her chin. "But I love it."

Ares chuckled, and Athena slipped away from Odysseus and steeled her spine.

In the center of the arena, Rhadamanthys squared up. The Judges wouldn't wait much longer. Athena exhaled. Rhadamanthys was the only judge without a weapon. Aeacus carried some kind of silver scepter with beautifully honed and twisted edges, finely wrought lines of razor that would slice flesh like corned beef at the lightest touch. Minos had weapons built in: his sharpened horns had a good ten-foot reach.

Athena, Odysseus, Ares, and the wolves leapt up and out in different directions, scattering before the Judges with no plan and no steadying "on three" count. Both Athena and Odysseus went for Minos. She grabbed hold of one of his horns and wrenched it upward; Odysseus slid through the gap between his feet and trailed his sword. One judge on one knee. A solid job of hamstringing.

Something in Athena's gut told her to duck, and she hit the floor just in time to feel Rhadamanthys' massive arm pass over her head. A wolf yipped and Panic went sailing through the air. She glanced back: Oblivion was still on its paws, feinting and charging Minos where he knelt, bleeding.

"Up, wolf!" Odysseus scooped up Panic and made for the stairs but Rhadamanthys was there first, his leg stomping down like a tree trunk in their path. Athena didn't think, she just leapt as the judge aimed a blow at Odysseus and the wolf. She caught his wrist in her stomach and doubled over his arm as it swung, watching the floor and walls fly by until she struck one and all the wind left her body. She slid straight down and landed on buckled legs and her ass, sucking as much air into her deflated lungs as she could. Ares bellowed to her left, engaged with Aeacus and his razor scepter. Every inch of Ares' exposed skin was painted red. He didn't know how to dodge. Aeacus swung and Ares took it, a blunt instrument, digging in and pushing back and losing pints. He'd never shake loose enough to get to the door.

And maybe he doesn't want to. Maybe he wants to stay until the Judges lie still on the floor.

Idiot. Pick up a spear at least, you dope.

Athena rolled right in time to avoid Rhadamanthys' elephantine stomp and leapt back toward the center of the arena. She ducked another of his grabs. The bastard was fast, despite his size.

"Oblivion! Panic! Hands!" she shouted to the wolves and they jumped to it, each sinking teeth into one of the giant's hands and clinging there. They wouldn't be able to hold long, but at least the walls were far enough away that he couldn't crush them against the marble. Athena ran to the stairs and used them to kick off, launching onto the judge's back and scrambling for his neck. It would take one whole arm to choke him out and maybe part of the other.

If Heracles could manage with the three heads of Cerberus, I can manage just this one.

Her arms wrapped around Rhadamanthys' massive neck and squeezed.

The judge could hold his breath, she'd give him that. Whether it would be his throat that gave or her arms came down to the wire, but just when her muscles began to shake, he dropped to his knees and then onto his face.

"Nice," Odysseus shouted as the wolves let go. He jogged to her from a prone Minos. While she'd been choking Rhadamanthys, Odysseus had apparently hamstringed Minos' other leg for good measure.

On the other side of the room, Ares stood over Aeacus, bludgeoning him with his own scepter. Odysseus winced when the scepter made contact with the judge's skull. They'd had to take them all down after all.

"Come on," Athena called to Ares from the base of the stairs. "Before they pop back up like jack-in-the-boxes."

Ares smiled, covered in cuts, and brandished the stolen scepter. She had to give him credit. She'd thought she was going to have to run to his rescue.

Odysseus slipped his hand onto the small of her back as they headed up the stairs. How he loved trouble. He'd never want a quiet life, or a safe one. Looking into his exhilarated face, Athena could almost believe that they suited each other, and that it would last forever.

She paused at the door. It was the end. Behind it was the way out. She jerked it open and looked out at the damp rocks and dirt of the tunnel leading up. Wind hit her cheeks. Real wind.

"Amazing." Odysseus grinned and stared into the flame of a torch. "Light. And the smell of regular water. It's been so long."

Athena smiled. She looked at the scepter in Ares' hand. "Minos' scepter. You should toss it back inside."

"But I like it," Ares said, and held it up to the torchlight. With a closer look, Athena saw that the lines of razor didn't stop at the handle. They twisted and worked all the way down the grip. To wield the scepter turned the fighter's hand into hamburger.

"You would like it. It's monstrous. But it isn't yours."

Ares squeezed the handle one last time, and blood ran down his wrist. Then he tossed it back into the arena before pulling the door shut behind them. One glance at his hand turned Athena's stomach; it didn't resemble fingers and palm so much as a pile of julienned tomatoes. They'd have to wrap it. She reached for Odysseus' sword and cut a strip off the back of his shirt.

"Hey, my shirt," Odysseus protested, but he looked as green as she did, watching Ares tie the bandage.

Athena took a breath. All that stood between them and the living world now was a leisurely walk up smooth stone steps. She started up, and stopped. A familiar sound was coming from somewhere farther up.

"Do you hear that?" she asked.

"Hear what?" Ares asked. But it wasn't her imagination. The wolves stood at attention, ears pricked forward. They heard it, too. "Hear what?" Ares asked again.

Athena leapt forward with a shout.

"Hermes!"

16

THE MOTHER COUNTRY

Despite the fact that Thanatos had sprung for a suite, the room felt cramped. Cassandra had been on the road for too long, on the run for too long, on the hunt for so long that she couldn't remember sometimes what was more important, the hunting or the running. She was tired of crappy water pressure and shampoo that never lathered enough. She was tired of the way Calypso hummed through every task she performed. And she was tired of Thanatos. Of the way he looked at her sometimes. Like he could see through her skin, all the way down.

He probably can. He's the god of death, for Pete's sake.

Cassandra looked out the window. They'd been in Athens for two days. Down on the streets, mopeds slipped easily through late-afternoon traffic. Up on the hill, the lights surrounding the Acropolis were on, and the ruin glowed. Athens was beautiful like she'd always thought it would be, back when she daydreamed about going someday with Aidan, when she thought it was just an ancient city. Before she knew the bitch it was named after.

Thanatos called it "the Mother Country." It wasn't. Not really. But it was all they had left. The last trappings of lost glory, a handful of crumbling buildings mostly poached of marble. And somewhere in the midst of it, the god of the dead lived out his final days.

There hadn't been a plague. No rash of illnesses or packed hospitals. No hastily dug graves or backed-up crematoriums. No deaths that could be called out of the ordinary for a city of Athens' size. They'd checked when they arrived, and found not so much as a fish kill. Cassandra should have been relieved. But she'd been so sure there would be traces of Hades and his illness that the lack made her pause. In her mind, he'd been a moldy black spot on the map.

Thanatos was out there now, scouting, determining where Hades was and what paths they should take. Looking down at the crowds of pedestrians, she thought she might catch a glimpse of him maneuvering through the shadows, but there was no sign, not of him nor of Calypso, either. Cassandra was alone, a princess in an ivory tower, waiting patiently to slay her dragon.

The door to the suite opened and Calypso entered, carrying a large plastic bag of food with her good arm. Souvlaki stuffed with French fries. It smelled good, but it looked as though she'd bought enough to feed Hermes.

"Is he back yet?" Calypso asked.

"No."

Calypso set the bag down on the table and Cassandra rifled through it.

"Lamb and chicken both," Calypso said. "But no way to tell which is which without unwrapping." She flicked a lock of Cassandra's hair over her shoulder. It was a familiar, affectionate touch—Odysseus used to do it, and suddenly the weight of his absence hit Cassandra square in the chest. It must have hit Calypso, too, because her fingers lingered on Cassandra's shirt. Cassandra grasped them, to squeeze and comfort, but what she felt made her jerk away. Calypso's fingers were half-rotten bone, and left wet streaks on her skin.

That's just my imagination.

Imagination and not imagination. Since the vision after the Fury attack, a shadow stretched across Calypso's face like a caul. Sometimes her hair fell out. Sometimes her teeth. What was seen couldn't be unseen. Cassandra's eyes re-created it from all angles, and when she slept her brain re-created it, too, turning it over in dreams a hundred times worse. They enhanced it with smell, and sound, and left her woozy and uneasy after waking.

Since they'd been in Athens, Calypso seemed happier. She laughed more, and left the hotel for hours at a time to wander. She came back smelling of stray dogs she'd found and fed. And when they crossed over the sea, she'd stared at the stunning blue so intensely that Cassandra knew she was remembering a time from before, when she'd used to swim in it.

It was one last turn on the carousel. The last act in Calypso's long goodbye.

Or so she thinks.

After the gods were dead, Calypso wouldn't want to join them. Enough time would pass for her to see she had things to stay for. Friends who cared. Cassandra's brain laid these ropes of reason around her vision of Calypso's death, around and around in a slow, quiet noose. And always the vision lashed back. You can't change fate.

But I can. I'll learn.

"We're not really so far from Ithaca," Calypso said. She sat near the window picking fries out of her pita and dipping them in *tzatziki*. Ithaca. Odysseus' island. "I hated that island," she went on, "for taking him away from me. And now I'd give anything to go and find him there."

Cassandra said nothing. Anything she said would come out wrong, or hollow, or just plain stupid. She knew. She'd heard enough from other people after Aidan died.

"If I turn my ear the right way into the wind," Calypso said, "I can almost hear him. A memory on the air. Ithaca must remember him even after all this time. Or at least I'd like to think so." Calypso looked down. "Can you feel Aidan? In this ancient city?"

"I haven't been listening."

Calypso nodded. "Too busy sniffing out Hades."

"Yes. But not only that. The Aidan who would haunt Athens wouldn't be Aidan. He'd be Apollo."

"They're one and the same."

No. They weren't. But Calypso needed to think so. Because she needed to believe that Odysseus was the same boy who had loved her beside the sea.

"Yeah, well," said Cassandra. "I hate him as many days as I love him, anyway. Maybe that's why I don't want to kill myself now that he's gone."

Calypso stopped chewing.

"I didn't mean it to come out that way," Cassandra said. "I get . . . pissed off at the drop of a hat, these days."

"I know. I understand."

"I didn't mean to make you sound—" *What? Pathetic? Go ahead, idiot, stick your foot farther down your throat.*

"It's all right, I said." Calypso pushed a piece of meat into her mouth and went back to looking out the window. Conversation over. They ate the rest of their lunch in silence.

By the time Thanatos returned, Cassandra had fallen asleep on the couch watching a European version of MTV. She woke to the sound of the shower turning off. The rest of the suite was empty. Calypso had taken enough of her crap and fled.

The bathroom door opened. Thanatos poked his head out and peered at her.

"Did you find him?" she asked.

"Where's Calypso?"

"Don't know." Cassandra shrugged. "Did you find him?"

He pulled the towel off his shoulders and ran it through his hair.

"I found his house. Without him in it."

Acid churned in Cassandra's gut and heat flooded her fingertips. They'd come all that way to find an empty house. On another continent. Across an ocean. She was up and pacing before she knew it, back and forth, back and forth.

"So where did he go? Ant-fricking-arctica?"

"He didn't go anywhere, really. He went underground. Off the map underground."

To the underworld. Cassandra narrowed her eyes. Had someone tipped him off? Had he run?

"I know what you're thinking," Thanatos said. "And yes, he probably knows you're coming. But he wouldn't run from you. Hades wouldn't run from anything."

"So he'll be back?"

"He'll be back."

"Good. We'll go to the house, then, and wait. He might not expect that. What? What's that look for?" She narrowed her eyes, and he looked away.

"You don't think I can kill him," she said.

He threw his towel over the back of a chair.

"Can I?" she asked. "Or is he like you? Have you known this was impossible the whole time?"

"He's not like me," Thanatos said. "He's the god of the dead, not death himself. You can kill him. What I'm beginning to wonder is if *he* can kill *you*." He closed the distance between them in a few slow steps. Not sad or worried, but curious.

Don't be stupid. He's a god. And death, besides. It doesn't matter how many times he's kind, or if he's saved my life. Death is what's underneath. He's not wondering if Hades can kill me. He's wondering if he could do it himself.

"Why are you helping me?" she asked. "Why are you here?"

"I'm here because a girl with a broken heart came looking. And I have a soft spot for girls with broken hearts." He reached out to touch her hair. His face was so charming and harmless when he smiled, like a pinup in a girls' magazine. You could take the god of death home to meet your parents, as long as he was smiling when you did it.

"Maybe I looked into your eyes and couldn't say no," he said. She knocked his hand away, and he chuckled. "Maybe I like being with you, moody as you are. Maybe you're the first living girl I've ever met who I'd like to stay living."

"Cut the bullshit."

He smiled again.

"Or maybe I just want to know what you are."

Hades' house looked more like an abandoned building: a great, dirty slab of white, with windows spotted with fly dirt. Half of it had been torn down, or had fallen in. At any rate, the top three floors of the eastern side were missing, the hole covered over with black tarps and drop cloths.

"This is it?" Cassandra asked doubtfully. "I expected columns. Maybe some gold and gilding."

"You'll find that inside. Richness abounds." Thanatos stood beside her, and Calypso behind. They had armed themselves lightly with knives bought in one of the flea markets. The one Calypso carried was purely ornamental, not even sharpened. But if she pushed hard enough, it would do the job.

On the doorstep before them lay three dead rats. The cat that might have eaten them lay dead in a nearby planter box. Except for the flies and squirming maggots under their fur, they looked as though they had fallen asleep, a happy ending to a quaint fairy tale of dancing predators and prey.

"How did you get in before?" Cassandra asked. Thanatos nodded toward the side of the building.

"There's a broken window. It was cracked when I arrived, but I smashed it clean through. You'll be able to climb in."

He led them to it, and they picked their way through the slivers of glass. Thanatos went first, jumping up and through with all the grace and balance Cassandra knew she didn't have. It took her almost two minutes to navigate the window and stay clear of the glass edges.

Once her head was inside the house, it was all shadows and stale air, and she suddenly wanted to ask what had killed the cat and the rats. But then Thanatos held out his hand, and she took it.

When her eyes adjusted to the dimness, they still weren't much use. They'd come into an interior hallway and, except for the white shaft of window light behind them, it was completely black. Nobody home, Thanatos had said. No servants or watchdogs.

No dogs because you wouldn't need them. Who would think to rob the place?

Her foot crunched something as she edged down the hall, and she twisted her toe hard into the floorboards in case it was a cockroach stuck to her shoe.

"You didn't see any squatters here, either?" she asked.

"None," Thanatos replied. "There's a body on the third floor, but it's stuffed."

"Stuffed?"

"Stuffed. You know. Taxidermied."

Cassandra's hand went to her mouth. Almost instantly, her nose invented the smell of that taxidermied corpse, and it didn't matter that she didn't really know what it would smell like. *At least if I throw up here the vomit will be right at home.*

She peered in every door she passed. Each room was filled with enough knickknacks to stock several gift shops. Many of them shone silver and gold in the scant light from the windows. *Expensive knickknacks. Museum-gift-shop quality.*

Silver and gold. Hades loved them well. No wonder so many kings tried to buy their way out of the underworld. She wondered if Hades might try to buy his way clear of her.

He could offer me every jewel in this house. The contents of every bank account. It wouldn't be enough.

Ahead of them, the hallway ended and opened on a large central room, cut through by a winding staircase. Silhouettes of dense oak tables and lamps stood like sentries. It was difficult to reconcile the finery inside with the desolate façade of the building outside. She expected dust and got oiled wood. Expected cobwebs and found polished marble. And there wasn't a single roach or rat to be seen.

But don't forget the stuffed body upstairs.

Cassandra glanced at a gold candelabrum with white candles. If only it would sing, and dance, and talk in a French accent to lighten the mood. Disney enchantments were never around when you needed them.

"There's no one here," she said suddenly, and loudly. "So why are we creeping? Can't we get some light?"

Thanatos and Calypso moved to light candles. They might have tried the light switch. It wouldn't have surprised Cassandra to find the electricity on. But she supposed the candles attracted less attention.

"Where is the best place to wait?" she asked as they walked up the stairs.

"No telling how he'll return. Through which door he'll come," Calypso mused. "Perhaps we should just squat. Make ourselves at home. As long as we avoid the tarp-covered wing, it should be as comfortable as the hotel."

She swept the candles across a dark shadow and Cassandra winced when the light shone on the oily eyes and bared fangs of a stuffed wolverine.

"I don't know what hotel you've been staying in," Thanatos said. He brushed passed them to recheck the hallway, and Cassandra headed for the windows. She craved the light. The natural light of the sun, to remind her that outside still existed.

It's only a building.

But that was a lie. It was Hades' house. Death and decadence around every corner, and the idea of staying more than an hour, let alone sleeping there, made her stomach clench and flutter.

Maybe if we knocked all the windows out. Let air move through the place.

She took a deep breath against the cool pane of glass and abruptly spat it back out again. No less than two dozen dead flies and moths lay in piles on the exterior sill. Dead when they came too close. Like the cat and the three rats.

Like the three of us.

But not exactly. Thanatos couldn't die, and Cassandra suspected that Hades' death wouldn't rebound on her. Even if he was a ticking time bomb of bubonic plague, of Ebola and smallpox, cholera and Spanish flu. But Calypso— Cassandra looked over at her, where she stood studying a tapestry of a unicorn woven with gold thread. Calypso should go. As soon as they caught a glimpse of him, they'd send her away, just to be safe.

"Clear," Thanatos said, emerging from the hallway. "Plenty more floors. If you don't want to see the stuffed doorman, hang by the stairs for this next one."

Cassandra didn't need to be told twice. She and Calypso stayed close together and made small talk with their eyes until he finished his sweep. Thanatos didn't ask if Cassandra was all right. He didn't put his arm around her, or walk two protective steps ahead. And she didn't know why she wanted him to, when she could take care of herself.

They passed so many floors that by the time they made it to the last she'd lost count. But she'd begun to feel better about being inside. The air on the upper three floors was fresher, thanks to the missing walls. Now that they could see under the tarps, it was clear that a cave-in had occurred. Large chunks of plaster blocked the hallway. Hades hadn't bothered to clear the damage.

"Top floor," Cassandra said. She stepped off the stairs into a wide open space. No hallways here. Only the shadows of what looked like rows and rows of shelves and cases. Calypso leaned forward and her candlelight flickered feebly in the dark. Heavy curtains had been drawn shut against the sun.

"May I?" Cassandra asked, and Calypso handed the candles over. They walked past the first row of shelves together, heading toward the windows to let in some light. But when the flame illuminated a severed head floating inside a jar of cloudy liquid, Cassandra squeaked and dropped the candles. The wax extinguished the flames at once, leaving them in complete darkness.

With a head. A severed head in a jar. Cassandra bit her tongue and cheek hard to keep from screaming.

What does it matter if I scream? It's not like I can wake it.

She bit her cheek harder to shut her brain up. She'd had less than a second to look at the face behind the glass, but her imagination filled in the blanks: waxy skin around the mouth, and eyes like pickled onions behind half-closed lids. A tongue as gray as a storm cloud.

"It's all right." Thanatos threw the curtains back from

one set of windows and then another until cold white light ruled the room.

They stood in the center of a row of shelves. Each shelf held six jars. Each jar held a head. Cassandra wasn't well-versed in plagues and disease, but Thanatos said that the head she'd glimpsed in the candlelight had belonged to someone who died of the Spanish flu. Another face covered with blisterlike pustules appeared to have succumbed to smallpox. And in the center, a bloated, twisted skull floated in an oversized jar, the victim of whatever disease had taken down the Elephant Man.

Thanatos said it was all right. But the hell it was. They stood surrounded by death and disease, preserved body parts and grotesque medieval books on anatomy. Covered petri dishes lined three rows, each labeled lovingly in fancy, hand-written calligraphy. She thought she read ANTHRAX below the nearest one and stumbled away. Calypso caught her by the shoulders and steadied her until they passed the shelves.

A large white bed lay near the windows.

"This is his bedroom?" Cassandra asked, and shuddered.

"He's the god of the dead," Thanatos said. "He'd sleep like a baby here."

"And so would you, I suppose?"

He kept his eyes on the window. Not exactly a denial, but no admission, either.

"Having second thoughts about facing him?" Calypso asked Cassandra.

"No," Cassandra snapped. But the place had her rattled. From the dead cat and friends on the stoop to the taxidermied butler to the cavalcade of heads, she would have liked to smash everything and run screaming, even if she would likely die of bubonic plague, yellow fever, and botulism before she made it out the door. "But Calypso, maybe you should go. This isn't exactly the safest place."

Calypso smiled and nudged her shoulder, as though that was the silliest suggestion in the world. "I'll stay with you. You know that."

Cassandra glanced into a shadowy corner at what looked to be the entire mummified corpse of a woman, and couldn't help being relieved. Having Calypso there was comforting as a soft breeze. But she wished even more for the warmth of Aidan's hands.

Calypso turned to Thanatos.

"How long do you think, until Hades comes home?" she asked.

Thanatos shrugged. "I don't know. He's still underneath. I should've drunk the rest of Megaera's blood. Maybe then I would've been able to pinpoint him."

"It would have put you on your ass for days. What use would you have been to me then?" Cassandra grumbled. She looked away. She sounded cold, like Athena.

"What use will I be to you now?" he asked. "I said I'd bring you here. And here you are."

"But . . . you're not leaving?"

He smiled. "One minute a murderess and the next a frightened girl. I don't know how you manage to pull off so many things at once." The smile faded, and he looked at her in that way he had, as though he could see the future better than she could. "I don't know how much longer you'll be able to."

"It will be dark soon," Calypso said. "I'm going to gather more candles."

It was probably too much to hope for something with batteries. A camping lantern or, hell, some extravagant electric chandelier. Cassandra approached Hades' king-sized, white-blanketed bed and ran her hand across it.

"How likely am I to catch hepatitis if I sit on this?"

Thanatos smiled. He went to the bed and sat. Cassandra sat on the side opposite.

"You've been vaccinated, right?" he asked, and she chuckled nervously.

"Asshole."

They talked quietly, with one eye each trained on the setting sun. The other they kept on Calypso, who set lit candles around them until the room looked less like a lab at the CDC and more like the apse of a church. It was almost pretty, if they ignored the way the firelight lit the gaunt cheeks of the formaldehyde-soaked heads.

Time passed. The candles burned down by half, and Cassandra's eyes grew heavy. She thought it monstrous that Hades slept in the same room as his shelves of death, but the bed was so soft. Thanatos touched her arm.

"I'll stay awake if you sleep," he said.

"Mm," Cassandra muttered. She couldn't stay awake forever. Who knew how long it would be before Hades returned.

"What was that?" Calypso asked suddenly.

"What was what?"

Cassandra hadn't heard a thing. But both Thanatos and Calypso sat upright and stared through the candles to the shadows near the stairs. Cassandra trained her ears in the same direction. There it was: a papery whisper, like old parchment rubbing together.

It might have been nothing more than air moving through the building and stirring the pages of an open book. It might have been the sound of the tarps covering the collapsed walls. But it wasn't. It was too deliberate.

Cassandra rose off the bed quietly. Thanatos stood with her, and Calypso, too, but Cassandra held her hand out in front of Calypso's chest.

Cassandra's eyes tracked over the floating heads, the preserved digestive tracts in sealed plastic. But the noise wasn't coming from them. The flickering candlelight only made them *appear* to move. She walked through the rows of shelves, heat flowing to her fingertips. Fear lent itself to anger with comforting ease.

Whatever it was whispered again. A meatier sound this time, and closer. Not paper rubbing together, but leather. She should have brought a candle. But Thanatos was beside her, and his preternatural eyes could see where hers couldn't. She looked deep into the far corner, toward the preserved, shriveled corpse of the woman.

It wasn't there.

Cassandra grabbed Thanatos' arm.

"What?" he asked.

"There was—" She paused. How could she explain it? She'd barely looked at it before, out of sheer aversion. Part of her thought she'd imagined it, or gotten the placement wrong. "There was something there before." She pointed into the dark. "A body. It isn't there now." Thanatos came close and she leaned into his chest, not caring whether it was something she should do. "Why would Hades move it?"

The leathery whisper issued from somewhere to their left, in the shelves.

"He didn't." Thanatos dragged her back toward Calypso and the candlelight. He held her tightly. "It's not Hades."

They retreated fast into the circle of candles and stumbled against the side of the bed. Calypso had drawn her knife. Thanatos held Cassandra by the wrist and kept her carefully behind him.

The corpse of the woman ran. It ran, letting them glimpse it through jars of formaldehyde. Then it disappeared. All was silent for a span of minutes. When it moved again, it was much, much closer.

"Can I kill that?" she asked Thanatos. "It looks like it's already dead, so can I kill it?"

"No," the corpse laughed. "You can't kill it." She stepped out from between the glass cases, a beautiful, dark-haired girl in a black dress and high boots. A Fury.

"Alecto," Thanatos said.

The girl smiled, and Cassandra flinched. Alecto of the Unceasing Anger. The Fury they'd taken such care to avoid.

Or no care at all, considering we drank her sister like a bottle of Coca-Cola.

Thanatos lunged, and knocked up against the shelves of dead and diseased things. Cassandra held her breath while they rattled and rocked. If anything fell and shattered, she wasn't sure if she could control her panic.

Alecto laughed and danced easily out of his grasp. She moved too fast to be seen. Even Hermes might have had trouble getting his hands on her.

But he would have eventually, and Cassandra wished he was there.

The Fury stepped into the light again. Her face was

sharper than her sisters' and her eyes smaller, the dark irises so large Cassandra could barely make out any white.

"What? Just one charge?" She clucked her tongue. "I would very much like to see you bull your way through this china shop."

Alecto traced her fingers along the row of petri dishes. Surely most of the specimens were dead, but Cassandra had heard stories of mass plague graves that authorities were afraid to disturb even sixty or a hundred years later.

"Hades would be displeased," Calypso said. "If you damaged his collection."

"More displeased than if I left you here to try and murder him?"

"It's not murder. It's an assassination," Cassandra said.

"Semantics," Alecto hissed, and gave them a view of her blackening teeth, so mismatched with her beautiful face. But that was her true form. The girl was an illusion stretched over the top of decaying wings.

"What are you doing here?" Thanatos asked, and Alecto slipped behind them, fast as a light going out. She stayed just long enough for them to spin and stumble against the bed before flashing back to hide behind the stacks. She was too fast. Trying to follow her movements felt like a case of whiplash.

"I'm here to do what Furies do."

"Your sister's dead," Cassandra said. "Let it go."

"Let it go?" Alecto screeched. "Like you have let Apollo go?"

"Your sister was a monster."

"We are all monsters here."

Cassandra stepped forward. If Alecto wanted to join

Megaera, then so be it. What was one more Fury? Thanatos was there. He would move when she did. Alecto didn't look that much more terrible than Megaera had. Cassandra didn't know what they'd been so afraid of.

"A little girl who presumes to kill gods." Alecto grinned. "Who kills them with her hands. And with her heart."

"What are you talking about?" Cassandra asked.

"I'm talking about your . . . Aidan," the Fury said. Her eyes lit up when she said the name, and Cassandra grimaced. It felt as if Alecto had reached into her head and torn his name out with clawed fingers. "Your Aidan, whom you killed."

"I didn't kill him." Her hands burned. "But I'll kill who did."

"You killed him as sure as you stand before me."

"No."

"He died for you. Because of you. He never would have been there. Never would have fought. And one mortal girl lives, while a god lies dead."

Cassandra's vision swam and ran hot. Everything blurred around the edges, whether from tears or rage she couldn't tell.

"Cassandra, don't listen." That was Thanatos' voice. Far away and unimportant.

"He died a mortal's death. Demeaned on the side of a road." Alecto burrowed into Cassandra's mind again and pulled the memory out by the root. "A branch shoved through his chest. Sputtering about love on a cloudy day."

"Shut up!"

"You made him nothing. Made him fallible."

"I didn't ask for any of that!"

"But it's your fault. He died for you. Because of you."

"I never asked him to," Cassandra screamed. "He never listened to anything I wanted. He was a god! A stupid, stupid god!" Fire licked up and down her arms. Pure, clean hate. "He didn't die for me. To save me. He died to clear his own conscience, and he got what he deserved!" Tears rolled down her cheek. "For what he did. For what they all did."

"Cassandra," Calypso said, her soothing voice, like music, pale as an echo. Everything spun and burned before Cassandra's eyes, ready to explode. To send glass and disease flying.

"And now Athena returns," Alecto whispered. "Alive and well. With Aphrodite and Ares by her side. Friends. Allies. Your Aidan forgotten."

"Athena?" Calypso asked. "Alive? But how?" She stepped closer to Alecto, looking for a miracle, but Cassandra couldn't see her. Her world had turned red. Athena was with Aphrodite. She was with Ares.

I always knew it. I always knew she'd go to them.

Cassandra's palms bled where her nails dug in.

"Cassandra, we have to go! We have to see." Calypso was in her ear, imploring and so damn hopeful. "We have to—"

"You want to help them!" Cassandra whirled and grabbed Calypso by the shoulders. Thanatos screamed for her to stop, but it was too late. Angry as she was, it only took a touch.

And Alecto laughed, and disappeared.

TWO WARS

17

STAIRS UP, ALL TOGETHER NOW

Hermes led Andie and Henry deeper and deeper into the belly of Hephaestus' house. The only sounds were their footsteps and rapidly huffing breath. He held the Shield of Achilles ahead of them at chest level. What must they look like? What would Hades think when they burst into the underworld, a scrappy army of three?

Doesn't matter. Just get them down. He looked back. *And be ready to catch them if they stumble.*

They had run over two hundred stairs and still saw no sign of the bottom. If they took a fall, it wouldn't be pretty.

"Slower," he said. "We've gone far enough now. We can take it easy." He thought of his friend above, Hephaestus in the grip of the Moirae. But when Hephaestus had told them to go, he'd meant it, knowing what it would cost.

"How much farther?" Andie asked.

"Don't know." He cupped his hands and hooted down

into the dark, heard it echo five times before going out of earshot. "Long way."

Andie puffed, hands on her knees. "Guess I shouldn't have stopped going to hockey practice."

"It doesn't help that much, actually," Henry puffed beside her. "Can I see it?"

It took Hermes a minute to realize he meant the shield.

"Of course." He handed it over. "You won it. It's yours."

His. But not his. He saw it in Henry's eyes the moment he held it, studying the intricate carvings. It took Henry two arms to keep it aloft. Achilles could have flung it like a discus.

"Andie," Henry said. "Do you want to see it?"

"No." She turned her shoulder. "I don't care."

Henry frowned, and Hermes took the shield back. Of course she didn't want to see it. It wasn't hers. Her lot was to be the war wife, all over again.

But it might turn out different, this time.

"Did you hear that?" Henry asked.

"Hear what?" Andie asked.

"It sounded like someone shouting, from down there." He pointed down the stairs.

Hermes stilled, and listened.

"Did it sound like torture?" He asked. "Maybe we're closer than I thought, and coming in on the Tartarus side."

They started forward again, this time easy and ambling. Apprehension grew in Hermes' chest with every step. They weren't much of a match for anything that might crawl up to the gates. The sound of tramping feet reached them and Hermes wished for more light, or a few stretched-out shadows to serve as warning. Judging by the noise, they were about to be overtaken by a herd of Cape buffalo.

"Turtle up," he said, and set the shield in front of them. No time like the present to find out what it was worth.

Ares' face, smeared with blood, came into view first. There was just enough time for Hermes to think, *Oh, shit*, before Athena shouted, "Get out of my way," and pushed past him. Hermes let the shield roll, let Henry scramble to keep it from bouncing down the million or so remaining stairs.

It was Athena. It was his sister.

Hugging her felt so good it seemed imaginary, even if the impact of her rattled all the bones in his body.

When Athena threw her arms around her brother, she thought she'd never let go. She was afraid it was all an illusion, that they'd never escaped the underworld at all and any moment Hermes would dissolve into molecules right beneath her fingers.

"I'm sorry," she said.

"Shut up. You're here. You're back. I found you." He squeezed her tighter. "Though admittedly I wasn't really looking."

"Odysseus? *Odysseus!*" Andie shouted and stumbled on jelly legs down the steps to put her hands on his shoulders in disbelief. "You're alive."

"Thanks to her." He grinned at Athena. "And him, if you can believe it."

Ares tipped an imaginary cap with his mangled hand.

"What are they doing here?" Henry asked, glaring at Panic and Oblivion.

"It doesn't matter now," Athena said. She held Hermes at arms' length. He looked thinner. More pale. And weary. He looked incredible.

"Where's Cassandra?" Odysseus asked. "And Cally?"

"Finding their way back," Andie answered. "At least that's what Demeter said when we went to see her in the desert. We haven't seen them since the fight on Olympus. We thought they were dead. We thought you all were."

Athena nodded. So Cassandra and Calypso were together. Good. At least they weren't alone. And it was good, too, that Cassandra wasn't with Hermes. She'd have killed Ares if she was, and Athena owed him more than half a trip up the underworld's stairs. But they would find her. And soon.

I won't pick sides.

But that felt like a lie.

"If you weren't looking for me," she asked Hermes, "what are you doing down here?"

"The Moirae," he said. "They're up there with Achilles. In Hephaestus' house. They've got him. We were after the shield and we got it. But we had to run. Athena." He grabbed her arm. "I stood against them. They're weakening. Hephaestus told me to come back, if I found help."

Athena thought quickly, remembering how it felt to have the Moirae in her head on Olympus. How easily they'd forced her to her knee. But Hermes had faced them down.

And I stood, too, when I had to. When Odysseus fell.

"We have to go back up." Hermes tugged her gently. "Hephaestus was trying to help us."

"Then we won't lose him." She nodded to Ares, and he sprinted ahead at once. Athena choked down the urge to tell him not to do anything stupid. Wasted words.

Odysseus flipped his sword in his hand, but Athena pressed it to his side.

"Don't face him," she said.

"Not going to face him. I'm just going to give back this sword, and we'll call it quits."

"I mean it. You'd lose."

"Yes," he said. "But it'd be closer than you think."

Athena knew long before she got inside Hephaestus' house that it was over. Ares hadn't even bothered to battle cry.

The sight when she reached the top of the stairs was sad and strangely empty. The fireplaces still burned. Hermes pressed a hand to a motorized chair and declared it still warm. No doubt the blood was warm, too, where it lay in streaks and puddles. Everything about the scene felt immediate, as though if they'd gotten there a blink sooner they'd have seen it all. But Hephaestus was gone. Vanished. Not even a twisted body remained for them to mourn.

"I can't tell if he left alive." Ares studied the tracks of blood covering most of the floor. If Hephaestus left alive, he'd done so in pieces. "There's too much corruption to the trail. The Moirae dragged themselves through it. Maybe they dragged him along behind. Or maybe he dragged himself, and got away." He leaned in and sniffed a spray of red. "Not all of it's his. Good on him."

"Will you cut the CSI," Hermes snapped. "Goddamn it."

"I'm saying he might be alive," Ares snapped back. "Look here, at the palm print. There was weight behind that."

"Do you want me to get you a black light and those little flags with numbers on them? And get your damned wolves out of it!" Hermes darted to the desk and threw a paperweight at Panic and Oblivion. It landed among their paws and shattered. They whined and trotted away licking red muzzles.

Ares set his jaw and squeezed fresh blood from his mangled hand.

"Hermes," Athena said. "Someone should try to track him, if he can be tracked." She nodded reluctantly at Ares, as if to say, *Let him do it.* She didn't want to leave the others, in case the Moirae or Achilles decided to double back.

"Where are we?" she asked, and hoped no one gave the obvious answer of Hephaestus' house. That much she could tell. From the welded girders decorating the ceiling to the double fireplaces burning hot, the whole place felt like him. Blacksmith of the gods. It even smelled faintly of iron, though that might have been the blood.

"Buffalo," Henry supplied.

Buffalo. So close to home. So close to her own bed she could practically feel the pillows rising up to meet the backs of her shoulders. She wouldn't even make them hitchhike. They'd spring for a car. Hell, they'd spring for a driver.

She took a deep breath, and doubled over coughing. Minutes out of the underworld and the feathers came on fast. A bundle of them in her chest all at once, twisting through lung tissue and rib meat like flowers blooming in time-lapse photography. She hacked and spat and bled down deep, holding Odysseus at arms' length when he tried to help. He couldn't help. It had to run its course.

When she finally caught her breath, she'd worked up three medium-sized feathers and crunched them in her fists. Another wormed its way out through her third and fourth ribs. That one she yanked, foolishly and too hard. The gash it left was twice as big as if she'd been careful.

Odysseus finally got close enough to put his hand on her shoulder. She smiled at him with bloody teeth.

"Welcome home."

Ares couldn't find a trace of Hephaestus. There were no real clues as to whether he had managed to escape, though the sheer amount of blood on the walls and floor suggested he hadn't. Ares returned empty-handed from following the trail ten minutes after leaving, and a search of the massive home had to be abandoned when they realized they'd be lost in the labyrinth in minutes.

Athena gritted her teeth. Another friend missing and probably lost. Her death of feathers returned with a vengeance. Not a great way to return to the world above. Adding insult to injury, they could not, as it turned out, get a car with a driver. That was thanks to the wolves. Nobody would allow them in a vehicle without being secured in crates, and Ares wasn't about to secure Oblivion and Panic in crates. So Athena rented an SUV, and drove home with Odysseus sitting shotgun. Ares lounged in the rear seats and smeared blood over everything. The wolves they stuffed into the back cargo space.

Athena glanced into the rearview mirror at Hermes, behind the wheel of the Mustang with Andie and Henry. She wished he'd ridden with them, but he didn't want to leave Andie and Henry by themselves. And no one could've convinced Henry to let Ares or his wolves set finger or paw inside his car.

Then again, maybe it was better. Even with steel and road between them, she couldn't think of what to say. Part of it was tension, and Ares' presence like a big, bleeding elephant in the room. But mostly there was simply so much. Where to begin? And once they started, where would it go? Farther, probably, than any of them had the energy for at the moment.

The house. Her house. Athena watched it grow larger as they approached, eyes wide and fingers hugging the steering wheel like an excited child. She wanted to stick her head out the window like a dog. Ares and the wolves had slept on and off during the drive back, but she couldn't have, even had she not been driving. Odysseus didn't sleep either. He'd spent too much time unconscious and she'd been below for far too long.

I never want to leave this place again.

But she would, if she survived. She'd seen enough things change during her long life to know that change was the only certainty. Just then, though, she let herself believe that pulling into her driveway was truly coming home. She and Odysseus and Hermes were home.

"I'm ordering from Stanley's Wok." Hermes popped out of the Mustang and pulled out his cell. "Any requests?"

Odysseus leaned his head back and moaned. "God, I missed Stanley's Wok! Just get . . . the entire left side of the menu."

"So the usual, then, plus sesame beef for Athena."

"How are their chicken wings?" Ares asked, leaning on the open rear hatch. He'd let the wolves out to stretch. Panic and Oblivion loped side by side in the yard, snapping jaws at each other. They looked like dogs, except that when they stretched their necks, their shoulders popped out a bit too wide.

"Find somewhere else to eat," Hermes snapped.

"Hermes. Get him some chicken wings." Athena stood in front of her house and breathed in deep. Spring had sprung. The yard smelled of loamy earth and wet roads and bands of warmth woven between layers of chilly air.

Henry and Andie got out of the Mustang and stretched their weary limbs. The Mustang was many things, but it wasn't roomy, and Henry had been cramped in the backseat the entire ride with the shield across his lap. It took a minute to wrangle it out of the car, and when he got it loose, it slipped from his fingers and clanged onto the driveway to wobble like a fallen top.

Athena frowned. She knew Henry was tired and unused to the feel of it, but watching him fumble still felt like a bad omen. She walked over, toed the shield, and flipped it up into her hand like a skateboard. The Shield of Achilles. It hadn't aged much since she'd last seen it. Hephaestus must have taken it out of the world of men as soon as Achilles' line died out. She squeezed the edges to test the metal, to see if she could bend it. But of course she couldn't. And she shouldn't want to. The Shield of Achilles was a formidable asset. The metal taco shell of Achilles didn't have the same ring.

Besides, it's Henry's now. He claimed it, fair and square.

She wished she'd been there to see him do it.

"You'll train him with this?" Andie asked, and nudged the edge of the shield.

Train him. How could she train him? So they could start right back where they'd been? So she could use them up again, and run them headlong into impossible odds?

Athena shook her head slightly, and tilted the shield into Andie's hands. The mortals' lives weren't hers to play with.

"Are you and Henry—?" Athena gestured with her eyes and kept her voice low, cloaked by a light breeze and Ares' wolves snarling.

Andie's cheeks went rust.

Athena snorted. "Good."

"Are you and Odysseus?" Andie asked. She arched her brow and made the same gesture with her eyes. Neither excelled at girl talk. "I mean, you jumped off a mountain for him, so, the cat's out of the bag on feelings."

Yes. Feelings. Except feelings didn't change what was.

"I just know I couldn't let him go," Athena said. "And I still can't."

Odysseus caught her eye and smiled. He looked different to her now. Fragile. The untouchable hero of her memory was gone, and maybe he'd only been a delusion to begin with. Or maybe it only felt that way because she'd lost the power to protect him.

"I still don't understand how you're not dead," Andie said to Odysseus.

"The banks of the underworld kept me in limbo after we

jumped off Olympus," Odysseus replied. "And then good old Ares showed up with magic beans. Water from one of the rivers of Olympus. It let me heal. Brought me back."

"Did he piss in the bottle first?" Henry muttered.

Hermes snorted, but Ares laughed full force, with just a bit too much wicked mirth in it. Odysseus turned faintly green.

"Hope you don't mind if we take off," Andie said. "It's been a long trip. We want to get home. Henry, you should probably leave that."

Henry had been holding the shield, and looked disappointed to have to let it go. But it would be a lot to explain, and impossible to sneak in under his shirt.

"We'll take care of it. Until you come to train."

As he backed out of the driveway, Henry waved. Just a little wave, and no smile. Athena waved back. Something had changed while she'd been gone. Henry had finally thawed to them.

Well. Maybe not to all of us.

Ares stood alone, his good hand stuffed into his pocket, studying the house. She thought he'd sneer at its lack of grandeur, but he didn't. Maybe he was too tired. Whatever it was, the expression he wore took her a moment to place. He looked at the house like he wanted one. Like he wished it was his. Or at least he did until he caught her looking.

"The wolves and I will take the basement," he said.

"You'll take whatever I give you," she said. *And that means somewhere you can be watched.*

18

MANY HAPPY RETURNS

It always happened with gods. You left the house in the morning for a simple meet and greet and returned in the evening after a battle, an impromptu obstacle course, and a trip halfway to the underworld.

Henry's stomach growled loudly and he mumbled, "Excuse me."

Andie shrugged. "What for? It's just your stomach. Not like you can control it, or even like it smells bad."

He grinned. "Next time I'll let a burp fly. Isn't it nice that we can make out and somehow still talk like this?"

"It's not that nice. I'm a lady, for Christ's effing sake." She laughed. He loved to watch her laugh. Teeth out, like a donkey yawning. It was the prettiest thing he'd ever seen.

"Can you come in for awhile?" he asked. "Or do you have to go home?"

The slightest flush crept into her cheeks.

"I can come in."

Had he not been so focused on Andie, thinking ahead to her warm curves on the soft, familiar surface of his bed, he might have noticed that something was different about his house. That yellow light flooded nearly every room. That it looked like a house again instead of a vacant building. But he didn't even notice that Lux wasn't barking.

He and Andie opened the door with their hands and lips already on each other. The awkward, embarrassing sound of their mouths smacking apart when his mother shouted would replay in Henry's brain for days afterward.

"Henry!"

At first his mom's face was all he could see. Her smile stretched so far across it might literally have gone from ear to ear. That smile was rare. He'd only seen it a handful of times in his entire life. The question in his mind—what could be that good?—was answered less than a second later, when he saw Cassandra on the couch with his dog half on her lap.

"Oh my god," Andie whispered. Then she shouted it, and ran to hug her friend. Lux disengaged and came to snuffle Henry's hand.

"She came back today," his mother said. "Just came back. Showed up on the front steps with . . ." Her voice trailed off, and she looked farther into the den, to where a stranger stood.

A god.

Not one they'd ever seen before, but Henry saw past the college-boy clothes in an instant. It was hard to believe that his parents hadn't. But then, they'd had far less practice.

"Zack," the god said. "Thanatos."

Zack. Cassandra's eyes flickered vaguely at the name.

That's not a name she's heard often. Just something made up? For our benefit?

"Henry." His mom gestured for him to come closer, but his feet stayed planted. Sitting on the couch, one hand held limply by their dad, Cassandra looked like a ghost. She looked like a rag, worse even than she had in the days following Aidan's funeral. Whatever had happened to her after Olympus had been bad to the point of trauma, and his parents' smiles seemed at best mismatched and at worst wildly inappropriate.

"Cassandra." The god who called himself Zack stepped up and knelt beside her. "I'm going to go, so you can be with your family. But I won't go far." He and Henry's parents stood. It seemed to take forever for his father to work up the nerve to shake the boy's hand.

"Thank you," his dad said. "For bringing her home."

"Sorry I couldn't convince her to come back sooner." And he sounded like he meant it. When he walked past, Henry grabbed him by the arm.

"Where are you going?"

"I thought I would stay at my cousin's place."

Henry looked into his eyes.

"She has a lot of cousins."

Thanatos looked back. "Not as many as she used to."

A minute after he left, Henry heard a car start somewhere on the street. They must've driven right past it without noticing.

With the stranger gone, the tension in the room was plain. No one knew what to do after so long apart. His parents puttered around Cassandra like square pegs navigating round holes. They wanted to yell and scold, but were too happy to see her. They wanted to baby her and stuff her full of food, but it wasn't right to coddle a runaway.

"So you and Athena came home," Henry said.

Cassandra looked at him. Wherever she'd been, it was sunny. And hard.

"Hi, Henry."

"Hi, Cassie."

They all looked to him for what to do. As if he knew any better than they did. He was sick of being the one to figure it out and hold it together. But everyone else seemed ready to break.

Henry took a deep breath.

"What do you say to a double-cheese Hawaiian pizza?"

Even though it was an odd meal, eaten between estranged and hated family members, Stanley's Wok had never tasted better. Not even the sound of Panic and Oblivion crunching through chicken wing bones could put Athena off her food.

"The house looks great," she said.

"What?" Hermes asked. "You thought I was going to trash it? I'm the only one who does any cleaning around here. And now it's going to smell like dog."

Ares scowled near the kitchen sink and fed Oblivion another wing. The wolves didn't, in fact, smell like dog. They smelled like blood if they smelled like anything.

She'd need to decide what room to give to Ares. And he'd need a few sets of clothes. Nothing Hermes had was likely to be of his taste, and probably wouldn't fit anyway.

Ares had several inches on Hermes around the shoulders and chest, even before Hermes started to lose weight. Odysseus' shirts would be tight, too. But maybe something of Henry's.

She stuffed the last of her sesame beef into her mouth and pushed away from the table. Her room, her bed, and her widow's walk called her name.

Everything in her room was exactly as she'd left it. Exactly. Nothing had been moved, from the items on her dresser to the blanket on her bed hanging slightly askew. Hermes had preserved it like a shrine.

The door closed behind her, and she turned. Odysseus leaned against it. He looked good. Healthy. Freshly showered, and his T-shirt clung to his chest from the damp. Athena cleared her throat.

"It's good to be back," she said.

"It is." He crossed the room to her, hands fluttering in his back pockets, eyes everywhere but on her. "Only we're not back."

"What do you mean?" she asked.

"We're not back," he said. "Not back to playing at goddess and hero."

He looked up at her from under his brow. They were alone, and all at once that seemed to take on another meaning, as if the French doors had bricked over and all the furniture but the bed had tramped out on wooden legs.

"I know," she said.

She thought it would be all the encouragement he needed. But instead he stood there, as awkward as she felt. She rolled her eyes.

"What?" he asked.

"Nothing." She shrugged. "I just thought . . . that you would handle this part."

"This part?"

"You have this reputation, after all. Calypso, Circe, even Penelope. Odysseus, the man of many ways. Slayer of Cyclops. Seducer of women."

Odysseus laughed.

"I've never had to seduce a woman in my life. They see me and fall into my lap."

Athena rolled her eyes again, but she laughed, too.

"You're the difficult one," he said.

She crossed her arms and nodded. She was difficult. And she'd been the one to blur the lines between them in the first place, kissing him in the sleeper of that truck, something that it felt like had happened forever ago and as close as yesterday. If she hadn't done that, he might never have pressed the issue. But it had felt so natural there, waking beside him in the afternoon light. As right and as easy as resting her head on his shoulder on the banks of the Styx. She stepped closer, barely a shuffle of feet. If she could just get close enough, maybe it would feel that natural again.

He stood still, as though he was worried any movement he made would scare her off. But his breath came faster, and she could hear his good, strong heartbeat.

She lifted her arm and slipped it around his neck. It was harder than anything. Heavier than any sword or shield she'd ever lifted. And she trembled. What guts this took. What a fool she'd been, to think Aphrodite was ever weak.

Odysseus raised his hands to her hips, and then to her sides, careful to avoid the fresh feather wound over her ribs.

They stood that way for long moments, statues except for the blood rushing under their skin. Athena sensed his wanting in the eager grip of his fingers, and his rising and falling chest. But still they stood, and went no further.

"I love you," she blurted, and his eyes opened wider. "I just wanted to tell you, in case. In case you didn't know."

"I knew," he said. "I don't remember much from the fall. Just the wind in my ears and you, wrapped around me. Your heart beating faster as mine slowed down." He pushed her hair away from her cheek.

"I love you, too, Athena," he said. "Always have."

He looked into her eyes. If he kissed her now, she would let him. More than that, she would kiss him back. They both knew it, and neither moved.

It's because he knows it's wrong. He feels it, like I do. Our hearts, our desire will never be stronger than what stands between us. We are two different things. But oh how I want it, this time we have left.

Athena let her hands slip from behind his neck down to his shoulders.

"Don't," he said. "Don't let go of me. I haven't worked up the courage yet, but I will."

"You never lacked for courage," she said, and pushed gently away. "It's because it's real now. And now that we can have it, you know it's as wrong as I've always said."

"That's not it. That's not it at all."

He reached for her, as if he would prove it.

"Athena!" Hermes said, and burst into the room.

"Not now, mate," Odysseus groaned. "There's a sock on the door."

Hermes narrowed his eyes and tore it off the knob.

"There's not anymore," he said, "and you two had better get downstairs."

He turned on his heel and left, and Athena and Odysseus followed. When the stairs turned toward the entryway, Athena was greeted by a very unexpected sight.

Standing on her welcome mat, dressed in a navy plaid button-up with sleeves rolled to the elbows, was the god of death.

Athena had last seen Thanatos in Los Angeles in 1972. She'd been living there then, in a small, dusty apartment above a biker's lounge. Most of her nights she spent on a stool, belly up to the bar and a line of empty beers, watching a band called Steve Hunger Road Show do their best impression of America. Steve Hunger Road Show. She couldn't remember the last time she'd thought of them. Steve had been sort of a douche, but Mickey and Jim hadn't been half bad. They'd been her friends.

And then one night she'd seen Thanatos' pale face across the room. She'd invited him over for a drink, even though he made her skin shrink two sizes. They talked, and laughed, and she'd teased him a little, called him the "Goodnight Prince." Seductive Death, always trying to make what he was seem beautiful instead of necessary. Before they said goodbye, she'd squeezed his hand.

The next morning, without word or notice, she abandoned her beloved dusty apartment. What became of Steve Hunger Road Show she never knew. Probably nothing. Or maybe Thanatos had been there for them, and the bar had burned down that night with them inside it. It didn't matter. Where Thanatos was, she had no desire to be.

And now he's here in my living room. Drinking my brother's wine.

She didn't even know Hermes had wine. He certainly never offered anyone else any. But it was the obvious choice. Even in rolled-sleeve plaid, Thanatos looked like a vampire god. She kept a close eye on his glass of wine as he sipped, curious to see if he could stick a finger in it and turn it into blood.

"Thanatos," she said. "What are you doing here?"

"Isn't it obvious?" Ares interjected. "He's here for us. Death come to claim the dying gods."

"Shut up, Ares." Not that it would have surprised her. Thanatos' eyes flickered over every inch of them as he sat, reclined comfortably in a chair. He lingered on Hermes' gaunt face, on Ares' seeping, mangled hand, on the dark circle of blood staining the side of her shirt.

"Did Hades send you?" she asked.

"I haven't seen Hades. I came with Cassandra. She's at her house now."

"Cassandra?" A quick look passed between Athena, Hermes, and Odysseus.

"She found me in California," Thanatos explained. "I've been trying to help her. And I've been failing." The story slipped out of his mouth in low tones: Cassandra's intention to rid the world of gods, Megaera's end in the basement, and the Fury attack on the road. "And then we went to Athens. After Hades."

Athens. Athena's city. Hades was living in her city.

Athena chewed her cheek until she drew blood; it tasted musty, like the inside of a birdcage.

So what? Athens isn't mine to protect anymore. I couldn't protect it, anymore.

"And then?" Hermes pressed.

"And then Alecto told Cassandra that Athena had taken in Ares and Aphrodite."

Panic whined loudly from behind Ares' knees. If Cassandra was home, she'd know Ares was there soon enough. The last time Athena got between them it had cost her a shoulder's worth of feathers. This time would be much worse.

"She won't come for you," Thanatos said.

"The hell she won't," Ares spat.

"Wait." Odysseus pressed closer. "Where's Calypso? Did she stay with Cassandra?"

Thanatos set his wine down on the coffee table. His long fingers rubbed against the legs of his jeans.

"Calypso is dead. Alecto killed her."

The room went still. Athena reached for Odysseus and found air. He was gone before anyone had time to think of something to say.

Calypso. Dead.

She didn't have any right to feel so bad about it. But she did anyway.

"Is Cassandra all right?" she asked.

"No." Thanatos hung his head. "But at least she's almost done."

Cassandra ate as much pizza as she was able. It was funny how comforting her parents found watching her eat a decent meal. It had been too long since they'd been able to feed her, or tell her things, or make sure she was safe. They intended to make up for it in spades, and she would let them, for as long as she could.

But who knew how long that would be? Seeing the confused relief in their eyes was terrible. Knowing she would do it to them again was worse. It hadn't been her idea to come home. After she'd murdered Calypso with her bare hands, Thanatos had scooped her up and made the plans without discussion. They hadn't even taken Calypso's body. It was probably still lying in Hades' house, among the other dead things.

Unless Alecto had returned to take it to her sisters, to defile it somewhere, tearing it apart and cackling in a ruthless, satisfied circle.

Cassandra closed her eyes. Whatever the Furies did to the corpse was irrelevant.

I killed my friend.

"You're going to have to do summer school as it is," her dad said, and poured her more soda. "For a few weeks at least. You can't disappear without consequences." But what those consequences were, he didn't say. Neither did her mother. They tiptoed around it and talked themselves out of it with every slice of pizza. It could wait until tomorrow, they thought. She'd had a hard year, but at least she was safe, they thought.

They were poor punishers due to lack of practice. Seventeen years without enforcing anything more than two days' grounding would do that to a parent. The closest they came to scolding that night was telling Andie she couldn't stay over.

"We kept your room closed off," her mom said gently. "But I went in to straighten up. Sometimes. Of course now you can do it yourself."

Cassandra touched her doorknob and made a silent wish that she'd open it and fall through into a void. Out of existence, just like that, with no memory of her left behind for her family to mourn over.

"Do you want me to make pancakes in the morning, Mom?" she heard herself ask.

"That would be nice. Cassandra?"

"Yes?"

"I know it was hard. I won't pretend to know what you felt. But I know what I felt when you were gone, and if it's anything like that, I—" Her mother paused and looked at her, hard. "It's not okay to make us feel like that. It's not okay to do that to us on purpose."

"I know. I should've come home."

"You should never have left."

"I know. That's what I meant."

Her mother hugged her tight, and Cassandra could feel her heart beating fast, as though just saying those words had scared her to death.

"I love you, Cassandra. You're a good girl."

No, I'm not. Not anymore. Now I'm a monster.

19

DEATH AND THE DYING

I'm afraid to open the damn door.

Athena stood outside Odysseus' room. She'd waited as long as she could, given him as much space as she knew how, only to stand motionless with her hand on the knob. *Screw that.* She swung the door open and stepped inside.

"So, when do you want to kill Alecto?" she asked.

Odysseus looked up at her.

"What?"

"When do you want to kill Alecto? We can go as early as tomorrow. I might be dying, but I can still tear the wings off a couple of overgrown harpies. She's dead. Say the word."

He didn't say anything. He sat on his bed with his elbows on his knees. If he'd wept, she couldn't tell. If he'd thrown anything, she couldn't tell, either, as his room was generally messy.

"You can say something. Anything you want to. I know you loved her."

He ran his hand roughly across his face.

"I didn't love her," he said. "That's the bitch of it. But she always loved me, and I sure did like her a lot, and that seems like the shittiest thing in the world."

He toyed with something between his fingers: a dried white flower. A gift from Calypso? Or something he'd kept, that she'd worn in her hair?

Athena swallowed, disliking the way the sight of the flower made her feel.

He has every right to mourn. Every right to feel whatever he feels. But then, I suppose, so do I.

"I never loved her," he said. "And I never cut her loose. She knew it, but she would've been happy with me anyway, even knowing that I loved you more." He looked at Athena, but she turned away for fear of resentment. "You said let's go kill Alecto. But what if I said let's go find Calypso? What if I didn't believe she was dead?"

"Then we'd go. We'd find her." It felt stupid in retrospect, coming in and declaring war on the Fury. All bluster and balls and no heart.

"Because it doesn't feel like she can be gone," Odysseus said. "She's always been here."

"We'll do whatever you need to do."

He rolled the flower between his fingers and clenched it in his fist. Ten minutes ago they'd been in Athena's bedroom with their hands on each other. So close. Ten minutes ago. It felt like light-years.

"I just need some time, okay?" he said. "I'll be fine."

She nodded. He didn't want her to stay. He didn't need her to. It was how he'd always been. But after she left, she couldn't stop thinking that she should have asked.

"This is good. This is good news. Not about Calypso, of course, but Cassandra is home. There's that, at least." Hermes sat surprisingly still, considering the unease he felt at having Thanatos in their home, eating the last of their egg rolls. He'd babbled on and off since Athena left to check on Odysseus, but neither Thanatos nor Ares took much notice. Which was fine by him. He'd never cared much for Thanatos. None of the gods had. As for Ares, well, if Cassandra made short, bloody work of Ares then all the better, no matter what deal he and Athena had struck.

"Hermes." Ares nodded at him. "You're sweating."

"So? At least I'm sweating sweat. You're sweating blood. And you"—he eyed Thanatos—"you don't have any body heat to begin with." How had he wound up there, playing polite host to two gods he disliked or downright hated?

While two murderous . . . wolves, for lack of a proper word, lounge on my recently shampooed carpet.

Panic did a decent impression of a dog, flopped over on its side. But Oblivion rested its snout on its forepaws, eyes open and unblinking.

Ares sighed lazily and leaned back against the couch cushions. Hermes chucked a coaster at him before he could set his leaking hand down on the upholstery.

"What happened to you, anyway?" Hermes asked.

Ares studied his wounded fist with affection. He

squeezed it together, and blood ran down his wrist to soak into the sleeve of his shirt.

"One of the judges of the underworld had a scepter with razor edges. I bludgeoned him, but it cost me my hand. Athena wouldn't let me keep the scepter. Go figure." He shrugged. "It'll heal."

Hermes glanced at Thanatos. It might heal. But certainly not as quickly as Ares was accustomed to. A cut was ready to open on his forearm, too. It spread across the skin like red ink and would burst in the next few days.

"What were you doing, Hermes?" Ares asked. "When we met you on the stairs?"

"Running for our lives from Achilles and the Moirae. I told you."

"But why were you there?"

"To get the shield. Have you been paying *any* attention?"

"I think what he's looking for is, why the shield," Thanatos said.

"Because we needed it for Henry," Hermes muttered. "Because he's the only one who can kill Achilles and have him stay dead."

Thanatos made a face. "The only one?"

"Yeah, according to Demeter. Why? Does that piss you off?"

"A little," Thanatos admitted. "Then again, if it's possible for one, it's possible for another."

"What's he going on about?" Ares asked, and reached for the lone remaining egg roll.

Hermes had to admit, it was a good question.

"Why are you here, Thanatos?" Hermes asked. "Why are you helping Cassandra?"

"I don't know," Thanatos replied. His eyes lost focus. It wasn't a look Hermes remembered ever seeing on Death's face before. "Maybe because she's like me. She's becoming like me."

"Like you?" Hermes asked, but Ares barked laughter.

"What is it about that girl?" He hit Hermes in the shoulder. "Are you in love with her, too?"

"Don't be stupid," Thanatos said. He drained the last of the wine and stood. "I'm not in love with her. That's not possible."

Hermes watched him walk to the kitchen, the god of death in jeans and Hollister plaid. Thanatos might not love Cassandra. But he certainly did like her. The college-boy costume he wore had never seemed a truer fit. He looked cagey, nervous, caught in the headlights.

I should be afraid for her. People he grows fond of have a habit of wilting like cut flowers.

But if wilting was in Cassandra's blood, she'd have done it already. It was Thanatos who was in danger here. *Love.* Hermes snorted. It made you a moth to a flame, they said. More like a bird to a plate-glass window. And for Thanatos it would be worse, because his very touch could kill her, if he wasn't careful.

And you'll want to do it, too. Maybe not at first, but eventually. It's in your nature. It is your nature.

"I don't get you," Ares sighed. "The lot of you. Getting so *attached* to these people. Even if we survive, you're just going to lose them."

"Then you shouldn't get attached to anything, Ares." Thanatos poured a splash of wine and drank it down. The sound of the glass when he set it on the counter was so brittle Hermes half-expected the stem to crack. "Nothing lasts forever. You're walking proof."

Ares frowned. "But it's just how they're made. They're made to die. I don't get it."

"Well," Thanatos said. "Agree to disagree."

"You think you get to keep her," Hermes said softly. And then louder, "You think Cassandra's like you. A god of death."

Thanatos stared at his hands. His voice when he spoke was firm, but patient.

"That's exactly what she is. Haven't *you* been paying attention?"

When Cassandra's phone chirped, she almost didn't know what it was. It seemed like a long-dead corpse, come back to life after being plugged into a wall. She grabbed it off her bedside table with a little distaste. People could reach her again. She was back on the grid.

The text was from Athena.

I'm in your backyard. Can you come?

Cassandra sighed. If she left the house, even to stand in the backyard, her parents might have tandem heart attacks. They probably weren't even asleep. They were probably lying there listening for telltale scrapes of canvas against carpet or suitcase zippers. She typed back:

I'll let you in. We can talk in the kitchen.

Minutes later, Cassandra had robed up and sat across the kitchen table from a distracted-looking Athena. The goddess looked like crap. Worn around the edges. And she hadn't bothered to clean herself up: the shirt she wore had a fat bloodstain on the side and she hadn't put on a jacket.

"I gather you've been gone since Olympus," Athena said quietly.

"Yep. And until two days ago, I thought you were lying dead at the foot of it."

"You thought?" Athena asked. "Or you hoped?"

Cassandra's palms tingled and she pulled them into her lap. She shrugged. It didn't make much difference.

"Are you all right?" Athena asked. "You don't look all right."

"It doesn't matter. I'm here."

"Do you want me to smooth things over with your parents? I could, you know."

Athena could charm them. Use her god's tricks to muddle their brains and make everything seem like a reasonable dream.

"No. I don't want you to do that." Cassandra nodded toward the bloodstain. "How are your feathers?"

Athena pulled the shirt away from her side. The darkest part of the stain stuck to her skin. She was still bleeding.

"They're a bitch, as usual. Had a little break from them in the underworld. But now they're back. And they're angry." She smiled. Talk of feathers shouldn't have made her smile.

"You were in the underworld?"

Athena nodded. "Odysseus is alive."

Cassandra straightened in her chair. It couldn't be. She'd been there. She'd seen that sword fly into his chest and come out his back. A brief flare of joy rose in her chest; she nearly jumped up to go see him. But it flickered out. All she could see was the hope in Calypso's eyes.

"Ares saved him, the bastard," Athena went on. "He made a deal, and saved him, and got us all out of there in one piece." Athena's eyes stayed on the blood on her shirt; her fingers fidgeted with it. When she looked up, she didn't look anything like the Athena Cassandra remembered. "That's why Ares is here, Cassandra. That's why I let him come. Because he gave me Odysseus back."

"And Aphrodite?"

"She stayed below. The underworld holds everything in check, it seems. Or at least it slows everything down. Down there, she's barely crazy."

"She'll always be crazy," Cassandra said. The heat from her hands felt like it might send the whole table up in flames. She clasped them together tight.

"I know. The deal is just a deal, Cassandra. It doesn't mean they're forgiven."

Cassandra saw the way the goddess' eyes tracked up and down her shaking arms.

"Odysseus will want to see you," Athena said. "He'll be . . . glad. That you're okay. But . . ."

"But what?"

"Thanatos told us. About Calypso. That Alecto killed her."

"Alecto . . . God," Cassandra whispered, and closed her eyes. How could she ever face Odysseus, after what she'd done?

"Is he—?" she started to ask, but didn't know how to finish. Of course he wasn't all right. Odysseus had loved

Calypso in his way. If he ever found out what Cassandra had done, he might strangle her.

"It'll take time," Athena said. "A visit from you would be welcome."

"Soon," Cassandra lied. "Maybe tomorrow."

"Why are you back?" Athena asked calmly. "Thanatos said you were seeking Hades. To kill him. You should have come looking for me instead. Hades was with us, in the underworld."

"I must have just missed him," Cassandra said. "The blood of a Fury sent us to his home in Athens."

"I ruined your plans again."

"No. It doesn't matter. I don't—" Cassandra started, and stopped. "I'm done."

Athena looked relieved, as if she thought Cassandra might grab her throat and demand another boat ride to the underworld.

"You seem tired," Athena said. "But you must be glad to be home. How was it, seeing Andie and Henry?"

"They're together now," Cassandra said, and her arms began to relax. "A couple. They think I don't know. That I can't tell. But the way they look at each other. When Henry looks at Andie, the scar on his cheek turns bright red. I can't decide if it's gross or sweet."

Athena chuckled, another thing about her that was softer than Cassandra remembered. Whatever happened in the underworld was transforming. Or perhaps seeing a sword through Odysseus was transforming.

"Did you know?" Cassandra asked.

"I just found out. We got back today, too."

"You and me," Cassandra said. "Blown dimensions apart

after Olympus only to come home on the same day. Does that feel like the hand of Fate to you?"

The light in the hall flipped on, and Cassandra's dad poked a groggy head into the kitchen. When he saw Athena, he woke up fast and his face hardened.

"It's her first night home," he said. "She needs to sleep."

"I know," Athena nodded. "I just wanted to make sure she'd settled in okay."

"That's not your responsibility. You need to leave now."

Cassandra watched as Athena stood to go. Her dad had never spoken to her like that before. She really wasn't using any tricks.

"How did she get in?" her dad asked after Athena was gone.

"I let her in the back door. She just wanted to talk a minute."

Her dad huffed. "I've got to talk to Henry about that fat dog of his. He's really starting to slack off."

20

HELL-BENT FOR LEATHER

They approached with stealth. A whisper of sand here, a glimmer of steel there. Just slow enough to make her doubt what she'd heard and seen, to convince her she was dreaming or perhaps just truly getting old. She'd felt safe in the desert for so long. Underneath the same star-speckled black sky. The darkness cloaked her; it settled on her weathered, stretched skin like the softest of blankets. So she was confident, and comfortable. Levelheaded enough to talk herself out of gleams from the shadows. Enough even to push it away as imagination when she felt their feet press her edges into the sand. Not even the sting of that first slice woke her completely. It took four, five, six, seven, the shears cutting so fast and sharp that it felt like being burned by hot pokers.

And by then it was too late.

———

"Demeter!"

Athena jerked upright in her bed. Her arms struck out, idiotic panic punches at nothing but the warm, quiet air of her room. Had she screamed? She thought she'd heard herself shout as she woke, or maybe that's what woke her. She felt back for her pillow. It was soaked with sweat. Her hair, too, was wet. And when she made to swing her legs out of bed they were hopelessly tangled in damp sheets. She turned for the bedside lamp and saw a thin, moonlit face standing inside her door.

"Hermes." She flipped on the light and rubbed her hand across her face. "Did I wake you? Did I scream?"

"We both did." Hermes was pale. The whole of him was covered with sweat. His T-shirt stuck to every hollow of every rib.

"We both?" Athena extricated her legs from the sheets and slipped her feet out.

"Demeter in the desert," she said, and Hermes nodded. "She was asleep and they—they cut her apart with their shears." She saw it again as soon as she said it. Twin silver blades, racing through Demeter's skin. Clean cuts all. They moved through her like razors through wrapping paper, so fast it took seconds before the wounds realized they should bleed.

"They were so sharp," Hermes whispered.

She looked at him. He was more than terrified; he was close to crying. She wondered if he could taste the blood and desert dust in his mouth like she could.

"It doesn't mean anything," she said. "It doesn't mean it's true. It's just a dream."

"We don't have just dreams."

No, they didn't. And certainly not the same dream at the same time. The Moirae were doing it. They were killing them all. *Aunt Demeter* . . . Athena closed her eyes.

"Do you think they did it because of what happened at Hephaestus' house?" Hermes asked, shaking. "Because I stood against them? Because we fought?"

"I think they did it because they're mad," she said quietly. "And I mean mad like nuts. Not because they were angry with you."

"But they were. They had to be. You didn't see the way they broke Hephaestus' bones. The way Atropos *smiled*—" His breath hitched and he hugged himself. Sweat beaded on his forehead and upper lip.

"Hermes."

"You didn't see!" And just like that he collapsed at her feet.

"Hermes!"

He flopped and jerked and bit his tongue; blood shone red and slick on his teeth and lips. She shouted for Odysseus, for anyone as she held him down, ignoring how hot his skin was and how many bones she could feel.

"Is this it?" she heard herself screaming, and it made no sense. He was sick, that's all. He was sick and he'd upset himself. Any moment he'd be still, and take a breath, and his eyes would roll back the right way.

"Oh, shit."

She looked up; Odysseus stood over them.

"Help us!" she shouted, and he knelt and took Hermes' head in his hands.

"He's burning up. Hermes, can you hear me?" He slapped his cheeks lightly. Hermes bucked in her grip.

"Give him here." Ares bent and scooped him up, keeping his head clear of Hermes' flailing arms. "Get ice."

"What are you doing?" Athena blinked confusedly as Odysseus dashed for the kitchen.

"We've got to get his fever down," Ares said.

Athena darted past them in the hall and opened the bathroom door wide, noting absently that Hermes had found time to fix it since she'd ripped it off its hinges. After the first time she'd heard him fall.

She tore half the shower curtain off its rings pulling it back.

"Cold water," Ares barked. "Push the plug down."

Ares set their brother down gently. The water touching his bandaged hand churned pink and Athena winced when he splashed it over Hermes' thin arms and shoulders. It must've been so cold. Such a shock.

But Hermes didn't shiver. He didn't take great gulps of air. He lay in the frigid water as though he was dead. But at least he stopped thrashing.

"What's going on?"

Athena glanced over her shoulder and saw Thanatos standing in the doorway with wide eyes.

"You get out!" she shouted. "Get out of my house! Now!"

He backed out slowly. Goddamned Death.

"Ice," Odysseus said. He emptied three trays of cubes into the bath before Ares stopped him on the fourth.

"Keep that one. We might need it later. And refill the rest."

"Is it working?" Athena asked. "Is he cooler?"

"I don't know."

Time flattened. The sound of water rushing into the tub

went on and on into forever, and she couldn't tell if it cooled her brother, even as it cooled the air against her face. Her mind spun, it raced ahead and put coins over his eyes. She could actually see them, silver circles sunk into his cheeks.

Ares pressed ice to the back of Hermes' neck, and his lids fluttered. They fluttered, and the eyes underneath swiveled back and forth, slower and slower, until he blinked. When he opened his eyes again, they fixed on her face.

"Hey," Athena said.

"Hey yourself," Hermes whispered. "This feels nice."

Her heart thudded in her throat, and she gripped Odysseus' fingers where they held her shoulder. Hermes was fine. It was just a scare. Just a bad night after too much running and too many bad dreams.

"Ares," Athena said. "How did you know to do this?"

"You knew it, too. You just panicked." He pressed more ice to Hermes' forehead. "You love him too much," he said gruffly. "It makes you stupid."

The pulse in Ares' neck jumped like a grasshopper. His expression was as worried as theirs. He loved their brother, too, she realized. No matter what he said.

They lay Hermes onto the couch with ice packs and damp towels, and covered the whole mess with an insulated blanket to slow the melt. Athena spent the rest of the night sitting on the floor, watching him sleep. Odysseus did his best to stay awake with her, but by daybreak she and Ares were the only ones left. Odysseus snored softly with his head in her lap, and Panic did the same with Ares on the other sofa. Oblivion slept beside the armrest. Or she thought it did. Its eyes were still open, but it hadn't moved in hours, and occasionally twitched its paws like it was dreaming.

They didn't talk, though their whispers would've woken no one. Athena didn't know how to say thank you, and she didn't want to hear the other thing. The thing that she knew. That Hermes was worse. That ice baths and an insulated couch were not a cure. They'd fought their way out of the underworld in just enough time to watch their brother die.

No. I'll save him. I should be able to save him.

Maybe if she'd been there. If she'd stayed in the fight that day instead of diving off Olympus. Hermes had had to do everything without her.

But then Odysseus would be dead. And damn it all, she couldn't trade one for the other, even in her imagination.

She hadn't heard a peep from Thanatos. She assumed he'd listened and left. Good. But now and then, when Odysseus stopped snoring and everything seemed too quiet, she'd imagine him in the basement, motionless as a wax figure, waiting for her to calm down.

"I'm going to change the ice." Ares stood and stretched, dislodging Panic, who yawned. "And then I'm going to take the wolves out to run. They don't do well kept in one place for too long. Start taking bites out of each other."

He switched melted ice for fresh and subbed in a few frozen gel packs they'd accumulated for the mortals' post-training-session swelling. He did it so well and so carefully that Hermes didn't even mumble in his sleep.

"Come on." He clapped his hand to his thigh softly for the wolves to come.

"Don't go far," Athena said.

She'd told him about the dream she and Hermes had shared about Demeter, murdered in the desert, but wasn't sure whether Ares believed it was true. He'd said that the desert was days away anyhow. On a map, it was days away. Yet the Moirae had been in Buffalo yesterday, and slicing into Demeter by nightfall.

"I'll go to the woods," said Ares. "And I won't kill anything that anyone will notice. You don't need to watch me every minute." He shrugged into a jacket and headed for the back door.

"Ares," she called softly, and his shoulders slumped, ready for a lecture. "Be careful."

He looked back. Sometimes Ares seemed so much like one of his wolves. But just then he seemed more like a kicked dog, surprised by an offered Milk-Bone.

"I will be."

Cassandra and her mother met with the principal for an hour and a half. For forty minutes of that time, the district superintendent sat in as well, for no other reason than to convey the gravity of the situation. Or at least that's how it seemed. She said nothing of note, just sat in a charcoal suit and drank a cup of coffee. But they let Cassandra back in for the rest of the term. Summer school was on the docket, too, as her father had predicted. Consequences.

Cassandra and her mother timed their arrival and departure to avoid crowds in the halls. Her mom's idea, and a great one. The few kids they did see weren't ones she knew, and didn't seem to recognize her. When she officially returned to classes, it would be a hassle. She'd have to give the same explanation over and over, for friends and for people who suddenly considered themselves friends because they wanted to know the gossip. She could've hugged her mom till she was blue for sparing her one more day of it.

Of course Andie and Henry would spread the news as much as they could. But it wouldn't be the same as hearing fantastic runaway stories straight from the runaway's mouth.

"Do you think you'll be okay, to catch up?"

"What?" Cassandra asked. "Yeah, Mom. I'll have to study a lot, but what else is new."

Her mom shook her head. "For a few minutes there, I thought we might have to switch schools. The way Superintendent Russell was looking at you. Like she'd just caught you outside the walls with an open can of spray paint."

"She was just trying to see if I was trouble."

"Just trying to be a jackass, more like."

"Mom!"

"Well. It's not as though you've been in any trouble before. A detention here and there, sure. But you've always been an excellent student. And we participate in the damn bake sales just like everyone else."

Cassandra laughed. They walked through the front doors and out to the visitor's lot. Thanatos stood beside their car.

"Zack," her mom said, and it took Cassandra a few seconds to connect the name to his face.

"Hi, Mrs. Weaver. Hey, Cassandra. How'd it go?"

"She's back in. Starts back tomorrow."

"That's great!" Thanatos smiled. Cassandra wondered if her mom noticed the way his smile never touched his eyes. It didn't seem like she did. "Can I treat you guys to lunch?"

Her mom checked her watch. "I can't. I've got just enough time to run a few errands before I go back in to the office. But I suppose you could take Cassandra, if you'll drop her at the house right after."

Her mom got into the car and smiled at them as she buckled up. They waved as she pulled out onto the road.

"Odd how she lets me out of the house unsupervised with the boy who just brought me home from god knows where," Cassandra said.

"Well I'm sure she wouldn't, if she knew I was Death."

Cassandra frowned. "What are you doing here?"

"I wanted to see you. To see how you were. And Athena kicked me out of the house."

"Why?" she asked, and almost chuckled at the image. Standing in the familiar spring sunlight of the town she'd grown up in, Thanatos looked different. She could almost forget the way they met. She could actually feel her brain trying to superimpose a normal explanation over the true one.

Thanatos sighed.

"Because I am what I am," he replied. His brows knit. "There's something wrong with Hermes."

"What? What's wrong with him?"

"He's dying."

"He's been dying." But something in Thanatos' eyes told her this time was different. Hermes was dying now.

When they pulled into Athena's driveway, Cassandra had a moment of doubt. A flash that going inside wasn't the best idea. Ares was bound to be there. It could all blow up. But she had to see Hermes.

She knocked at the door without knowing why. She'd always gone straight in. Times had changed.

Odysseus answered, and after his face lit up, he pulled her into a hug. Her arms stuck out behind him like brittle twigs. He was alive. Alive and unhurt as if nothing had happened.

And Calypso will never know.

"Odysseus," Cassandra said. She could only bear looking into his eyes for a few seconds. "Athena told me you were alive, but I almost didn't believe it."

"Yeah, well, this bloke told us about you, and I almost didn't believe it, either." He touched her hair. "I'm glad you're okay. I'm sorry about Cally."

Cassandra squeezed her eyes shut. He was the last person in the world who should say that.

"Is Hermes . . . ?" she asked.

Odysseus nodded over his shoulder.

"Stick around, after," he said. "I want to hear all about your time on the road. God killing."

Cassandra let him lead her into the house. The kindness in his voice was terrible. It was only because he didn't know. Once he did, their friendship would be over. She deserved that. But she couldn't help wanting to put it off.

Hermes lay on the couch, covered from chin to toe by a slab of blankets. They'd packed something in with him that made boxy bunches beneath the fabric. She didn't know what it was, but it hid his thinness well enough. If she didn't know better, she'd think he had just come down with the flu.

That's a lie. His gaunt face had gone the color of ash. *If I didn't know better, I'd think he was already dead.*

Athena stood beside the couch. She'd changed out of her bloody shirt, but the way she stood said the wound still hurt. A dark spot above her collarbone hinted at another feather working toward the surface.

"You brought him back here," Athena said, staring at Thanatos.

"He's not the cause of this." Cassandra spoke carefully. Anyone could see Athena was barely hanging on, and Thanatos was an easy target. But Athena knew the truth when she heard it. She backed up a step so Cassandra could get to the front of the couch.

"Hey," Hermes whispered as she knelt. "We've been looking for you. Went all the way to the desert to ask Aunt Demeter where you were." Cassandra felt the cold emanating from beneath the thick blanket. They'd packed him with ice, and still his eyes shone bright with fever, and sweat dripped down his neck. "They killed her, you know. The Moirae. Sliced her into confetti."

Cassandra pressed her hand to his shoulder. "How long has he been like this?"

"Since last night. Since we dreamed of Demeter's murder." Athena hugged herself tightly, and Odysseus went to stand beside her. "The fever broke for a few hours this morning. But it won't stay gone."

"Is there anything we can do?"

"I don't know." Athena wiped a tear out of her eye. "Maybe if we found a way to kill that." She gestured toward Thanatos, who did his best to look innocent.

"Can't." Cassandra smiled softly. "I already tried."

Athena scoffed and rolled her eyes. "Perfect."

The back door opened and closed. Cassandra knew who it was before she saw him, even before she heard the wolves scramble into the kitchen, just by the way Athena stiffened. Cassandra drew her hand back fast from Hermes' shoulder and took a long, slow breath.

Control it.

But she couldn't. It burst from her as soon as Ares stepped into her peripheral vision. His wolves whined and slunk behind his legs. Cassandra breathed, in and out. In and out as fire licked up her arms.

He should be dead. He should die. It was what she'd waited for.

Control it.

She told herself again. To control it like she hadn't been able, when she'd killed Calypso. When she'd murdered Calypso.

Athena stepped slowly around the back of the couch, her arm stretched wide to block Cassandra's way, or maybe just to separate them. Not that it would do any good. One touch and there'd be nothing left of Athena but the remains of a pillow fight.

"It should've been you," Cassandra heard herself say. Her legs drove up from the ground and she vaulted toward Ares and Athena both. "It should've been you! Not her!"

Ares stepped back, and reached for Athena as though he might shove her closer. The coward. But his hand wrapped around Athena's arm and pulled her to his side, so maybe he meant to use her as a human shield instead.

"Cassandra!" Thanatos jumped forward and caught her around the waist. She'd come so close. The terror in Ares' eyes was incredible. Exhilarating.

"Thanatos, be careful," Athena shouted, but he paid no attention. He wrangled Cassandra from the room. Just like he had in Hades' house.

21

NO TIME TO HEAL

"That went better than I expected." Athena shook loose of Ares and returned to Hermes.

"What just happened?" Hermes asked when she knelt.

"Nothing." She checked his shoulder where Cassandra had touched him. It was no worse. "Just Cassandra, come to check on you." She felt Odysseus' and Ares' eyes glued to her back and willed them to shut up. There wasn't any need to worry Hermes.

Sure, Cassandra had exploded into a bloodthirsty monster in their living room. Sure, the way her face had seemed to elongate in that moment, the way her *teeth* seemed to elongate, was bound to keep them all up nights. But considering Athena had figured on losing most of an arm to feathers during the exchange, it really had gone much better than she'd hoped.

Still, they'd have to find a way to keep Cassandra and Ares apart.

Odysseus closed the front door, left open after Thanatos had dragged Cassandra out. There'd been a tense few seconds when she'd clawed into the jamb and it seemed that she would scratch her way back in. But her fingernails gave way instead.

Athena reached for Hermes' forehead and watched her hand shake.

"Ares, would you and the wolves stay with him a few minutes? There's—" She looked around the living room as though she was surveying her kitchen cupboards. "There's nothing here to eat. Nothing that's good for sick people. The grocery store's only a few miles away. Odysseus, will you drive?"

She tossed the keys to the SUV at him and headed for the back door without really knowing why. Maybe to avoid the invisible trail Cassandra seemed to have left. Maybe just to feel farther away.

"Good thing we still have the rental," Odysseus said as he buckled up. "I guess Hermes didn't bother to bring the Dodge back from where we parked it. I wonder if anyone's found it yet. Maybe it's giving the cops something to puzzle over: a stolen car covered with inhuman prints."

"I doubt that they'd bother to dust a stolen '91 Dodge for prints. Besides, our fingerprints look as human as anyone else's." She didn't bother with her own seat belt. She didn't want to be gone long. Just long enough for the twitchy feeling to leak out of her bones, and to find something palatable for Hermes to eat, if there was such a thing.

"So," Odysseus said carefully. "Cassandra seems different."

"Whatever do you mean?" Athena looked at him slantways.

"Oh, nothing." He smiled. "Just that she sent the temp up by ten degrees. And after she was gone I swear it smelled like . . . ozone? Is that what they call the smell before a thunderstorm?" He shook his head and turned onto Alderwood Place. "She didn't even look like herself."

"She looked like a monster. A demon. And how much, do you think, did we have to do with that?"

"All of it. None of it. And what do you mean by 'we'?" Odysseus blinkered for the grocery store and hit the brakes abruptly. He still had trouble sometimes with driving on the right side of the road. "Besides, it's probably for the best anyway. We can use all the monsters we can get."

"I thought you were her friend," Athena said.

"I am her friend. But the Fates are slicing and dicing your aunt, we'll be next on their list, and Hermes is laid up on the sofa. So you'd better start finding uses for the assets we've got."

Athena sat quietly as Odysseus pulled into a parking space and killed the engine.

"No," she said.

"No?"

"I'm not leading. I'm not going to use them anymore. Your lives are your own. From now on, they'll make their own choices."

Odysseus stared at her. But how could she make him understand? She still felt like Athena, goddess of battle and wisdom. But she wasn't. If she was, she wouldn't have almost gotten them killed. Gotten *him* killed.

"I'm sorry," she said. "I shouldn't have asked you to drive me here. You have too much on your mind. Calypso—"

"I'll mourn Calypso for the rest of my life," he said, and grabbed her shoulder when she moved for the door. "But I need you. We need you."

"No you don't," Athena said, jerking the handle and stepping out. "I had to learn that. And now so do you."

Henry squeezed Andie's hand before they got out of the Mustang. Her fingers were cold and clammy. They'd been stuck in school for hours after Cassandra texted, saying that Hermes was sick and she was going over to see him. Knowing she was there already eased Henry's conscience, as though she was an ambassador for all Hermes' human friends. Andie wanted to ditch out on the rest of the day and go at once. But they were just about out of good excuses.

He can't be that bad.

The words repeated in Henry's mind but refused to come out of his mouth. Hermes probably wasn't that bad. They'd just seen him, for Pete's sake, and he'd been fine. Thin as ever, and maybe a little feverish, but he had run fevers on and off since the day they'd met him. But every time Henry tried to say something to reassure Andie, his tongue went numb. What did he know about the deaths of gods?

When they finally got to Athena's, Andie was first through the door, and not for the first time Henry regretted that she was so tall. He couldn't see a thing.

"Get away from him," Andie said.

Ares had dragged the ottoman nearer to the couch. He sat on the edge, leaned over Hermes, and pressed a wet cloth to his forehead. He paid no attention to Andie's order, just regarded them in a lazy, irritated way and kept sponging. Henry's throat tightened. What right did Ares have to take care of Hermes, when whatever had gone wrong was probably his fault?

"Where's Athena?" Henry asked.

"And Cassandra?" Andie added.

"Athena went out for food," Ares replied calmly. "As for Cassandra, Thanatos dragged her out of here. I guess that means I owe him one."

"Thanatos?" Andie asked.

"The guy Cassie came home with," Henry said. *The god she came home with.*

"Yeah," Ares said. "Thanatos. You know. God of death."

Andie glanced at Henry. He knew exactly what she was thinking. Where the hell had Cassandra hooked up with the god of death? And why?

In the five seconds since Cassandra had been back, they'd barely had a moment with her that didn't involve one of their parents. She hadn't told them anything. That morning she'd made pancakes before Henry left for school, and he'd practically choked on them, sitting across from her pretending to be nothing more than her relieved brother.

"She really doesn't tell you much, does she?" Ares smirked.

"She will," Henry said. No matter how curious he was, he had no desire to hear anything from Ares.

Hermes shuddered beneath the blankets, violent as a seizure. Every one of them moved closer, ready to do who knows what. Andie nudged past Ares and stepped over Panic's back. Henry started to tell her not to get so close, but she edged her toe underneath its rump until it whined and jumped away to lay someplace less pokey. She pressed the back of her hand to Hermes' cheek.

"He's so hot."

Henry stood over the back of the couch and looked down. Hermes' cheeks and eyes had fallen in. Had he really been so healthy yesterday? Or had they imagined it, refusing to see how much of him had wasted away? His skin was so pale. Almost blue.

How can skin that color be hot? How can it have any blood in it at all?

"What happened?" Andie asked. "He seemed fine when we left. He was so happy to see Athena."

"They had a nightmare," Ares said. "From what I understand, they saw the Moirae kill old Demeter." He flipped the cloth on Hermes' forehead to the cool side. "I guess it set him off. Or maybe he was just waiting for his big sister to get home."

Henry gritted his teeth. What was that in Ares' voice? Resentment? Regret? He wanted to shove him, take the damp cloth and throw it in his face. Being nursed by Ares was the last thing Hermes would want.

"Is there anything we can do for him?" Andie asked. She tucked the blankets tighter around his chin, and his eyes fluttered.

"Not unless you can kill the Moirae."

"So you believe it then," Henry said. "I know Hermes does. But you do, too?"

"Believe what?"

"That if the gods kill each other . . . if you kill the Moirae, you'll get better. He'll get better."

Ares shrugged. "Maybe. But fuck, why not? I haven't heard any better suggestions. And even if we don't get better, with them dead at least we can live out the last of our days without worrying about a pair of shears to the guts."

"So how do we find them?"

"Henry," Andie whispered, like she didn't want Hermes to hear. But Hermes couldn't hear anything. Henry could've shouted it point-blank into his ear and he wouldn't have flinched. He was so close to gone. And Athena wouldn't take that sitting down. She might be playing nursemaid with chicken soup and Tylenol for now, but soon enough the goddess of battle would remember who she was. They'd be on the road after the Moirae before they had time to pack socks, and they'd better have a good idea about which way to go.

"If they were in the desert last night, do you think they'll stay there?" Henry asked.

"Henry, shut up!"

He couldn't. He wished he could hold Andie and tell her he was still scared, that he knew Achilles would be waiting. Maybe he would later, when Ares' mocking eyes weren't assessing every inch of his frame for signs of trembling.

"Hermes is our friend," he said. "It's going to come down to it sooner or later, so why not now, when some good might come out of it?"

Ares smiled, cockeyed. For a second, he looked a little like Odysseus, only dim instead of clever. He stood. With his knees locked, he and Henry were almost the same height.

"You look a little like me," Ares said. "I didn't notice until you grew some balls."

"He doesn't look anything like you," said Andie, but she had to be blind to think that. They had the same broad shoulders and deep chest. They'd even dressed in similar T-shirts. With the scar on Henry's face, and the fresh cuts surfacing on Ares' neck, they looked more like brothers than Ares and Hermes did.

"He looks a *lot* like me," Ares said. "But that's where the similarity stops. I'm the god of war. You're just a kid. And I don't know what they think you're going to do against Achilles except die."

"I'm the only one who can kill him," Henry said, and hated the way his voice sounded.

"You?" Ares shook his head. "Not you. Hector of Troy maybe, but not you."

"I know what you're saying," Henry said calmly. "And I'm not doing it. This is as close to Hector of Troy as you're going to get."

"Not even if it would give you the juice you need to stay alive? Haven't you noticed that you past heroes who die and come back with your old memories tend to wake up . . . supercharged?"

"Supercharged," Henry whispered, remembering how Odysseus had taken out Famine in the tunnels of Olympus. How he'd managed to survive a sword through the chest long enough to fall all the way to the underworld. Achilles, Cassandra, and Odysseus. They were all more than they were before. They weren't just heroes. They embodied their myths. Odysseus, once only clever and quick, was now fast enough to take down wolves, clever enough to hide Achilles and his own strength for most of a year.

Cassandra, once a doomed prophet, was now the doom of gods, with eyes to the future that rivaled the Fates'.

And Achilles. The myths said he was invincible, and now he was impossible to kill.

The myths also said that of all others, only Hector could stand against him. What would that Hector be now, if not the one who could truly destroy Achilles?

Henry looked at Andie. She stared at him with wide brown eyes and shook her head.

"Why would you tell me this?" Henry asked Ares.

Ares shrugged.

"You seem to care about my brother, so maybe I want you to live. Or maybe I could just tell that you didn't want to know." He shrugged again. "I just do things. Let other people figure out the whys."

Cassandra was so angry she thought her fingers might melt together. She wanted to hurt something so badly she was moments from hurting herself. Her fingernails were bloodied and cracked from breaking across Athena's door, and their sharp edges dragged up and down her wrists. But it wasn't enough. Her wrists itched down deep. She'd have to claw her way under the skin if she wanted to scratch it.

"Why did you bring me here?" she shouted.

"This is where you needed to go," Thanatos said quietly.

"I'd almost gotten it down. I'd almost swallowed it." She wasn't making sense but it felt good to yell. To hell with the right words. Screaming eased the itch in her chest. Yelling loosened the tightness in her throat.

In the car she'd started to feel better. Breathed deep and closed her eyes, let the cold wind come in through the window and blow Ares right off her shoulders. Calypso, too, had helped. She'd closed her eyes and thought of Calypso.

Then Thanatos turned the car into the cemetery and pulled her by the wrist to Aidan's grave.

"You can't swallow it," Thanatos said. "You almost killed them back there, going after Ares. You'd have gone through Athena. You'd have stepped on Hermes' chest if it would've gotten you closer. Did you really want to kill Ares so badly?"

"Yes, I wanted to kill him! I want to kill all of them. Athena, Hermes, Odysseus. All of them. I hate them." She paced in front of Aidan's grave. The letters on his headstone curved down in pity. She ran at it and shoved it hard. Two hundred pounds of marble fell over in the grass. It seemed to Cassandra that it flew.

"I hate you," she said, and then she screamed until she thought her vocal cords would rip, would snap like weak twine. "I hate you!"

What else she said in the next several minutes, what expletives, what names, what elaborate curses, she didn't know. Maybe it was none of those and she stood screaming nothing in an empty, sunlit cemetery.

Thanatos stood to the side and ignored her until she was through.

Wrung out and guilty, she felt sort of ridiculous, and her broken fingernails throbbed. But when she glanced at Thanatos, his expression was neutral. Her lip curled to say something like, *What was that? Death therapy? Should we hug it out now?* but her voice was too tired for it. Instead she asked, "Am I crazy?"

"If you are, people have gone crazy for less." He looked at Aidan's headstone, helpless on its back. It reminded Cassandra of a lobster she'd seen in a tank once, hopelessly flipped over, no longer trying to right itself. Why bother? It was headed for a pot of hot water anyway.

"Thanatos?"

"Yeah?"

"Am I evil?"

He looked at her with calm eyes. This was what he'd been trying to puzzle out this whole time. What she was.

"I'm not sure yet," he said.

Cassandra smiled shakily. "Me neither." She flexed her hands. They didn't feel like her hands. So much power in little bones and skin. It was strange to have that power and still feel so powerless.

"I'm angry about everything," she said softly. "Angry that Aidan's dead. Angry that he deserved it. Angry that these people, these *gods*, showed up one day and made everything *hard*. Athena stuffed a bad life into my head. Made me fight when I didn't want to fight. Hurt my friends. *Became* my friends.

"And I feel guilty for being so angry." She sighed. "And I can't control it. And I killed Calypso."

"It doesn't make it any easier that she wanted to be dead," Thanatos said.

"No. And she wouldn't have wanted to die, if she knew that Odysseus was alive. She hoped, at the end. I saw it in her eyes. Maybe that's why I did it. Maybe I killed her on purpose because I hated her hope. I wanted him to be dead because Aidan was dead. So I wouldn't be alone."

"You're adding to your own memories," Thanatos said

gently. "You weren't really thinking that. It happened too fast." He said those things to comfort her. But he didn't say it was an accident, or that she hadn't meant to do it. He didn't lie.

"I have to learn to control this," she said. "I have to learn to swallow it."

Thanatos bent to retrieve Aidan's headstone. He lifted it one-handed and set it carefully back into its place.

"You can't swallow it, Cassandra. You have to let it go."

22

THE WAR UNSEEN

Thanatos dropped Cassandra in the Applebee's parking lot to meet her dad for an early dinner and a movie. Her idea. Making up for time lost being a jackass, she told herself. Not a tactic to avoid Andie and Henry, though that was a bonus. She didn't know what to tell them about Calypso, or about almost murdering everyone in her path.

She remembered testing her touch on Andie, when they'd visited Henry in the hospital after the wolf attack, and her stomach twinged with shame.

"Are you sure you're all right?" Thanatos asked. "We can go somewhere else. Talk."

"I'm fine. And thanks. But what about you? Where are you going? Think Athena will let you back in the house?" Or perhaps he was leaving. Back to California. It surprised her how much she wanted him to stay.

He can't go. He's my only witness. The only one who knows what we did.

He ran his hand through his hair and ruffled it like he was tired.

"You won't leave?" she asked. "Town, I mean."

He touched her shoulder lightly. Just a fast touch from cold fingers. If he'd lingered any longer, she might have walked into his arms.

"I'm not going anywhere," he said. "But I won't go back to Athena's. I'd wake up in the middle of the night to find her staring down at me with a hatchet. I'll find someplace else to stay."

"There's not much to choose from. There's a Motel 6 off the highway that seems pretty popular with gods."

Thanatos chuckled and pulled a face. "Or maybe I'll rent a house."

He pulled out of the lot just as Cassandra's dad pulled in. They honked at each other and did the guy salute.

Throughout dinner her dad did a good job pretending that she hadn't been gone at all, and pretending that meeting at Applebee's for smothered chicken and potato skins was something they did often instead of never before. Sometimes he went overboard with cheerfulness and she had to force her cheeks to go along with it. But it made her sad that he tried so hard to keep her happy, as though keeping her happy would keep her home. He blamed himself, and he'd do it again the next time she ran away to fight in one god's struggle or another.

"Do you want dessert?" he asked. "Or would you rather get something at the movie?"

"I'm stuffed. Maybe some Sour Patch Kids at the movie. Or some Cookie Dough Bites."

"And probably some popcorn," he added. "Medium soda."

"Dad?" she said. "Thanks for not locking me in a basket."

She could tell the word choice confused him, but he smiled anyway.

"Sure, kiddo. But do it again, and I make no promises."

When they pulled into the driveway, Andie's Saturn was parked on the street. As she went up the stairs Cassandra thought of ways to dodge uncomfortable questions, but when she reached the second floor hallway, Henry's door was pulled firmly shut. A lucky break.

She could hear them inside, and was briefly grossed out before she realized they were arguing.

I should find out about what, she thought, but instead turned and went through her bedroom door.

In her room, she twisted the knob tight and leaned against her door, grimacing even at the soft *whuft* the wood made sliding into place. But no one came. Andie didn't burst from Henry's room like a Valkyrie demanding answers. Lux didn't even bark.

She started to take off her cardigan when an insect crawled up her nose.

"Ungh!" She swatted and exhaled as hard as she could, trying to stop the million legs from scrambling up her nostril. Any moment and the bug would turn, take the down chute, and head for her throat. She'd be able to hack it up onto her tongue and spit it out. The thought filled her with adrenaline and disgust. All those legs in her mouth, cling-ing to her lips.

Cassandra stumbled to her vanity dresser and stared into the mirror, expecting to see the back third of a red-brown centipede hanging from her face.

There was nothing there. And the bug had settled down inside, too.

She tilted her face up, more scared than she could re-member being in a while, bracing herself for bug legs nes-tled firmly up her nose.

Nothing.

"I really am going crazy."

(No. Not crazy. Just unused to having us inside your head.)

Cassandra lurched back from the mirror. That voice. She recognized the way it boomed from the center of her brain.

"The Moirae."

(Not all of us. Only Clotho. And now Lachesis.)

"Now?" Cassandra asked, and felt another bug start to fight its way in, this time through her ear. That was worse than through her nose, though she hadn't been able to imag-ine worse moments before. It drilled and squiggled and scratched its way right past her eardrum, and she couldn't tell how many legs it had but it felt like a lot. By the time Lachesis finished working her way in, Cassandra lay curled up and sweating on the carpet.

She took a breath and her stomach clenched in a hard dry heave. Clotho and Lachesis waited for it to subside. Cassandra could feel them sitting behind her eyes, their presence as heavy as two fat, furred spiders bouncing on a web.

(Get up, Cassandra.)

Their voices wove together as one, so loud and encompassing that Cassandra mistook it for her own thought. She'd hooked her elbow onto the vanity table and dragged herself halfway onto her knees before she realized it wasn't.

"Get out of my head."

(Not just now. Now we need your legs. Ours have become . . . unreliable.)

A flash then, of skin twisted and melted together, bones joining to other bones as tributaries into a larger river. The image couldn't be hers. She'd never seen that part of the Moirae. The legs uncovered. And even in her darkest thoughts, she couldn't have conjured something so painfully wrong.

"What do you want my legs for?" Cassandra looked at her reflection. A single dot of blood hung on her upper lip. She touched her ear and her fingers came away dry.

(To ferry a message.)

"Forget it." She wiped the blood away on her sleeve. "Get out." Except she didn't mean it. Not really. The longer Clotho and Lachesis sat inside her mind, the more at home they seemed. It wasn't crowded, or an invasion. It was company. When one or the other or both of them took control of her legs and stood, Cassandra went pleasantly slack inside.

Sort of lovely, to not have to do things on my own.

(Yes. Very lovely. You are very lovely, Cassandra.)

Cassandra smiled into the mirror. One half of each eye had turned green.

"Should we go to Athena's, then?"

———

Hermes' fever held steady. He didn't wake. Aside from swallowing and shivering when Athena spoon-fed him bowl after bowl of hot broth that evening, he hadn't moved at all.

"Hermes," Athena whispered. "Can you hear me?"

She listened so intently for a response that she jumped at the sound of Odysseus' shoes on the floor.

"Come on," he said, and squeezed her shoulder. "Let's get you some air."

He led her upstairs into her bedroom and straight through to the widow's walk. The cool night hit her square in the chest. Odysseus moved to the railing beside her.

It had been tense in the house with Hermes ill, and tense between Athena and Odysseus. The ghost of Calypso was around every corner. Sometimes, Athena passed Odysseus in the kitchen and felt the pressure of a hundred things keeping them apart. Other times, such as there on the walk with him, they felt closer than skin to skin.

"We shouldn't stay up here long," she said. "Ares is out running the wolves, and I don't want Hermes to wake up alone."

Odysseus said nothing. But it hung in the air anyway. Hermes might not wake up. She might never hear his annoying, wiseass voice ever again. The fever was high and mean. A mortal would have been dead hours ago.

Odysseus bent his head and kissed Athena's shoulder. He turned her toward him and kissed her cheeks, her closed eyes, and finally her lips. He slipped his arms around her and held her tight, kissing her deeper until her mind was a blank, until she was nothing but body.

"It's not wrong," he said. "I was just afraid."

"It is wrong," she said, but she kissed him again.

A branch snapping underfoot made them draw apart. It was Cassandra, walking slowly across the grass.

"Good thing Ares is in the woods," Odysseus said, and waved, but Cassandra didn't look up. She didn't look at much of anything.

Athena's hackles raised with every step the girl took. Just before Cassandra disappeared from view, her eyes flickered to the widow's walk.

Brown eyes gone half green.

She grabbed Odysseus' arm.

"That's not Cassandra."

They dashed down the stairs. Odysseus grabbed a sword off the wall and made a good show of being ready to use it.

"What do you mean it's not Cassandra?" he asked. "Who the bloody hell is it, then?"

Athena leaned down and, as gently as she could, shoved the couch and Hermes away from the door as far as it would go.

"I don't know who exactly. But I think it's the Moirae. Wearing her face."

Whoever it was knocked. Three times. Odysseus swore. Athena shook the fist out of her hand and walked to the entryway.

She took a deep breath, ready to knock the Moirae flat on Cassandra's ass. But when the door opened, Cassandra simply stood there without a jacket on. Wet dirt and trampled grass stuck to her bare feet. Beneath the weak house lights it was hard to tell that something was wrong with her eyes. If she hadn't looked up at the balcony, Athena might not have noticed at all.

"What is it?" Odysseus asked, and the thing wearing Cassandra smiled a wrong smile, as though it hadn't figured out quite how to use her face.

"Aren't you going to invite us in?"

"Who are you?" Athena asked.

"Clotho," a voice that wasn't quite Cassandra's voice replied.

"And Lachesis," added a voice that wasn't quite Cassandra's voice but wasn't exactly the first voice, either.

Athena waited a long beat before asking, "But not Atropos?"

They shook their head.

"It is she we come to discuss. But we have to hurry. We don't have much time."

Cassandra sat mute inside her mind. She felt Clotho and Lachesis' reactions as if they were her own, and heard every thought they had. Athena looked so frightened. She wished she could tell her that there was no guile in these Moirae. That they meant her no harm.

Walking into the house, she saw Odysseus standing in front of the couch where Hermes lay. A sword was in his hand, gripped tight. It seemed somehow amusing to Cassandra, and she wanted to wave to him from inside her mind. Inside her mind, as through a window. But when she tried, Lachesis pressed her hand gently down.

Clotho and Lachesis. The Moira of Life and the Moira of Destiny. They maneuvered Cassandra's body poorly; one eye tracked later than the other, and the way they walked had a strange side-to-side tilt. Beneath the lights of her living room, Athena saw that strands of red and silver-blonde hair had twisted into Cassandra's brown.

"What are you doing with Cassandra?" Odysseus asked. "Is she all right?"

"She is fine. Here with us. We would not harm her." They looked around the house, jerking Cassandra's head like a puppet.

Athena wanted them out. Out of her living room, and out of Cassandra, and she wanted them out now.

"Then what do you want?" Athena asked.

"We want to tell you what is." They made their way to the middle of the room and stopped, seemingly content to stand and go no farther.

"Tell us what is?" Odysseus asked. "That's all? After you tried to kill us?"

"We did not. But some of you have died." Cassandra's head turned, a little too far. A joint popped, and her head turned back quickly, as though the Moirae were surprised by the limit. "It is Atropos who kills you. Atropos who would kill us all."

Athena remembered how the Moirae had looked on Olympus. Clotho and Lachesis were two deflating balloons, bleeding into their dark-headed sister.

"All this time we have struggled with her in secret," they said. "Our sister is sick. And when the Moirae of Death is ill, she spreads her sickness down. To all her leaves and branches." They peered past Odysseus, to Hermes, lying still on the couch.

"He's unwell," they said. "He'll be gone soon."

Fast, angry tears blurred Athena's vision. A fat lot of nerve they had, coming into her house and telling her that her dying brother was dying. A fat lot of nerve, coming to them now. When it was too late.

"We need to kill her," said Clotho, or Lachesis, or perhaps both. "Kill Atropos."

"So kill her," Athena said.

"She is weakened. But she will not go easily."

"So kill her harder."

The Moirae inside Cassandra frowned. They looked at Athena the way a parent looks at a child they've just discovered has been spoiled.

"You have other brothers," they said. "Other sisters. Think of them."

Athena wanted to tell them where they could stick it, but only clenched her fists.

"You'll help us now," Clotho and Lachesis said. "You and Cassandra. You'll help us kill Atropos to win your lives back. And in exchange for your lives . . ."

In her mind Athena ransacked the house for any weapon she could use to batter the Moirae out of Cassandra's body. They came with balls the size of grapefruits, demanding help and payment for their lives besides.

"What the hell can you possibly want?" Athena asked.

"After Atropos falls," the Fates sighed. "Cassandra will join us."

"Join you?" Odysseus said. "What do you mean, 'join you'?"

"The Moirae are three. Life, Destiny, and Death. We can cut Death out. But Death must replace her."

Athena looked hard into Cassandra's eyes, trying to see any of her in there. Could she hear? Was she trying to fight while they stood there talking? Was she afraid? Angry? But no matter where Athena looked, all she saw were the Moirae. They'd invaded Cassandra's head and taken over, and before they were through, they would take the rest of her, too.

"She is ours, anyway," the Moirae said, and shrugged with Cassandra's shoulders. "Our perfect creation, brought into being by us, given the gift of prophecy by us, and touched with the hand of Death. It was all put into motion so long ago."

The Moirae pursed Cassandra's lips and crooned inwardly to her, as if crooning to a pretty bird they'd recently swallowed.

A perfect creation. But that's not what Athena saw. Athena saw a girl with too many lives inside. Too many pains and wrongs and losses. A girl her brother Aidan had loved and ruined, but mostly loved.

I promised to take care of her. And even though she hates me, she's still my friend.

"Would you take me instead?" Athena asked.

"What? No. No, they won't take you instead!" Odysseus stared at her as though she'd lost her mind. She wanted to look at him, to try to explain, but if she did that she'd never be able to say what she had to.

"I can take lives as well as she can," Athena said. "I'm strong. You can give me the sight."

"Understand what you offer, goddess," said Clotho. "To join us is to become us. To join us is to disappear."

And that's what you intended for Cassandra. To put her through all this shit, just to lose herself anyway.

"Of course I understand," Athena said. "I'm a goddess. Not a stolen girl."

The Moira wearing Cassandra considered the trade. And nodded. An obsolete goddess of battle would become the Moira of Death. It was more than fair, on all sides.

"Athena, you can't do this," Odysseus said. "How do we even know they're telling the truth?"

"As a token of good faith," Clotho said in her Cassandra-but-not-Cassandra voice, "we will tell you a very great secret."

"What's that?" Athena asked.

"Achilles is here. Now. In Cassandra's house."

23

ACHILLES

"Don't. Linger." Andie brushed Henry's fingers away from her bare belly. "On my scars."

"Why not?" he asked, and walked his fingers right back where they'd started. Four clean cuts slashed across her belly, gently pink.

"Because I don't like to think about them. I rub fricking Bio Oil on them twice a day hoping they'll disappear."

But they never would. They would remain, shiny and smooth, with small pockmarks at the edges where the stitches had grown into the skin. Henry hadn't realized how close he'd come to losing her that day in the road, when the Nereid raked its claws across her stomach. Nobody had until it was over, and Hermes noticed all the blood that had soaked into her shirt.

"So close," he whispered.

"Yeah. Close to spilling my guts out across the hood of

your old Mustang." She covered her eyes with one hand, reclined on his pillow. She talked tough, but her stomach clenched beneath his palm. It had to be a strange thing, to know what it felt like to almost be disemboweled. Henry could relate. He knew what it felt like to almost have his jugular torn out.

He touched the scar on his cheek.

"Yours is prettier than mine," she said, and touched it, too.

"Handsomer, you mean. And no it isn't. I'd rather have yours. Tiger stripes."

She laughed. "Tiger stripes. You're so full of it." She pulled him close and wrapped her arms around his neck. They kissed, and the house was quiet. He'd thought he heard Cassandra come home a while ago, but couldn't be sure. At the time, he'd been trying to keep an angry Andie from storming out. But Andie thought she'd won. That she'd convinced him to stay himself, and not die and come back and let Hector in. But letting Hector in was the only way. When he was a true hero, she would see that.

Something mood-killing and cold dug into his side: Lux's wet nose.

"Ew. Go away, boy."

"He's mad." Andie smiled. "We're taking up the whole bed."

Lux whined and paced around a minute before turning to stare at Henry's closed door.

"Maybe he has to go out." Henry hauled himself up and opened it, motioning for the dog to go through. Lux lowered his head and backed up two steps.

"Come on, what's the matter?" Henry made to clap his

hand to his leg and stopped. Andie sat up nervously. Now that the door was open, the house was too quiet. There were no sounds from downstairs. No muffled TV or clinking dishes in the kitchen.

Lux stared into the dark hallway, pinning and unpinning his ears. Henry knew enough of his language to understand. *Something is out there. Don't go out there.*

"HECTOR!"

Andie clapped her hand over her mouth.

"HEEECTORR!"

Henry held his breath.

It was Achilles. Achilles was in their house.

There were no wolves in the woods except Ares' own. No coyotes, no bears. Nothing more interesting than a couple of city raccoons and a few dozen of his sister's reflector-eyed owls.

Ares listened to the quick steps of Panic rustle through the brush. Oblivion trotted behind, but made no sound. In their wake, the ghosts of Famine and Pain howled miserably, unable to catch up. His poor, missed wolves. He'd let the Moirae use them, and he'd paid the price.

Ares looked up at the cold yellow moon. He'd been running beneath it with Panic and Oblivion for over an hour. It was something he'd always loved to do. Aphrodite had never understood that. She'd rather he be an indoor dog, free of dirt and draped in expensive clothes. But he went out to run anyway. Under the moon, like their sister Artemis.

He remembered Artemis' blood splashed across the jungle. It was probably still there. Wet. Dead.

But that was the only memorial she would want. And if she had to die, that was the death she would want.

If she had to die.

Ares flexed his hand. Parts of it had scabbed over, but the scabs around his knuckles and the folds of his palm broke easily. Artemis had gotten the death she wanted. The death she deserved. Would he? Aphrodite certainly wouldn't. Aphrodite would die mad, frothing at the mouth, when she should die in his arms. Looking into his eyes. Knowing who he was.

He wiped blood across the front of his shirt. He'd probably never see his Aphrodite again, and if he wanted the death he deserved, he would have to go seek it out.

The scent of carrion hit his nose. The wolves had opened their mouths to taste the wind, their eyes fixed back the way they'd come. It was their breath he smelled.

"What is it?" he asked.

Guests, the wolves replied.

"The ladder in Cassandra's room," Andie whispered. His parents had a fire ladder installed outside Cassandra's window when they were children. Who knew if it still worked? But Henry didn't intend to check. Achilles was in his house, and that filled him with rage as well as fear. He regretted that he'd let Athena hold on to the shield.

How he ached to face Achilles with that. And beat him with it.

Henry edged into the hallway and felt his dog quick by his side. A low growl rumbled through Lux's body even as his tail tucked between his legs. Henry put a hand on his head and scratched.

"Andie," he said, and nodded to the dog.

"Henry," she hissed back, but she understood. *Take care of Lux.*

Every time his foot hit a creak on the stairs, his heart stopped.

It doesn't matter. He knows where you are anyway. And he's too much of a dick to sneak an attack from behind.

"Hec-tor," Achilles sang out, and the light turned on in the den.

"My name is Henry."

"No it isn't. Not down deep. Down deep you're him as much as I'm me."

"I'm pretty sure Achilles never had an Australian accent."

Achilles laughed, and the sound made Henry grind his teeth hard enough to taste dust. He wasn't Hector, but he still hated Achilles. How much must they have hated each other back then, for it to carry through their blood for so many thousand years?

He took the last step and walked down the hall to the den. Andie came behind him with her hand on Lux's collar. When she saw inside the room, she gasped.

Achilles had taken two chairs from the kitchen and set them with their backs to the TV. Then he'd strapped Henry's parents to them and gagged them with cloth. His dad's nose was broken. His mom wept.

"I'll kill you," Henry growled.

Achilles laughed, free and easy until the smile that went along with it slid off his face.

"That's the spirit, mate." He reached into his back pocket and drew out a long, silver knife. To demonstrate its sharpness, he cut off some of Henry's mom's hair.

"You fucking prick!" Andie shouted.

Achilles paid no attention. He jerked Henry's mom's head back and slid the knife down her temple. He seemed worse, somehow. More unhinged. More wrathful. Perhaps it was something the Moirae had done. Perhaps they'd been infusing him with hate on his way to godhood.

"Doesn't even know who you are, does she?" Achilles asked. "Her own son."

"Let them go."

"Before I tell them?" he grinned. "Before I make you pick one?"

Henry looked to each. Even though his brain screamed that he could never choose, he knew he would.

"Eye for an eye, as they say."

"Hector killed Patroclus," Henry said. His parents looked so confused, and helpless. "And you killed Hector. You killed Hector, and so many more."

"Yeah, well. Some people are worth more eyes than others." Achilles spun his knife, twisted, and, before Henry could move, carved a scar to match Henry's into his father's cheek. It bled horribly. The sight of so much red, so much of his father's blood, made Henry dizzy. Behind him, Andie quietly began to cry.

"You killed Patroclus," Achilles said. "And you stole my shield. As if you were worthy of it." He bared his teeth. "I'll be having it back now. Is it here?"

"I can take you to it," Henry said. "You can have it. I know it's yours."

Lux whined and squirmed in Andie's grip, maybe smelling the blood.

Achilles sighed.

"No, I suppose they wouldn't let you keep it here," he said. "I suppose they won't even let you use it, now that Athena's back. She'll be the one to face me with it, and that will really be something." Achilles wagged his knife back and forth. "Much more gratifying than this. I thought this would be fun. But it's cruel.

"And it really isn't fair, making you choose when I've already cut this one up." He grabbed Henry's dad by the shoulder and turned the knife in his fist, angling the blade downward and raising it over his head.

Henry's mind flashed on Michael Myers. On the shower scene from *Psycho*. He screamed as the knife came down. They all did. His dad closed his eyes. His mom shouted through her gag.

The windows behind the TV shattered, and an enormous black wolf rose up on two legs. Panic came through the second window and used Oblivion's distraction to knock Achilles away. They crashed into the TV and rolled through broken glass. Achilles made no sound, but Panic yelped miserably when Achilles shoved the knife through its side.

Henry darted forward and dragged his dad's chair out of the way. Andie did the same for his mom, taking her far across the room with a shell-shocked Lux in tow.

"Hector!" Achilles shouted and leaped, so damn fast, and Henry stood between him and his father, no time to think about the eight inches of steel about to be buried in his stomach, or his neck, or driven right down into his head.

What was done would be done, and maybe he'd leave the rest of them alone.

I wish Andie would close her eyes.

"Achilles!"

Ares jumped through the broken window. His arm shot out and grasped Achilles' wrist. The way his knuckles whitened, Henry knew the force of the grip would have broken a normal person's arm. But Achilles didn't even drop the knife. The point hung suspended, inches from Henry's chest.

"God of war," Achilles said, and looked up at Ares from under his brow. "It's an honor."

"You stabbed my wolf." Ares shoved Achilles hard and sent him skidding nowhere near far enough. Oblivion circled around behind, but didn't attack. It seemed to know it would catch a knife in its throat. Instead it hunkered low on its paws and blocked as much of Henry's mom and Andie with its body as it could.

"He-Henry," Ares barked, like he'd just remembered Henry's name. "Do you have anything to cut into this prick with?"

"No."

"Here." Ares pulled two knives out of his back pocket and tossed one end over end. Henry reached out and caught it by the handle—barely. He swallowed. He'd almost grabbed it wrong and skewered himself like an idiot.

He had to focus. On his training. He'd trained with Athena. He'd even trained with Achilles.

Henry stared at the knife in his hands. He wasn't afraid, exactly, though he knew he should be. He was just . . . numb. The knife felt fake. Made of rubber. So out of place in his grip that he didn't know whether to laugh or cry.

"Taking hostages." Ares clucked his tongue. "The old Achilles was a warrior. Not a whackjob."

"The old Achilles died." Achilles grinned. "This Achilles can't. This Achilles is a god."

Ares spun the knife in his fingers. "Don't get ahead of yourself."

Ares stepped forward; Achilles stood his ground. Henry walk-stumbled around the side of the couch. Anyone bothering to look would have seen the tip of his knife shaking. All his anger had leaked out with his father's blood.

When they jumped, Henry meant to go with them. But they were too fast. They hit in the center of the room like a thunderclap, and he stood frozen, watching them wrench and tear at each other. No tentative cuts. Ares shoved Achilles away and he flew into Oblivion, into his mother's chair. Achilles reached back and slashed at anything he could find. Andie dragged Lux out of the way and screamed when the knife cut through the muscle of her shoulder.

That made Henry move. He crossed the room fast, ready to throw himself onto Achilles' knife. With some luck, the blade in his chest would give him enough time to land a stab of his own.

And he'll die. If I can find his heart, he'll die and stay dead.

But Achilles didn't drive his knife into Henry's chest. He flipped it and brought the handle down on the top of his head.

"Later," he whispered as Henry buckled at his feet.

The room blacked in and out. Henry heard sounds, shouts, words, Lux barking. Ares and Achilles struggled again in the middle of the room, their movements too fast for Henry's spinning vision. He heard something like a growl, and Achilles' hand stuffed into Ares' gut.

There's a knife on the end of that hand.

Another moment flickered past, and Achilles jumped through the broken window. Henry couldn't be sure, but it seemed that Achilles had been holding something in his arm. Something loose, and wet, and pink. Achilles had been holding his own intestines in his hands.

"Andie," Henry said, right before he lost consciousness.

PART III

ONE FATE

24

LIES CAVE IN

"Did you kill him?" were the first words out of Henry's mom's mouth when Andie yanked her gag. "Did you kill him?"

"No," Ares groaned. "He can't be killed."

"What are you saying? Of course he can be killed. You cut through his stomach. He's probably out there now, on the ground."

Henry's head pounded, but he hauled himself up and un-gagged his dad, then started working on the knots in the rags used to tie him to the chair.

"We need to call the police," his dad said.

"We need to call Athena," Ares corrected. "She'll coordinate . . . hospitals." His voice was low and far away. Henry glanced at him, fearful he'd see the god losing consciousness, or holding his own guts in his hands. The idea brought back a flash of Achilles, diving through the window with ropes of intestine looped over his wrist. Henry gagged.

But Ares wasn't holding his stomach. His gut wound looked like a clean stab, just leaking blood and nearly forgotten. Ares looked down at the floor, where Panic lay limp.

"Damn it." Henry finished with his dad and wadded some of the rags together to press to the cut on his cheek. "Andie?"

"I'm okay," she said. "Lux is okay. Your mom is okay." She had finished with the knots holding his mom's feet and started on her hands. Her left arm was a sleeve of red, but her hand was steady.

"Where's Cassandra?" his mom asked. "Is she all right? Did any of you see her upstairs?!"

"I didn't think she was home," Andie said. But before anyone could really panic, Athena kicked in the door and ran inside, with Odysseus and Cassandra behind her.

"Cassandra! Thank god!"

Cassandra blinked hard twice. The sight before her eyes made no sense. Overturned furniture. Her parents wearing bracelets of rags. There was a blood-soaked bandage on her dad's cheek. And in the center, Ares stood motionless over the body of a red wolf.

"Where were you?" her dad asked, though she thought the answer was a little obvious. Athena was right beside her. She'd been with Athena.

Only that wasn't quite true. Clotho and Lachesis had been with Athena. Cassandra had last been in her room, where they'd wormed inside her head. But they were gone now. Back at Athena's house, two creatures that resembled translucent, elongated crustaceans lay ground into the carpet. One had fallen out of Cassandra's nose. The other from her ear. She'd crushed both beneath her feet and listened to them crunch like hard candies.

Henry lurched from behind their father to kneel over the top of Panic. He pressed a reluctant hand to its chest.

"He's not dead," he said, and Ares knelt beside him. "He might be okay, if we get him to a vet."

"It isn't a dog," Ares said. He sounded slow. In shock. Blood had soaked one of his pant legs all the way to the knee.

"Well, can it pretend to be a dog?" Henry asked, and the wolf whispered an answer. "Talking isn't a good start," Henry said to it. "I'll take him. Ares, you have to stay here. The vet will take one look at your gut and send you to the ER." He heaved the wolf up in his arms and made a face when the creature rose onto two feet to help. Oblivion nosed closer, mostly on all fours.

"Stay." Henry pointed at it, and it lowered its head.

"What does he mean? What's wrong with your gut?" Athena asked. "Are you all right?"

"I took a stab. Nothing to write home about." Ares stood straighter while Athena lifted his shirt. The wound was deep and bad. It pulsed blood and opened like a mouth every time he breathed.

"What were you doing here?" Athena asked.

"He saved us," Cassandra's mother answered for him. "Him and his dogs. They jumped through the windows and stopped him. That boy—that boy was going to kill your father."

"I'm okay, Maureen." Cassandra's dad went to her and hugged her tight. "We have to call the police. That kid, whoever he was, can't have gotten far."

"Oh, you can bet he'll be miles away," Ares said.

"No," said Cassandra's mother. "He couldn't be. I saw you cut through his stomach. He was holding his . . . his . . ."

"Yeah, well. He'll have stuffed all those back in by now. Just a little nick for him. Won't even leave a scar."

Cassandra watched her parents. They were surrounded by familiar faces, but each became more foreign and confusing with every passing moment. She knew how they felt. It had been the same for her, when Aidan had suddenly become something different.

"We're going to have to get you all to hospitals," Odysseus said. "Andie, come let me look at your arm."

"Henry should go, too. He was hit on the head. He might have a concussion," Andie said while Odysseus and Athena studied the deep gash on her shoulder. It looked as though someone had taken a hatchet to her.

Cassandra felt like vomiting. Achilles had come into her home and defiled it. Everywhere she looked there was blood. Splashed across her family's den. Sinking into the carpet. The people she loved stood afraid inside their own walls. Achilles was forever an invader. A sacker of cities. He snuck in quietly and brought red death with him. Only this time her family hadn't died.

Ares and his wolves had saved them all.

Cassandra chanced a look at Ares, half-expecting the same old hate to flare into her hands. It didn't.

"We can stitch Ares up," Odysseus said. "But Andie and Tom should go to the clinic."

Athena turned to Cassandra's mother.

"Maureen," she asked. "Are you okay?"

Cassandra watched her mom sputter.

"And it feels strange to say this in such a crowd," Odysseus said, "but I think we're shorthanded. Cassandra, do you know how to get in touch with Thanatos?"

"Um, no, I—" She didn't know where he was. And had no phone number to contact him. They should have thought of that, it seemed. But every time she'd needed him, he'd just been there.

"Never mind," Athena said. "He's right behind you."

Cassandra looked over her shoulder and, true enough, Thanatos walked in through the broken doorway.

"The Moirae?" he asked.

"Gone," Athena replied.

"I'll take Andie to the hospital," Odysseus said. "She's got to go now."

"What are we going to say?" Andie asked.

"I don't know. That you fell on something sharp. I'm a great liar. Don't sweat it." He took the keys to her Saturn and nodded to Athena before they ducked out the door.

"What is going on here?" Cassandra's dad asked after they went. "Why do they have to make up a story? And why isn't anyone calling the police?"

Athena looked at Cassandra. This wasn't something to cover up. They'd seen too much.

But could she use her god's tricks and lie it away? Would that be easier? Could we go back to before? The family we were before.

"We've got butterfly bandages in the first-aid kit,"

Cassandra said. "I'll go. You start talking. And don't leave anything out."

Cassandra bandaged her father's cheek together as best she could. Athena might have done a better job, but it felt like she should do it. He was her father.

For the next hour, Athena talked to Cassandra's parents in a low, reasonable voice about mad, unreasonable things. They scoffed at first, and then their eyes bugged out of their heads. Ares showed his wounds. Athena showed her feathers. At one point, Oblivion rose up on its hind legs and spoke. They told them everything. What they were. Who their children were. When Athena told them about strangling Cassandra to death in the woods, her mother put her fingers to her mouth and wept. Slowly, the gods' tricks reversed from lies to truth.

"We should go now, to the clinic." Athena stood. "You can go yourselves, if you think you can handle it."

"Yes," her dad said. "We'll tell them I was working in the garage and my hand slipped." His eyes were tired, and mostly vacant. They passed over the mess and carnage in his house. He pulled Cassandra's mom to her feet and clamped his arm around her shoulders.

When they walked past Cassandra it was as if they'd never seen her before.

Her mom stopped.

"But—Henry is still our Henry, isn't he?"

Athena frowned. "Cassandra is still *your* Cassandra. Don't misunderstand."

"Of course," her mom said. They walked out and got into the car.

"Will they come back, do you think?" Cassandra asked.

"They just need time," Athena said. "Like you did with Aidan. They're your parents."

"*Your* father abandoned you," Cassandra said.

"Yes. But he was a god. So, sort of a shit to begin with."

Cassandra felt the goddess' hand on her shoulder. Past them in the den, Thanatos moved through the room righting chairs and collecting bandage wrappers for the trash. So much had been broken. So much to repair. And Cassandra wouldn't be there for any of it.

"I heard what you said to the Moirae." She turned out of Athena's grip and looked at her dead-on. "I was there. I could hear, even though I didn't care." She remembered the euphoric, blurry feeling of having them in her mind, of being on the inside of her own face as if inside a mask.

"You don't need to worry," Athena said. "They agreed to the deal. I'll take your place."

"That's not what I was going to say."

"Listen, it doesn't matter. This is our mess. And besides, I made a promise to Aidan."

25

BLOOD STAINS

When Athena returned to her house, Hermes greeted her from the couch.

"Where've you been? What's all the excitement?"

The shock of hearing his voice made her knees buckle, but she got her legs underneath her fast enough when he looked ready to jump from the couch and help.

"Stay!" She pointed. "Stay there. I'm fine. None of the blood is mine. Most of it is Ares'."

"Most of it?"

She went to the couch and pressed her hand to his forehead.

The fever was gone. He'd kicked all of the ice packs onto the floor like a child.

"You're so difficult," she said, smiling. "You wake at the worst times. I wanted to be here. I didn't want you to wake up alone."

"I knew I wasn't alone. Packed into all these blankets? And my mouth still tastes like broth."

"You must want real food. And maybe a hot bath? Or a warm bath?"

He put his hand on hers.

"I want to know what's happening."

"No. You don't want to know that," she said, trying to spare him. But he made a stern face, so she told him anyway.

"I've slept through my part," he said when she was through. "I wasn't here to keep you from making false promises."

She squeezed his thin hand. He wouldn't be there to stop her from keeping them, either.

"Where's Ares?" he asked.

"Hanging around outside Cassandra's house. He's convinced that her parents are going to return with the National Guard. And he's worried about Panic."

She hoped the wolf made it. They owed it now, and Ares and Oblivion, too. Even Cassandra knew it.

"Isn't he injured?" Hermes asked.

"Yeah, but he stitched it up himself. It was pretty disgusting."

Hermes pushed himself into an upright position and reached for a cup of water.

"What's there to eat?" he asked. "Or should we order out?"

"There's a ham in the refrigerator. And a few dozen sandwich rolls. What do you think you could eat?"

"At least a few dozen ham sandwiches. Be a peach?"

"There's no need to bat your eyes." Athena hauled herself

up. But before she let go of his hand, she leaned down and kissed his forehead. He tasted of sweat and sickness. Hermes was awake. But he was not well. He was not better.

Athena pulled the ham out of the refrigerator and grabbed two knives: one for the bread and ham, and another for mayo. As she assembled sandwich after sandwich, she stole glances back into the living room to make sure his eyes were still open.

Headlights flashed in the driveway. Andie, dropping Odysseus off at home.

"It can't be," Odysseus exclaimed when he came through the door. "You're awake!"

Athena smiled at their reunion, full of laughter and fond insults and manly embraces.

"Where's your sister?"

"In the kitchen."

Odysseus rounded the corner and grasped her around the waist, lifting her half a foot off the ground.

"A bad night turns good," he whispered.

"A good night all around." She looked into his eyes. "Hermes is awake, and nobody died. Except maybe Panic."

"Panic's set to make a full recovery. Andie heard from Henry while we were at the hospital. The mutt'll be out in a day."

"How's Andie?"

"Stitches. Another scar to add to her collection. But you're right. It could've been worse." He nodded toward the plate of ham buns. "Any of those for me?"

"Maybe one." She held it up and walked around him to take the rest to Hermes. Odysseus caught her by the elbow.

"I won't say anything tonight," he said. "About your mad plan. Because your brother is well. But tomorrow . . ."

Odysseus. His eyes were still bright from their kiss upstairs. He wasn't afraid. He didn't think she'd be able to leave him. Athena's heart hammered in her chest.

"Tomorrow," she agreed. "For now, let's just enjoy a night of small favors."

Cassandra had been on her hands and knees for forty minutes with hot water and sponges and carpet spray, but the blood wasn't coming out. Still, she kept scrubbing, wiping sweat from her brow and pretending that the minutes weren't crawling by as she waited for someone, anyone, to come home.

She raised her head at a set of headlights. They didn't slow. Maybe none would. Maybe her parents would go to the emergency vet and grab Henry and drive away without looking back. They'd check into a hotel and send the police for her. The girl who was no longer their daughter.

No. She glanced toward the entryway, where Lux lay with his nose on his paws. *They'll have to come back for him, at least.*

"Should we not have told them?" Thanatos asked from where he knelt, scrubbing at another stain.

"There was no choice," Cassandra said.

"That doesn't mean you can't resent the fact that you had to."

"I know. And I do." She sat back and blew a few wet strands of hair out of her face.

"We've got a steam cleaner around here somewhere," she said, and got up. "How did you know to come anyway? Did you feel them? The Moirae?"

"Yes," Thanatos said. "But I didn't come fast enough. I was worried for you."

"Were you? Or were you curious? Thought they might have solved the puzzle of what I am?" She wiped at her hands with a pink-stained towel. "They did, you know," she said. "They crawled into my head and solved the mystery. Told me straight up."

Thanatos' eyes were somber. His fingers were stained red as the towel, and he'd stayed with her after the rest had gone. He'd stood beside her when her parents had walked past without a second glance.

"Congratulations," she said coolly. "In a few days, I'll be a goddess of death. I'll be like you."

Thanatos set down his sponge.

"Was this what you suspected?" she asked.

"Yes," he said. "And what I was afraid of."

He was doing it again, looking at her, and into her. Only now his curiosity was gone. He looked at Cassandra as if he wanted to remember every curve and color of her face.

"I didn't think death was afraid of anything," Cassandra said.

"Not many things. And not often." Thanatos reached out, slowly, and touched her throat. He drew closer until both hands were on her and he was near enough that Cassandra could feel the cool of his skin. She wondered what his kiss would feel like. She wondered if he could still kill her that way. But before she could protest, he dropped his head to her shoulder and gently brushed his lips against her collarbone.

Her heart didn't stop. He was cool but not cold, and when she shivered it wasn't because of a chill.

"What are you doing?" she asked. It had been a long time since anyone had touched her like that. Her hands slid around Thanatos' waist and grasped his back.

The Saturn and the Mustang pulled into the driveway.

"Something foolish," he replied, and kissed her fingertips.

Lux got up and scratched at the door. It bounced back and forth. It wouldn't close properly anymore. Athena had broken it.

When Andie and Henry came into the house, Thanatos tried to leave, but Cassandra took his hand. There was a lot to tell about her time on the road hunting gods, and Athena's plans for the Moirae. About Calypso. She could use a shoulder to lean on.

Cassandra's mom flinched whenever their hands touched. She didn't even try to hide it. They needed time, Athena had said. But her parents glanced at each other like prisoners in a yard, plotting escape. Maybe not today, or this month, but eventually Cassandra would come home from school to find an empty house, and a note on the kitchen table if she was lucky.

She didn't blame them. But she wouldn't wait around for it, either. After she and Athena had dealt with Atropos, she would join the Moirae. Cassandra would disappear again, only this time, they wouldn't worry or search. This time they'd be relieved.

Henry sat at the table eating bacon, half a strip for him, half a strip for Lux, in a slow, salty pattern. He hadn't said much since she'd told him about the Moirae's plan. And about Calypso. The truth about Calypso.

But she hadn't told him everything. Her intent to join the Moirae she kept to herself. Because no matter how wrong she was, or how tainted, he and Andie would want her to stay.

There was still life here worth living. Cassandra looked down at the dishrag in her hand. If only her mess could wipe away clean.

"You guys are being jerks," Henry said. Everyone in the kitchen turned, but he was only talking to their parents.

"Henry?" their mom asked. "Are you all right?"

"Am I still your kid, you mean?" He frowned. "Yeah. I still am. And so is she."

Their parents looked down at their feet, ashamed as children caught teasing a dog.

"Of course she is," their dad said. "It's just strange knowing . . . all of this."

"I know," Henry said. "It was strange for me, too. But I didn't act like a total dick."

"I don't know how you think we're supposed to respond—"

"Better," he said. "The world's the same as it was yesterday. You just know about it now. I know you haven't had much time to process, or whatever." He stood up and put his backpack over his shoulder. "But both of your kids might be dead tomorrow. So you might want to speed it up."

"Dead? What do you mean 'dead'?!" Their mom chased him out the door, but he was in his car and out of the driveway before she made it down the front steps.

"Cassie," her dad said. "What did he mean, 'dead'? Tomorrow?" He took her by the shoulder and tucked her hair back. Her mom came back inside and grabbed her phone.

"What are you doing?" Cassandra asked.

"Calling the police."

"Mom. You don't want to do that."

"Why not?"

"Because we know a lot of the police. And they'll all get killed."

Her mom hesitated with the phone halfway to her ear.

"This isn't real," she said, and hung up.

"It is," Cassandra said softly. "But it's almost over."

Her dad squeezed her shoulder.

"I need you to tell us everything," he said, and she nodded. There was fear in her mom's eyes, but not fear of her. It would be all right. Cassandra looked into the driveway, where the Mustang usually sat.

Henry. Always the peacemaker.

26

NEW VS. OLD

Hermes texted Henry before he got to school, so Henry headed for McDonald's and looped back around toward Athena's house. He hadn't figured on going to many classes anyway.

"Henry." Odysseus sat up when he walked in. "What're you doing here?"

He held up a greasy paper bag. "Egg McMuffins." He held up another bag. "Pancakes and hash browns. Hermes texted. When did he wake up?"

"Last night."

"Where is he?"

Odysseus' face darkened. "We moved him to his room so he'd be more comfortable. And less underfoot." He smiled sadly. "You've never seen a worse patient. He's lobbying for one of those little bells."

"I thought he might be . . . up and around."

Odysseus shook his head. Hermes would never be up and around again.

"Can I go in?" Henry asked. "Or is Athena there?"

"Athena's out back, waiting for Ares to get home with the mutt." Odysseus cocked his head. "You surprised me last night, when you helped him. I mean, I know you've got a soft spot for four-legs, but that same four-leg put you and your dog in the hospital this winter."

"I guess saving my parents' lives goes a long way."

Odysseus nodded. "Guess so."

Henry walked down the hall, trying to decide what face to wear when he saw Hermes. How happy was too happy, and too hopeful of recovery? How sad was too sad, and insulting about the way he looked?

"Don't bother knocking, just get those bags in here," Hermes called. "I've been smelling that greasy wonderful crap since the minute you walked through the front door."

Henry walked in, holding up the bags like Santa's sacks, and Hermes held his arms out eagerly, all bones. The god in the bed was a skeleton with stretched-out skin. He looked so weak. It made Henry second-guess the favor he'd come to ask.

"You're a godsend," Hermes said, and tore into the first McMuffin. He'd asked for a variety pack of sausage and egg, and Henry had taken the liberty of sneaking in a few bacon, egg, and cheese biscuits. "Are you hungry? Do you want half a hash brown?"

"No," Henry said. "I'm fine. Is there anything else you need?"

"Well, you could butter my pancakes."

"God. Odysseus was right. You're a terrible patient." He

reached into the bag for a handful of butter packets and a plastic knife.

"I've missed you, mortal," Hermes said. "And your little girlfriend, too."

"We were here," Henry said. "We came to see you. You had us worried."

"I should have been the one worried," Hermes said. His chewing slowed. "I'm sorry I wasn't there when Achilles came. I looked after you well enough until you really needed looking after. Then I passed out."

"That wasn't your fault."

"Maybe not." Hermes shrugged. "But nothing ever seems to be. Not my fault, and not my doing. I wasn't the one who brought our sisters home. Or got us out of Hephaestus' house. Or even got you that fine shield. You did that. I drove."

"You can't think that way," Henry said. "You did everything we needed you to."

"I won't be there," Hermes said. "I didn't even make it to the end. You'll be alone. You and Athena."

"Don't talk like you're already gone. You don't know that."

"My heart hurts every time it beats. Like a countdown. And I know when it's going to hit zero, Henry." He sighed. "Athena will make it all right. She'll make sure you're okay. Even against Atropos, I'd lay money on my sister any day of the week."

Henry sat on the foot of Hermes' bed and bit into a cooling hash brown. He wasn't sure whether Athena had told Hermes that when the battle was over, she'd be gone, joined into the Moirae, but somehow he doubted it.

"She won't be able to help me," he said.

"What do you mean?"

"She'll have her hands full fighting Atropos." He regretted having to ask a favor of a dying friend. But there was no one else to ask. "I saw Achilles last night. The way he moved. The way he fought. I can't beat him."

"You can. Demeter said so."

"She said I could kill him. And maybe that's true. But I'll never get close enough. Not like this."

"Henry," Hermes said through a cheekful of pancake. "What are you talking about?"

"Ares says that the reason Achilles is so strong, the reason they all are—even Odysseus and Cassandra—is because they embody the myths. Because they died and came back with a hero inside."

Hermes pressed deeper into his pile of pillows. Henry thought he saw his heart beating through his T-shirt, and looked away fast.

"And you believe Ares?" Hermes asked.

Henry shrugged. But how could he see Cassandra and Achilles and not believe?

"But," Hermes sputtered, "you and Andie always said that you were yourselves. And you can fight. We trained you, and honestly, you sort of could to begin with. Probably why you both had such stellar ice-hockey careers—"

"Hermes. I'm asking you if you have the energy." He nodded toward the god's thin hands. "And the breath to bring me back."

Hermes looked him in the eyes for a long time. But Henry wouldn't change his mind.

"All right," Hermes said. "Odysseus is in the living room. If I don't have the breath for CPR, I'll shout for him."

Athena sat on her back patio, foot up on the damp cushion of a cheap plastic chair. The sun shone bright on young grass, merciless in a cloudless, blue day. Spring gave way to summer already. Beside her, a bucket of beer bottles sat insulated with the ice packs they'd used to cool Hermes.

She took a breath and smelled drying earth and warming leaves. The neighborhood was peaceful. Softly quiet. No indication of the violence that had erupted last night, less than a mile away.

If I was the god I used to be, I'd spur a storm. Something great, and black, and blasting. My winds would tear that little rabbit out from whatever tree he hid under. I'd string him up by his innards and watch him kick.

Wishful thinking. And impossible, even if she possessed the power. Achilles wasn't shivering somewhere in the woods. He was back with Atropos.

The message from Clotho and Lachesis would come soon. Athena knew it as surely as if they'd touched her with the sight already. The message would come, and they would go. Achilles would fall alongside his mistress of death, and Athena would take her place. She hoped not literally.

Clotho and Lachesis had implied that with Atropos gone, the disease and corruption would also be gone. Athena hoped that meant they would go back to separate bodies. She said she would join them, but not at the hip.

The latch on the back gate lifted; a dark-as-night snout pushed through the privacy fence. Oblivion. Even under a bright sun and clear skies, its coat sucked up light like a black hole.

"I thought you'd be back sooner," Athena said.

Ares started, surprised to find her waiting.

"Panic's been cooped up and bandaged too long," he said. "It needed to eat a few raccoons."

The red wolf came into the yard, walking a little stiffly. But it wasn't dead. Its jaws hung open and dripped blood-stained spit. Pieces of the raccoons were stuck in its teeth.

Terrible, wicked wolves. Who saved our friends' lives.

Terrible and wicked, like their master. Athena looked at Ares and noted the fresh blood over the wound in his stomach. What had he ever been, except what he was? What right did she have to expect otherwise?

"How's your stomach?" she asked.

"Hole in it," he said, and shrugged. "Not healing as fast as I'd like." He came to the patio table and shoved her foot off the chair opposite to sit down. He shoved a little harder than necessary, and she hid her smile behind a turned cheek.

"Is this how it is for you?" he asked. "Is this how it is to play the hero? A knife in your guts and a half-dead wolf, and she hasn't even said thank you."

"She hasn't tried to kill you again, either."

He laughed. "That's what passes for gratitude? What a state these mortals are in." He watched his wolves circle each other in the yard. Oblivion snuck in to steal a lick from Panic's reddened teeth. They were grotesquely sweet.

"Not long now, is it?" he asked.

"Nope."

"That why you're out here? Soaking up the rays, making a toast to the first casualty of war?" He nodded to her beer, and squinted skyward at Aidan's sun.

"Making jokes about him now?" Athena asked, and her jaw clenched. "When it was your girlfriend who killed him?"

"It wasn't easy to hear that," he said, voice going lower, and louder. "No matter what you think. He was my brother, too. And Aphrodite didn't know. She didn't."

"But she did it."

Ares made a fist, and Athena took a deep breath. Aphrodite killed Aidan. Aidan killed Poseidon. Cassandra killed Hera. And on, and on, one to the other. The only constant was that they were dead.

"I don't want to do this," Athena said. "I was waiting for you as much as anything."

"Really?" he asked, and she almost laughed. He sounded all of eight years old. The little brother forever in her shadow.

"So," Ares said. "What do we have, besides ourselves? What can we turn to our advantage? Location? Weapons? You should have let me keep Aeacus' scepter."

"So he could pound down our door looking for it? No." Athena took a swallow of beer.

"I wish we still had Uncle Poseidon's head," Ares sighed. "We could call the sea. Recruit an army of Nereids."

"You had Poseidon's head?"

"Right." Ares smiled. "You jumped off the mountain before that part."

"Well . . . where is it?"

Ares frowned. "Aphrodite stashed it when we were on the run. She buried it in a hole in Rhode Island. Two days later she went to dig it up and the whole place was a salt-water marsh. It's gone. Lost."

"You lost our uncle's head?"

"Yes. You turned him into a head, and we lost it. Either way, we can't count it amongst our assets."

"He probably wouldn't have been too big a help anyway, even if we hadn't killed him," Athena said. "The Titans' children seemed to suffer worse than us." She picked at a scab near her neck and tore out a feather like a ragged splinter before tossing it into the yard. Blood leaked hot down her chest. "How do you think Dad died?"

"Zeus? What makes you think he's dead? With the ego on him, he'd probably explode. We'd have heard it, or dreamt it. Or died right along with him."

Athena curled her lip. Ares always put too much stock in their father. She glanced to the yard, where the wolves circled the bloody bit of feather.

"Don't let them eat that," she said, and he shooed them off.

"You should let me carry Achilles' shield," Ares said. "The kid will only get killed and stripped of it." He waited, eyes sharp as though he hoped she'd argue.

"If Henry says you can take it, you can take it. I don't know if Henry will want to go at all."

"Want to?" Ares asked, puzzled. "Who cares if he wants to? And why aren't you planning? Battle strategy. That's your bag of tricks. What's gotten into you?"

"I messed up," Athena said. "I can't be in charge of their lives. I won't be. I'm a soldier now, just like you." She laughed bitterly. She couldn't believe she'd had to say that, and to him of all people.

She reached down into the ice bucket and brought out two fresh beers. Ares looked at her skeptically.

"A little early, isn't it?"

"No, brother. It's late."

Hermes' hands trembled around Henry's neck. Not because he lacked the strength. He might not be able to hold himself upright, but he was still god enough to cut off a mortal's air supply. He was still god enough to crack right through a mortal neck.

But Hermes looked at his thin fingers wrapped around Henry's throat and trembled. They were numb and graceless as dry twigs. He had to be careful, oh so goddamn careful.

"There has to be a better way to do this," he stammered. "Julia Roberts and Kiefer Sutherland made an entire crappy movie about it in the '80s."

"Hermes. You have to."

"I don't have to. *Flatliners*. That's what it was called. Terrible." He squeezed down gently, testing. "And fantastic. Like most things in that decade."

"Hermes."

"I don't know why you had to ask me. I'm your friend. You think I won't mess this up, but I could, I really could—" As he spoke, his grip tightened, and as he kept talking, Henry stopped. Henry turned first red, and then purple. He hit Hermes in the chest. Hermes knew he would, that his blacking-out body would try to defend itself, but it still made the act that much worse. But if he stopped now, Henry would make him do it again on an already bruised neck.

"It'll be all right, when you wake up," Hermes whispered.

"What are you doing?!"

Andie's voice was such a shock that he let go. She stood in the open doorway, eyes wide and furious. Then she shoved him back into the pillows and knelt over Henry, rolling him over and slapping his face.

"Odysseus!" she shouted over her shoulder, and then glared at Hermes. "What were you doing to him?" She pressed her ear to Henry's chest, felt his wrist for a pulse. "Wake up, Henry. Wake up."

"Is he still alive?" Hermes asked.

"You were trying to kill him?" Her face grew as red as Henry's had been a moment ago. "Because you're dying and you think your sister needs another soldier? I should cut your head off!"

At her feet, Henry took a great, whooping breath and started coughing. She knelt and helped him sit up, tugged at his shirt collar as if it could give him more room to breathe.

"Hermes, you stupid asshole," Andie spat. "I don't care if you're dying. I'm glad you are. We're your friends!"

Henry's coughing slowed, and he sat quietly, one hand to his forehead, blocking his eyes. Hermes didn't know if Henry's heart had stopped, but if it had, even for a few seconds, it might have been long enough.

"Andie," Henry said. "I told him to do it."

She drew back as though he'd slapped her in the face.

"Henry?" Hermes asked. "Or Hector?"

"It would be both," he replied. "If he came back, it would be both. But it's just me."

"What do you think you're doing?" Andie asked. "We decided!"

"That was before he tried to kill my parents," Henry said

as she got to her feet and backed away. "That was before I realized I can't beat him. Andie—"

"So you were going to *Invasion-of-the-Body-Snatchers* yourself without even saying anything?" She held up her hands. "Don't. I am so out of here. And don't even think about following me. I don't need a domestic on my record right before college applications."

Odysseus caught Andie by the arm as she darted for the door.

"Oy. What's going on?"

No one responded, but there were many eyes, shooting many daggers. Odysseus sighed.

"Time for a family meeting."

Despite the loss of Aidan and Achilles, the backyard circle had grown larger. Athena looked around at the new faces: at Thanatos, pale beside Cassandra. At Ares and his wolves. They left a space for Hermes, too, who listened through his open window.

They were waiting for Athena to start. To lead. But she refused. And after a moment, Odysseus spoke, catching Cassandra and Thanatos up.

"So," Cassandra said. "If Henry dies, and is brought back, he'll have more than just his memories? I thought it was just me and Achilles."

"So did I," Athena said. "Odysseus hid his strength from us, and not even your ability to kill gods was apparent right away."

She met Cassandra's eyes and saw the smolder there, the

readiness to jump in front of Henry if Athena made the slightest move. Athena shook her head.

"I did hide it," said Odysseus. "So who told?" He looked at Athena, but Ares straightened.

"I did," Ares declared. "I figured it out." He punched Athena in the arm. "And you always said I was stupid."

"Ares," Odysseus muttered. "You dick."

"They had a right to know," Ares said. "To choose. And this one's chosen, so someone choke him out and bring back Hector. We could use him."

"Athena," Odysseus said. "Say something."

"It's Henry's choice," Athena said, and looked around at them. "Your choice, if you want to fight at all. Your choice what to do." She swallowed hard. It still wasn't easy to say. "I'm not your leader. I never was. You don't need us. We needed you."

"She's right," Cassandra said. "We are the weapons here. Me against Atropos. Hector against Achilles. It won't be for the gods to tell us what to do." She nodded to Athena. "We'll wait for the vision from Clotho and Lachesis. And then we'll decide."

27

THE LAST VISION

Cassandra and her parents sat in the kitchen, like troops awaiting orders. Soldiers sitting in a U-boat, ears strained toward the first sounds of exploding shells.

Upstairs, Henry blasted music. He'd locked himself and Lux in his room after he'd explained to their parents for an hour how and why he had Hermes try to squeeze the life out of him.

"Like watching a pot try to boil," Thanatos said from the doorway. "Take a walk with me?"

"It's not like a walk is going to free anything up," Cassandra said, but went out with him anyway, into the faded light of early evening. "I'm not giving birth. It'll come when it comes." But it would be soon. She knew it the same way she knew what side a coin would fall on.

They walked companionably down the block together. The sky was clear and still. There was no breeze.

"Let Athena take your place," Thanatos said.

"No."

"You won't be you, after it's over. You'll be gone."

"So they say," Cassandra muttered, and kicked a pebble.

"You're acting like a stupid kid."

"I am what they think I am," she said. "What they created. I can't let someone take that fate for me. Not even Athena. Besides, I owe Odysseus. A girlfriend for a girlfriend." Cassandra closed her eyes and thought of Calypso's face.

"Why?" Thanatos asked. "Why do you want to be a Moira?"

"It's not that I want to be one," she said. "I already am one."

The Cassandra that used to be, before the gods descended like locusts, felt so far away she might as well have made her up. That was another girl. Aidan was gone and she was, too.

"How do you even know you'll be able to do it?" Thanatos asked. "That you'll be able to call up your power? Since you lost control with Ares, you haven't been the same."

He stopped her, took her by the arm. His fingers were so cold, even through her shirt.

"It didn't feel bad," she said, "to join with them. It didn't hurt." She squeezed her eyes shut.

She was stronger. In control. She could hold her power between her fingers as if it were a candle.

"Isn't this what you wanted me to find, when we met?" Cassandra asked. "Control? Balance? To bring death from someplace other than a place of hate?"

"I didn't want you to find it right before you disappear,"

Thanatos whispered. He touched her cheek, knuckles cool against her skin.

Cassandra looked into his black eyes. He was different from Aidan in every way. Perhaps that made it easier to like him. He would never be a replacement.

"I used to think I was angry at the gods," she said. "But I was just angry. Angry at Apollo for painting a target on my back. Angry at Aidan for being gone."

"You still love Apollo," Thanatos said.

Aidan. Apollo. He couldn't undo the past, but he'd tried to make up for it.

"I guess I do," Cassandra replied. "Why?"

"I don't know," Thanatos said. "I find that I'm jealous. Maybe it's leftovers from Calypso's spell."

He stood before her, a god dressed like a boy. She saw through it now. If Aidan were alive, and came knocking on her door, she'd know him for what he was in an instant.

"If I let you kiss me," she said, "would you try to kill me?"

"No," he said, and pushed his fingers into her hair. "If I kissed you now, I wouldn't. But I would someday."

Someday. But they would never have a "someday." Their time would end when she did.

She pressed her hands to his chest.

Birds chirped loud in her ears. A hundred. A thousand. Too many to populate the elm trees on the sides of the road. It was the vision.

"Birds," she said, and pushed away from Thanatos. "What are you trying to tell me? That you're staying in an aviary?" But the chirping wasn't birds. The wings coming toward her face flapped too fast, and dipped up and down. Birds didn't have fur, or pinched little rat faces.

Bats. They screeched their way past calcite formations and subterranean waterfalls. Cassandra felt the breeze from their wings, felt the warm skin of them pass against her cheeks. If any of their claws caught in her hair, she was going to scream, vision or not.

"What is it?" Thanatos asked.

"Cave system. Adirondacks. There's a newly opened entrance." She could see them, too. The Moirae. Or more accurately, she could feel them, beating like a heart in the center.

28

WALKING STRAIGHT INTO AN AXE

"How's Hermes?" Odysseus asked. He'd come out on the widow's walk to stand with Athena in the dark.

"Sleeping. Ares is with him now."

Odysseus squeezed the wood railing and it groaned. It was a wonder the balcony still stood, after all her pacing and pushing.

"How much longer does he have?" he asked, and her throat tightened.

"Not long." Hermes' breathing had been strained for the last few hours, and the fever was back. He was still conscious, but so weak he could hardly keep his eyes open.

"I'm sorry," Odysseus said. "I know it's hard."

"It shouldn't be," she said bitterly.

"Letting go of anyone is hard."

"No, I mean it shouldn't *be*," she said. "Aidan fell in *battle*. That was bad enough. But Hermes is just lying there. Wasting away while I stand here with my hands tied, waiting to serve the thing that's killing him." Her fingers gripped the wood and rattled it. "Why haven't they told us where to go yet? Why couldn't they have shown up a day earlier? And why do I wish he was already gone, so I wouldn't have to do this knowing that my brother is dead and that wherever I am, I wasn't with him when it happened."

"However he'd die . . . it wouldn't make it easier."

"Stop saying stupid things!" she shouted.

"Why are you yelling at me?" he shouted back.

"Because they've already won. Don't you get it? This isn't a battle. They cost everyone *everything*. And they still win." Athena twisted the railing in her hands and splintered it, wrenching the whole thing loose. It hit the walkway below and cracked. She stared down at it. In the dark, the wood looked like bones.

I wish they were mine. I wish they were mine and Cassandra's both, and we'd leave them with nothing.

"You're not the only one losing everything," Odysseus said angrily. "In fact, I'd say you got the best end of it. You get to sew yourself up with Clotho and Lachesis and come out a butterfly on the other side. A shiny new Atropos in an Athena skin. You won't remember Hermes. Or me. Or if you do, you won't care."

"You'd rather I let Cassandra become the Fate of death?"

"I'd rather you thought of something else!" he shouted. "You're afraid. I get it. You messed up on Olympus and you don't think you have the right to lead them anymore, but you're wrong, Athena. This isn't noble. This is giving up."

He turned and struck the side of the house hard enough to rattle it.

"Just like you and me," he said. "That was giving up, too."

"Odysseus—"

"You never would have done it, if you thought you were going to survive. For you, telling me you love me is the same as saying goodbye."

Athena stepped away from the edge. She regretted tearing the railing down; her hands itched for something to lean on.

"I do love you, Odysseus."

"I know," he said. "But I thought that you and I were real. Not just a dream that I was having."

Ares knocked on her door sometime later.

"Is it Hermes?" she asked.

"No. It's Cassandra. She's here. She's had the vision."

"But is Hermes?"

"Still sleeping."

They went downstairs to find Cassandra, Henry, her parents, and even their dog standing in the living room.

"Is Andie on her way?" Athena asked.

"I sent Thanatos to go get her." Cassandra motioned for her parents to sit, and they did, clutching each other at the elbow, eyes big and round as wall clocks. Athena crossed and uncrossed her arms. The notion that she should offer Cassandra's parents something to drink popped into her head. *Ridiculous.*

Cassandra began, recounting what little there was. Headlights flashed through the window and signaled Andie's arrival just as she was wrapping up.

Athena bit the inside of her cheek, her teeth worrying at

the quill of a feather. Twisting it back and forth sent shock waves of pain through her gums and down her neck. No matter. The feathers would be gone forever in a few hours.

"What's going on?" Andie asked as she came in. When no one replied, she took her place behind the sofa.

"No one has to go who doesn't want to," Cassandra said. "Only me and Athena."

"You can't take Atropos alone," Ares said, though he sounded impressed that she wanted to try.

"And you can't face Achilles," said Henry. "Only I can do that."

"Only Hector can do that," Odysseus corrected. "And you're not him. Unless . . . ?"

"No," Andie shouted.

The room dissolved to bickering, until Cassandra shouted over the top.

"Athena," she said. "What do you think we should do?"

Athena blinked. "I don't know."

"Yes, you do," said Odysseus.

Athena studied them. They were all staring at her. Even Cassandra's parents. Even Ares. Her throat went dry.

Andie gave her a nod.

"We were all there," Andie said. "On Olympus. And we're still asking, anyway. We still trust you."

Something tightened Athena's chest. Gratitude. Sentimentality. She looked at Odysseus, who seemed proud, and finally at Cassandra.

"I never trusted you," Cassandra said. "But I'm still asking."

Athena held her breath. Odysseus was right. She was afraid.

"Look," Cassandra said. "We've all decided to go anyway."

Athena dug her fingernails deep into her palms.

Caves. The Moirae burrowed into the ground like moles, and wanted them to stick their hands in blindly after. No thanks.

"I don't think we should go to the caves," Athena said. "No holes or wells or mazes. We ought to take the high ground, with open space and cover."

"I didn't think they were giving us a choice about location," Cassandra said.

"I didn't, either. But aren't you tired of following other people's plans?"

From behind the couch, Andie smiled. "I'll get food, water, and supplies," she said. "The first-aid packs from the basement." She slapped Henry on the arm. "Let's go get your shield."

"What are you doing?" Odysseus asked Athena from across the room of mobilizing bodies.

Athena wasn't quite sure. But whatever they did, they would do it on their own terms.

"I need to ask you to do something for me," Athena said. She sat before Cassandra's parents, her weight making the coffee table creak.

"You mean we're not coming?" Tom asked. "It feels like we should. I want to go."

Athena nodded. He did want to go. To be a dad and protect his kids. But his eyes were wide and bewildered. He wouldn't know what to do if she agreed.

"I know you want to. But I was hoping you would do something for me here."

"What is it?" Maureen asked.

"Hermes is upstairs in his room. We can't move him. And we can't wait for him to . . ." She paused and let the tightness in her throat pass. "He's not going to last much longer. And I don't want him to be alone."

They looked at Cassandra, and their eyes went unfocused as they thought of Henry. Then they nodded.

"When will you be back?" Maureen asked.

"Your kids will be back. Soon." She touched them fondly on the knee and on the shoulder. "I have to go say goodbye to my brother."

Hermes lay still. He was so thin, he barely made a shape underneath the blankets.

Athena sat on the edge of the bed and held his hand, careful not to disturb him even though he wouldn't wake up. She'd said his name three times to no response. She should have been happy about that, that he was unconscious and not in pain. But she would have given anything for one more word. One more smile. All this sleep and slowness didn't suit him.

Ares sat in a chair on the opposite side. When she'd come in, he'd made to leave her alone, but she'd told him to stay. Hermes wasn't awake. She didn't need to be alone with him, and truly, having another god in the room felt like comfort, even if it was Ares.

"Knock knock." Andie poked her head in. Henry and

Odysseus stood behind her. "Can we come in to say good-bye?"

Athena nodded, and stepped back to give them room. She didn't listen to what they said. She just saw them laugh, and wipe tears, and touch Hermes' shoulder. Andie kissed his cheek.

If he were awake, he'd tell me to keep them safe.

"Cars are packed. Ready to go," Odysseus said.

"We'll be down. Soon." She leaned down over Hermes as they filed out of the room, and kissed his forehead. It felt strange. She thought there'd be more to say. But Hermes knew everything he ever would. And the cars waited downstairs.

Ares stood.

"I'm not going with you," he said. He hung his head a second and gestured weakly to his stomach. "He cut me up worse than I thought. It isn't healing."

"Let me see." Athena put her hands out, but he caught them.

"The day I get examined by you," he said, and smiled. He looked down at Hermes. "I'm going to stay with him. Make sure they don't check here first and do something you wouldn't want them to do."

"I thought you'd want the blood," Athena said.

"Make no mistake, I want the blood," said Ares. "But leaving him alone doesn't seem right. And I didn't catch a knife in the gut saving those two downstairs," he nodded to the door and down to Cassandra's parents, "just to let them get skinned two days later."

So much for his bitter words about playing the hero.

"After he's gone, I'll come and find you," he said. "I'll stash the parents and pick up your trail."

"We're headed up the southern face of Mount Emmons. I'll look for you."

"If something goes wrong," he said. "If Atropos can't be stopped. What do you want me to do?"

She looked at Hermes on the bed, so pale he'd turned gray. They'd come so far. She'd led them here.

"I'm not your general, Ares. I never have been. But if I were you . . ." She took a slow breath. "I'd spring Aphrodite from the underworld and spend as much time with her as I could. Someplace warm. I'd run and I wouldn't look back."

They stood beside Hermes' bed together for a long time. Athena had been unfair to Ares, and he to her, for as long as she could remember, but it didn't matter. Ares would look after their brother, and Athena would trade herself so Ares could heal.

"So long, Ares," she said, and he flinched when she touched his shoulder, like she might hit him. It made her smile. They would never be friends. But they were family.

Cassandra watched Athena's house recede as Thanatos backed out of the driveway. Inside, a god she'd hated from the moment she laid eyes on him sat beside Hermes' bed, and protected her parents.

"Are you sure we can trust him?" she asked, and in her side mirror, she saw Athena glance up to the house.

"You killed his mother and he saved yours," she replied. "That earns him at least a little slack, don't you think?"

Cassandra clenched her teeth. But it wasn't Ares who weighed on her mind. The instinct to go where her vision indicated was so strong it pulled. Strings tightening around her heart.

29

NO HIGHER GROUND

Their caravan drove northeast, racing the dawn for higher ground. Where Athena intended to take them, there were no good trails. No cleared paths at all, save the ones made by deer. But their legs were fresh, and their fear would keep them sharp. For a little while at least.

Somewhere ahead, Mount Emmons waited in the dark, one of the high peaks of the Adirondacks. They'd push their way up and wait for Atropos and Achilles to come up behind. With luck, they'd hold the high ground, and maybe find cover to dig into.

"What if they don't come?" Cassandra asked. "What if by not going where we're told, we're spoiling Clotho and Lachesis' plans?"

"What if," Athena said. Her teeth caught the edge of an emerging feather and she winced, but she felt strangely elated. "I think it was when we deviated," she continued after a moment. "I think that's when it changed."

"What are you talking about?" Cassandra asked.

"Fate isn't fate anymore. The Moirae grow weak. We turn away from their plans, and they don't turn us back."

"That's all in your head."

"No," Thanatos said from the driver's seat. "I feel it, too."

Cassandra turned. Her eyes shone in the dark like marbles. "You both know how this is going to end."

Athena smiled.

"I don't."

Henry followed Athena's car down back roads that turned from blacktop to dirt, and finally to not much more than twin tracks. He didn't know how she knew where they were going. Maybe the gods' innate sense of direction. Maybe Athena had used part of her long, immortal life to commit every inch of the globe to memory. However they did it, Henry kept the Mustang close to the rental's taillights.

Andie sat beside him, still not speaking much. She hadn't said she'd forgiven him for trying to become Hector. He wasn't quite sure if he forgave her for not understanding why he should have. But there'd been a moment, at Hermes' bedside, when she let him put his arm around her.

Brake lights lit up ahead, and Thanatos turned off the road completely. The cars bumped and lurched through fields of greening grass and mud. Trees popped up in the Mustang's headlights, and he couldn't see the sky ahead anymore in the face of the mountain. Just when he thought they couldn't go any farther, Thanatos' brake lights lit up and stayed lit.

Henry threw the Mustang into park. The ground felt too soft even behind the wheel. If they survived the fight, they might return to find the cars sunk in up to the tire rims.

Andie opened her door.

"Hey," he said, and popped the trunk. "Are you going to stay mad at me the whole time?"

She turned and kissed him.

"I'm not mad at you. Just nervous. It's not every day I have to fight an insane hero of legend."

She got out and walked around to the trunk. Henry followed.

"What do you mean you're going to fight?" he asked. "I'm the one who has to do it."

"Who has to kill him. Right. But no one ever said you had to do it alone." Her eyes narrowed at him in the light from the trunk, and Henry wasn't about to tell her no.

Odysseus walked out of the dark and reached in for a bag of supplies.

"Did you tell him?" Odysseus asked Andie.

"Why else would he have that look on his face?"

Odysseus smiled. "Come on, Henry. You didn't expect us to just sit up on the wall, did you? He put a sword through my chest. That needs answering."

"And with us along," Andie said, "you might not die."

Cassandra looked up toward the summit of the mountain. The cave where the Moirae lay was hours away. The pull of it made her chest ache, and the dark part of her mind throbbed like a burn.

"Are you all right?" Thanatos put his hand on the back of her neck and it felt like a bucket of ice water.

"I'm just hoping we don't break our legs walking up a mountain in the dark."

"It won't be dark for much longer."

Her eyes strained. After a minute it seemed that the sky grew lighter.

We're wasting so much time. Clotho and Lachesis need us. Now.

Her brain screamed it. But her gut told her to take Athena's advice. To do something contrary. Something outside the plan. Even if it was only defiance for defiance's sake.

"I'll take point with Henry and Andie," Odysseus said.

They'd assembled and armed themselves, loaded down with backpacks of supplies and first aid, swords and spears drawn or strapped to their backs. The Shield of Achilles rested against Henry's leg and gleamed in the headlights.

"Cassandra and I will sweep behind." Athena looked at Thanatos. "Are you fighting?"

"I don't know," he said, and glanced at Cassandra. "I don't think it's my fight. But I will if—"

"Just don't get in the way," Cassandra said. She reached into the car and killed the headlights. A moment later, flashlights clicked on, and they started up the mountain.

For a long time, the only sounds were their feet breaking through twigs and crushing pine needles and grass. And then of breathing, as they began to tire.

Athena kept her ears wide open, and couldn't help checking over her shoulder. At any moment, the Moirae could crash down like a sack pulled over their heads. She hoped they had enough of a lead that the attack wouldn't come while it was still dark. And as the light around them turned first gray and then silver, she hoped the Moirae would strike soon, before the strength in their legs gave out, or they lost their nerve.

No one broke an ankle in the dark, but it was a wonder. In the predawn light, more and more exposed roots and fallen branches came into view.

Cassandra adjusted the medical pack on her shoulders. She'd taken it from Andie an hour ago, when the weariness on Andie's face was too much to bear.

Cassandra looked back, down the mountain. Surely they'd gone far enough. They should start looking for someplace to use as a sort of stronghold. But Athena kept going up and up, and glancing over her shoulder far too often, unsure as a sheepdog without an owner to command it.

(Athena breaks her word. She runs. But don't fear. We can be anywhere we need to be.)

Cassandra stopped short and blinked hard. But Clotho and Lachesis weren't lurking behind the nearest tree. They hadn't wriggled their way up through her nose or into her ear. It was only their voices. In the dark part of Cassandra's mind, a curious itch started, like an oiled gear clicking around and around. Turning from a cave in some other mountain to a cave in this one.

Cassandra stole a look in Athena's direction. The goddess

continued to walk. She gave no indication of having heard or sensed anything.

Cassandra exhaled, and the knot of strings in her chest began to relax.

30

ONE FATE

They stopped for a light breakfast, using a fallen log for both bench and table. No one ate much. They nibbled at granola bars and sipped from plastic bottles, and tried not to look as tired as they felt.

Athena perched on the edge. The Moirae should have come by now. She'd thought they'd be enraged that they'd tried to run, that they'd have spurred Atropos and Achilles, driven them out of their cave as horses harnessed to a chariot.

She looked over the sweat-streaked faces of Andie and Henry. She couldn't keep them going for much longer. They'd have to find a good place to make their stand, and wait.

Or we could just keep on running. The hell with the feathers in my lungs and their plan for us. We could run like Hermes, fast as we could, until they couldn't even track the dust behind us. Maybe with that much defiance, I could defy even my own death, and we could go on like that together. Forever.

Forever was a very pretty word. A very pretty, very bull-shit word.

Odysseus caught her eye, his cheek stuffed full of granola.

"Has anyone else noticed," he asked, "that all of the birds stopped chirping five minutes ago?"

Everyone stopped chewing. He was right.

"Stay together," he said calmly, and popped a piece of dried apple into his mouth. Athena watched Andie and Henry carefully. They wanted to bolt but neither moved. They trusted Odysseus like they trusted Athena.

The sound of the hatchet slicing air gave only a second of warning before Athena saw it, aiming end over end for Andie's chest. Odysseus barely had time to pull her clear.

"Where is he?" Henry shouted. He dragged Andie back behind the shield with him, and Odysseus frowned. That wouldn't do, in the fight that was coming.

Achilles' laughter rang out from somewhere in the trees. Thanatos edged in front of Cassandra, and Athena eyed him carefully. Could she count on his help? She didn't think so. He'd stand against Achilles, but not the Moirae. Athena scanned the woods below. In the Moirae's present state, they'd be hard to miss. No trunk in the forest was broad enough to hide their twisted form.

Something else cut through the air: a spear this time. The throw was better; it sliced Odysseus in the shoulder as he spun out of the way.

"We can't just stand here and let him toss things at us," he said. He pressed his hand to his arm and it came away red. His eyes sought Athena's. *Don't worry about me*, they said. *There's something bigger headed your way.*

"Then let's go out and meet him," said Henry. He stood and hefted the shield. Another spear launched through the air and he jumped toward it and leaned in. It bounced off harmlessly, and he laughed out of sheer surprise.

"This shield you left me isn't half-bad," he shouted, and in the next second Achilles was there, running up on them, faster than Athena remembered even in paranoid nightmares.

She braced, ready to help, maybe to toss him like she'd tossed him in Australia. She might have done it, despite the damage he'd have done to her, if it hadn't been for Thanatos' shout.

"Cassandra! Don't!"

When Athena turned the girl was running off into the trees, east and down the mountain.

"Cassandra!" Athena shouted, and glanced between Cassandra and Achilles. He'd be on Henry in a blink.

"Go," Odysseus said, and his sword was beside her cheek. "Just don't go far."

Athena turned and ran.

Henry didn't breathe. There simply wasn't time. The first blow that Achilles landed rang the shield like a cathedral bell and sent Henry wheeling backward. Panic fluttered through his limbs. The impact told his legs to buckle, but that wasn't an option. If he lost his feet, it was all over.

He stepped back, and his ankle turned on a root. He went down and landed hard on his hip.

This is it.

Achilles' sword would slice through his exposed neck, right above the protection of the shield. It would shear his head clean off, foolishly as a turtle caught out of its shell. Henry wondered if he'd feel it.

"Just like back in Troy." Achilles laughed. "You stumble and fall."

"Back in Troy I was tricked," Henry said. He got his legs under him and stood, stifling the urge to use the shield to help. The damned thing was so heavy. It pulled his shoulder down despite the adrenaline. "Back in Troy I was alone."

Odysseus and Andie closed in cautiously on both sides. Achilles kept his eyes on Henry, as though he was trying to decide whether Henry's accepting help was practical, or cowardly.

The sword in Henry's hand was slick with sweat. Even if he could swing it, it might fly from his grip like a wriggling fish.

Achilles didn't look the least bit concerned that Odysseus and Andie had him cornered. He looked every bit the warrior, right down to the blond hair ruffling in the wind. He didn't carry a shield of his own. Probably because he intended to strip his old one off of Henry's dead body.

"What happened to you, Achilles?" Henry asked. "They called you a hero. You used to be a hero."

"I still am a hero," Achilles said. "Avenging my friend's murder for the second time. It's all a matter of perspective."

"And what about what you did to me?" Odysseus asked. "Putting a sword through my chest. You avenge one friend and fuck all to the rest?"

"I didn't enjoy doing that," Achilles said.

"And I won't enjoy doing this," said Odysseus.

Cassandra ran between trees, skirting and ducking branches, moving closer and closer to the Moirae, as though she was attached to the end of a string.

"Cassandra!"

"Cassandra, stop!"

Athena and Thanatos were close, too. Cassandra didn't turn when they called, but it was good. She might need Athena, at least, to do what needed doing. She didn't know how strong Clotho and Lachesis could be. They were so shriveled. So deflated.

A branch caught Cassandra in the eye and she blinked away pain and water. It didn't matter. A few more strides. Maybe just over the next rise, or past the next tree trunk.

It's almost over. I'm almost done. The gods will leave, and my family will be safe. The Moirae will be whole. We'll be whole.

She ran faster until it felt like flying. When her foot came down on a pile of brush and she fell right through, straight into the heart of the cave, she was only slightly surprised.

Athena saw Cassandra disappear. One second she was there, and the next gone, as if the earth itself had swallowed her up. Between herself and Thanatos, she didn't know who yelled louder, but she reached the hole first.

"Cassandra!"

She didn't answer, but Athena saw her down there, in

the circle of light let in by the cave opening, paddling and sputtering in the middle of a blue-green cave lake with bits of leaves and sticks floating around her.

"Are you hurt?" Athena shouted, but Cassandra had already started swimming for the rock ledge.

"Dammit." Athena looked around at the trees. The hole Cassandra had uncovered was fairly broad, eight by ten feet at least, and the edges were smooth, gray stone.

"Thanatos," she said, and gripped his arm. "Go get rope. Tie it off on the trees and lower it down."

"Did we bring rope with us from the cars?"

Athena closed her eyes. She couldn't remember.

"If we didn't then there's some in Henry's trunk. Go!"

"But—" he started, but he didn't get to finish. Athena stood and jumped down into the cave.

Odysseus attacked first. Henry thought that he should have been the one to do it. Or maybe that Achilles should have. But it seemed they might have stood there talking until Cassandra and Athena dealt with the Moirae. If no one attacked, no one had to die.

It wasn't brave to think those things, watching Andie dart in on Achilles' other side. But as Achilles held them off, with grace and with such goddamn ease, Henry couldn't help thinking it. He couldn't help seeing the young man in Achilles' face. Neither one was older than the other. And both had their reasons. When it was over, one of them would lie dead. One of them always lay dead.

Henry took a breath and brought his sword down, his eye carefully trained on the expanse of Achilles' exposed form.

But the blade struck steel. Achilles moved faster than them all. Much faster than Henry and Andie. Even faster than Odysseus. He attacked as quickly as Henry could block, and they were all driven back. Henry's shield arm ached miserably.

Andie and Odysseus kept on, though their faces grew strained and nervous. Achilles treated them as an afterthought, holding them off and hurting them just a little. Blood ran from Odysseus' nose. Andie limped from a shallow gash above her knee. All of his wrath he saved for Henry. Had any one of his blows struck outside the shield, the part of Henry that met it would have been cleaved in two.

And he talked. Spat words of hate that chilled Henry's blood.

"I'll smash your skin, break the bones against each other." He would feed Henry's cheeks to Ares' wolves.

And still, Henry didn't want to fight him.

Henry braced the shield against his shoulder and made his swing, swung his sword hard and steady as he could. It was a good blow. It felt like it had been waiting, curled up inside his chest the whole time.

The blade sank deep, deep into Achilles' side.

When Andie and Odysseus saw the wound, they stopped mid-attack, their eyes no wider than Achilles' own. Achilles went down on one knee, barely believing the blood that already dripped past his lips. Henry didn't pull out his sword so much as Achilles fell off of it.

Achilles pressed his hand down hard. Blood dripped through his fingers.

"This isn't how it ends," he said. He stood and stumbled

backward, staring at Henry like he'd never seen him before. And then he fled down through the trees.

"Do we follow?" Odysseus asked.

"No," Henry replied, relieved to find none of the hate in his heart that he thought might be there.

Athena hit the water and kicked up hard, shoving wet strands of hair out of her eyes, looking for Cassandra on the stone bank. But when she saw her, she almost wished she hadn't.

Cassandra stood, drenched and shaking, not ten feet from the Moirae. The Moirae stared down at her with three sets of eyes: two murky green, and one murderous red. Five arms twitched like spider legs in their massive, monstrous form. Three of the arms held wicked, shining shears, all pointed at Cassandra's chest.

They led her here. They led her here to take her apart. It was all a trick.

The shears were long, and bore razor edges on both sides of their blades. They could slice as well as they cut, and it would take them less than a minute to reduce Cassandra to a pile of girl-colored confetti on the cave floor.

"Leave her alone!" Athena shouted, and swam fast to the edge. Her fingers slipped once on the stone and she cursed. In the corner of her eye, the tips of the shears weaved through the air like the heads of dancing snakes.

She hauled herself out of the water and took two strides toward Cassandra before stopping short. Something was different. The power to kill gods coursed through Cassandra's entire body. Athena felt it in the air, in waves. And she had almost run up and grabbed her.

The girl nodded and it took Athena a moment to realize the nod wasn't meant for her.

Cassandra was speaking to them.

"Cassandra," Athena said. "Come here to me."

Cassandra's head cocked over her shoulder. "Athena. You're here."

"I am." Athena kept her eyes on the tips of Atropos' shears. Not even Hermes would be fast enough to snatch Cassandra out of the way from that distance.

"Do you see her? The disease in the middle?"

Atropos hissed. Aside from the bloodred eyes, her face didn't look diseased at all. It was only below her chest, where her legs had grown into her sisters'. Where her stomach had absorbed Lachesis' arm all the way to the elbow.

Athena trembled. She was afraid. She stood before the failing, dying gods of her father, and she was afraid.

Zeus rose up to throw down the Titans. I can rise up against the Moirae.

Cassandra leapt forward and Athena screamed. Atropos' shears took aim for Cassandra's throat, ready to open her up like a slaughtered pig. Athena's hand fumbled at her side for a knife: it wasn't much, no weapon of legend, but in her haste to get to Cassandra, it was all she had.

She ran full force, even as Clotho and Lachesis took hold of Atropos' arms with surprising strength and jerked them back tight. Athena ran so fast that she and Cassandra struck the Moirae at almost the same time. Hermes would have been proud.

Her knife stabbed into Atropos' shoulder. Atropos shrieked. Athena shouted, too; her hip had bumped Cassandra and pain sprang sharp from the bone along with a rush of hot blood. Feathers. A mass of them by the feel of it. Pain sent her to the floor.

She looked up. Cassandra had latched on and Atropos was screaming, but not enough. Atropos' lungs heaved underneath stretched skin, but didn't shrivel. She didn't flake away, or turn to dust. She was the Moira of death. She weakened, but she resisted.

"How do I help her?" Athena shouted, and Clotho and Lachesis answered in her mind:

(With the shears. Help her. Help us. With the shears.)

Athena ran in and grappled with Atropos, careful to avoid Cassandra. The edges of the shears sliced into her cheek and made her vision swim, as if the edges were poisoned. But even through the drug of the Moirae she heard Atropos hissing.

(TRAITORS! SISTERS! BETRAYORS!)

Athena chuckled groggily.

"Strong words coming from someone who's been eating them."

(DOWN, GODDESS.)

Athena heard the words, and her legs buckled even as her fingers closed around the handles of Atropos' shears.

"Stay up!" Cassandra shouted, but she didn't try to pull her. The girl was thinking clear. Both hands stayed on Atropos' chest. Cassandra's teeth bared and clenched. Sweat stood on her forehead. She and Atropos traded death back and forth.

(Help us. Cut her out. Help us.)

Athena groaned and forced her legs to stay. She turned the tip of Atropos' shears inward and sliced. The sound Atropos made was inhuman and terrible. When her sisters' shears joined her own, it became a wail.

Three sets of razor edges cut through Atropos. Lachesis hacked her own arm free, leaving a gaping red wound across Atropos' stomach. When they started on her legs, the brutality was too much to bear. Athena and Cassandra stepped back. Clotho and Lachesis cut and cut until one mangled form became three, each bleeding from the hips down.

Clotho and Lachesis lay on their bellies, legs damaged, their faces and arms withered and graying as blood left them. Atropos wavered on her feet, wobbly as a mermaid who'd lost her tail. Blood covered her in a broad skirt.

"Athena! I've got the rope!"

The rope dropped and almost at the same time she saw Odysseus' foot, ready to climb down.

"No!" she shouted. "Thanatos! Don't let him come!"

"Athena! Don't you do it," Odysseus shouted as Thanatos pulled him back up. "Don't you leave me!"

There was so much love in his voice. He was wrong, what he said on the widow's walk. She would have been with him as long as she could, if there had been a choice.

"Cassandra!"

"Cassie!"

Andie and Henry up there, too. They were all right. How Athena wanted to see all of their faces again. Just once more. But Atropos wasn't dead yet.

"Now what?" Athena asked Clotho.

(The shears. She dies by her own shears. The one who kills her will take her place.)

Clotho and Lachesis lay sprawled, clutching their own shears in their hands.

"You heard them," Cassandra said. "Give them to me."

"What?"

"Give them to me." She held her hand out. "It's what's supposed to happen."

Athena stared at her, open-mouthed.

"Come on," Cassandra said, and smiled. "You've got a life now. Up there. This wasn't meant for you."

"No," Athena said. "We made the deal."

Cassandra's smile changed. It disappeared.

"Give them to me!"

Athena jumped back, favoring her injured hip. Cassandra fell and her hands caught Athena at the knee. Athena thought she would black out from the pain of so many feathers bursting through the joint.

"Stop this, Cassandra." Athena moaned. "It's only them in your head. You don't want this."

"Nobody wants this," Cassandra said as she got to her feet. "But I *am* this." Her fingers hooked into claws but this time Athena was faster and managed to dodge.

"Get out of her head!" Athena screamed at the Moirae.

"Cassandra. You're not death. You killed gods because you fought—"

"I killed Calypso!"

Athena stopped. Cassandra's eyes were wide and hateful. Full of regret. In the midst of all that had happened, Athena had missed how much of Cassandra's hate had turned inward.

"I put my hands on her," Cassandra shouted. "And she died. Her hair turned white, and then yellow, and then it shed off of her skull. Her face turned to leather in front of me!"

Above, Athena heard Odysseus speak, but couldn't tell what he said.

"You didn't mean to do that," Athena said, and knew it was true. Cassandra had cared for Calypso. It was in her eyes for anyone to see.

Athena sought Atropos in the back of the cave. The cold weight of the shears in her hand felt good. Solid. She opened and closed them once, and Atropos hissed.

Athena moved fast, but Cassandra's hands slammed down on her back. Feathers cut through her lungs, through her liver, through the skin and muscle that held her together. It brought her to the ground.

Athena turned over and looked up through the cave entrance, hoping to see a scrap of sky, wishing she wasn't there, in a hole that felt so much like a grave.

"Athena!" Odysseus shouted. He started down the rope and then let go and fell the rest of the way to splash into the lake. He came up sputtering, and she recalled how cold it was. It seemed a long time ago that she had been in the water.

Cassandra's shadow fell across her torso. She bent down to carefully take the shears from Athena's hand.

"I don't want to kill you," Cassandra said. "After it's over, I think you'll heal."

Poor Cassandra. The girl who killed gods. They'd put her through a world of shit, and she proved herself tough as nails. Athena understood why Aidan had loved her so much.

"No," Athena whispered. "You'll heal."

Athena jerked the shears closed, and severed half of

Cassandra's ring and pinky fingers. The sound of the tips falling to the cave floor was covered by her scream.

Athena rolled away. The feathers made it hard to move. Hard to breathe. But she did it anyway, and scrambled across the stone. She raised the shears high over her head, and brought them down in Atropos' chest.

Something flooded through her. Something dark.

"No. No, goddamn it." Odysseus dragged himself out of the lake.

Athena knelt beside the wall of the cave with her head down, one arm out to hold herself up. Her other hand clutched the shears. Her shears.

Cassandra's head swam. Atropos was dead. Athena killed her. And suddenly, Clotho and Lachesis weren't talking to her anymore. But she could still hear them as they begged their new sister for help.

(Join your blood with us. Heal us. Help us.)

Athena grabbed her head as though she was trying to block them out. Trying to fight. But she wouldn't be able to for long.

Cassandra stared at Clotho and Lachesis. They were pathetic, shriveled sacks. Weak. Dying. They'd done so much to bring her there. They'd created her. The Fates.

She got to her feet and wiped the blood from her severed fingers on her shirt. It was all right, the lost fingers. She only needed one good hand anyway.

When she plucked the shears from Lachesis' hand, Lachesis looked at her curiously. It wasn't until she brought the point down between her eyes that anyone started screaming, and then it was only Clotho. But soon enough, Clotho stopped as well.

Cassandra backed away from the dead Moirae, away from the blood that leaked from their sliced-open legs and from their heads. She held the shears carefully. They were so very, very sharp.

"Go see if she's okay," she said to Odysseus, and he went to Athena's side. For a moment, Cassandra wasn't sure. The next thing she saw might be the tip of Atropos' shears through Odysseus' back. But Athena wrapped her arm around him, and he helped her stand.

Cassandra heard her whisper, "Fucking feathers," and smiled.

"What did you do?" Odysseus asked. He looked at Cassandra with wonder.

"What I was put here to do," Cassandra said, and felt the dark part of her mind click shut.

EPILOGUE

Athena stood in her kitchen, making sandwiches. One black nose and one red one pressed close to the countertop, so she tossed the wolves each a slice of roast beef.

"That's plenty," she said when it seemed as if they'd beg for more. She smiled. If she forgot that they could walk on two legs and speak, she could almost become fond of them. And with their deaths gone, they weren't nearly so disgusting. Panic's red coat was almost pretty.

"Is that for me?"

Hermes poked his head around the corner.

"Make your own," she said, but pushed the plate toward him. Old habits died hard. She might be following him around with sandwiches forever even though he didn't need them. His cheeks were back, and his arms and chest were on their way. He was well.

"Tell me the truth," he said with his mouth full. "When Ares didn't show up to fight, you thought he had run off."

"I didn't think that," she replied. "And you wouldn't think that, either, if you'd seen him at the end." The back door closed. Ares, coming back from the woods after the wolves. "He was by your bedside like a nursemaid, eyes big and wet as Henry's German shepherd." She smirked and handed Ares a sandwich over her shoulder.

"The hell I was," Ares muttered.

"The hell he was," Hermes agreed.

They stood in the kitchen and ate in silence. The space felt crowded with so many gods inside it. So many true gods. Over the course of one battle, they'd outgrown the house.

"I'm leaving tomorrow," Ares said.

"For where?" Athena asked.

"The underworld. To spring Aphrodite," Ares said. He chewed for a moment, and cleared his throat. "If Hades gives me any trouble . . ."

"Gives you any trouble?" Hermes scoffed. "After we just saved every god's life? He'd better fall down groveling and shower you with pomegranates. He'd better shove a bunch into a fruit basket and send it over here posthaste. Trouble."

Athena smiled. "If he gives you any trouble, you know where to find us."

Ares nodded, and she thought she saw the corner of his mouth turn up. Just a little. Then Odysseus' feet sounded on the stairs, and Ares stuffed the last of his sandwich in his mouth and left. Hermes, too, took his plate and waggled his eyebrows.

"Was it something I said?" Odysseus asked as both gods and two wolves walked past him. He slid his arms around Athena's waist. The feathers had fallen out and healed without a scar. Before long, she might not even remember what they felt like twisting through her skin.

She put her hands over his. He was her hero, as he'd always been.

"Well, goddess," he said, and kissed her. "Where to now?"

"Weather's getting warmer. Everyone says we're going to have a hot summer. I thought about bringing flowers, maybe in a pot, but if I don't get here for a few days I don't want them to wither. Of course, maybe you could do something about that?"

Cassandra stood before Aidan's grave, talking to him, as she had every day since they'd returned. Every day. But it wouldn't be that way forever. Eventually the visits would slow, and then stall out. That was just how it was. No matter how much you loved someone.

"You're not here anyway," she said. "Under that rock and all that dirt." She looked up into the sky. Aidan was there. The sun. He was in the light, and the wind. And he was with her, too. In memories, and even the fat gold coin in her pocket. The past never left.

"Your sister is thinking of selling her house. But I don't think she will. I think she'll keep it, as long as we're still here." But Athena wouldn't stay. She, Odysseus, and Hermes would move on, and soon. Andie said that every time she and Henry went over, it felt as if they might walk in and find the place vacant. Cassandra hadn't seen any of them in days. Only Thanatos. Thanatos lingered, and looked at her in that way he had that told her he wasn't going anywhere. Cassandra didn't know whether Athena would bother to say goodbye, or if she would ever see her or Hermes again after they left. But she was surprised to find that she hoped she would.

A horn sounded. She turned and saw the Mustang, with Andie and Henry inside.

"Guess that's my cue," Cassandra said, and looked down at the grave. Walking away was always hard. She was glad that it hadn't gotten easier. But she did it.

As she left the cemetery, she reached into her pocket for the coin, and twisted it between her healing fingers. Heads and tails winked in the late afternoon light. She flipped it high and watched it spin end over end.

She had no idea on which side it would land.

ACKNOWLEDGMENTS

The end of a trilogy. When I started writing, I never had any designs on writing a series of novels with overlapping characters, let alone an actual trilogy. And then *Anna Dressed in Blood* happened, and then *Girl of Nightmares* went pretty well, and I thought, I can probably do a three. And truth be told, I'm happiest with the last two legs of the Goddess War books, which is a nice surprise. There was plenty of pain trying to wrap up this last one, don't get me wrong, but par for the course, I don't remember exactly what that pain was, only that it was there.

But here it is, and it is done, and there are so many people who have had a hand in that, who have put their work in, their minds in, their sweat in, and I've got this horrible paranoid thought that I'm going to forget someone. If that someone is you, trust that I am sorry, and that one day not far from now I will wake from a dead sleep, with blood-shot eyes, screaming your name.

Seriously, though, that paranoia is probably unfounded. How could I forget any of these folks, who have done so much?

Melissa Frain, editor of editors. Never have I received one of your editorial suggestions with any other reaction than, "Duh! Of course!" and smacking myself in the head for not spotting it myself. You are right on. Brilliant, and amazing to work with. Thank you for making these books. It's a true team effort. They're ours.

Adriann Ranta, super agent. You are always one hundred percent on top of things, and that's no exaggeration. You are also brilliant, and amazing to work with. Thank you for having more faith in my writing than I deserve.

Alexis Saarela, publicist supreme. Thanks for being flex-ible with me this year, and not wringing my neck when I had trouble coordinating all those tour dates. Thank you for coordinating all those tour dates. You are so good at what you do. I've been lucky, lucky to have you.

Seth Lerner, the art team at Tor, and Eithné O'Hanlon, the artist who created the redesigned cover art, thank you for making them pretty.

Thanks to Amy Stapp, for mailing me things and stay-ing on top of production schedules and being all around kind and accommodating. Also for being a willing partici-pant in any Mel-pranking that may need doing . . . I'm sort of being presumptuous here.

Thanks to Lauren Hougen, for an excellent set of copy-edits. You caught a lot of stupid, and made me remember who got injured and where.

Kathleen Doherty is just about the best publisher anyone could ask for, and she gives excellent advice on dog ownership to boot. Thank you, Kathleen.

Thanks to amazing author April Genevieve Tucholke, for her sense of adventure, welcoming spirit, and many, many interesting and lucrative career alternatives. The beefalo call us, April. One day we'll heed them. And ride them.

Thank you to the librarians, who get books into folks' hands every day. Thanks to the bloggers, who love reading and love forcing their love onto other people.

Thank you to the readers, who, if you are reading these words, have truly made it through to the very end of the Goddess War trilogy. You stuck it out. Made the journey with me, and Athena, and our troubled and troublesome Cassandra. That means so much. I hope you'll come along to a few more places yet.

Usual suspects roll call: my brother, Ryan Vander Venter, thanks for toting me around whenever I need a media escort in Minnesota. You are a good brother, even if your popcorn is too salty and you make me listen to you recite sports champions in chronological order. Susan Murray, who reads everything even though she forgets it all and has to read it over again. Infinite reads! Missy Goldsmith, who has no time to read anything anymore, but once the kids are older I know you will read them all on a magnificent bender. Mom and Dad, you guys are more supportive than the very best Wonderbra. Dad, apologies for comparing you to a bra. You are more supportive than the very best . . . athletic supporter? And finally to my first reader, and great pop pop, Dylan Zoerb, for luck.